DEATH, YOU JABRONI

BY

RANDALL J. FUNK

<u>ALSO BY RANDALL J. FUNK</u>

Death is a Clingy Ex

Death Lives Across the Hall

Death Wears a Big Hat

Death is Sleeping with My Wife

Death Stole My Ride

Death and the Fanboy

Death is a Real Killer

Death Will Be Brief: Joe Davis Mystery Tales

Published in the United States by Ghost Light Press, LLC

www.randalljfunk.com

ISBN:

Cover design by Ann McMan

First edition

Special Thanks to:

Michelle Hughes, for her help in preparing the manuscript.

Ann McMan, for her usual awesome work on the cover.

Jim Cornette, Rip Rogers, and Mike Mondo, whose podcast and Twitter pages are an education in wrestling.

Greg Gagne and Jim Brunzell, aka The High Flyers; the reason I started to love this incredibly unique business called professional wrestling.

Everyone who has bought the previous Joe Davis books and helped me along on this adventure.

For Jay Urmann, Jerry Loew, Evan Jackson, Kelly Wells, Matt Berdahl, and other "true believers" who love this crazy business as much as I do.

CHAPTER ONE

The thing about professional wrestling is that it's a lot like porn: more people are into it than they're willing to admit.

Though pro wrestling has been around for over a hundred years, has been at the forefront of entertainment advancements like TV, cable, and the internet, and has filled arenas all over the country, a large portion of the population wants to pretend it doesn't exist. And it's not limited to the elitists who turn up their nose at such a thing. It's the fans of the business as well. Just as two guys will exchange a knowing and embarrassed look whenever names like Katie Morgan or John Holmes come up, so will pro wrestling fans pretend they have no idea who CM Punk is. It's like a secret society that exists in plain sight (like the Yakuza or Trump supporters).

Sometimes, it's like pretending there is no elephant in the room. Sixty thousand fans show up for an event and no one talks about it. Three million people watch a wrestling show on TV, but no one admits it. It's like Justin Bieber albums or Lindsey Graham's presence in the Senate. Somebody has to make this possible.

Just don't ask me about it. I will confirm or deny nothing.

My name is Joe Davis. I get paid to write stuff like that.

Right now, I do not have to disguise my love of professional wrestling. When one attends a wrestling event, they are joyously in the company of likeminded believers in the faith. You don't have to hide who you are or what you do. This must be what A.A. meetings feel like.

"I can't believe we're here," my friend Mike says, his big bulldog head bobbing up and down as he walks, "We're *finally* going to check this out."

Our friend Carol pulls her black trench coat tight around her. "This looks…interesting."

We're heading up the front walk toward the Midwest Championship Wrestling Sportatorium (formerly Fuller's Roller Rink Emporium). It's just off University Avenue in St. Paul, not far from the State Fairgrounds. It's bordered by an apartment building on one side, a copse of trees behind the arena, and a gas station across the street. Not exactly upscale, but it will do. It's a misty April night, one of those days where the weather isn't sure if it's winter or spring, so it just gives you a little of both. Still, it doesn't dampen, so to speak, the spirits of the people lining up to get inside. The big metal doors to the entryway are open and the line for tickets spills outside. Carol, the most professionally attired and dignified among us, looks like she's approaching a several hour-long gynecological appointment.

"You're going to get a column out of this, aren't you?" she asks.

"Maybe," I say, "It *is* the kind of thing I do."

I make my living (such as it is) as a thrice-weekly columnist for the *Daily Bugle*, an independent newspaper that gave the finger to luddites a few years back and now operates exclusively as a website. My column, *Cup o' Joe*, covers a variety of topics: pop culture, sports, movies, TV, social mores, politics, what have you. The same stuff with which I would hold court at the school lunch table (to a rapidly diminishing crowd of three or so).

As we go up the walk, we dodge people holding signs, guys playfighting and general drunkards lurching about. (Fellas, hit the bar *after* the show.) I have to admit: I've always like wrestling more than I've liked wrestling fans. Particularly when it comes to live events. Carol folds her arms, hugging herself.

"You guys are really into this?" she asks.

"Ever since college," Mike says, sticking his hands in the pockets of his black leather jacket.

I huddle into my peacoat. "Every Monday night, a bunch of us would get together in the dorm commons and watch."

"Such a period of growth for you young men," Carol says, rolling her clear blue eyes.

She didn't know us back in college, but she's heard enough to get a picture of what things were like. Mike and I met about five minutes after freshman orientation and have been best friends ever since (seventeen years and counting). If Carol has a picture of wrestling night as a bunch of bros getting together to be dudes, she's largely accurate.

"How many times have you guys been here?" Carol asks.

"To Midwest Championship Wrestling?" I say, "Actually, we've never been here. We've only seen the TV show."

Carol mutters, "Lucky you."

I wag a finger at her. "Just remember, you're here to support a friend."

"He's the ring announcer," Carol says, "You really think he needs my support?"

Before I can answer, one of the guys in front us, a bald guy with a hooked nose and a black windbreaker, turns our direction.

"You guys know Purple Suit?" he asks.

Mike and I hang our heads. "We do," I say.

Windbreaker (is that how I want to put that?) turns to his buddies and shouts, "Hey, these guys know Purple Suit!"

Instantly, a chant of *Purple Suit! Purple Suit!* goes up from everyone around us. Carol, Mike, and I inadvertently huddle together. The scene is starting to resemble something out of a Todd Browning film. (Google it if you don't get the reference.) The chant, though, dies off and everyone goes back to their business. Carol looks around.

"What the hell was that?" she asks.

"Lars is now donning a purple suit," I say.

"Why would he do that?" Carol asks.

"Why does he do most of the things he does?" I ask.

It feels weird, but this is something we've barely talked about. Lars didn't tell us he landed the gig as Midwest Championship Wrestling's ring announcer. Mike and I had to find out by watching the television show. I was initially offended that he didn't tell me, his upstairs neighbor. But he swung us free tickets, so I let him off the hook.

The line moves up, leading us into the entryway of the arena. It's a thin hallway with the box office window on the far side and to the left of that, the entrance into the lobby of the arena. For Carol, the entrance might as well have a sign reading, *Abandon hope all ye who enter here.*

"How often do they do these shows?" Carol asks.

"Twice a week," Mike says, "They tape TV every Tuesday night, and do a weekly show here every Friday."

"This is the weekly show we're going to?" Carol asks.

Mike nods, his brush of brown hair bobbing. "That is the case."

We reach the box office, grab our complimentary tickets and a couple of programs, and step into the large lobby. Black rubber mats cover the concrete floor (likely left over from its days as a roller rink). There's a concession stand and beer garden to our right. On the opposite side of the lobby, a couple of long tables have been put together.

"What are those?" Carol asks.

"Gimmick tables," Mike says, "The guys come out after the matches—or maybe during intermission—and sell t-shirts, pictures, wristbands, stuff like that."

"When you're working for an independent promotion," I say, "the gimmick table can make you more money than the actual wrestling."

Carol twists her mouth to one side, her contemplative look. "What is an *independent* wrestling promotion?"

"Back in the day," I say, "it would have meant a small, locally owned company that wasn't affiliated with one of the major promotions: the UWE, the PWA, the GAWF. These days, the only major promotion left is the UWE."

"The UWE," Carol says, "I've heard of them."

"Most everybody has, whether they admit it or not," I say.

"What does UWE stand for again?" Carol asks.

"Universal Wrestling Entertainment," I say, "But don't call them that. They don't like it. They just go by the initials now."

"Why is that?" Carol asks.

"Because they want to expand into movies and reality TV and books," I say, "They'd rather be known as an entertainment brand than a wrestling company. They don't even like using the words *pro wrestling.*"

"Sports entertainment," Mike says, using the same tone of voice my redneck uncle Mel uses when saying *liberals.*

"They produce wrestling for content," I say, "That's why they get big contracts from the networks."

Mike jumps in. "But they don't give two shits about the wrestling itself. That's why their shows are unwatchable."

We step out of the lobby and into the arena proper. The place has a huge arched roof, reminding of the Memorial Building, the hockey arena in my hometown of Porter's Bay. The ring sits in the middle of the floor. Rows of metal folding chairs extend away from it on all four sides. The floor seats eventually give way to bleachers. We walk down the aisle leading from the lobby. There are ramps to the left and right of the ring, each leading back to the dressing rooms. Fans are filling the seats, creating an increasingly loud buzz in the arena. The place probably holds about a thousand people. We make our way to our ringside seats, located near one of the ring posts. The arena is warm, despite the relative chill in the weather. Carol studies our proximity to the ring.

"Are we going to get sweat on us?" she asks.

"If we're lucky," Mike says.

Weirdly, this does *nothing* for Carol's enthusiasm. A distraction presents itself, though. Our friend Lars appears, walking down the aisle from one of the dressing rooms. As advertised, he wears a purple suit, completed by a lavender shirt and a purple necktie. Coupled with his lanky frame and his quasi-pompadour, he looks like The Joker has chucked the whole *life of crime* thing and taken up work a game show host. Another chant of *Purple Suit! Purple Suit!* goes up. Lars shakes hands as he goes, completely in his element. He makes his way around ringside. When he finally gets to us, he throws his pipe-cleaner arms wide, his horse-toothed grin showing through his (for once not scraggly) beard.

"Greetings and salutations, my friends," Lars says, "You ready for a great show?"

Carol frowns. Mike, as usual, ignores the suffering of others. "How the hell did you land this gig?" he asks Lars.

"Just a little luck," Lars says, adding a modest wave (or as modest as his giant flipper-like hand allows), "I work out at the same gym as one of the wrestlers."

Mike's jaw drops. "You work out with a wrestler?"

Carol's jaw drops. "You work out?"

"I started a few months ago," Lars says, "I had to get rid of my winter weight."

That's interesting. I've known Lars for seven years and his frame has best resembled the Scarecrow from *The Wizard of Oz* the entire time. If my experience means anything, most of Lars's *winter weight* could be taken care of with a haircut. Mike's eyes light up.

"Which wrestler?" he asks.

"Lance Mack," Lars says.

Wow. Lars isn't just working out with *a* wrestler. He's working out with *the* wrestler in Midwest Championship Wrestling. Lance Mack has only been in the business a couple years, but he's clearly on his way to bigger things. Right now, he holds the Midwest Heavyweight Championship, the top title in the promotion. Mike, for one, is impressed with the name, if not the person attached to it.

"Lance Mack," he says, with less enthusiasm than he might, "Holy shit."

"Indeed," Lars says, "He's a great guy. We met when he pulled a weight bar off my chest. My fault. I should have used a spotter for bench presses."

"How much were you benching?" I ask.

"Just the bar," Lars says, "Anyhoo, Lance saved me, and we got to talking. Turned out Midwest Championship

Wrestling needed a ring announcer, and he thought I would fit the bill."

"Based on what?" Carol asks.

"According to Lance, I have a big mouth and no shame."

I'll hand it to Lance Mack: he's perceptive. The three of us may have known Lars longer, but we've all reached the same conclusion. More shouts of *Purple Suit* fill the air, signaling Lars it's time to move on. He hesitates.

"Say, brother, I'll want to talk to you soon," he says to me, "I've got something interesting to discuss. Gotta go. See you at intermission."

He gives us a little bow and moves down the line, continuing to work the crowd. Carol, Mike, and I slide into our seats. Mike's leg bounces a hundred times a minute, something he does when excited or restless. I take off my peacoat and push up the sleeves of my black long-sleeved tee. I'm feeling a little unsettled. Lars wanting to discuss something is never good news. It's like your father coming to you and saying *I want to give you the blow-by-blow details of having sex with your mother.* You know nothing good is going to come of it and there's a distinct possibility you're going to be sick to your stomach by the end of it. Carol flips back her shoulder-length dark hair and watches the crowd trickle into the arena.

"This seems like a pretty good turn out," Carol says, "Is this good for an…independent promotion?"

"They're doing okay." I say, "Back in the day, a thousand fans would have been considered a failure. Today, it's pretty decent."

Mike leans in. "Midwest Championship Wrestling isn't your typical indie. Most of the others rent out an American Legion Hall or a National Guard Armory. They might have a You Tube channel, but that's it. MCW has their own arena and their own spot on local TV. As far as indie promotions go, they're bigger than most."

"Why is that?" Carol asks.

"Bobby Cronus," Mike says.

Carol cocks her head to one side. "Okay, who is Bobby Cronus?"

"Probably the greatest wrestling manager of all time," I say, "As well as a brilliant promoter and booker."

"Booker?" Carol asks, "What's that?"

Hoo-boy. This is going to be a long night. Back when I was in college, I had a class on the life and death of languages. During one of the units, we talked about secret languages; languages that are used to provide cover for a secret society. (Google *Polari* sometime if you're curious.) I argued that professional wrestling lingo, which was created to keep the general public in the dark about the inner workings of the business, constituted a secret language. I don't know if my professor agreed, but she found my reasoning fascinating, nonetheless. No word on whether she ever became a professional wrestling fan. Still, it's no fun speaking a secret language when you're barely aware it's a secret language and you're not trying to keep anything from your companions.

"It covers a lot of things," I say, "For now, let's just say it's the guy who decides who wins and how."

Carol inclines her head, perhaps accepting that she's looking into a world she will never understand. Lars rolls into the ring. He takes his place in the middle and swings one long arm toward the crowd, his hand open.

"Welcome, welcome, welcome all!" he bellows. His voice is an octave deeper and much more boisterous (even by Lars's standards) than usual; the ringmaster of this particular circus. "Welcome to another exciting evening of Midwest Championship Wrestling! I am your ring announcer. My name is Lars!" The crowd breaks out into a chant of *Purple Suit! Purple Suit!* "This first match is one fall…" The crowd answers with a cry of *One fall!* Lars continues, "with a twenty-minute time limit."

So, the fun begins. The first match features two guys probably fresh out of wrestling school. They open by engaging in a dance off. Mike and I roll our eyes and Carol giggles, but the crowd eats it up.

"All this stuff is scripted in advance?" Carol asks.

"Not all of it," I say, "Just the ending. Most of the rest they call in the ring."

"Like improv stage combat?"

"More or less," I say, "These days a lot of guys like to go over the matches in detail. Bobby Cronus is the kind of booker who wants them to call most of it in the ring. That way, they learn to feed off the fans."

Once the wrestlers finally get the match started, they exchange high flying moves. The crowd is attentive but quiet. Noises echo around the arena: the clatter of ring supports, the clacking of the ropes as the wrestlers bounce off, the grunts and groans as they sell the action. Early in the match, one of the guys breaks a hold by running up the turnbuckles, pushing off the top rope and arm dragging his opponent across the ring. Carol watches the move and mutters, "Whoa." That's a good sign. Otherwise, the opening match is largely forgettable. One guy wins with a Sunset Flip. Ho-hum. Between the first few matches, Carol looks over the program.

"Lance Mack isn't even in the main event," she says, "Are you sure he's a big deal?"

"That's because Nick Diamond and Jack Blades are in the main event," Mike says.

"And who are they?" Carol asks.

Wow. We really *are* dealing with a novice. Mike's big bulldog head flushes, as if he's about to have a stroke (and let's not rule that out). I put a hand on his shoulder, slowing his roll. Best to be patient with the non-believer.

"Nick Diamond is one of the greatest wrestlers of all time," I say, "The guy could do it all. Great in interviews. Great in the ring. One of the biggest box office attractions of his day. One of the best heels ever."

"Heels?" Carol asks.

Mike jumps in. "Pro wrestling lingo for a bad guy."

"What about the good guy?" Carol asks, "What's he called?"

"A babyface," Mike says, "Or just *face* for short."

"If this Nick Diamond is such a big star, what's he doing here?" Carol says.

Mike and I exchange an uncomfortable look. "He and the IRS have had a few disagreements," I say, "The IRS tends to win those, so Nick still works from time to time."

"He and Bobby Cronus are friends," Mike says, "And Nick's daughter is on the card."

Carol runs a finger down the program. "Ashley Diamond. That's her, I assume?"

"You assume correctly," I say.

"What about Jack Blades?" she asks, tapping the program.

"One of Nick Diamond's best opponents," I say. Then I turn to Mike, "Remember that feud they had over the PWA World Title?"

"I was ten," Mike says, "Watched it that whole summer. Classic stuff."

Carol waves her hand like she's erasing a blackboard. "Wait, they were wrestling when you were ten? One of them has a daughter who's a wrestler. How old are these guys?"

Mike and I try to do the mental math, something neither of us is particularly good at. I take the first shot.

"Let's see, when they had the PWA Title feud," I say, "Diamond had been wrestling for about fifteen years and Blades for about thirteen. If my math is correct, Diamond is pushing sixty and Blades is a few years younger."

Carol tries to clear her ears. "These guys are AARP members and they're still wrestling?"

Mike looks at Carol as if she just called Santa Claus a big fat bastard. "Hey, they love it and they're still good at it. Let them do what they want."

Carol holds up her hands, suitably chastened (but quietly amused). The second match, also featuring a couple young wrestlers, and is only slightly less forgettable than the first. A big, masked wrestler named the Super Destroyer spends his time throwing a significantly smaller guy around the ring and playing to the crowd. He finishes the smaller guy off with a Cobra, best described as a full nelson but with one arm pulled across the guy's throat. The match might not have been pretty but at least it was over quickly.

We perk up for the third match, which features the aforementioned Ashley Diamond. Shelly Blaze, Ashley's opponent, comes out first, sneering at the crowd. Lars gives her a perfunctory introduction. The crowd responds with a round of jeers. A few moments later, the chugging guitar of *Barracuda* by Heart kicks in. A tall, lanky woman with long blonde hair and an hourglass figure emerges from the babyface dressing room. Mike and I are on our feet, caught up in the general excitement of the crowd. Ashley throws her arms out and does a sort of cheesecake turn. Lars lets the cheering build to a fever pitch before getting on the mic.

"And her opponent, hailing from Hollywood, California. The number one contender to the Midwest Women's Title. The Next Big Thing…Ashley Diamond!"

Ashley slaps hands with the fans as she walks to the ring. She gets up on the ring apron, stretches out one long leg and glides between the top and middle ropes. Ms. Blaze tries to trash-talk her, but Ashley just strolls past and climbs up on one of the turnbuckles. She throws her arms wide, striking a pose that seems to say *Yep, I'm a big deal.* A second later, Shelly Blaze hits Ashley with a forearm to the back and we're off the races.

It goes about five minutes and is a tale of two matches. Ms. Blaze spends the first few minutes alternating between pounding Ashley Diamond and shouting at the crowd. Ashley sells like a champ, registering the pain on her face and in her body language. The turning point comes when Ashley is whipped into the corner and comes out with a desperation clothesline, driving her arm across Shelly's chest and sending them both to the mat. The crowd erupts. Ashley gets to her feet first and starts delivers a beatdown to Shelly Blaze. Ashley finishes the match with a version of her father's finishing hold: the Diamond Clasp. Essentially, Shelly's legs are grapevined around one of Ashley's long legs, then Ashley steps over Shelly, flipping her on to her stomach. Ashley then squats slightly to apply pressure. It plays like an all-out assault on the legs and lower back. Shelly screams in pain before finally tapping out. Ashley drops the hold and throws her arms wide in the middle of the ring, soaking up the crowd's adulation.

"Star power, man," Mike says, his eyes wide, "She's going to be huge."

Before Mike can gush further, another woman approaches the ring. She has a small gold title belt slung over her shoulder. She's not as tall as Ashley but is clearly the product of some quality time in the gym. Her long dark hair is pulled back and she wears a black leather jacket and black jeans. She scowls at Ashley.

"Who is this?" Carol asks.

"Vanessa," Mike says, "The Midwest Women's Champion."

Ashley leans on the top rope and returns Vanessa's glare. After a few seconds, Vanessa walks back to the dressing room, leaving the fight for another day. Ashley triumphantly climbs the turnbuckles and returns to her pose. The crowd eats it up. Ashley returns to the dressing room. Mike's eyes follow her all the way up the aisle. Lars hops into the ring.

"Wasn't that a match?" he shouts, "We're going to take a fifteen-minute intermission. Be sure to visit the concession stand and the merchandise tables. And after intermission, we've got a big announcement for you!"

Lars rolls out of the ring and heads our direction. The crowd noisily files toward the lobby. Lars slaps hands with more fans at ringside. His quasi-pompadour is drooping slightly as the heat in the arena causes him to sweat profusely. He stops in front of us and rocks back on his heels.

"What do you think?" he asks.

I offer a fist bump. "You do good work, my friend."

Mike steps in front of me. "What's the big announcement?"

"Oh, you'll have to wait for that," Lars says, wagging a finger at Mike.

Before we get any farther, someone approaches us. He's middle-aged with a full head of graying hair and a large pair of glasses dominating his face. The haircut is outdated, as are the glasses. His walk is slightly pigeon-toed. Beneath his mustache is a row of big white teeth. Mike and I recognize him.

"Lars," the guy says, his voice smooth and professional (an announcer's voice if I've ever heard one), "I take it these are your friends?"

"They are, indeed, Mr. Russell." He turns to us. "Lads—" Then a bow toward Carol. "And lass, this is   "

Mike beats him to it, lunging past me and offering his hand. "Gordon Russell," Mike says, "The owner of Midwest Championship Wrestling and the play-by-play announcer."

Russell gives that a self-deprecating chuckle. If this were a TV taping, he would be at an announce table at ringside. The weekly shows must leave him free to greet the people. I can't help wondering why he's chosen *these* particular people, though.

"Thank you for coming," Russell says, before turning his large lenses on me, "You're Joe Davis, aren't you?"

"I am, yes," I say.

"I thought so," Russell says, "I'm a big fan."

Carol power-rolls her eyes. My weenie bit of celebrity is a constant source of irritation to her and amusement to me.

Russell grabs my hand and pumps it in an overly gregarious shake.

"I love your column," he says, "I never miss one. I think you're hilarious."

"Thank you," I say, smooth as you like (which will only further irritate Carol).

"Are you going to write a column about this?" Russell asks.

"I'm just here as a fan," I say.

"No such thing as *just a fan*," Russell says, "I appreciate all of them. But maybe there's something you can do for us. How would you like to interview Bobby Cronus?"

If I had been holding something, I almost certainly would have dropped it. I wait to see if Russell is yanking my chain. But he's serious. It takes a few seconds before my jaw starts working again.

"Me?" I say. Because why not start with something pithy?

"Of course," Russell says, "Bobby would a great subject for a column. I don't want to tell you how to do your job. You do that well enough on your own. But you've made it pretty clear you're a big wrestling fan. I think your readers would be interested in a conversation between you and Bobby."

Huh. Seven years of writing my column and I've never interviewed a celebrity. It's allowed *me* a bit of celebrity but hasn't allowed me access to others. This would be a great opportunity. Assuming I don't have a nervous breakdown beforehand.

"When would we do this?" I ask.

"How about tomorrow?" Russell says, "We're having a training session here at the arena. I'm sure Bobby can carve out some time for you. Maybe in the afternoon?"

"Sure," I say. Then a thought occurs. "Does Bobby Cronus know about this?"

"He'll be fine," Russell says, "Bobby understands the value of publicity."

"Does he even know who I am?" I ask.

"I'm not sure," Russell says, looking away, "He might. I'll make sure he's filled in, though. Interested?"

Mike looks at me like I'd be crazy to pass it up. Carol looks at me like I'd be crazy to do it. Lars looks at me like he's just plain crazy.

"Sounds like a plan," I say, "Would two o'clock work?"

"Absolutely," Russell says, again pumping my hand, "I'll let Bobby know. Thank you!"

Russell finishes the handshake (thankfully, leaving my hand still attached to my arm) and ambles back to the announce desk. Lars slaps me on the shoulder.

"Good choice, brother," he says, "Mr. Cronus is a legend. I'm sure this will be a great interview. Now, if you'll excuse me, duty calls."

Lars circles the ring, working the crowd. Mike, Carol, and I return to our seats. I try to wrap my head around what I've just agreed to do. Carol, meanwhile, sets her program on her lap and turns to Mike.

"How's the new job going?" she asks.

For those not in the know, Mike lost his cushy real estate job about a year ago after he was caught diddling the boss's daughter. (It was as sordid as it sounds.) Since then, he's worked a couple of temp jobs and had a brief run as a delivery driver for a local Chinese joint (that last one also ended in a sordid fashion). His latest gig is temping for a company that handles class action lawsuits. It's a nice change, given that we all expected Mike to be the *target* of a class action lawsuit rather than an administrator.

"Going great," Mike says, "The work is easy, and I get along with everyone in the office."

There's something in Mike's tone that I don't like. I've heard it many times before. It's like he's fighting off a shit-eating grin. I prop an elbow on one knee.

"Everyone at the office, huh?" I say.

"Everyone," Mike says.

"Including your boss?"

"Especially my boss."

"She's happy with your work?"

"She's very happy."

"How happy?"

Mike squares me with a look. "We're fucking, Joe. Is that what you want to hear?"

I can't say it's what I *wanted* to hear, but it's certainly what I *expected* to hear. Carol drops her head into her hands (a frequent reaction when dealing with Mike). I look toward the lobby, wondering if I should go grab a beer.

"I don't have to tell you the dangers of getting involved with someone at work, do I?" I say, "We've been down this road before. Many times"

Mike, no longer holding back the shit-eating grin, gives that a flip of his hand. "It's different this time. I'm not hiding anything from the boss. Brigid *is* the boss. It's a no-lose situation."

Until such time as Mike actually loses. The man has an uncanny knack for finding ways to do that. He was a military brat who spent his formative years under his parents' very formidable thumbs. When he got to college and discovered his freedom, he went on the sort of rampage that would have made Hunter S. Thompson reconsider his life choices.

"I take it nobody at the office knows about this?" I ask.

"Fuck 'em if they do," Mike says, "I think people suspect. They see me in my office when they're stuck at a table. They see me getting the cushy assignments when they're backed up with work. They see me getting a raise and an extension on my assignment. They think *Hey this guy is nothing special. He doesn't know shit about this business. The only way he can get ahead is if he's sleeping with the boss.*"

"But you *are* sleeping with the boss," I say.

"Maybe *she* is sleeping with *me*," Mike says, "You ever stopped to consider that?"

The discussion comes to an end there (thank ye Gods) because something has gotten our attention. Bobby Cronus is coming down the aisle from the babyfaces' dressing room. Mike elbows me in the ribs and points.

"There he is," Mike says, "The man himself."

Carol is unimpressed. "He looks like a nerd."

She's trying to be insulting, but she's actually correct. It's been Bobby Cronus's gimmick for most of his career: the interfering nerd manager who runs his mouth, hides behind his guys, and desperately needs to be slapped by every man, woman and child walking the planet. A guy who is so good at his job that dyed-in-the-wool fans like me and Mike (and thousands of others) came to admire him for his work. He has maintained the same look even as he's transitioned out of his role as a manager and into a backstage role. He's about my height, which would put him at just over six feet. He's got thinning dark hair (going gray), and a rather bulbous belly. In the old days, when he was in his gimmick, he would be wearing a loud suit (something like red pants, a green shirt, and a blue suitcoat) and carrying a golf club. Now, he's wearing a simple black suit with a matching tie and a white shirt. He *does* carry the golf club, maybe as a sop to us fans who remember him from back in the day. The glasses cover a pair of slightly malevolent eyes. He doesn't look like a formidable presence, but that shouldn't fool anyone.

"The nerd thing was his gimmick," I say.

"Gimmick?" Carol asks.

"What you might call a *character*," I say, "In wrestling, your act is your *gimmick*."

Carol shrugs. Unlike the rest of the crowd, she remains in her seat, gazing at the program. There's a rising excitement in my chest. Bobby Cronus himself is only a few feet away from me. Sure, he's not the big star he once was, but nostalgia doesn't recognize these things. How many hours did I spend in front of the TV watching him? Sure, I hated him at the time. But I remember all those hours fondly.

Lars accompanies Bobby Cronus into the ring. Cronus gets his share of cheers, but he doesn't acknowledge them. The crowd is filing noisily back into the arena. It takes several rings of the bell, but they finally quiet down. Lars takes a dramatic pause.

"Ladies and gentlemen, Midwest Championship Wrestling is proud to announce that our annual spectacular, *WrestleShock*, will be held on Saturday night, April 30th! Here to tell you more about it is the general manager of Midwest Championship Wrestling: Mr. Bobby Cronus!"

That gets a huge round of applause. Cronus gives the crowd a waggle of the golf club. He waits for the noise to die down before speaking.

"As Lars said, we have a huge card coming up," Cronus says, his voice carrying a Southern twang, "And it will have a huge main event. At *WrestleShock* on April 30th, right here at the Sportatorium, the main event will feature our own Midwest Heavyweight Champion, Lance Mack—" That gets a mix of cheers and boos. "Defending his title against…" Pause for effect. "The winner of tonight's main event between Nick Diamond and Jack Blades!"

The crowd explodes. Mike and I have our eyebrows raised. I know where we'll be on April 30th. Carol looks up, probably making *other* plans for that date (wash her hair, walk the dog, buy a dog). Cronus hands the microphone back to Lars.

"Tickets go on sale tomorrow morning at ten a.m. for this huge event," Lars says, "Please go to our website or call the box office number on your programs. We expect to see you all here for _WrestleShock!_"

The crowd is still buzzing when the second half of the card begins. They more or less ignore the opening match, a forgettable tag team affair. When the match is over and the wrestlers go to the back, we have a minute to stretch before the main events. Carol checks her phone and grins. Mike leers over her shoulder.

"New guy?" he asks.

Carol drops the phone into her purse. "I suppose."

My eyebrows go up. "I hadn't heard this."

"Yep. Yep," Carol says, "That's the case."

"Who is he?" I ask.

"Just somebody I'm seeing," Carol says, flitting a hand, "Nothing important."

"Ah," I say, "You sound very...committed."

"No, he's a great guy," Carol says, her arms folded, and her legs crossed, "Great guy. I like him a lot."

Carol is pointedly not making eye contact. This is weird. Yes, you could chalk it up to Mike's presence. Mike and Carol dated once upon a time. It's been over for a few years, but their breakup came as a real shock. To Mike. Since then, despite claims he's _totally_ over Carol, he gets the bends every time she dates somebody new. But Carol has never been shy about mentioning a new guy around Mike. What can this be all about?

This speculation ends when the next match starts. *Chase* by Giorgio Moroder starts up and all eyes turn toward the babyface dressing room. A goth looking dude with spiky brown hair and sloppily applied black and white makeup (designed to look like war paint, I'm guessing) emerges. His black coat billows out behind him. He slides into the ring, snake-like, and sits in one corner, apparently brooding. Lars introduces the babyface as Jackson Darkfire. Darkfire stands and throws off the coat, revealing a sleeveless black bodysuit. (Save for the makeup, the dude could be going diving.) Suddenly, *Jump Around* by House of Pain kicks in. A mix of cheers and boos accompanies it.

"Here he comes," I say.

"Behold," Mike says, "the biggest tool in the universe."

Lance Mack emerges from the heel dressing room and strikes a pose. He's tall and muscular, with curly brown hair flowing past his shoulders and perfectly tanned skin. (Minnesotans aren't noted for coming out of winter with their tans intact, so I'm guessing Mack has invested in some tanning solution.) He wears a black leather vest covered with pins and emblems (sort of like a TGIFridays that's converted to a biker bar) and a pair of bright orange trunks (as if to advertise the aforementioned toolness). A gold title belt is slung over his shoulder, and he wears a pair of aviator shades. His self-satisfaction is visible from a hundred yards.

Carol's nostrils flare. "This is Lance Mack?"

"Sadly, it is," I say.

Mack swaggers down the aisle. He taps a big gold badge on his vest and shouts, "There's a new sheriff in town!" He climbs up on the ring apron. The mix of cheers and catcalls grows louder but Mack merely gives the crowd a faux puzzled look, as if to say *Who invited you jerks to* my *party?* Mack strolls to the center of the ring, forcing Lars to take a few steps to the side.

"And ladies and gentlemen," Lars says, with less enthusiasm than he might, "your Midwest Heavyweight Champion, Lance Mack!"

Mack takes off the shades and moves to throw them to the crowd. Then he reconsiders and tosses them to Lars. Vociferous booing follows. Mack also tosses the vest and the belt to Lars, forcing him to carry them from the ring. That ratches up the booing. Apparently, the crowd doesn't like the wrestlers messing with Purple Suit. Carol gives Mr. Mack an appreciative gaze.

"He's an attractive guy," she says.

"You gonna text your boyfriend about him?" Mike says.

"Maybe I will, Michael," Carol says, "He'll be happy to know I still have a pulse. Who'd have thunk it?"

Mike gives Carol the stink eye. Fortunately, there's a wrestling match to distract them from these things (which is one of the things wrestling matches are good for).

Unfortunately, the match is kind of a disappointment. Both guys are athletic, that's for sure, and the match is fast paced. But there's no ebb or flow to it. Just a series of moves that look a little too clean to be part of a struggle. It's like watching a car race where you just see cars blurring past but have no sense of who's winning the race. Carol watches closely at first, but soon she sits back in her chair, just like Mike and me. Similarly, the audience is into it for a minute then gets restless. At one point, I catch a glimpse of Bobby Cronus standing near the faces' dressing room. He paces back and forth, not looking pleased.

Finally, Mack is down and looks vulnerable. Darkfire pulls Mack to his feet, grabs him around the waist in a sort of gut-wrench, hoists him into the air and flips him over. Darkfire's intent is to drive Mack into the mat, back first, and pin him. (A finishing move he calls the Fire Bomb.) Mack, however, shifts slightly in the air and tucks Darkfire's head under his arm. After a couple of spins (in which Darkfire is nice enough to remain on his feet and spin *exactly* where Mack needs him to), Mack falls back to the mat, driving Darkfire's head in, face down. It's a move called a DDT (or a Tornado DDT, if you count the spinning). Mack follows up with a cover and gets the win, clean in the middle of the ring. My eyes flick to Cronus, who throws up his hands and stalks off. Mack stands and raises his arm, fist clenched.

"Oh," Mike says, feigning applause, "Joy."

Lars returns the title belt to Mack, who also relieves Lars of the microphone. He puts his fingers on Lars's chest and moves him away, drawing the wrath of the crowd. (Again, don't mess with Purple Suit.)

"Beat it, scarecrow," Mack says. Lars scurries out under the bottom rope. Mack turns his attention to the fans, his voice slightly whiny. "You did it again, Midwest Championship Wrestling. You can call it a co-main event, but who goes on last? I can tell you it's not the Real Main Event, the Showstopper, the Straw That Stirs the Drink…*your* Midwest Heavyweight Champion, Lance Mack."

Mack punctuates his speech by holding the gold belt over his head and slowly pacing the ring. Mike cups his hands around his mouth.

"Aaaaaassssssclown!" Mike shouts.

Mack snaps him a look. Mike quiets down. Mack brings the belt down to waist level and gazes at it.

"Since the winner of this match is supposed to get a shot at *my* Midwest Heavyweight Title," he says, "I figure I should keep an eye on things. I'm just going to take a seat at ringside and find out which member of the Geritol Express is going to get their ass kicked at *WrestleShock.*"

He drops the mic and rolls under the bottom rope, coolly making himself at home in a ringside chair. (The fact Lars has been using that chair does not seem to bother him.) Mack retrieves his leather vest and shades and puts them back on. He strikes an insolent pose on the chair. Lars picks up the mic.

"Lance Mack, ladies and gentleman," he says, with a half-hearted gesture toward the champ, "And now it is time for your other main event of the evening!"

That gets a roar from the crowd. Lars fades into a corner of the ring. A familiar guitar riff blasts through the PA system. *Bad to the Bone* by George Thorogood. All eyes turn toward the heel side. A second later, Jack Blades appears. Holy crap. The man is here. He's tall and his only concessions to age are a little belly and a craggy face. He wears black tights and a black leather vest. His thinning dark hair hangs down past his shoulders and a goatee covers the lower part of his face. He lopes down to the ring, his eyes slightly wild. He carries a small white towel in one hand, for reasons passing understanding. A few fans shout at him, and Blades draws back as if to throw a punch. The fans back off. Blades stalks around ringside, his walk slightly bowlegged. He shouts at the fans in his gravelly voice. Up close, you can see the scars in his forehead and the mashed nose that's likely been broken a few times. Carol remains in her seat, shielding herself. Mike and I are standing, stunned at finding ourselves just a few feet from Jack freakin' Blades. Carol doesn't quite possess the same awe.

"You two like this guy?" she asks.

"Just on a professional level," I say.

"Once the match starts, we're going to boo the living shit out of him," Mike says.

Blades ignores Lance Mack as he passes. The music fades out as Blades climbs into the ring. He calls us a bunch of Minnesota maggots, in a voice that carries even without a microphone. He takes notice of Lars and charges at him, causing Lars to bail out of the ring, a tangle of assholes, elbows and purple suit. Blade stalks toward the center of the ring and throws his hands up, the towel waving like a white plume.

That's interrupted by a soaring melody from the PA. *Pomp and Circumstance.* The crowd is on its feet. I grip the railing in front of me. All eyes turn toward the face aisle. Anticipation builds. And finally, there he is: Nick Diamond himself.

He wears a gorgeous blue robe lined with white sequins. His dyed blonde hair is swept back, covering a developing bald spot on the crown of his head. He throws his arms wide and slowly turns in a circle, letting everyone in the place admire his splendor. As he struts down the aisle, fans on either side bow in the *We're not worthy* gesture. Diamond steps up to the ring apron and turns toward the crowd. He looks uneasy. He's not used to being a babyface, but his status as an elder statesman guarantees the fans are going to cheer him.

Lars takes it upon himself to spread the ropes for Diamond, easing the great man's entrance into the ring. The second Diamond gets in, Jack Blades starts toward him. The referee gets between the two. Diamond laughs off Blades' attitude and struts around the ring, playing to the crowd. Lars waits for the noise to die down.

"Ladies and gentlemen, this match is one fall—" The crowd interrupts with a shout of *One fall!* It's one of the many wrestling chants that have sprung up in recent years which, frankly, I could live without. Lars rolls with it. "With a thirty-minute time limit. In the corner to my left…" He extends a long arm toward Jack Blades. "Weighing in at two-hundred-and-sixty-five pounds and hailing from Denton County, Texas. He is a former PWA World and World Tag Team Champion, as well as a former Western Heavyweight, United States, and International Heavyweight Champion. He is Wrestling's Most Dangerous Man. This is Jack Blades!"

Blades yells at a ringside fan who may or may not be heckling him. (He doesn't really need provocation.) Lars lets the reaction die down before continuing.

"And in the corner to my right," he says, provoking an explosion from the crowd, "weighing in at two-hundred-forty-five pounds and originally from Minneapolis, Minnesota." That gets a *huge* pop from the crowd. "He is a former PWA, UWE and GAWF World Heavyweight Champion. A man who needs no introduction in any wrestling arena in the world." Thus, Lars pretty much renders himself useless. But that's never stopped him before. "He is the True Living Legend. The Icon. Professional wrestling's all-time greatest champion. He is the Diamond Stud. Nick Diamond!"

Just when you thought the place couldn't hold any more noise, the loudest roar yet goes up from the crowd. Diamond greets it with another slow turn. Lance Mack remains motionless at ringside. Diamond undoes the robe, revealing a still lithe build. From the neck down at least, he could pass for a man thirty years younger. He carefully removes the robe, folds it lengthwise and hands to Lars. It takes only one look from Diamond for Lars to know he's holding precious cargo. Diamond turns, ready to go to the center of the ring for the referee's instructions. However, he's greeted by an attack from Jack Blades.

Blades starts with a series of punches then chucks Diamond out of the ring. Blades follows him out, and shoves Diamond into the ring post. Blades rolls back into the ring and plays to the crowd while Diamond slowly gets to his feet, now bleeding from the forehead. (More than ten thousand matches and Diamond has bled in nearly all of them. It's amazing he has any blood left.) Carol recoils.

"Please tell me that's fake blood," she says.

"Nope, it's real," Mike says, "The man is in love with the blade."

"Blade?" Carol asks.

"That's how they get juice, um, *blood.*"

Carol tilts her head to one side. "With a blade?"

"A little piece of a razor blade," Mike says, "They hide it in the tape on their wrists or on their fingers. Diamond gets thrown into ring post, he goes facedown and puts his hands up to his head. What the fans don't see is that he's exposed the blade and he's dragging it across his forehead. Then he either gets rid of the blade or covers it again with the tape. Easy-peasy."

Carol's mouth hangs open. "He cuts himself with a razorblade? On purpose?"

"That's how the game is played," Mike says.

I suppose to a relative outsider, a thing like that *does* seem strange. Then again, a method actor walking around a movie set and pretending he's an aristocrat from the 1800's because he doesn't want to break character would be defined as lunacy in everyday life. (Actually, it's defined as lunacy on many movie sets.)

Diamond rolls back into the ring. Blades tries to drop an elbow on him. Diamond keeps rolling, causing Blades to miss and crash into the mat. Both men get to their feet. Diamond hits Blades with a series of jabs. Blades falls through the ropes and tumbles to ringside. He flails around, punching at the air and staggering like a drunk; selling in a style that would be ridiculous if done by anyone else. Diamond follows, hitting Blades with a chop to the chest. Blades spins around and crashes into the ring post. He drops to the floor. When Blades comes up, he's bleeding as well. I guess we've gotten that out of the way early.

Blades scurries back into the ring. Diamond follows and hits him with a knee drop. Diamond goes for the pin. But Lance Mack springs out of his seat and slides into the ring. The move distracts Diamond, causing him to break the pin and go after Mack. The kid slides out of the ring and returns to his seat. Diamond follows and confronts Mack, who doesn't react. The referee orders Diamond to get back into the ring. Diamond reluctantly complies.

Blades greets Diamond with a low blow. Diamond crumples to the mat. Blades grabs Diamond's hair and sinks his teeth into his forehead. Diamond screams and grabs his head. Blades gets to his feet, his mouth now resembling a vampire's and spits some of Diamond's blood into the air. Carol watches this through her fingers.

"This is the most disgusting thing I've ever seen," she says.

"You want to leave?" I ask.

"Hell, no."

Blades hurls punches and kicks at Diamond, who is trapped in the corner. Diamond feebly holds up his fists, trying to defend himself. Blades starts slapping him across the face.

"Fight me!" Blades screams, "Fight me, you mangy yellow dog! Fight me, you banana-nosed sumbitch!"

The referee steps in front of Blades, moving him back, possibly getting ready to check on Diamond's fitness to continue the match. While the referee has his back turned, Lance Mack hits Diamond with a cheap shot to the ribs. The crowd screams at the referee, who remains preoccupied. (Rule #1 about pro wrestling referees: they're easily distracted.) Blades shoves his way past the ref and begins battering Diamond in the corner.

But with each blow Diamond's body language becomes more animated. The crowd senses it. Each blow hurts less and less. Blades pauses, befuddled. He loops a left hand, but Diamond blocks it and lands a punch of his own. Diamond fires lefts and rights and punctuates the flurry with a huge chop to Blades' chest. Blades spins in the air and lands flat on his back. The crowd erupts.

"Kick his ass, Nick!" Mike shouts.

Diamond grabs Blades legs and puts on the Diamond Clasp. He has Blades in the center of the ring. Blades can't get to the ropes and force the referee to break the hold. The end is nigh.

Lance Mack picks up the folding chair he was sitting on and slides it into the ring. Diamond breaks the hold and goes after Mack. The referee tries to stop him. Blades bellycrawls over to the chair and uses it to get to his feet. He drives the chair into the back of Diamond's knee.

Diamond crumples to the mat, screaming in pain and grabbing his leg. The ref is preoccupied with Lance Mack. Blades shoves the chair out of the ring before the referee can notice it. (Rule #2 about pro wrestling referees: they are not particularly observant.) The referee ushers Mack out of the ring. Blades stomps Diamond's injured knee. Diamond's face contorts in pain. Blades then twists Diamond's legs like a pretzel and bridges backward. It's the Indian Deathlock, Blades' finishing hold.

Diamond's screaming hits a new level, punctuated by a few cries of "Oh God!" He reaches for the ropes, hoping to break the hold, but he's not close. Blades straightens up out of the bridge and leans over Diamond, screaming for him to quit. Diamond responds by firing a short right hand into Blades' face. Blades wavers. Diamond hits him again. Blades straightens up, releases the hold, and falls over backwards.

While the referee checks on Blades, Mack slides in with the chair. He waits for Diamond to get to his feet. As Diamond slowly rises, Ashley runs down the babyface aisle and into the ring. Just as Mack raises the chair over his head, Ashley snatches it out of his hands. She bolts out of the ring with Mack in hot pursuit. She leaves the chair behind. The referee turns his attention to the chase going on outside the ring. Diamond grabs the chair and hit Blades over the head with a blow that sounds not unlike a rifle shot. (Audible to everyone in the arena except for the referee because Rule #3 about pro wrestling referees: if they didn't see it, they didn't hear it either.) When the ref turns around, the chair is nowhere to be seen. Diamond is Mr. Innocent himself. He goes for the cover. The referee drops down. The crowd counts along.

"One…two…*three!*"

The crowd explodes again. Diamond struggles to his feet. The referee raises Diamond's hand in victory. Ashley runs in and throws her arms around her father. Mike and I exchange a high five. Lars climbs into the ring.

"Ladies and gentlemen, the winner of this match: the True Living Legend, Nick Diamond!"

Diamond drops to his knees, his arms in the air. Ashley hugs him around the neck. Mack stands outside the ring, witnessing the scene. He disgustedly grabs his belt and stalks up the heel aisle. Before disappearing into the dressing room, he turns Diamond's direction and draws a thumb across his throat. Diamond extends a hand toward him, inviting Mack to bring it on. Mack disappears into the heels' dressing room.

Carol is on her feet, her face is flushed. "I can't believe he won!"

Mike and I smile. Yup, we got her hooked.

CHAPTER TWO

One element of pro wrestling that has always fascinated me—but can also be very difficult to explain—is the idea of maintaining the illusion at all times. Now, this is an outdated notion since social media makes such a thing impossible these days. (The evidence suggests wrestlers don't even try very hard.) But it was taken seriously back in the day.

It's a tricky concept. Despite what TV or the movies might tell you, most everyone who was a professional wrestling fan knew the sport was a work. The fans may not have known how things worked behind the scenes, but there was a sense that everything you were watching was pre-planned. The key to making it work was maintaining the illusion that it was spontaneous. Much like Napoleon's concept of history, professional wrestling was a lie, agreed upon. The result was the wrestlers had to maintain the illusion twenty-four-seven. This made their activities outside the ring just as important as their activities inside it. One snagged thread of exposure could unravel the entire tapestry of illusion.

So, except for the confines of the dressing room and maybe a few other chosen spots, wrestlers lived their in-ring gimmicks. Bitter enemies didn't ride in the car together or have cookouts with each other's families.

Heels didn't sign autographs or ever give you the idea they wanted to be approached. On the other hand, babyfaces, if they were of the smiling "Aw, shucks" variety, would always be willing to shake hands, sign autographs, kiss babies or do whatever the fans required of them (within reason…although, even then…). It was as if Sean Connery went out and really did some spying (or made fans think he was spying). It's what makes wrestling unique. In any other form of entertainment, you'd think someone was completely nuts if they tried to maintain the illusion outside the chosen medium. In wrestling, back in the day at least, you'd be considered nuts if you didn't.

I'm pretty sure Bobby Cronus is still committed to protecting this illusion. At least, that's the impression I get. And why I'm nervous as hell to meet him.

Lars volunteers to drive me to my meeting with Cronus. For once, I'm happy to have his company. He hums an unidentifiable tune as he navigates his piece-of-crap Oldsmobuick down Lexington Avenue, heading toward the neighborhood around the state fairgrounds. The weather is overcast and chilly. The heater, though, blasts warm air. (The heater is probably the only good thing about this car.) Lars has dispensed with the purple suit and is resplendent in his suede coat, slacks, bowling shirt and scarf. I try to take my mind off the pending meeting.

"You said you wanted to talk to me about something," I ask, "What's up?"

Lars strokes his goatee. "I've got a couple of things. I'll deal with the fun one first. It's a little business proposition."

Oh boy. Given Lars's propensity for get-rich-quick schemes, I can only face the prospect of him having a business proposition for me with dread. I put on my best (fake) smile.

"What did you have in mind?" I ask.

"How would you like to write a movie?"

I snap a look at him. If Lars had asked me to put together a fruit basket for the aliens who are visiting him this weekend, I couldn't be more surprised. (Actually, I wouldn't be surprised at all. This *is* Lars we're talking about.)

"A movie?" I ask, "What do you mean?"

Lars adopts a superior air (a common thing when he knows something you don't). "I have secured some backers to make a film. As you know, I've always wanted to do just such a thing."

"Truthfully, I didn't know that."

"Well, I have. It's been my ambition since I saw *Breathless* in college. And now I have the opportunity."

"How did you get this opportunity?"

"I met a couple fellow buffs at a film fest," Lars says, "Turns out they have money and a strong interest in making a film. All they needed was an expert to handle the nuts and bolts."

"But you're not an expert."

"I'm not an expert *now*," Lars says, "Just give me a little time and I'm sure I'll have the whole thing mastered. I know this much: you need money, you need an idea, and you need a script. I've got the money. I've got the idea. And I've got a writer friend who, I hope, will provide the script. What do you say?"

I have to admit, despite my better judgment, I'm intrigued by this. Lars isn't the only one who has always loved film. When I was in college, I took a copious number of film classes as electives and very briefly considered becoming a filmmaker. (One look from my father when I floated the idea at the dinner table dampened my enthusiasm.) Yes, I know anything involving Lars is going to end in tears. But at the same time…movie. Hmm…

"What is this movie idea?" I ask.

"It's still forming in my head," Lars says, "But I love to mix genres. I thought a combination horror film and heist film might be a fun idea. With some social commentary. I can lay it all out for you some other time. If you're interested."

God help me, I'm interested. But I've always vowed not to get too involved in Lars's crazy schemes. And by *not too involved*, I mean not involved at all. Still, the possibility of a film is tempting.

"Let me give it some thought," I tell him, "It's a pretty big undertaking."

Lars slaps the dash. "Sounds like a plan."

The Oldsmobuick crosses University Avenue. I look toward the corner of University and Lexington and try to picture what the neighborhood looked like when University was a main thoroughfare between Minneapolis and St. Paul and Lexington Park was the home of the original St. Paul Saints. We're only a few blocks from the Sportatorium now. I try to calm down.

"Are all the wrestlers going to be there?" I ask.

"Yep," Lars says, "Mr. Cronus sees Midwest Championship Wrestling as a training facility. Accepting training is a requirement of employment."

"Even Lance Mack?"

"Even him. Although I don't know how much longer Mr. Mack will be there. From what I hear, he's on his way to the big time."

"That's the consensus."

"The big time, indeed," Lars says, "Toppermost of the poppermost. *The* big *time*."

"You don't know what *the big time* in wrestling is, do you?"

"Not as such, no."

I could school him or berate him for getting a job in pro wrestling when he knows so little about the business. But I'm too tense. A few minutes later, we're at the arena. With the gas station and the rundown residential area nearby, the Sportatorium doesn't cut an impressive figure in the light of day, despite the charming copse of trees behind it. Lars slides out of the car and takes long strides toward the arena, his scarf trailing behind him, making him look like a particularly doofy Ichabod Crane. I try to keep my legs from shaking as we approach.

"Are we going to be able to get in?" I ask.

"Absolutely," Lars says. He drops a hand into one of the pockets of his suede suitcoat and comes out with a small set of keys, "I'm a trusted employee of Midwest Championship Wrestling."

"Really? Little ol' you, huh?" I say, "Who else has keys?"

"Let's see. Me. Mr. Cronus has a set. Mr. Russell, of course. Mr. Mack. Miss Diamond. Oh, and Nick Diamond and Jack Blades each get a set while they're in town."

"I see. So, just you and the greater part of North America."

Lars twirls the keys on his finger. "Membership has its privileges."

He unlocks the big front doors. We cross the entryway and step into the lobby. As soon as we do, the sounds of grunting and banging fill the air. Lars and I peek in the entryway to the arena. The place looks cavernous without a crowd there. Wrestling school in session.

Two wrestlers are in the ring. Other wrestlers occupy the seats around ringside. The two guys in the ring are running crisscross patterns, bouncing off the ropes and narrowly missing each other as they go. Cronus, wearing a black t-shirt and sweatpants, prowls around the ring, carrying a stopwatch. Gordon Russell stands several feet back of Cronus. Every now and again, one of the wrestlers drops down on his stomach and the other steps over him without breaking stride. I recognize one of the guys. It's Jackson Darkfire, sans black-and-white makeup and goth wear. The other guy looks familiar, though I can't quite place him. Their movement is mesmerizing but brutal. Welts are visible on both guys' backs. They're sweating and breathing heavy. Lars leans toward me.

"This is called—" he says.

"Running the ropes," I say, "I've heard of it."

My eyes drift away from the ring. Lance Mack is standing on the floor, several feet away from one of the ring posts. He's chatting with Ashley Diamond. I nearly didn't recognize her. Her hair is pulled back into a ponytail and she's not wearing makeup (not that this is a problem). Mack's smirk is ever-present (I guess that's not just a gimmick) and he leans close to her as he talks. Ashley's eyes slide away from him, and her arms are folded tight against her chest. Nick Diamond, wearing a sweatshirt and coach's pants rather than his usual tailored suit, watches them as well. His eyes narrow.

"Hey Ashley, why don't you come stand by me?" he says.

Ashley steps away from Mack and walks over to her father. Mack ignores the look he's getting from Nick Diamond. Bobby Cronus's voice cuts through the air.

"Lance, you want to join the rest of the class?" Cronus says, "It's kind of the fucking point of being here."

Mack gets a sort of shit-sniffing look on his face and trudges back to ringside. He drops into a chair and slouches with maximum attitude. Cronus glares at him then goes back to watching the wrestlers in the ring. They don't slacken the pace.

The running continues for a few more minutes before Cronus calls time. Both wrestlers stagger out of the ring. The taller one lumbers slightly and makes a movement that causes me to recognize him. He's the Super Destroyer, sans mask. With the lantern jaw and the beady eyes, I can see why he wears a mask. It gives him a presence he wouldn't have otherwise. He plunks down in the seat next to Lance Mack and the two fall into conversation. Cronus orders two other wrestlers into the ring. They begin doing the same exercise. Lars and I drift down the aisle and take seats in the first row of the bleachers. Jack Blades sits in the bleachers perpendicular to us. In the light of day, he looks calm and normal. He leans back in his chair, legs crossed, and studies the action in the ring.

Lars keeps his voice down. "I'm told that running the ropes is a fundamental exercise."

"Wrestlers need incredible cardio," I say, "And ring awareness. This helps with both."

We watch, rapt, while the wrestlers run the ropes. After a minute, Bobby Cronus catches sight of us. He walks over to Gordon Russell. The ensuing conversation is quiet, but if the gestures Cronus is employing mean anything, spirited. Russell puts his hands on Cronus's shoulders, giving him some sort of assurance, then makes a beeline over to us.

"Good seeing you, Joe," he says, throwing a furtive look back, "Maybe you'd be more comfortable in the office. Bobby can join you there shortly."

Ah. Bobby Cronus's reputation for protecting the business is well founded. I follow Russell out of the arena and across the lobby. There's a metal door right behind the box office. It opens on to a small, windowless office. A few old wrestling posters adorn the wall. There's a TV with a DVD player in the corner. No sign of a computer. Everything on the desk is neatly arranged. (Just my style.) Russell pulls out a chair across from the desk. There's just enough room for me to squeeze into it.

"Your office?" I ask.

"Uh, no, it's Bobby's," he says, tugging at his mustache.

"Oh. Where's your office?"

Russell's eyes search the room. "There's only one office in the building. I guess, in a sense, the whole building is my office. After all, I'm the owner."

I keep forgetting Gordon Russell isn't in the wrestling business full-time. He's a real estate agent by day and a pretty successful one from what Mike tells me (Mike having once been in the real estate business himself). Russell backs out of the room.

"Just make yourself at home," he says, "I can get you a soda from the concession stand if you like."

"I'll be fine," I tell him, "Thank you."

"Sounds good," Russell says, adding a nervous laugh, "Bobby will be in shortly."

He strolls back to the arena. I sit in the office for several minutes. It's like waiting in the doctor's office: a long period of boredom that ends with something you might not like. I fidget, trying to find a comfortable position. The wrestling posters are from the Seventies and only hold so much interest for me. I step out of the office and edge toward the arena, hoping Cronus doesn't see me. He's standing in front of the ring. The wrestlers gather in the seats nearby.

"The spot show is tomorrow afternoon in Mankato," Cronus says, but he mispronounces it *Man-kah-to*.

Russell holds up a finger. "Man-kay-to."

"I don't give a rusty fuck," Cronus says, staring at the clipboard, "It's spelled the same way on the map."

Lance Mack stands up, getting the room's attention. "And don't forget the party here tomorrow night, after we all get back. The Block is providing the booze. We were originally gonna have it at The Block, but somebody put the kibosh on that."

Mack returns to his seat. Cronus resumes looking at his clipboard. "Anyway, show's at two o'clock," Cronus says, "You need to be there by one."

The big guy sitting next to Mack raises his hand. "Can we get there a little early? Work on our matches?"

"No, Bill Walker, you cannot get there early to work on your matches," Cronus says, looking annoyed (although I'm thinking that's a perpetual look), "You'll get there at one, I'll give you your finish and then you guys will go out and call it in the ring. That's how it's done. That's professional wrestling."

Walker mumbles something. I'm too far away to catch it, but Bobby Cronus isn't. He tosses the clipboard into the ring.

"You can call it *old school* if you want," Cronus says, "I'm going to call it *professional wrestling*." Cronus paces in front of the ring. "You know what makes professional wrestling work? When it's taken seriously. When it's not a fucking clown show. Most of these independent promotions—these outlaw mud show goofs—they just run their shows to jack off and tickle their own taints. The gimmicks they use proves that. There's that fucking guy out there who wrestles with his hands in his pockets."

"Red Partridge," Bill Walker says.

"Fucking douchebag," Cronus says, "Sure, wrestling is a simulated sport. But the key word is *sport*, not *simulated*. You get some fuckwit with his hands in his pockets trying to wrestle. In what fucking sport would you find that acceptable? If you went to a major league baseball game, you think you're going to see the shortstop standing there with his hands in his fucking pockets? If some guy tried to fight Muhammad Ali by keeping his hands stuck down his trunks, Ali would have kicked his ass in thirty seconds and thought, 'Shit, that's the easiest money I ever made.' If it's not acceptable in an actual sport, it's not acceptable in a simulated sport. I don't see why it's so hard for these morons to understand that." Cronus looks at the clipboard again, then changes his mind and continues his lecture. "The problem today is everyone analyzes wrestling, and no one enjoys it. It's all critics and no fans. If you go to a movie like *Back to the Future*, are you supposed to analyze the lighting or the editing or the way the shots are set up? Maybe if you're a film student or a critic. But ninety-five percent of us are supposed to care if Marty gets back to fucking Nineteen Eighty-Five."

Cronus pauses for effect. Mack leans toward Bill Walker and, while ostensibly whispering, speaks loudly enough for the whole arena to hear him.

"Speaking of guys who want to go back to 1985," Mack says.

The room is quiet. Then a few of the wrestlers laugh. They're followed by a couple more wrestlers. Mack doesn't look remotely repentant. Cronus stalks over to Mack, his face going red. Mack doesn't react.

"Listen to me, chucklefuck," Cronus says, "You might have a future in this business. Might. But it ain't gonna happen if you keep sitting there thinking you know all about this shit. I been in this business thirty years and I've seen dipshits like you come and go and never draw a fuckin' dime. Because they got some athletic ability but no fucking brain and no fucking heart. You think you're an actor playing a role. Bad news for you, you prissy prancing, metrosexual looking fucking douchebag: that ain't the business you got into. You're a professional wrestler. Or at least you're trying to be. But until you get it through your head that cosplaying this shit don't cut it, you got no future."

Mack stands up. He's a few inches taller than Cronus, but Cronus shows no sign of backing down.

"I'm getting pretty fucking sick of you talking to me that way," Mack says, his voice whiny as ever (dude, just a little bit of bass, it's not that hard), "Maybe you need to shut up. Before I shut you up."

"Go ahead and try it, you weaselly little fucker."

Mack stands there, uncertain. It's as if he doesn't know how to start a fight. Then he steps toward Cronus and puts a hand on his face, getting ready to push Cronus down. Before he can do it, though, Jack Blades grabs Mack around the waist and tosses him back toward his chair with a little more force than absolutely necessary. Mack bounces up but doesn't seem anxious to get into a fight. Nick Diamond steps in front of Cronus and keeps him from going after Mack. Russell tries to keep things calm.

"Why don't we call it a day?" Russell says, "We can pick this up another time."

I speed back to the office, lest I get caught watching the scene. This doesn't make me feel any better. Bobby Cronus is many things but *approachable* has never been among them. I don't need him to be riled up on top of everything. I leave the office door open, maybe to give him the idea I've got nothing to hide.

After a few minutes, voices drift in from the lobby. I glance out the door, expecting to see Bobby Cronus walking my direction. But I don't see anyone coming. On the far side of the lobby, though, Nick and Ashley Diamond are in a furtive conversation. It doesn't look friendly. Ashley has tears in her eyes and her gestures punch the air very close to her father. Nick doesn't say anything, but he doesn't look happy. I can't hear what's being said. Ashley finally smacks her father on the arm and shouts, "I can take care of myself!" She stalks back to the arena. Nick says something in passing, but Ashley doesn't pay any attention. I turn back to the office.

A few minutes of squirming later, my guest (or am I *his* guest?) storms into the office. Bobby Cronus notices me and stops, his cheeks puffing out like he's come fresh from a fight (which is a distinct possibility). I'm worried I'm going to get thrown out of the office. Then Cronus softens ever so slightly.

"You're the reporter," he says, "The one Gordon wanted me to talk to."

"I am," I say, standing and offering him my hand, "My name is Joe Davis. And I'm more of a blogger than an actual reporter."

Cronus gives me a polite but exceedingly firm handshake. "Who do you work for?"

"*The Daily Bugle*," I say, "It's a website. Locally based." (As if that last part will somehow make a difference.)

I drop back into the chair as Cronus wedges himself behind the desk. He fishes a can of Sprite out of the minifridge behind him and cracks it as he sits down. He doesn't offer one to me, but I don't consider that a great loss. (I *do* wish there was coffee, though.) He takes a healthy swig of the soda.

"What's the article going to be about?" he asks.

Good question. I haven't given it a lot of thought. Sometimes I have an idea fully formed in my head. Sometimes I just blunder around until an idea presents itself. But I don't think that's going to hold any water with Cronus. The office suddenly feels very small.

"I'm thinking it's about a wrestling legend," I say, "helping out a local promotion."

Cronus snorts. "Helping out." He drums his fingers on the desk. "All right, go ahead."

I hold up my phone with the recording app open. Cronus nods and I set it down on the desk. I look down at my notebook.

"How did you first get interested in wrestling?" I ask.

Cronus looks toward the wall. "I used to catch Spike Atlas's show out of Indianapolis, back when I'd stay at my grandma's house during the summer. It was on late, on this snowy TV screen. Then I found a local wrestling show in Louisville. Then I started reading wrestling magazines. Pretty soon, I talked my mom into taking me to the weekly cards at the Louisville Gardens. And we were off to the races."

"Did you know right away that you wanted to get into the business?"

"Not right away, no," Cronus says, "I knew I wanted to get closer to it. My mom started working the concession stand and I'd help her out. Then I started taking photos at ringside."

"You were pretty successful with that."

His eyes light up, "If I hadn't gotten into the business, I could have made decent money just being a photographer."

I make a note. "What attracted you to wrestling? As a fan, I mean."

Cronus gives it some thought. Maybe he hasn't been asked this before. It's like me being asked what I like about writing. I know that I love it but trying to explain it can be a beast. Cronus speaks to the wall.

"I got caught up in the drama," he says, "I watched it as a pure fan. I had guys I liked to root for. Bob James, Jimmy Valentine, guys like that. Rooted against guys like Johnny King and Sam Bash. When it's done right, it's easy to get caught up in it."

"When did you get smart to the business?" I ask.

Cronus's face darkens. "When did *you* get smart to the business?"

That pretty much kills the jovial mood we were developing. "It was just…y'know…the internet," I say. And it doesn't even come out sounding *that* eloquent.

"Fucking internet geeks," Cronus says, "You gonna kayfabe this article?"

Hey, there's a word I know (though Bobby Cronus probably thinks I shouldn't know it). For those not familiar with the lingo, *kayfabe* is the line of demarcation between the illusion of pro wrestling's legitimacy and the real world. You could, for lack of a better term, call it the *fourth wall* for professional wrestling. But as I've discussed, that wall can extend out into the real world in a way the movies' or TV's fourth wall never could. Old school guys like Bobby Cronus treat it like Omertà. For younger guys like Lance Mack, it's a custom more honored in the breech than in the observance. In an era of the internet and the exposure of the business, it's difficult to say who is right. For the moment, though, I don't want to antagonize Bobby Cronus.

"I'm not sure," I say, "I'm going to gather information and decide from there."

Cronus pauses a second. "Just let me read the article before it goes to press."

"I'd be glad to," I say, "My editors don't even know it exists until I send it to them. If we have to kill it, nobody will know about it but us."

Cronus is satisfied with that and we continue the interview. We go through his early days, breaking into the business as a manager in Louisville, using an *incompetent rich kid* gimmick. We move into his first big break, getting hired by Cowboy Bob Watson in Louisiana and being put together with Tommy Corbin and Steve Ray to form The Nightmare Express. After setting records there, they moved to the PWA and became the top heel tag team in the business for over three years. As he reminisces, Cronus leans back in his chair, relaxed. But I'm about to screw that up.

I grimace. "And then…"

Cronus lets out a breath through his nose. "And then." He takes a sip of Sprite. "PWA is running out of money. They're taken over by Taylor Broadcasting. The corporate suits start running things. They don't know shit from apple butter about wrestling, but they think there isn't shit to *know* about wrestling. They decide they're going to be just like the UWE. Sign a bunch of muscle-heads, give 'em cartoony gimmicks, and use 'em to sell fucking ice cream bars to little kids. They didn't see any value in the Nightmare Express. They wanted to turn me into a fucking announcer. Bullshit. I had to get out. So did Steve. Tommy had a family. He needed the paycheck. That was the end of the Nightmare Express."

"But not the end of you in the business."

"Hell no," Cronus says, "I started my own promotion down in east Tennessee. That ran for a few years. It was fun, but it was a down time for the wrestling business. I couldn't keep the company afloat." He takes off his glasses and cleans them on his shirt. "Then I went to work for the UWE. Three fucking years. It was good money. I'll give it that. But it damn near killed me. Corporate atmosphere. Dealing with Terry Kennedy's whims. Cartoony wrestling. I had to get out. I talked them into letting me go back to Louisville and starting a developmental territory. Break guys in before they went up to the UWE."

"Kentucky Championship Wrestling," I say.

"We had some damn good talent there. Built a whole generation of stars for UWE." He frowns. "Then their creative staff started fucking things up. We'd send people up there and they'd get these ridiculous comedy gimmicks. It's what happens when your creative team is a bunch of failed sitcom writers. Then the new Head of Talent Relations made it worse. Started sending me guys he'd met on an airplane or girls he found in lingerie catalogues. People who didn't care about wrestling. They just wanted to be on television." Cronus puts a mocking little ring around *television.* "People like that fucking Joey Munson."

"I heard about that," I say, "That was the last straw."

"It was. Little puke started laughing during one of his matches. Like the whole fucking thing was a joke. The business I had been in for twenty-five fucking years at that point. I was running on no sleep and no food, and I had *no* fucking time for this little jackoff. When he got back to the dressing room, I slapped the taste out of his fucking mouth." Cronus flips a hand. "The little puke called the office and complained."

"And that was the end of that."

"The UWE cancelled the developmental deal," Cronus says, "We lost most of our talent. I sold the company to one of the trainers and moved on."

We go through the list of promotions Cronus has worked with since then. It tends to be the same story again and again: Cronus gets hired, does some brilliant work for the promotion, then runs afoul of someone (usually over some transgression of Cronus's idea of how wrestling should be) and gets shown the door. Wash, rinse, repeat. He's wrestling's version of Billy Martin (minus the alcohol problem). A guy whose genius for his business is matched only by his genius for pissing people off.

"And now you're here," I say.

"Gordon is a good guy," Cronus says, "I like him. Can't say that about everyone he's hired. Can't say this state is my favorite place to be. Cold as shit."

"I've heard that said."

"But it's a living," Cronus says, "I don't need the money. I made plenty in my time. I just…love the business, I guess." And here's his last chance to be in it, though I keep that to myself. Cronus keeps going. "Gordon at least understands how the business is supposed to look. This horseshit the UWE has been doing for years, now that they're the only game in town, it's killing the business. Bad wrestling and bad comedy. And it's bled down to the indies now. People think wrestling is supposed to be funny and silly. They laugh at all the people who used to like wrestling, say they were a bunch of gap-toothed yokels who thought this shit was real. At least they fucking *cared*. And they laid down plenty of fucking money *because* they cared, not because they wanted a fucking laugh. If you can't get people to care, there's no point in doing this shit."

I tap my pen on the paper. "What do you think his going to happen to the business? In the future?

Cronus finishes his can of Sprite, crushes it, and tosses it into a nearby wastebasket. "You ever heard of roller derby?"

"Heard of it," I say.

"Did you know it used to huge? Maybe even bigger than wrestling. Now, it's fucking dead. It might be a niche thing here and there, but it sure as shit ain't big business. Wrestling will go the same way. Maybe not in my lifetime, but it'll happen." I don't say anything to that. Cronus raises his eyebrows. "You don't think so?"

"It's just...the UWE is a billion-dollar company."

"So was Enron. How did that work out?"

He's got a point. A pessimistic one, but a point, nonetheless. I shift in my seat. I've got one more question, and I'm wondering if I should ask it. But what the hell? The worst he can do is throw me out. (At least, I hope that's the worst he can do.)

"Is there anything you'd do differently?" I ask, "With your career, I mean."

Cronus fishes another Sprite out of the minifridge. "Maybe being born ten years earlier so I could have gotten into the business sooner. The wrestling I watched growing up, that was what I wanted to do. Feels like I got into the business just in time to watch it change into something I hate. I've done my best to keep the old values around. But…I don't know." He props his chin in one hand. "I was doing a meet and a greet at a convention a few months back. I was there with Jack Blades. One of the fans was trying to thank us for putting our bodies on the line to entertain people like him. And he started crying and saying, 'It's still real to me, dammit.' I knew how he felt." Cronus says quietly, "It's still real to me, dammit."

If I was one of these good journalistic types, I'd press him with more questions. But I'm one of these lazy internet journalists. I turn off the recording app, and offer him my hand.

"Thanks for chatting with me," I say.

Cronus takes it without standing up. "Just make sure I see the article before you print it. Or whatever the fuck it is you do."

"I guarantee it."

"Close the door on your way out."

I do as I'm told. Once the door is closed, I'm alone in the lobby. I look around for Lars, but naturally, he's nowhere to be found. I take out my phone and text him. He replies with, **I'm in the WC. Be out in a few.** Swell.

I linger around the lobby, wondering if I'm going to run into any more wrestlers and what I would do if I *did* run into one. (Probably keep my head down.) Voices come from the entrance to the arena, echoing in the relative stillness of the building. One of them belongs to Gordon Russell. The other belongs to Lance Mack. I peek around the corner. They're the only ones there. This is clearly a private chat. A private chat I'm going to listen to. (I'm not eavesdropping. *You're* eavesdropping!)

"I'm sorry," Russell says, "but Bobby is my booker."

"He's out of touch," Mack says, "Maybe he was fine twenty years ago, but time has passed him by. It would be one thing if he was at least open to discussing shit. But the second you say or do something he doesn't agree with, he shuts you down. It's bullshit."

"I understand," Russell says, "but you also have to consider—"

"No, here's a thing *you* have to consider," Mack says, "I'm not the only one getting fed up. People are talking. I'd hate for something to happen. Screw up the deal you're working on."

There's a slight pause. "What do you mean?"

"You think the deal is still going to go down if everyone on your roster walks out?"

Russell sounds short of breath. "They wouldn't do that."

"No, that's *exactly* what they'd do," Mack says, his voice a purr that carries no charm, "And I'd be the one to lead them. You know Bruno Harvey over at the Minnesota Wrestling Federation? He'd love it if I was working over there. And if I went, most of the roster would follow me. You know that, right?"

"Yes, I do."

"Turns out MWF has a show the same night as *WrestleShock*," Mack says, "I wonder what *WrestleShock* will look like if most of the boys are working on the other side of the river that night?"

Russell's jaw drops. "You'd do that?"

"Yes, I would," Mack says, "Unless you get rid of Bobby Cronus. Understand?"

It's silent, then Russell says, "You realize the position you're putting me in?"

"I suppose," Mack says, "And I don't really care. You have to decide who's most important here. Your call, not mine."

Someone comes out of the faces' dressing room. Mack and Russell separate. Russell is coming toward the lobby. I take three giant steps toward the office, trying to make it look like I was over there the whole time (and *completely* out of earshot). Russell comes into the lobby and spots me immediately.

"Everything go well?" he asks.

"Jiffy swell," I say, "It was great meeting Bobby."

"Yes. He's a good…he's a guy." Russell clears his throat. "Did you get enough material?"

"Got a good start," I say, "I'd, uh, I'd like to keep coming to the matches. See what other material I can find."

"I'll make sure you have complimentary tickets to the TV tapings and the weekly shows," Russell says, "Just let me know how many you need. I'll be happy to get them for you."

I thank Russell. He walks back toward the arena. He passes Lars, who was likely the person coming out of the faces' dressing room. Lars bounds up to me.

"Everything go okay?" he asks.

"It was great. You have any idea what might be going on with Lance Mack and Gordon Russell?"

"A fantastic working relationship that makes Midwest Championship Wrestling tick."

I'm not going to get anywhere talking to Lars. While some are caught between what they know and their wish not to know it, Lars jumps right to the latter. I wave a hand toward the door.

"Shall we?" I ask.

Lars gives me a thumbs up. "Roger-dodger. We'll be back here soon enough."

That will be the case. I wonder if it's going to be the case for Bobby Cronus.

***

A thing you need to understand about Mike: women find him attractive. Really attractive. At first. He's a good-looking guy with a gift of gab. He dresses well when he puts his mind to it. He can even be funny and self-deprecating if he thinks that will aid in getting a woman naked. It's only when said women get to know him that the cracks begin to show. Still, it's rare that I'm surprised by Mike landing a date with someone.

"I'm going to get a drink with Ashley Diamond."

This is one of those rare occasions.

I nearly drop the bottles of Grand Brewing Maibock I'm fetching from my fridge. Mike leans against the breakfast bar on the other end of my narrow kitchen. His smile would be visible from the other end of a football field. I take a moment to recover myself before kicking the refrigerator door shut.

"There's very little chance that the Ashley Diamond we're talking about *isn't* the Ashley Diamond from the other night?" I say.

Mike scratches his head. "Meaning it *is* the Ashley Diamond from the other night?"

"Yes."

"Then yes."

This is not where I thought this little get together would go. We're hanging out at my apartment on Summit Avenue, a mansion-strewn artery of St. Paul that F. Scott Fitzgerald once dubbed *a museum of architectural failures*. (When you're privileged and drunk, you tend to think like that. I assume.) It's a one-bedroom, one-bathroom place on the third floor of a converted rowhouse. There are three arch windows at the front and a deck I haven't gotten to use all winter out back. It's a simple affair but it's all I need. Speaking of simple affairs…

"We spent a whole night playing trivia at The Tav," I say, handing him a beer, "and you wait until we come back here to tell me that?"

"Carol was there," Mike says, "You never how these things are going to affect her."

"Assuming they affect her at all. She's got a boyfriend."

Mike snorts. "A boyfriend she never talks about. That's true love there."

I'm tempted to argue but realize I can't. Though we don't do a great deal of talking during trivia at The Tav (our Sunday night tradition when football season is not in session), Carol *did* scrupulously avoid talking about her latest paramour. There was no way this was in deference to Mike. I suspect she enjoys torturing him, particularly when the guy she's dating is a demonstrably better catch than Mike (which extends to nearly every guy Carol dates).

"How did you land a date with Ashley Diamond?" I say.

"I asked her."

"Quit fucking around."

We retire to the living room. Mike drops on to the futon while I sit in the nearby comfy chair. My desk, where I write most of my columns, looms in the corner. Rain taps against the arch windows at the front of the apartment and the radiator below them is hissing. (Almost mid-April and I still need the radiator. You can warm up at any time, Spring!) Mike sets his beer on the coffee table, spilling some. He makes no effort to clean it up, forcing me to grab a napkin and do it myself. He ignores my work and continues with his story.

"After the matches the other night, I didn't feel like going straight home," he says, "So, I stopped into this bar near the arena. Place called The Block."

"I've heard of it."

"Some of the wrestlers were hanging out there," Mike says, "I didn't have the guts to approach them, so I took a seat at the bar. Ashley Diamond came up to get another drink and I started chatting her up. We hit it off. I asked her if she wanted to meet me for a drink sometime and she said yes. Done and done."

"Amazing," I say, reaching down to scratch Lenny, my alpha cat, on the ears, "How much did you have to liquor her up to pull that off?"

"Didn't have to at all," Mike says, "and fuck you. Ashley was drinking club soda the whole time."

"Seriously? You sure there wasn't something *in* the club soda?"

"There wasn't. She ordered two of them while we were at the bar. I'm willing to say she's straight edge."

"Huh," I say, contemplating this over a sip of beer, "Was her dad there?"

"He was," Mike says, "He came up to the bar a few times, but I didn't have the guts to talk to him. He was buying rounds of kamikazes for the house, though. I managed to snag one."

"But Ashley didn't drink?"

"Nope. She was the exception. A lot of guys getting loaded in there."

I sit back in the chair. "I heard they're supposed to do a bigger bash at the arena tonight. You didn't get an invite to that?"

"I did not. That's okay, though. I'm meeting up with Ashley tomorrow night at The Tav."

Lenny brushes up against my leg. I temporarily leave Mike to his self-satisfaction and give the cats a late-night snack. Two cats, littermates, run my household. Lenny, a handsome butterscotch tabby who may have been George Patton in another life, and Squiqqy, the nervous former runt of the litter whose black-and-white coloring and obsequious manner remind me of a butler. As could be expected, it's Lenny who goes about demanding the snack while Squiggy maintains a discreet distance. I scoop some kibble out of the big plastic container and deposit it in their separate bowls.

"How does this date with Ashley affect things with your boss?" I ask.

"What does one have to do with the other?" Mike says.

"You're currently shagging your boss and hoping, I assume, to shag Ashley."

"You assume correctly."

"These two things would seem incompatible," I say, returning to the comfy chair, "Unless, of course, your boss is cool with you seeing other people."

"Oh God, she absolutely is not," Mike says, "If Brigid knew about Ashley, she'd shit herself. And I'd be out of a job. Again."

"Then what's your plan?" I ask.

Mike throws his hands out, as if the solution should be obvious. "I don't tell Brigid about Ashley. What she doesn't know doesn't hurt her. Or me. But most importantly, me."

I press the beer bottle to my head, fighting off the pre-hangover headache Mike is giving me. When I pull the beer bottle away, I hold it up in a toast.

"Good luck and Godspeed, son," I say.

Mike clinks bottles with me and we each take a healthy sip of our adult beverages. Between Carol's mystery boyfriend and Mike's various surreptitious girlfriends, there's no shortage of excitement around here.

Speaking of excitement, Lars bursts through the front door. I forgot to lock it when Mike and I came in but that doesn't make a difference. Lars is the building superintendent and has the master set of keys. You can't stop him. You can only hope to slow him down. He doesn't seem willing or able to slow down at the moment. Hands the size of flank steaks saw the air. (I've often wondered if Lars's hands are really that big or if they just look more sizable at the ends of his pipe-cleaner arms.)

"I need your help," he says to me.

"All right," I say, "You need a beer? Is that the help?"

"No, no," Lars says. He looks toward the kitchen then the liquor shelf in the corner. "But let's not take anything off the table."

Come to think of it, Lars *did* seem a little preoccupied at The Tav. "What's the help?" I ask.

He puts his hands in the pockets of his cardigan sweater. "Okay, you guys remember a little more than a year ago when I had a meeting with this guy Peter? The one who was interested in reviving Les Bos?"

I *do* remember that night, though there were a few more important things going on (Carol being accused of murder, running from a contract killer, being pursued by the police, the usual). For those not in the know, Les Bos was one of Lars's entrepreneurial adventures. It was a strip club where the women stripped each other. Financially, its brief run was a sterling success. But said run was brief because Lars and his business partner, Chuck, forgot to obtain a liquor license (their individual devil frequently hiding out in the details).

"I remember that meeting," I ask, "You never told me what happened."

"Nothing happened," Lars says, "Peter was interested and wanted me on board. But didn't want Chuck. And Chuck, as you may imagine, had strong feelings about that. I told Peter I couldn't go ahead with it. I thought he accepted it like a gentleman. Turns out he's rather more a complete bastard."

Mike, whose interest in that venture far exceeded mine, sits up. "What did he do?"

"It's what he's *going* to do," Lars says, "He's reopening Les Bos. This time he's going to cut out *both* me and Chuck."

Mike asks, "Can he do that?"

Lars strokes his beard. "We're looking into it. And by *looking into it*, I mean I'm trying to keep Chuck from killing the guy. Once that's done, I'll open a more formal inquiry."

I wish I could help, but I don't know a hell of a lot about law. And even less about business law. I *do* have some connections, however.

"I can give you my brother Kevin's number," I say, "I don't know if he'd handle it personally, but he might point you in the right direction. Or just give you some general advice."

"I was hoping for that," Lars says, "Thank you, brother." He claps his hands. "Say, your dad's a business owner, isn't he? He must know something about this stuff. Do you think he'd help us out?"

Ah, this is a bit of a sticky wicket (and other Britishisms I find disgusting). It's one thing to set Lars loose on my brother

Kevin. I can enjoy some good comedy in the name of helping a friend. But my dad? I love my dad. He doesn't deserve having Lars sic'd on him. Besides, there *would* be repercussions the next time I visit my parents.

"I can ask," I say, "But he's awfully busy running the store."

"Any help would be appreciated," Lars says.

Guilt is seeping in. I know perfectly well my dad's industry these days extends to reading the paper and shooting the shit with his buddies while my brother Owen actually runs the family hardware store. So, his being busy is a little white lie I will have to compound with another little white lie about how he doesn't have time to talk to Lars. I think this is how Watergate started.

It's probably a good thing that Lars's cell phone rings. He's quick to answer. Whatever he hears causes him to totter. I'm afraid he's going to crash into (or possibly through) one of the arch windows. He gets it together enough to say, "I'll be there" before hanging up.

"What's going on?" I ask.

Lars takes in a breath. "Lance Mack is dead."

And there are those moments when a strip club isn't the biggest of your problems.

CHAPTER THREE

One of the most (if not the *most) effective storytelling techniques in wrestling is The Turn. It plays on the fans' emotions, both to the good and the bad. If done right, it sets up future matches and feuds and draws money. Like a lot of things in pro wrestling, it's simple in theory and challenging in execution. Here's how it works:*

As is commonly known in wrestling, you have good guys and bad guys. The good guys are called babyfaces *or simply* faces. *Bad guys are known as* heels. *The Turn involves a wrestler switching from one side to the other. Becoming a babyface is called a Face Turn. Going to the dark side is called a Heel Turn. See? Simple to describe. But here's where it gets complex.*

Turning a wrestler isn't as simple as deciding "Okay, Bob's going to be a babyface now." First, the fans must want *to see the wrestler turn, even if they aren't aware of it. Maybe the heel has been getting a smattering of cheers. Maybe the babyface has simply run his course and things are getting stale. Maybe the booker sees something in a particular wrestler and thinks, "If I turn them, they're going to be huge." It takes an astute booker to both give the fans what they want and tell them what they want without them realizing it. Again, simple in theory but complex in execution.*

Any guy who has ever tried to get a bra off a woman will know what I'm talking about.

News of Lance Mack's demise is like a Turn we didn't see coming. I'm not sure if it's a face turn or a heel turn, but it's certainly unexpected. We sit there, stunned.

"Lance Mack is dead?" I say, "What happened?"

Lars throws out his pipe cleaner arms and lets them fall to his side. "I don't know. That was Mr. Russell on the phone. He said Mr. Mack was found dead in the locker room at the arena." He sits on the arm of my futon. "I'm not sure why Mr. Russell called me. I guess he just needed to tell someone." He runs a hand through his quasi-pompadour. "Mr. Russell's at the arena, waiting for the police. He asked me to come over. I think he just wants someone there."

Mike drains his beer. "Maybe *you* need someone there, too."

I look to Mike. "Seems like the kind of thing we ought to do."

Yep, here we go again: finishing a night of drinking, rushing off to the scene of a crime. (Although, there have been plenty of nights of drinking that ended with us rushing *away* from the scene of a crime.) Lars tosses his scarf over his shoulder. Mike is already lurching toward the sofa to grab his leather jacket (which he deposited there rather than the coat tree, located conveniently near the door). I take Mike's beer bottle and put it in the recycling bin before grabbing my peacoat off the coat tree. (*Somebody* has to use the damn thing). In a perfect world, I'd be going to bed and dealing with everything in the morning.

Then again, what perfect world would involve Lars?

***

The police are still on the scene when we pull up to the Midwest Championship Wrestling Sportatorium. Lars parks in the dirt lot on the side of the building and leads us toward the front entrance. The wind blows cold rain into our faces. A group of cops are gathered near the front, discouraging anyone from getting into the building. (Although, it's the middle of the night. The task isn't exactly Herculean.) One of them, a dude with a blonde crew cut and a round face, approaches us.

"We're going to need you to keep back," the cop says, probably dropping his voice an octave.

Lars has scant respect or love for the police, who he consistently refers to as *the federales*. Ergo, it's no surprise when he draws up his scarf and looks away. Mike has a similarly dyspeptic view of law enforcement. He stands aloof. I guess it's up to me.

"We're here to see Gordon Russell," I say.

"You work here?" the cop asks.

"My friend does," I say.

Lars, though, refuses to speak to the cop. Mike is equally unhelpful, using a completely unnecessary finger to scratch the bridge of his nose. If the cop decides this situation calls for police brutality, I'm not going to get much help. I turn to Lars.

"Would you mind talking to them?" I say, "Or just letting Gordon know we're here."

Lars takes out his cell phone and places a call. "Mr. Russell," he says, "It's Lars. I'm outside with my friends Joe and Mike."

Lars thanks Russell and pockets the phone. Everyone is quiet until Gordon Russell appears. He looks haggard, his hair sticking up and his dress shirt half-tucked into his slacks. There's a faint smell of booze about him.

"It's okay," he assures the cop, "They're with me. I'd like to have them come inside."

The cop checks with someone on a radio then jerks a thumb toward the entrance. We follow Russell to the front entryway. No one speaks until the door closes behind us.

"Thank you for coming," Russell says, "Sorry to bother you so late. I couldn't get ahold of Bobby. I didn't know who else to call."

We push past the entryway and into the lobby. The first thing we see is a plainclothes cop. He's a short, balding guy with a sad bulldog face and wire-rim glasses. With his rumpled gray suit and clip-on tie, he looks like a slightly intense insurance salesman. I recognize him. It's Sergeant Frank Pike of the St. Paul Police Department. He gives a casual look my direction and does a doubletake when he recognizes me.

"Counselor," he says, "why did I know I'd see you here?"

Weirdly, that makes two of us. For the record, the *counselor* nickname hearkens back to my first meeting with Pike. Mike was accused of killing his neighbor (relax, he was innocent) and for reasons passing understanding, decided to introduce me to Sergeant Pike as his lawyer. The murder charge didn't stick, but the nickname has.

"I'm here with a friend," I say.

Pike eyeballs Lars. "And why is *he* here?"

"He works for the wrestling promotion," I say.

"Why didn't I see that coming?" Pike mumbles.

"What happened?" I ask.

Pike debates telling me. But we've run into each other a few times. He knows how this is going to play out. I'm going to be a bigger and bigger pain in the ass until he finally tells me what's going on. Pike sighs.

"Follow me," he says. We step into the lobby. The place seems empty. Pike turns toward me "This going to wind up on your little website?" he asks.

"Maybe. But only after the fact and only if there's a story to tell. I'll keep it to myself in the meantime."

"That doesn't really give me any comfort. But fine." He runs a hand through what's left of his hair. "Mack was found in the dressing room. Severe head trauma. Likely beaten to death."

Whoa. Mack is—was—a fairly-sizeable guy and an athlete to boot. Beating him couldn't have been an easy task. "How was it done?"

"We found a golf club," Pike says, "It had blood and brain matter on it."

I try not to gag. The instinct is overcome by another thought. A golf club. Bobby Cronus's gimmick. The concern must cross my face, but Pike doesn't notice. I glance toward the heels' dressing room.

"Who found him?" I ask.

"Gordon Russell," Pike says, "Says he was here for a little gathering. He left and came back. Apparently, he forgot something. He found Mack in the dressing room, lying on the floor in his underwear, already cold."

"His underwear?" I say, "What was he doing in his underwear?"

"I don't know," Pike says, deadpan, "You want to ask him, or should I?"

Great. Nice to know I can inspire what passes for Pike's sense of humor. I look around. "No idea who could have done this?" I ask, "Or why?"

"Not yet. Whoever it was went through Mack's stuff. The bag was on the other side of the room from the body. It was open and had been tossed." I don't think Pike is aware of the significance of the golf club. I don't want to tell him, but the look on my face gives something away. "Something on your mind, counselor?" he asks.

I slowly shake my head (if I did it quickly, he'd know something was up). "Nope. Just…thinking."

"Fine. You going to let me do my work now? And promise to stay out of this?"

I hold up my hands. "This is your show. I'm just here for moral support."

He eyeballs me over the top of his wire rim glasses. "I'd like to think that."

I stroll back out to the entryway. Russell is pacing and mumbling. Lars and Mike stand nearby. We're clear of any cops.

"Do you have any idea where Bobby Cronus is right now?" I ask.

Russell tugs at his mustache. "His apartment, I imagine. Why?"

"Because I think the police are going to ask you that shortly." Reacting to the stunned look on Russell's face, I add: "There was a golf club found at the scene. The police think it's the murder weapon."

Russell totters slightly, like he's going to pass out. Lars drops a hand on Russell's shoulder, helping to steady him.

"I…I didn't see the golf club," Russell says, "I just saw Lance and…I knew I had to call the police. It…do they know if it was Bobby's golf club?"

"They haven't said," I say, "But unless Rory McIlroy picked a really strange time to play through, I'm guessing it belongs to Bobby Cronus."

"Oh God, what are we going to do?" Russell says, "No top star. No booker. We are completely…" He struggles to say it, but it's the most accurate word choice. "Fucked."

"Maybe not," I say, looking back to make sure Pike isn't eavesdropping, "What happened here tonight?"

Russell takes a moment to collect himself. "We had a little party. Nick Diamond was bartending, so things got a little…insane. I had to take over for him, just to make sure everyone got home all right." Russell rubs his head at the memory. "It was just a few of us at the end of the evening. Bobby and me. Nick Diamond. Ashley. Jack Blades. And Lance, of course."

"What time did the party start to wind down?"

"About eleven-thirty," Russell says.

"And what time did you call the police?" I ask.

"About a half hour ago, I think."

It's just past one in the morning. Russell found Mack's body around twelve-thirty, roughly. Meaning Mack was murdered somewhere between eleven-thirty and twelve-thirty.

"What time did you leave?" I ask.

"About twelve," Russell says, "I got halfway home and remembered I had left some paperwork back at the arena. When I got back, Bobby wasn't here. I had already told him not to bother with a walkthrough, that I had done it already. Still, I decided to do another one. Just a compulsive thing, I guess. I saw a light on in the heels' dressing room. Then…I found Lance."

"Who was still here when you left the first time?" I ask.

Russell looks up as he thinks. "Everyone except Jack. I saw him leave earlier. Nick and Bobby were in the office, talking. Bobby had spent most of the night in there." He strokes his mustache. "I spent time trying to settle things between Bobby and Lance. I thought I was finally starting to make some progress. And now this."

I put a hand on his shoulder. "Did you see any of the others when you came back?" I ask.

"No, I didn't. And I did a reasonably thorough walkthrough. Lance was the only one."

It's safe to assume that at some point the party got down to just Lance Mack and whoever decided to corpsify same. There's an obvious candidate, but I don't want to believe it's him.

"You think Cronus is home right now?" I ask.

"I hope so," Russell says.

Lars steps in. "Unless he's on the lam, of course."

"Of course," I say, "Does Cronus live near here?"

"About four blocks away," Russell says, "He's got an apartment in the Techwood Complex."

"I'm going to go talk to Cronus," I say. Yes, it's a ridiculous hour, but this is a ridiculous situation.

"You sure that's a good idea, brother?" Lars says, "You might be dealing with a murderer."

"I don't want to believe that," I say.

"No, I mean he might kill *you*," Lars says, "For bothering him this late."

"I'll take my chances," I say, "You two want to come with me?"

Lars shivers (he's never been great with the chill), but says, "I'm in." Mike says, "As long as he kills you first…"

I get the exact address from Russell and ask him to keep my visit to Cronus on the downlow. He's hesitant but agrees. We take off down the slushy sidewalk. Lars and Mike look nervous. Whether they're more upset about the visit or the fact I've chosen to walk the four blocks (just as the rain is picking up) is anyone's guess.

***

The Techwood Complex is a collection of six buildings, none of them likely to make *Architectural Digest* anytime soon. They're squat, brick and beige. Bits of yellowed lawn are rimmed by melting snowbanks. It gives one the picture of an interior that is concrete bunkers with threadbare carpeting. Maybe the occasional cigarette burn. The perfect place to live if you like spending a lot of time at the office. I lead the way up the cracked, uneven sidewalk to building 2100; the address Russell gave me. It takes us farther into the poorly lit parking lot. The chill in the air is intensifying. Lars huddles into his coat and Mike blows on his hands. A rusty metal door separates building 2100 from the outside world. I look for a buzzer and don't see one.

"How are we going to get in there?" I ask.

Lars grabs the door and yanks it open. "Mr. Russell made these arrangements, and he isn't, uh…he isn't spending a lot on this place."

Obviously. We head the way up the stairs to the third floor. The carpeting is stained and faded, as are the lavender-colored walls. There's a faint smell of pot in the air. Bass thumping comes from an apartment at the end of the hall. (Bass thumping past midnight. There's a neighbor we'd all love to have.) Lars stops at an apartment in the middle of the hallway.

"This is it," he says.

A moment passes. No one does anything. "You going to knock?" I ask.

Lars fumbles with a tie he's not wearing. "I was hoping you would."

I look to Mike. "How about you?"

"I'm only useful when you want to break in," he says.

"*Somebody* has to fucking do it," I say. They both look to me. I roll my eyes. "Why does it always have to be me?"

"Why does it always have to be you sticking your nose into this stuff?" Mike asks.

"Hey, if I didn't stick my nose into this stuff, your ass would be in jail right now!" I say.

Lars steps between us, trying to keep the peace. "Hey fellas, calm down."

Mike waves a hand my direction. "Joe's the one getting pissy."

I slap at the hand. "I just want to know why one of you can't knock!"

Before that question can be answered, the door swings open, giving us a view of Bobby Cronus in a black t-shirt and tighty-whities. His face is red, his hair is disheveled, and his eyes laser beam through his thick frames.

"Or maybe you assholes could just stand there and fucking yammer on until I get sick of it and open the door myself," he says.

Mike and Lars back away, leaving me to face the wrath of Bobby Cronus. Thanks, assholes. I turn toward Cronus.

"I'm sorry for the late call," I say, "Gordon Russell told us where you're staying. Can we come in?"

"Why?" he says, looking as if I just suggested taking a dump on the welcome mat.

"Because Lance Mack is dead," I say, "And the police might be here soon."

There are many words, positive and negative, that have been said about Bobby Cronus over the years. *Speechless* has never been among them. Until now. He looks at me as if I've just sprouted a second head. It takes several moments for him to find the power of speech.

"Maybe you should come in," he says, stepping aside.

I lead the way into the apartment. It's spacious, I'll give it that much. The living room has high ceilings. There's a decent-sized deck. A thin hallway leads to what I imagine is a large bedroom. The kitchen is thin and has a teeny little breakfast bar (not nearly as charming as the one in my place). The apartment feels more spacious due the complete lack of decoration on the beige walls. A threadbare couch faces a big screen TV. A warped coffee table with a permanent ring on it completes the furniture. (I'm guessing everything but the TV comes from a thrift shop.) Cronus drops onto the couch, his eyes bleary.

"What the hell happened?" he asks.

"Gordon Russell went back to the arena after the party ended," I say, "He did a walk through and found Lance Mack in the dressing room. Mack had been bludgeoned to death."

"Bludgeoned? With what?"

"A golf club," I say.

Cronus's eyes get wide. He slowly rises from the sofa. (His movements are pretty fluid for an older guy with poor knees. I guess adrenaline helps.) "A golf club? My gimmick?"

"It looks like it," I say.

"The cops have my gimmick," Cronus says, his voice hollow, "And they think I killed Lance Mack."

I plunk down next to Cronus. "Did you do it?"

Cronus snaps me a look then sinks in on himself. "No, I didn't. Don't get me wrong. I'm not sorry the asshole is dead. But I didn't do it."

He'll probably want to downplay the *not sorry the asshole is dead* stuff when he talks to the cops. But I'm willing to believe him.

"What happened tonight?" I ask, "I know there was a party at the arena. I know you were in the office for a while before you left. Take me through what happened."

Cronus scratches his head, disheveling his thinning hair. "I was only going to drink a little. I wound up drinking a lot. It's what happens when you're around Nick Diamond. You get shitfaced, even if you start dumping drinks into the plants."

"I assume you saw Mack there?" I say.

"Of course I saw the jackass there. The whole fucking party was his idea. I tried to avoid him. He'd come by every now and again, give me some snide bullshit. 'Good to see you, *boss.*' I'd just ignore him or give him the finger."

"Did anything unusual happen?" I ask, "Arguments? Fights? Anyone make a scene?"

"No," Cronus says, "It was just a regular party."

"Gordon Russell was trying to smooth things over between you and Mack, right?" I say.

Cronus strokes the stubble on his face. "He tried. Didn't get too far. I could barely tolerate Mack's existence at the best of times. I sure as hell couldn't do it when I'd had a few."

"Did you do a walkthrough before you went home?" I ask.

"No. Gordon did one, and he didn't see anything."

"You were talking to Nick Diamond in the office," I say, "What did you two talk about?"

"Ashley. He's nervous about her. Wants to make sure she makes the right decisions. We didn't get too deep into it."

Cronus seems profoundly uncomfortable with this topic, so I let it go. Maybe I can ask Ashley or Nick Diamond about it. The bass thumping can be heard, faintly, down the hall.

"Did you see Nick Diamond leave?" I ask.

"I did," Cronus says, "He went out the front door. Said goodbye to me."

"When was this?" I ask.

"Maybe five minutes before I left."

"What about Ashley?" I ask, "Did you see her leave?"

"No, I didn't. I might have seen her in the arena before I left. I don't know exactly."

Mike shuffles his feet, uncomfortable. His new interest in Ashley Diamond clearly works against his recognition she might know something about the murder.

"Do you normally leave your golf club at the arena?" I ask.

"Yeah. I got a shitload of them. I'm not attached to any one."

"Do you remember where you left it?"

"Probably in the faces' dressing room."

Interesting. Mack was found in the heels' dressing room. The murder weapon must have travelled from one dressing room to the other. Likely in the possession of the murderer.

"Did anyone see you leave?" I ask.

Cronus considers it. "I don't think so. At least, I didn't see them if they did." He takes off his glasses and tosses them on the coffee table. "Why shouldn't it end like this? Last stop in the whole fucking wrestling business. Right here in this frozen fucking hellhole. No offense."

"None…taken?" I say, in the fine tradition of repressed Minnesotans everywhere.

"I am fucked. Being out of wrestling is one thing. Being in fucking jail is another."

"It might not come to that," I say.

"Oh?" Cronus says, "Who's going to fucking get me out of it?"

I was afraid he was going to ask that. Because I know the answer. I look toward Mike, who stuffs his hands into his coat pockets. Lars remains noncommittal. I turn toward Cronus.

"The police will come by," I say, "Once they figure out the murder weapon belongs to you, they're going to have some questions."

Cronus holds his hands out. "I didn't kill the motherfucker."

"I believe you," I say.

And I do. Maybe it's only because I want to. It's the same thing people go through when a celebrity is accused of something. (Hello, O.J.) They just don't *want* to believe it's true.

"Tell the police the truth," I say, "Tell them everything you told me."

"And I won't get arrested?" Cronus asks.

"Probably not," I say.

Cronus stands. "*Probably* not?"

"If they do, I'll go to bat for you."

That doesn't bring him a lot of comfort. "*You* will go to bat for me? You write a fucking blog. Are you a private detective on the side or something?"

I'm not sure what to say. (Throw a guy a lifeline and he questions your credentials?) Mike clears his throat.

"He's, uh, he's got some experience that direction," Mike says, "You can…" He mumbles the rest of it. "Trust him."

Lars glides out of the kitchen, having just made himself a sandwich. "He's done some good work. You may not realize it, Mr. Cronus, but you've fallen into very good hands. Joe has helped out Mike, gotten our friend Carol out of trouble, rescued his cousin Micky from some crooked cops, and saved a contract killer's job."

"What was that last part?" Cronus asks.

I hold up a hand. "Ignore that."

Lars drapes an arm around me. "The point is, what Joe might lack in cunning and cleverness, he more than makes up for in determination and dumb luck. You're going to be fine."

If the *Who Farted?* face Cronus is sporting means anything, he's not convinced. Given Lars's description of my talents, he has no reason to be. But Lars is only being largely accurate. I reach to pat Cronus on the shoulder but think better of it.

"The guy who's probably going to talk to you is named Frank Pike," I say, "Just play it straight with him. Tell him everything. Even the stuff about hating Mack. Just…maybe don't be so vehement about it."

Cronus sinks back on the couch. Lars wraps the sandwich in a paper towel and stuffs it in his pocket. We step out into the hallway. The bass is still thumping away. Mike looks back at Cronus's apartment.

"You really think he's innocent?" he asks.

"I guess we're going to find out," I say.

"*We're* going to find out?" Mike says, "As in, *you're* going to find out?"

"I guess so."

We're quiet until we start down the stairs. Behind me, Mike mumbles, "Here we fucking go again."

CHAPTER FOUR

Part of the reason kayfabe is so important to professional wrestling is that it is necessary for suspending disbelief. The audience has to believe, on some level, that the wrestlers are who they purport to be and the action happening is what it is purported to be. Any break in that and the illusion comes crashing down and the fabric of the pro wrestling illusion becomes unraveled.

That's why old school guys like Bobby Cronus still protect kayfabe. They don't believe they can do their job effectively unless kayfabe is maintained. It's why comedy wrestlers get so much heat from the old school guys. It's why they don't like the sight of a one-hundred-and-twenty pound woman kicking the ass of a guy twice her size. It's why they don't like wrestlers executing moves that require obvious cooperation. If the audience finds the action absurd, the wrestling is not doing its job.

Of course, that argues a couple two-hundred-pound guys beating the hell out of each other for more than half-an-hour is believable in the first place. But you have to pick your battles.

Sometimes, real life has a way of intruding on kayfabe. It starts with Lance Mack's death, which hits the local media.

The involvement of the police tells said media this is the real thing and not a pro wrestling angle. If there is any doubt on that score, Bobby Cronus being brought in for questioning the following day certainly eliminates it.

"Gordon Russell was able to arrange bail?" I say, running a block of gruyère over a cheese shredder.

"No need," Lars says, watching me from the breakfast bar, "Mr. Cronus was brought in for questioning but was not arrested. Mr. Cronus *does* have orders not to leave town."

Huh. I thought for sure Pike would arrest Cronus once he discovered the connection to the murder weapon. I wonder where Pike's thinking is at. I haven't had a chance to talk to him yet, so I'll satisfy myself with Cronus's freedom.

I finish shredding the gruyère and move on to the block of cheddar. I didn't invite Lars to lunch, but the man has a sixth sense for knowing when a meal is in the offing. It's not unlike the sense Lenny and Squiggy have. ("He twitched slightly in his sleep. Soon, he'll be awake and feeding us.") Still, a grilled cheese sandwich is not hard to make, and it always feels like a waste to make only one. I'll share my bounty with my idiot neighbor.

"The TV taping is tomorrow night, isn't it?" I ask, "Any idea what's going to happen? With the show, I mean?"

"I'm afraid not," Lars says, "Mr. Cronus will think of something. You're going to be there, aren't you?"

"Most definitely," I say, "Mike and Carol are coming, too."

"Righteous." Lars does a complete turn on the stool. "You made a decision on the movie, brother?"

I pause in shredding the cheese. I knew I would have to deal with this sooner or later. I drop the shredded cheddar on a plate and put my hands on the breakfast bar.

"I'm in." Yeah, even *I'm* surprised that's my answer. I gather my strength. "Couple things we need to get clear on right away."

"Of course," Lars says, stroking his beard with the back of one hand.

"First, we are *partners* in this thing. Collaborators. That means we're both going to produce the movie. I'm not doing this if I don't get significant say in the matter."

"Understood, brother. Wouldn't want it any other way."

"That also means I get approval on the director and the actors."

I'll confess to feeling like a jerk. Lars is so willing to meet my demands. He doesn't realize I'm making them because I know where things will go if I leave him completely in charge. His idiot friend Chuck will wind up in the director's chair and the cast will be a collection of people he met at a party. I'm not anxious to get an Alan Smithee credit.

"Dust in a windy street, my friend," Lars says, "I *want* you to be a big part of it. In fact, I was hoping you'd come along to meet our investors."

Ah. Lars has called my bluff. I yammer on about wanting to be a big part of the thing and then he presents me with a chance to meet important people. Which was not the part I was concerned about. But I am stepped in blood (or likely another bodily fluid) so far…

"When will this be?" I ask.

"Does Wednesday night work?" he asks.

I consult my mental social calendar while checking the two frying pans on the stove. They're heating up nicely and my social calendar is completely clear. I just *have* to be in a dating slump right now, don't I?

"What time and where?" I ask.

"About seven o'clock, over at their place in North Oaks. We can ride together. They're great people. Real patrons of the arts. And loaded." Lars looks me over and frowns. "I should consult you on wardrobe. You've got to dress for success."

Coming from a guy whose current occupation involves wearing a purple suit. "I can dress myself, thank you very much," I say.

I butter one side of each piece of bread then cover the other side with mustard. That done, I put the mix of gruyère and cheddar between the slices of bread and toss both sandwiches on one of the frying pans. I gently set the bottom of the other pan on top of the sandwiches. Now, it's just a matter of waiting for them to grill.

Of course, this is the time Mike chooses to buzz my apartment. I let him in then set about making another sandwich. A few seconds later, Mike swings in the front door, and makes his way to the breakfast bar.

"You making lunch?" Mike asks.

"I guess I am," I say.

"Good," Mike says, "I'm starving."

As I suspected. I do up another sandwich and take my position at the stove, waiting for the first round of sandwiches to be complete. I turn toward Mike.

"What are you doing here?" I ask, "Shouldn't you be at work?"

"I'm on special assignment," Mike says, "I'll be out of the office for the rest of the day."

"What kind of special assignment?" I ask.

"It involved a couple of things," Mike says, stepping over to the refrigerator, "First, going back to Brigid's place. Then fixing her a drink. Then giving her the ride of a lifetime. After that, I was told I could spend the rest of the afternoon out of the office."

"Uh-huh," I say, "You think anybody at the office is buying that?"

Mike fishes out a grape soda. "Fuck 'em if they don't. Fuck 'em if they do. There's only one person I'm worried about fucking."

"Didn't Don Henley write a song with those lines?" I ask.

I take the top frying pan away and slide the sandwiches on to two plates. I add some potato chips and set them down on the breakfast bar. I go back to make the other sandwich. Mike and Lars dig in, neither of them bothering to thank me. I toss a look over my shoulder.

"You still planning on going out with Ashley?" I ask.

"Absolutely," Mike says, his mouth full, "I'm meeting her at The Tav tonight."

Isn't that interesting? Ashley was at the party where Lance Mack was killed. In fact, she's the only one whose exit was not accounted for by either Bobby Cronus or Gordon Russell. Seems like the kind of thing I should discuss with her.

"When are you meeting?" I ask.

"Around nine," Mike says, "Why?"

"Feel like having a guest?" I ask.

"Not remotely."

"Ah," I say, "Sucks to be you. Because I'm coming along."

Mike hops up off the stool, leaving his sandwich behind. "No, you're not. I've got a date with a blonde amazon. I don't need you coming along and talking murders and shit and cockblocking me. No way, no how. You can hang out here tonight with your friends: Jergens Lotion and PornHub."

"I see." I mime picking up the phone. "'Hello, is this Brigid? You don't know me, but my name is Joe Davis. I'm a friend of Mike Griffin's. I understand you and Mike are currently riding the hobby horse, likely in violation of several company policies. And you might be interested in who else he's violating.'"

"You wouldn't," Mike says. I cock an eyebrow. "You would," he says, sitting back down, "All right, fine. You can come along. But you ask a few questions, make sure you don't kill the fucking mood—and I mean the *fucking* mood—and then you get the hell out. Understood?"

"Roger that," I say.

Lars finishes his sandwich and chips in record time (as per usual) then goes to the sink and deposits his plate. "Sounds like a good time. Maybe I'll stop by."

"The hell you will," Mike says, "This is supposed to be just me and Ashley. I don't need The Hardly Boys screwing it up."

I slide my grilled cheese on to a plate and grab some chips. Despite the number of times in college when I adhered to the *sock on the door* rule and even ran interference for him when he was cheating on his girlfriend, Mike still thinks I'll screw up his love life. I'll just have to know, privately, that I have Mike's best interests in mind.

Probably.

***

I hate being a third wheel. And that's when a couple *wants* me along. Dropping in on Mike and Ashley, unannounced and unwelcomed, is a whole different game of ball. While I could question Ashley in my guise as a reporter (of sorts) doing an article on the wrestling promotion, I think she'll be a little more forthcoming in a (seemingly) casual chat. I explained this logic to Mike, but he was more focused on how I had coerced him into this. (Sorry, but sometimes you catch fewer flies with honey than you do with blackmail.)

The Tav is my favorite neighborhood watering hole. It's a combination sports bar/pub. Picture windows face Selby Avenue. Big screen TVs hang from various corners. A pool table and a few dart boards can be found near the back. The atmosphere is cozy, the staff knows me and there's a collection of quality craft beers. What's not to love? The place is also a little quiet tonight, given it's a Monday. The odds of someone bothering Ashley for being a minor celebrity are pretty long. (The odds of someone bothering her because she's tall, blonde and gorgeous are, perhaps, not as long.)

I walk in, say hi to Nick the bartender, and grab a pint of Grand Brewing Maibock. Mike and Ashley are at a high top near the pool tables. Ashley has her back to me, so Mike is the first to see my approach. He breaks into a large (and completely fake) grin.

"Joe!" he says, "I didn't know you were going to be here tonight."

"Got bored sitting around the house," I say, unbuttoning my peacoat, "Thought I'd stop in for a drink. Didn't expect to see you here."

"Hanging out with a friend," he says.

Ashley stands to greet me, offering a hand. I fight saying *Whoa*. I'll never get over how much larger wrestlers look in everyday life. I'm six-one, but Ashley has a few inches on me. She wears a brown leather jacket over a tight-fitting white sweater and equally tight-fitting jeans. *Statuesque* doesn't begin to cover it. Her blonde hair tumbles past her shoulders and her bright smile reveals a set of perfectly straight teeth. We exchange a quick handshake before she returns to her seat. Mike uses his foot to push out an empty chair.

"Care to join us?" he says, "*Just* for a minute or so?"

"Sure," I say, "But just for a minute. I don't want to interrupt."

"How kind," Mike says, extending his middle finger across his pint glass.

I drop into the offered chair. Mike straightens the black dress shirt he's wearing (which could really use a wash). A club soda sits in front of Ashley. If she's annoyed by my presence, she doesn't show it.

"You're the one doing the article, right?" she asks, "The friend of Purple Suit?"

"That would be me," I say, "We've been friends with Lars for a while."

"That's what Mike was telling me," Ashley says, her voice bubbly, "Lars is such a great ring announcer. He picked it up so quickly."

"He's an idiot savant," I say.

"Or half of that," Mike says.

"I'm surprised you have a night off," I say, "I thought things were busy at MCW."

"Not as busy as you'd think," Ashley says, "We do TV on Tuesdays and live shows on Friday. But other than a spot show here and there, we mostly train."

"I'm sure you'll be busier when the UWE comes to call," I say.

Ashley crosses her fingers, though the gesture seems rehearsed. Mike props his chin on his hand, accepting this date-interrupting-bullshit as part of the program.

I slide my pint glass around the tabletop. "Must have been a shock. What happened to Lance and all."

"It was," Ashley says, her face freezing slightly, "Nobody can believe it."

She seems more shocked than dismayed. I can't help thinking about Mack's conversation with her at the training session and the confrontation with her father that followed it. Mike mouths. *Get on with it.* Great. No pressure.

"When was the last time you saw Lance?" I ask.

Ashley snaps me a look. "What do you mean?"

"Oh, I'm just..." Failing miserably? You bet! "I don't know about you, but when somebody passes away suddenly, I always get that *But I just saw them* sort of thing. I was wondering about you."

She tilts her head, giving me a sort of apology. "There was a party at the arena that night. Lance was there. Hell, everybody was there."

"Your dad, too?" I ask, as if I didn't already know the answer.

"Oh yes. He's not going to miss a party. He'll start one if he needs to." Ashley's face darkens for a moment, then she sips her club soda. "But like I said, everybody was there. It was a good time. Mostly."

"Did you talk to Lance at the party?" I ask.

Ashley's eyes slide away. "For a minute or two. I talked to a lot of people. Like I said, it was a fun time."

I sip my beer, trying to seem casual. "You didn't notice anything unusual with Lance? Given how things…turned out, it makes you wonder."

"No, I didn't see anything," Ashley says. Then gives me a shy look. "Are you going to put the stuff about Lance in the article?"

"Probably," I say, "If I'm going to write about the company, it would be kind of strange to leave it out. Right now, we're just chatting. This doesn't have to be on the record."

"I don't know what I can tell you anyway," Ashley says, "The party seemed normal. Until I heard about Lance the next morning."

"How did your dad take it?" I ask.

Her face falls. I'm not sure the source of it. Maybe Ashley is like a lot of children of celebrities, constantly met with, *That's great about you. Now, about your dad…*

"He was fine, I guess," she says, "He didn't know Lance all that well. He's mostly here as a favor to Bobby. And to me."

"And maybe to him," I say, "He still gets to wrestle."

"That, too," Ashley says, "I mean…ah, you probably already know. It's on the internet. Dad has his issues with the IRS. He needs to keep working."

I bow my head. "I have heard that."

"He's doing his best," Ashley says, "But it's hard. We used to have this great big house in North Carolina. He lost that a few years ago. It was a great place. It had a huge pool. Me and my friend Tricia…" Her face clouds. "Anyway, the house is gone."

Things feel a little uncomfortable. This is underscored by the glare Mike is giving me. I try to get us on to more pleasant topics.

"Your dad takes an interest in your career?" I ask.

"Oh, yes," Ashley says, drawing out the *s*, "Sometimes, he acts like he's starting his own career all over again. I think he always wanted one of the kids to follow in his footsteps. And then after…after Shane."

Ashley looks down for a fraught second. There's the very real possibility she's going to start crying. The grief for her brother runs close to the surface. She takes a quick breath and looks up. Her face is calm. Mike lays a hand on hers.

"I'm sorry," he says.

"It's okay," she says, "Shane was like my best friend when we were growing up. Dad was on the road over three hundred days a year. We saw him maybe one weekend a month. Maybe a week at Christmastime. Every time he'd come home, he'd say, 'God, I can't believe how big you're getting.' It's the same thing my grandparents would say when they hadn't seen me for a while." Her voice gets quiet. "Didn't seem like the sort of thing your dad should say."

"How did you deal with it?" I ask.

"When I got older, I dealt with it by drinking. And other stuff. Shane and I would get messed up together. Spend a whole weekend like that. The house was big enough that our mom didn't know what was going on. I'm sure she suspected, but…" She shakes the club soda, the ice rattling in the glass. "I've gotten my act together. I'm glad for that. So is Dad."

"Must be nice to spend more time with him," I say.

"It *has* been nice," Ashley says, "Being around him, it's like a master class in wrestling. And he's proud of me."

"I don't mean to pry," I say, even though that's exactly what I mean to do, "but I saw you having an argument with your dad at the arena. On Saturday. When I stopped by to talk to Bobby Cronus."

Ashley tears a few corners off her bar napkin. "Dad gets too protective sometimes. He wants me to make a name for myself and I appreciate that. But I get tired of it every now and again. That's what the argument was about."

"Did it start because you were talking to Lance?" I ask.

Ashley's eyes flick toward me, briefly. "Yeah, because of that. To tell the truth, Dad didn't have a high opinion of him. He thought Lance had a good look and was a good athlete. But he needed a lot of work as a wrestler. You have to get the psychology of it. Know how to tell a story. Lance didn't really get that. And he didn't seem interested in learning."

"Was that your opinion, too?" I ask.

Ashley bobs her head as she thinks. "More or less. Lance could be a decent guy. But he thought a lot of himself. Made him hard to be around."

"And that was the only reason your dad objected to you talking to Lance?" I ask.

Ashley runs a finger around the rim of her glass. "Not just that, no. Lance had a reputation for partying. That whole thing at the arena was his idea. He liked getting together with everybody and having a drink or several after the matches. Dad didn't really like that lifestyle."

Mike's jaw drops. "*Nick Diamond* had a problem with someone's lifestyle?"

He might be risking his standing with Ashley, but the man is spitting facts. Nick Diamond's gimmick is that of a high-flying, hard-living playboy. He could go an hour in the ring, party all night long, then do it all over again the next day. But the act wasn't just for show. According to legend (and some court documents), it was how Nick Diamond really lived.

Ashley, though, doesn't seem offended. "It's funny, isn't it? It's like, what, the pot and the kettle? But that was dad's thing. He didn't want me around Lance."

"Did *you* want to be around Lance?" I ask.

"Not always," Ashley says. Then she looks up at me. "But I'm going to miss him. When he was in the mood, he was a decent guy."

The last part sounds perfunctory. I sip my beer, letting the mood settle. Mike drums his fingers on the table. His look says: *Don't kill the mood here, doofus.* I flutter my fingers, letting him know I'll tread lightly.

"Did you say anything to Lance before you left?" I ask, "Last words, anything like that?"

Ashley's face freezes again; the deer-in-the-headlights look. "No. Just small talk."

"About what time did you leave?" I say.

"Quarter after twelve," she says.

I make a mental note. "Who was still there when you left?"

"Jack Blades. He had left but then he came back to talk with me. Just about training stuff. I don't remember anyone else."

"Did you see Jack leave?" I ask.

"No, I didn't." Ashley tilts her head slightly. "Is that important? Are you going to put that in the article?"

I wave off her concerns. "Just asking."

Thankfully, Ashley doesn't know the difference between a professional journalist and an amateur buttinski. She seems relieved. I've played this out as far as I can. And I can't take any more of Mike's glaring. I down the rest of my beer and get up from the table.

"I should get going," I say, buttoning my peacoat, "It was nice bumping into you, Ashley. Hope to see more of you."

"I'm sure you will," Ashley says. Her smile looks like it takes effort.

I clap a hand on Mike's shoulder. "Sorry for interrupting."

Mike says, under his breath, "Like I had a fucking choice."

I wish them both one last good night and head toward the door, waving at Nick the bartender as I go. I glance back toward Mike's table. He takes Ashley's hand; the pose one takes when apologizing for an idiot friend.

How to Lose Friends and Piss Off People, a Self "Help" Book by Joe Davis.

CHAPTER FIVE

Many professions have their own way of honoring the fallen. The military, who tends to specialize in the fallen, does this better than most. Say what you will about Taps, *but it's stirring and sad. The police using bagpipes at funerals never fails to send a chill down my spine. And I'll be honest, I still shed a tear when Spock is sent to his final (but not really) resting place in a photon torpedo while Scotty plays* Amazing Grace *on the bagpipes in* Wrath of Khan. *(Just don't tell anyone. Beyond the people I've already revealed this to. Oops.)*

In boxing and wrestling, the fallen are honored with a ten-bell salute. The crowd is asked to remain silent and then ten intermittent gongs ring through the otherwise silent arena. It's a moment when the worked nature of pro wrestling is set aside, and the fans and wrestlers mourn as one. Wrestling may be cheesy to some (even to those of us who love it) but the power of the ten-bell salute cannot be denied.

Again, don't tell anyone. We wrestling fans wouldn't want anyone to know a thing like that. (Beyond the people I've already told. Nuts. I've really got to work on my keeping secrets.)

I can't help wondering if whoever killed Lance Mack is as moved by the spectacle as the rest of us.

Mike, Carol, and I are on the front row, standing with the rest of the crowd and waiting for the show to start. The Sportatorium is nearly full. Well, full on three sides. The side nearest the lobby is empty because that's where the hard camera is located for the TV taping. (No point in putting people there if the camera can't see them.) Everyone is wondering how Midwest Championship Wrestling will handle Lance Mack's death and how it will affect *WrestleShock*. Carol pulls her pleather jacket closer around her.

"This is a TV taping?" she asks.

"It is," I say, "That's why you saw the big TV production truck outside."

"How is it different from the regular Friday show?"

"TV sets up the Friday shows," Mike says, "The tapings are free, so they're used to set up the angles and build interest for the shows that charge admission. That's how wrestling has always used TV. At least, that's the way wrestling is *supposed* to use TV. The UWE gets caught up in the ratings sometimes and gives away stuff on TV."

Carol tilts her head to one side. "Angles? What are those?"

"You'd probably call them *storylines*," Mike says, "They're used to build interest for a match. Maybe a bunch of matches. Fundamental stuff for selling tickets and getting ratings."

"And who thinks up the angles?" Carol asks.

"The booker," I say, "In this case, Bobby Cronus."

"One guy does all that?"

"In a promotion this small, yeah," Mike says, "Someplace like UWE has a whole creative team and a talent relations department. Committees of people to do the work of one guy."

"That sounds…inefficient," Carol says.

"I guess they're happy with whatever makes their programming unwatchable," I say.

Wrestlers and staff file into the ring. I pull my Porter's Bay hoodie over my head and deposit it on my seat. Many in the crowd begin removing their hats. A sense of anticipation is building. Something catches Mike's attention. There's a guy near the lobby entrance, watching the scene. He's short, thin and hairy. I'm not certain the last time he bathed, but sometime before winter seems a good guess. His arms are crossed, and he looks on with disdain. He's not as face-slappable as Bobby Cronus in his prime, but he's in the ballpark.

"Bruno Harvey," Mike says, "The guy who runs the Minnesota Wrestling Federation."

"The indie over in Minneapolis?"

"The very one."

From what I know about the Minneapolis Wrestling Federation, it's not on the level of Midwest Championship Wrestling. It doesn't have its own arena or a spot on local TV. It doesn't have a world class trainer like Bobby Cronus. But it's got ambition and some money behind it. Bruno Harvey is a wannabe big-time wrestling manager, booker and promoter who's been buying up all the indie talent he can find. I can't imagine he's welcomed at an event like this.

"What do you suppose he's doing here?" I ask.

"Getting thrown out, if Bobby Cronus sees him," Mike says.

We turn our attention back to the ring. Gordon Russell stands at the front. Lars is one step behind him, clad in his purple suit. Nick Diamond and Jack Blades flank him on either side. Ashley stands behind her father. Bobby Cronus is conspicuous by his absence. Ordinarily, Russell would be pumping the crowd up, getting them ready so there would be screaming and cheering when the show opens. Instead, he's content to let silence rule. He waits until getting the cue from the cameraman then brings the microphone to his mouth.

"As I'm sure you're all aware, our Midwest Championship Wrestling family has suffered a huge loss," Russell says, "Lance Mack was a young man with a very bright future in this business. Tonight, we continue the work of Midwest Championship Wrestling. But we do so with heavy hearts. And we do so to honor our friend, who loved this business. We ask for a few moments of silence while we honor Lance Mack."

The place is absolutely silent. Everyone waits for the mournful toll to begin. Several wrestlers and fans are fighting tears. Before the tolling can begin, though, a familiar voice booms out over the PA.

"To hell with this nonsense!"

Everyone in the ring and every fan in the arena looks around. We're all wondering where the voice is coming from, though we're certain who it belongs to. Bobby Cronus strolls down the center aisle, coming from the lobby. His golf club is over one shoulder. He wears a loud suit consisting of a red sports coat, red slacks, a green shirt, and a yellow tie. There's a certain jauntiness in his stride. I've seen this version of Bobby Cronus before. It's the _uber heel manager_ gimmick he used when I was a kid.

"What are we doing here?" Cronus says, "Who the hell are we celebrating? You think anybody liked this idiot?"

There's a rumbling of dissatisfaction among the fans. It's part shock, part indignation. Russell looks profoundly uncomfortable.

"Bobby, this really isn't the time," Russell says.

"No, I think this is exactly the time," Cronus says, "We're going to stand here and pretend we liked an arrogant piece of crap who didn't care about anybody but himself." The crowd is booing. Cronus looks around with disdain. "I'm not going to let everyone stand out here and be a bunch of hypocrites. I hated Lance Mack, and I'm glad he's dead."

That brings a cascade of boos down on the ring. The wrestlers and staff break into conversation. Russell looks indignant. Lars seems stunned. Russell looks down at Cronus.

"Bobby, we're talking about a member of the family," Russell says.

"Your family, not mine," Cronus says, climbing up on the ring apron. He takes the golf club off his shoulder and uses it to gesture to the wrestlers and staff. "The ten-bell salute isn't happening. Thank you all for coming but get the hell out." The wrestlers hesitate. Cronus waggles the golf club. "You heard me. Get the hell out! You want to still have jobs tomorrow morning, you'll do what I'm telling you. Go on! Git!"

Slowly, the wrestlers and staff disperse, giving Cronus sullen looks as they go. Gordon Russell steps between the ropes and makes his way over to the announce table, set up in one corner of the ringside area. Nick Diamond looks over at Jack Blades, who doesn't return it. Blades climbs out of the ring. Cronus points his golf club at Diamond.

"Hold on, Nick, I've got some news for you," Cronus says, climbing into the ring, "Looks like we have to book a new main event for *WrestleShock*. You earned a shot at the Midwest

Title. But now you don't have an opponent. I guess it's my job to give you the Midwest Title by forfeit."

Diamond holds a hand between the ring ropes. Lars hands him a microphone. "I won a lot of championships, Bobby," Diamond says, "People weren't always happy about it, but they respected me. I've earned everything I've ever gotten. You've known me a long time. You know I'm not gonna accept anything being handed to me."

The crowd gives that a nice round of applause. Cronus pumps a fist, agreeing with them.

"I figured that's what you'd say," Cronus says, "I'm going to make you a deal. You can earn the Midwest Title this coming Friday night. You and Jackson Darkfire in the main event. Winner becomes the new Midwest Champion." The crowd greets that with an anticipatory buzz. "And just to make sure nothing goes wrong, I'm going to be at ringside, keeping an eye on everything." He offers Diamond his hand. "I'll see you on Friday night."

Diamond thinks about it. The crowd shouts for him to avoid cozying up to Cronus. Diamond takes Cronus's hand, briefly. Cronus claps him on the shoulder. Diamond climbs out of the ring. Cronus twirls the golf club, steps out the other side of the ring, and strolls up the aisle toward the lobby. Carol looks over at us.

"Am I missing something?" she asks, "Or is Bobby Cronus…"

"Using his being implicated in killing Lance Mack as an angle?" Mike says, "That's exactly what he's doing."

"Huh," Carol says, then she turns to me, "He's not making your job any easier, is he?"

I look back at Cronus. As he reaches the lobby, he walks right past someone standing in the entryway, watching the proceedings. It's Sergeant Pike. Cronus doesn't look his direction. They don't exchange any words. I sigh.

"No," I say, "he is not."

Maybe this is what I get for taking on a lost cause. It just becomes more lost.

***

One advantage to having a friend who works for a wrestling promotion is the ability to hang around when other fans would be ushered out. The TV taping doesn't go much more than an hour (the whole broadcast show is less than an hour). Carol, Mike, and I are standing in the lobby, waiting for Lars. Pike skulks around, though he keeps his distance. Bobby Cronus is out in the production truck, wrapping things up. Gordon Russell locks the front door. The arena is quiet. When Russell returns to the lobby, he doesn't look happy. He takes up position outside Bobby Cronus's office. Lars slinks into the lobby a few seconds later.

"I don't think Mr. Russell is pleased," Lars says, trying to keep his voice down.

Russell is red-faced and sweating. He tugs at his mustache and loosens his tie. This is probably the closest thing he's got to a fume. (Or it's constipation. Kind of hard to tell.) Mike looks toward the entrance to the arena, waiting for Ashley. I make my way over to Pike, his rumpled suit and his orchestra. He watches me approach.

"Counselor," he says, with less than his usual snark, "What is it that you need?"

"Enjoy the show?" I ask.

"It was interesting."

It doesn't sound like he's going to elaborate on that. "I was surprised you didn't arrest Bobby Cronus," I say.

"There's still time," Pike says.

"Why didn't you do it?"

"I'll keep that to myself," he says, "Sort of like how you kept the information about Bobby Cronus's golf club to yourself."

Eep. I wasn't going to be able to keep that to myself for long. I ignore the cop stare Pike is giving me.

"It slipped my mind," I say, "Did you find any prints on the golf club?"

Pike waits a second, then says, "No, we didn't. Either the killer wore gloves, or he wiped the thing clean. Either way, we're not IDing him through the golf club. And the drugs aren't getting us anywhere."

I snap him a look. "Drugs?"

"Rohypnol," Pike says, satisfied to know something I don't, "Commonly known as roofies. It was found in Lance Mack's system."

"Roofies? The date rape drug? Someone was going to rape Lance Mack *and* kill him?"

"I don't know," Pike says, "I just know what toxicology found."

"I don't think Bobby Cronus did that."

"You might be right."

My heart rate picks up. "That's why you didn't arrest Cronus, isn't it? You're not sure he's guilty."

"I didn't say that. And I better not read that in your column."

I don't blame Pike for wanting to control publicity—however weenie it may be—when he's got an investigation going on. And I'm not going to put stuff like that in my column until the investigation is complete, for my own sake if nothing else.

Still, the information is interesting. Cronus is supposedly drunk and filled with rage. He grabs the best weapon he can find and unthinkingly beats Lance Mack to death with it. A crime of passion. But he thinks to either wear gloves or wipe the golf club clean in order to cover his crime. Then, having taken so much care to obscure his misdeeds, *he leaves the damn thing at the crime scene?* This doesn't feel like a crime of passion. This feels like…

"A frame-up," I say.

"I didn't say that," Pike says.

"I know. Just an idle thought."

"Well, keep it to yourself."

I hold up my hands, surrendering the point. "Anything else interesting?"

Pike's face tightens. "Off the record?" I nod. He lowers his voice. "Lance Mack had ten thousand dollars deposited into his bank account the day before he was murdered."

Holy Decent Chunk of Change, Batman. "By who?" I ask.

"Olani Holdings. You ever heard of them?"

"Not at all," I say.

"We're going to do some looking into them," Pike says, "We'll see what we find."

"And you'll let me know."

"No, I won't," Pike says, "Because it *still* won't be any of your business."

Assclown. I breathe through my nose. "You have any other suspects?"

He bobs his head, debating an answer. "I'm going to ask around. But I might not find anyone else. And your friend is still my best option. For now, I'd appreciate if you stayed out of my way, counselor."

"You won't even know I'm around," I say. I leave the *Or know what I'm up to* unspoken, though I'm sure Pike is aware of it.

I wander back to my friends. Pike steps into the arena. Cronus finally stalks in through the front entrance. The jacket and tie are gone, but he still bears a striking resemblance to a Christmas tree skirt. There are large sweat rings under both of his arms. He carries the golf club but without nearly the same panache. He goes straight for the office. Russell starts talking as Cronus passes.

"I thought the plan was to do the ten-bell salute and *then* you'd interrupt," Russell says.

"I changed my mind," Cronus says, "Thought it would play better if I didn't let it happen. I was right. You felt the heat we were getting out there."

Cronus unlocks the office and goes in. Russell follows him. The rest of us move forward, so we can better hear the conversation. (Apparently, I'm not the only buttinski on the scene.)

Russell straightens his glasses. "It's just…it's in bad taste. That's what I think."

"Bad taste?" Cronus says, "Of course it's in bad taste. I'm a fucking heel. I'm trying to get heat, not become Miss fucking Congeniality."

"I get that," Russell says, tugging at his tie, "But isn't there any other way?"

"Maybe," Cronus says, "But this is the best way. Besides, I've already started. You can't put the toothpaste back in the tube."

Russell swallows, consumed with impotent rage. I'm torn myself. On the one hand, Cronus is right. Heels are supposed to be distasteful people who do distasteful things. You shouldn't like them or sympathize with them in any way. Then again, some of the things, historically, that have been used to draw heat are racism, jingoism, misogyny, and sociopathic violence. *Drawing heat* covers a multitude of sins. Russell sees only the sins.

"I wish you had thought up another way," Russell says, "You have a perfectly good replacement match with Darkfire and Diamond. We could have main evented *WrestleShock* with that, instead of just doing it on Friday night."

"No one would care," Cronus says, "They just watched Mack beat Darkfire flatter than a plate of piss last Friday. Nobody thinks he's in Nick Diamond's league. You want to draw money at *WrestleShock*, you gotta give people something they want to see. Not just throw something out there because you can."

Russell concedes the point. "Then what *is* the main event for *WrestleShock?*"

Cronus taps a pencil on the desk. "Still working on it. But I'll think of something."

The place is quiet. Russell leaves the office and goes outside for some fresh air. I'd like to talk to Bobby Cronus. But I'm hesitating. Ashley Diamond strolls into the lobby. Her hair is still wet from the shower, and she has a large gym bag over one shoulder. Mike's eyes light up. She stiffens. She's not smiling, and her eyes are furtive. Mike stops.

"Um, hi," he says, "I think."

Before Ashley can respond, a voice floats in from the arena. "Ash? Everything okay?"

Ashley calls over her shoulder. "I'll be right back." She whispers to Mike, "I'm sorry. I don't want my dad to find out about us. It just…it would make things harder. I hope you get it. I'll talk to you soon."

Ashley walks back into the arena, giving Mike a finger wave behind her back. A scowl lines Mike's face.

"You believe that?" he says, "*Pappas Interruptus.*"

Carol spins toward Mike. "You know Latin?"

"That's Latin?" Mike says, "I thought it was Klingon."

Before the Katzenjammer Kids can banter on, Carol gets a phone call. She steps away to take it. Mike buries himself in his own phone. Lars paces the lobby, whistling *Classical Gas.* I step over to the office. Cronus sits behind the desk, staring at the wall and tapping a pencil against a pad of paper. He doesn't acknowledge my presence. I lean in the doorway.

"I'm going to prove you didn't kill Lance Mack," I say, "But you're making the job more complicated."

Cronus seems nonplussed. "I appreciate that, but I got a job to do, too."

"You sure this is the best way to go about it?"

I'm risking an argument here, but I need *some* cooperation out of Bobby Cronus. He swivels his chair toward me and tosses the pencil on the desk.

"Jerry Scott broke me into the business," he says, "Jerry used to have a sign on the wall of his office. It said, *Personal issues draw money.* And Jerry's booking drew a fuckload money over the years. People think I killed Lance Mack. Fine. We can draw money with that. Because it doesn't get any more personal."

"I sincerely hope people won't be disappointed if I prove you didn't kill him."

Cronus smiles. "I haven't told a lie so far. I didn't say I killed Lance Mack. I just said I'm glad he's dead. Truth is, I'm not all that disappointed about it."

Ugh. I knew this wasn't going to be easy. But I didn't think Cronus would actively work against me. Still, there's no talking him out of this angle. Cronus knows his business and he's nothing if not stubborn. I fold my arms and lean on the doorframe.

"Just out of curiosity," I say, "what *was* the main event of *WrestleShock* supposed to be?"

Cronus thinks about it for a second. "Ah hell, it won't hurt to tell you now. Lance was supposed to beat Nick Diamond clean. Afterwards, they were going to shake hands and Nick would hold up Mack's arm. Pass the torch. Turn Lance from our top heel to our top babyface."

"Wow," I say, "And you were cool with doing that?"

"It was my idea. Lance was starting to get cheers. No better time to turn him. No matter how insufferable a son of a bitch he could be."

Yeah, that would have been interesting. Cronus having to push a guy he genuinely hated in a way that would make the fans love Lance Mack. Assuming Mack even wanted to work with Cronus or that Nick Diamond would put him over. Speaking of which…

"Do you think you could get me a meeting with Nick Diamond?" I ask, "He was one of the last people in the building the night Mack was killed. He might have seen or heard something. I'd just like to talk to him."

Cronus seems wary. I don't blame him. He and Nick Diamond have known each other a long time. Cronus doesn't want to believe Nick Diamond is a murderer. But the fact is *somebody* killed Lance Mack and that person is likely someone Cronus has known for a long time. He runs a thumb and a forefinger over his nostrils.

"I'm sure I can set something up," he says, "Just go easy on him. He's a good friend."

"I'll do my best."

Cronus pulls the pad of paper closer to him. "I got work to do. You can see yourself out."

"Got it," I say, "What's going to happen on Friday?"

"You'll find out when everybody else does." He gazes toward the lobby. "Your friend is a halfway decent ring announcer."

"The fans seem to like him," I say.

"They really do," Cronus says, tapping his pencil on the tablet. Then he snaps out of it. "Anyway, feel free to show yourself out."

Huh. So glad I'm getting this inside peek at professional wrestling. It's a whole new place in which to be dismissed and thrown out. Variety really is the spice of life.

I step back into the lobby. Mike is still staring at his phone. Carol is talking on hers. Something she says catches my attention. A name. *Rick.* I step toward her. She doesn't see me approach and keeps right on talking.

"Okay, I'll see you in a little bit," Carol says, "I'm looking forward to it, Mr. Michaels."

Carol rings off and drops the phone into her pocket. She turns and sees me. She gets a stricken look. I point to her phone.

"Rick…Michaels is the boyfriend's name?" I say, "That's funny. I used to know a guy named Rick Michaels."

"It's not that funny," Carol says, "And he used to know you, too."

I tap the name on my hoodie. "Then this is Rick Michaels from Porter's Bay?"

"Yes. It's that Rick Michaels."

Holy shit. *That* Rick Michaels. Not just a dude from Porter's Bay but a celebrity of sorts. I'm gobsmacked. (Yes, I find that word disgusting. But smacked in the gob is the only way I can describe the feeling.) I should be annoyed that Carol kept this from me, but I'm overcome by the *Hey, I know that guy* feeling.

"You and Rick Michaels?" I say.

Carol pulls her ponytail out and lets her hair flow to her shoulders. "Yes."

"How long has this been going on?"

"A couple weeks. We met at a party. Hit it off. I had no idea he was a friend of yours."

"Of all the gin joints in all the towns in all the world."

"Pretty much."

In a school like Porter's Bay, where athletic excellence was the coin of the realm, Rick Michaels was an oddball. He was a jock, yes. He played wide receiver on the football team, left wing on the hockey team, and first base for the baseball team. But he never really fit in with the jocks. He didn't chase cheerleaders. He didn't hang out with other jocks. He wore his letter jacket about as often as a marine wears dress blues. He seemed more comfortable hanging out with theatre nerds and other assorted geeks. He had no interest in seeming cool. He wasn't shy about letting people know he had a brain. It was like someone from the chess club happened to be a decent athlete. Rick admitted being a fan of my column and copiously quoted from it.

"Rick said we were friends?" I ask.

"Why?" Carol asks, "Weren't you?"

"I liked to think so. I always thought he was cool. It's nice to know he considers me a friend."

"He does."

Which brings us to the big question. "Why didn't you tell me you were dating Rick Michaels?"

Carol searches for the words. "Because you know me."

Huh. Carol is not the first person to consider knowing me to be a liability, but I thought we'd gotten past that. I put my hands in the pockets of my hoodie.

"What does that have to do with anything?" I ask.

"It means when I meet a new guy, I try very hard to create a…persona."

"I get that."

"I'm not being fake. I'm just putting my best foot forward and keeping other things…in the background."

"I do the same," I tell her.

"But you *know* me. You know stuff about me. Normally, that doesn't matter because you don't say much more than *Hello* and *How are you doing* to the guys I date. But you and Rick will have some catching up to do. You'll talk. And that might…compromise things."

"Worried I'll rat you out, eh?"

"Not intentionally," Carol says, "But you and Rick could be talking, and something could just…pop out of your mouth. It's been known to happen."

"Excuse me?" I say, "I think you have me confused with the Impulse Control Problem Brigade over there." Mike and Lars are both oblivious.

Carol squares me with a look. "Did you just come up with that or have you been working on it?"

"I think I just came up with it. I'll have the consult the archives."

"At any rate," Carol says, drawing it out slightly, "I don't think it's a good idea for you and Rick to talk. Not yet. Just let us get a little more established."

"How long are you thinking?" I ask.

"I don't know. A year. Maybe five."

I roll my eyes (normally Carol's job). Then a thought occurs to me. "Wait a minute, I thought Rick was married. Last time I ran into him was the ten-year reunion and his wife was with him."

"He *was* married. They're divorced. A couple of years now."

"Huh. That's a shame. I didn't chat with her much, but she seemed really nice. Quite a looker, too, as I recall."

"I'm so sorry that your friend is coming down in the world," Carol says, her voice getting icy, "If you're so entranced by his ex, she's on the market again."

No, the situation is complicated enough, thank you very much (and I think Carol knows that). I stroke my chin with the back of my fingers and drop into the scratchy voice that is the signature for my impression of Marlon Brando as Vito Corleone.

"What have I done to earn such disrespect?" I ask.

Carol's head drops to one side. "Are you trying to sound like The Godfather?"

"If you had come to me in friendship, then your enemies would be my enemies."

"You realize that sounds more like Krusty the Clown, don't you?"

"Never ask me about my business, Carol."

"Okay, that's a *Michael* Corleone quote, dingus."

True, Carol can be a little crusty herself at times. But she knows her *Godfather*, so I'll let it slide.

"We should all get together sometime," I say, "I seriously don't think I've seen Rick since the reunion. Even then, it was just a quick chat. I'd love to catch up with him. And I promise I will say nothing compromising."

Carol doesn't respond, but her body language gives the unmistakable impression she considers this an idea on par with a root canal performed with rusty fishing knives.

"You're talking a double date?" she says, "Who would you take?"

"You said Rick's ex was available, right?"

"Joe…"

"I'll find somebody," I say, "Or I'll be a third wheel. No worries."

Carol twists her mouth to one side. "I don't know. Let me think about it."

"You worry too much," I say, "I'm not the worst guy in the world." Mike strolls over to us. "That job is taken," I say.

Mike looks from Carol to me. "I don't know what the two of you were talking about but fuck you."

It's a fair cop. We decide to go out to the parking lot and be on our way. When we get to the lot, something catches Mike's attention. He gestures toward the side of the building.

"Bruno Harvey," he says, "And he's talking to one of the wrestlers."

Mr. Harvey is indeed standing near one of the side doors, chatting up a wrestler. It takes a second, but I recognize the guy: Bill Walker aka The Super Destroyer. Their conversation is just out of earshot. I take a few steps that direction, trying (and failing) to look casual. Bits of the conversation carry over to me.

Harvey is speaking. "…does to my show? What about my money?"

"I'm sorry," Walker says. He starts to mumble, making him hard to hear. I only get snatches of the conversation: "play it safe…a barrel…gas…UWE." Before I catch anymore, Harvey looks our direction and clams up. Walker ducks back into the building. Harvey crosses the parking lot, walking past us without acknowledging us.

"What do you suppose that was all about?" Mike asks.

"Good question," I say.

I relay what I caught of the conversation. Carol twists her mouth to one side.

"Gas?" Carol asks, "You think someone gassed Lance Mack?"

"No," I say, "Mack was drugged, but it was an ingestible. I don't know what gas had to do with it."

"I seriously doubt they were talking about OPEC," Mike says.

He's right. But I don't have an answer. Maybe they weren't talking about Lance Mack at all, though he's certainly the topic of the moment. With no solid answers, we decide to get going. As we pull out of the lot, Sergeant Pike walks out the front door of the arena. He eyeballs us as we pass. I can't help wondering what he's found or what he's thinking.

And how long he's going to wait before going after Bobby Cronus.

***

"They're really great people, both of them," Lars says, his hands gliding around the steering wheel, "And they love movies. It's a perfect fit."

I sit back in the passenger seat, trying to find a comfortable position. "You said you met them at a film fest?"

"I did. Then we went and hung out at Steamers night club downtown. We had a huge corner booth to ourselves.

Pretty soon we were hitting all the clubs downtown: The Corner, Revision, NDs, the Hacienda."

"Wait a minute," I say, "I thought the Hacienda was closed."

"It is. Great place for an afterparty, though. Long as you don't mind the smell and you leave most of your valuables in the car."

Here's a promising start. As if I don't have enough on my mind. Maybe this thing is a mistake. I don't mean the movie or the investigation, necessarily. I mean my entire adult life.

I certainly can't complain about the meeting place. Our potential investors' home is in North Oaks, a snooty, enclosed community lodged in the suburbs north of St. Paul. A thin road winds through the community, hinting at house after house though a screen of trees. The temperature has plummeted to the point there are a few snowflakes in the air. Lars insisted on driving and his piece of crap Oldsmobuick could not look more out of place. It's like my wastrel uncle Gordie showed up at a cocktail party wearing his pizza delivery uniform.

"What are their names again?" I ask.

"Fabio and Frankie. They're twins."

"And they're cool dudes?"

"Frankie's a girl."

"Ah." I look out the window. "Speaking of business, how are things with the new Les Bos?"

Lars scratches his cheek. "Chuck and I talked about it, and we decided to mount a vigorous attack. We will spare no expense to protect our property."

"I'm not sure it's still your property,"

"That's fine. We have no expenses with which to protect it. We tried talking to Chuck's friend Barry Rose. See if he'd take us on."

"He's a lawyer."

"A law student," Lars says, "Self-taught. By which I mean, he watches a lot of *Law and Order* and has seen *A Few Good Men* twelve times."

I put a hand to my head. "Please tell me he turned you down."

"No, he was anxious to take us on. *I* decided to turn *him* down."

"Really? What made you decide that?"

"His plan was to bring a class action suit against the owners of Les Bos. When I told him Chuck and I are the rightful owners of Les Bos and why we had closed the place, he thought he had a real case for the people who felt defrauded by us."

"Wait, he was going to bring a suit *against* you guys?"

"That is the case. After that, we didn't believe Barry—who is a perfectly nice guy—was the one to act in our best interests. Chuck says he'll think up something."

On the one hand, I'm relieved they've chosen not to work with an incompetent "lawyer." On the other hand, they have their least competent person working on a backup plan. For the moment, though, there's the movie to think of, so I'll let Chuck and Lars stew on the club.

We eventually find the driveway we're looking for. It winds back through a wooded area and ends at a four-story house with a circular driveway and a surprisingly small garage. The outside lights are on, revealing a couple of columns flanking the front door. There are plenty of windows, though all the shades are drawn. Lars ditches the car in the driveway. (The pavement is completely clear of slush and dirt. I'll have to compliment them on whoever maintains it. Assuming they know who those people are.) We walk to the front door. Lars looks comfortable in his Nehru jacket. I tug at the sleeves of my peacoat.

"How old are these friends of yours?" I ask.

"Mid-twenties, I'd say."

"And they're living together? Brother and sister? Doesn't that seem kind of weird?"

"Not at all. Two parents, two children. That's your basic nuclear family, isn't it?"

I stop. "They still live with their parents?"

"Yes," Lars says, "It happens. Sometimes, you run into a situation where you have to move back in with your folks.

Although, I'm not certain they've ever lived away from home. We'll have to ask them."

"Are the parents going to be here?" I ask.

"I'm not sure. Why?"

I let it pass without comment. I don't want to tell Lars that, for possibly the first time in my life, I'm craving adult supervision. Lars presses the doorbell. After several seconds, a long-haired dude in his twenties answers.

"Lars!" he says, his voice somehow excited and laid back at the same time, "Thanks for coming, man. Step inside the casa."

We cross into the foyer and get our first look at the interior. It's all hardwood floors and glass cabinets. The walls are beige, sporting the occasional Matisse print or family portrait. Everything is tastefully decorated and spotless. The lighting is low and moody. I've known our host for five seconds, but I'm assuming he's not responsible for the lovely condition of the home.

"Fabio, my friend, thank you for having us," Lars says.

Fabio and Lars exchange some kind of complicated handshake. Lars is accurate in saying the dude is probably in his mid-twenties. His hair is dark and long, curling at the ends, suggesting some product use. His face is lean and angular. His grin is easy—if hazy—and reveals a set of straight white teeth. He wears a simple white dress shirt, open to the middle of his chest, and tucked into his black slacks. He and Lars complete the handshake.

"This is my friend, Joe," Lars says, "He's going to be the writer on this project. You might say he's my righthand man."

I force a smile. "*You* might say that."

Fabio sticks his hand out. "Good to meet you, Jo-Jo."

I swallow the bile that rises when I'm called *Jo-Jo*. I take Fabio's hand and we try to do the same complicated handshake. I make a hash of it. I often joke about how my father must have come out of the womb a fifty-five-year-old man. I suddenly feel like he's not the only one. Fabio flips open the closet.

"Just throw your coat in there, Jo-Jo," he says.

I put my peacoat on a hanger in the closet. I give myself a quick look in the mirror in the foyer. Black dress shirt, jeans and a black suitcoat. Hair in place. Clean shaven. This is as good as I clean up. Certainly better than my business partner, who looks like Elvis touring Bombay.

"Where is the meeting going to be?" Lars asks, looking around as if he's casing the joint.

Fabio jerks a thumb over his shoulder. "We're going to be in the dining room."

"Lead the way," Lars says.

We walk down a short hallway and find ourselves in the aforementioned dining room. It's dominated by a long wooden table surrounded by straight-back chairs. The family's good China is in a cabinet along one wall. Curio cabinets with various knick-knacks sit in two corners. A buffet table stretches along the far wall. The table is set for six. There are three unlit candles in the middle of the table. A half-consumed bottle of red wine rests on one corner, nearest the only other occupant in the room.

"This is Frankie," Fabio says, waving a hand toward his twin sister, "She's my partner."

Since this is supposed to be a business meeting, I avoid giving Frankie an appreciative look. It takes an effort, though. She's not an identical twin to Fabio—her nose is a little larger than his and she's half a head shorter—but they're very similar. Frankie's dark hair is slightly longer than a bob and frizzed out at the ends. Her eyes are bright, and there is a wicked set to her mouth. Her tan blouse is open maybe one button past modest and her black skirt stops just short of her knees. Fabio turns to me.

"This is Lars's friend, Joe," Fabio says, "He's the writer."

Frankie reaches across the table, offering me her hand. "Nice to meet you Lars's friend Joe the Writer."

The handshake lingers. Frankie watches me the entire time. Judging by the way Fabio's and Frankie's faces are flushed, the open bottle of wine on the table isn't the first of the evening. I gesture to the additional place settings.

"Is someone joining us?" I ask.

Fabio pours a healthy amount of wine into a glass goblet, "Our parents are going to be here. They kind of have to be."

"Have to be?" I ask.

"It's their money, right?" Frankie says, as if it should be obvious,

I sneak a look at Lars. "*Their* money."

Lars claps a hand on my shoulder and whispers, "It'll be great, brother. Just relax."

Frankie empties the bottle into her glass then leaves the room, presumably in search of another bottle. Once she's gone, a prim middle-aged woman in a chef's outfit brings food into the dining room, arranging it in chafing dishes on the buffet. At first, I assume she's a servant, then I catch the *Lunds Byerlys* logo on her outfit. Lunds Byerlys is a local upscale grocery store that does catering as well. If I'm not going to fed out of the family kitchen, this is likely the next best thing. Once the food is on the buffet table, the woman lights the candles on the dining room table then steps back into the corner, hands folded in front of her.

Frankie does indeed return with a new bottle of red. She pours a couple of modest glasses for me and Lars and rather larger portions for Fabio and herself. We do a quick, silent toast. Frankie's eyes linger on me.

"These must be our guests."

The voice belongs, I assume, to the male parental unit in the house. He's a few inches shorter than me, but the coldness on his face gives him a formidable presence. His graying hair is worn a tad long. His face is full, and his nose is a little large. His head is still, and there's a penetrating quality to his eyes. He wears a simple blue suit with a striped tie.

"You *are* the filmmakers?" he asks.

"We are," Lars says, adding a slight bow, "A pleasure to make your acquaintance."

Lars offers a hand across the table. The father stiffens up. Fabio's and Frankie's mother appears next in the dining room. She's taller than her husband. Her olive complexion and black hair more closely resemble the children. Like her husband, she has a look of cold formality. Unlike her husband, the formality seems less scrutiny and more disinterest. She wears a black blouse and a matching skirt reaching to the ankle. Her hands are fidgety, as if she'd love to have either a martini or a cigarette in them (perhaps both). Her eyes are glazed slightly, and I can't help wondering if she's partaken in the wine (or perhaps something stronger). Since her husband shows no inclination to take Lars's hand, she steps into the breach. Lars grandly bows and kisses the offered hand. The mother withdraws it like a small animal bit it (and she's not far off).

"Charmed," she says, not sounding entirely like she means it.

"It looks like dinner is served," the father says, edging toward the table, "Why don't we have a seat?"

The father, naturally, positions himself at the head of the table. The mother sits to his right, Fabio to his left. Lars sits next to Fabio, and I sit next to Lars. Frankie is across the table from us. We're silent while the Lunds Byerlys catering person fills our plates. (Chicken and roasted vegetables. I can deal with this.) The father sips a glass of ice water.

"Mr..." he says.

"Lars."

"Lars. Do you have a last name?"

"Lars is fine," my idiot friend says, smiling good-naturedly, "And you are..."

"Dr. Piper."

"Of course." Lars spins toward the wife. "And this would be..."

The mother barely opens her mouth. "Mrs. Piper."

"I see," Lars says, "That stands to reason."

I wish there was a hell of a lot more wine in my glass. The feeling is doubled by Frankie staring at me over the top of her glass. I shift my focus to Dr. Piper, who carefully unfolds his cloth napkin and lays it in his lap.

"Mister…Lars," he says, "why don't you tell me about this movie idea of yours?"

"Gladly," Lars says, wielding the silverware, "It is a multi-genre concept that blends the visceral excitement of the horror movie with the vicarious thrills of a heist movie. The sort of independent film that festivals drool over. I think it has an excellent chance of being picked up a major distributor."

Dr. Piper appears unmoved. "What does the plot involve?"

Lars pauses in his chewing. "Plot? That's more the province of the writer. My buddy Joe can talk to you about that."

That will be a real trick since we haven't had a single conversation about the plot of the film. The room feels very warm. I pour myself a refill of the wine.

"My initial thinking," I say, "and bear in mind, these are just ideas, is that it would it involve…vampires."

Dr. and Mrs. Piper exchange a look. The vibe is akin to somebody having cut one right here at the table. Dr. Piper waves his knife in my general direction and says, "Vampires?"

Well, I'm in this far… "Vampires, yes," I say, fighting off flop sweats, "But the twist is, nobody knows they're vampires. It's like a secret society. You become part of it when you're bitten by a vampire. But you don't know you've been bitten. We're not doing the old *bite marks on the neck* thing. You don't realize you're a vampire until it's too late."

Dr. Piper slices his chicken with care and precision. "I see."

I take a big ol' sip of wine. "Our main character has all these strange things happen to him: he hears blood rushing, he has weird dreams, he develops an aversion to going out in the daytime. But we never *see* a vampire or anything like that. It's like a vampire story told from the inside out."

Fabio and Frankie seem impressed. Dr. and Mrs. Piper remain completely placid.

"Where does the heist come in?" Mrs. Piper asks, pouring herself some wine.

"The heist?" That's right, there's another fucking genre Lars wants me to use. Thanks, asshole. "The heist is what the main character is planning. Him and some friends. Turns out the guys they're trying to rob are the vampires. They're posing as…respectable businessmen. The vampires, I mean."

Reactions vary around the table. Frankie's bright eyes are on me. Lars has a self-satisfied air, as if I've only relayed what he himself had thought up. Fabio mutters, "Far out." Dr. Piper turns to Lars.

"Mister…Lars," Dr. Piper says, "What is your experience in the film industry?"

Lars wipes his mouth with a napkin. "I have wanted to make movies ever since I saw *Breathless* in college. Have you seen it? Brilliant film. Since then, I've worked in a number of capacities in the film industry. I've been a critic, a performer, a production assistant, a teacher."

Dr. Piper's head tilts slightly. "You've taught film? At a school or a university?"

"I have taught."

The doctor's eyes narrow. I try to think of a way to help Lars. Something brushes my leg. For a moment, I think it might be a cat, though I seriously doubt this family would have a pet. I peek under the table and see a foot stroking my calf. I look up and see Frankie raising her eyebrows slightly. Oh great. Lars is ignorant of this (as he is of most things) and carries on defending himself to Dr. and Mrs. Piper.

"I have been intimately involved with many members of the Twin Cities film community," he says, expertly spearing a chunk of sweet potato, "Also, I am an expert in the fields of film theory, history and critique, as a routine check of my library account will show." He tosses the sweet potato in his mouth with a flourish. "I hope I've made my case clear."

"Abundantly," Dr. Piper says, "You've been talking for however long and you haven't said a thing."

Lars contemplates this as he chews. "It's a gift."

The parents seem to be wondering if it would be gauche to throw us out before dessert. Mrs. Piper takes a slug of wine. Fabio leans over to Lars and whispers, "You got any ganja on you?" I start laughing, for absolutely no reason other than to cover Fabio's question and Lars's possible response. Unfortunately, just as I start doing this, Frankie runs her foot up my leg again, causing my laugh to come out as a high squeak. What's worse, this brings me back to the attention of the parents.

"And Mr. Davis," Mrs. Piper says, "What is your experience in writing?"

I'm on safe ground here. I don't have to make anything up. "I'm mostly known for writing a column in *The Daily Bugle*. It's called *Cup o' Joe*. That's…I'm Joe."

That last part might not have come out quite so awkwardly if not for Mrs. Piper literally looking down her nose at me and Frankie tickling my calf with her toe. (She should probably clip her nails, but that's the least of my worries.) Mrs. Piper considers gives my resume.

"I've heard of *The Daily Bugle*," she says, "I'm not a fan."

Well, isn't that the tops? I clam up, since I don't really have any desire to justify my existence. Frankie's foot has made its way to my thigh and I'm wondering where, precisely, she's going to stop. Lars and Fabio give each other little hand signals, silently discussing their drug deal. Dr. Piper sets down his cutlery.

"I'm sure you're both very…passionate about this project," he says, "And as I'm sure you can see, I make a large indulgence for my children. They're both intelligent and driven. In their own way. I've tried to give them a start in life. The results have been… indifferent."

Frankie pauses in playing footsie with me. (Although, to be more accurate, she's playing footsie *at* me since I'm not participating.) "Here we go again," she says.

Dr. Piper is unfazed. "I don't wish to disillusion you gentlemen, but this would not be the first project my children have invested in. To date, they have been involved in a nightclub, a restaurant, a think tank, a design firm, and an alpaca farm. I'll spare you the details, but none of these projects have proceeded very far."

Lars gives that a flip of his hand. "The key is persistence. Lincoln had a string of failures at the beginning of his career and looked how that turned out."

"That's very true," Dr. Piper says, "But if you'll pardon my saying, Mr. Lars, I don't see a Lincoln at this table."

Mrs. Piper mutters into her wine, "You're goddamned right about that."

Frankie's foot hits the floor with an audible *smack.* "God, Dad, do we have to talk about this stuff again?"

Dr. Piper ignores her. "I'll be honest: I am extremely dubious about this venture. At the same time, I want to give my children a chance to succeed."

Mrs. Piper looks toward the wall. "Or at least move out of the house."

"I don't want to dismiss this idea out of hand," Dr. Piper says, "I'd like to talk it over with the children and then I'll make up my mind."

Lars strokes his beard. "I'm not sure—"

"We can accept that," I say, "Absolutely. Definitely. Very generous of you, really."

Dr. Piper resumes eating. Mrs. Piper pours herself more wine. Fabio leans over to Lars and whispers, "Okay, seriously, man, about the ganja…" Frankie runs her fingers along her tan blouse, sliding it back and giving me a peek at the lacy black bra she's wearing. There's a buzzing in my leg, very near my crotch. Then I realize it's my phone.

I retrieve the damn thing. Per the caller ID, it's a number I don't recognize. But it's not listed as spam and frankly, I'd chew my own leg off to get out of this particular bear trap. I stand up from the table.

"Sorry," I say, waving the phone, "I've got to take this."

I step into the hallway and answer, trying to keep my voice down. It's Bobby Cronus. (Honestly, if Captain Kirk had shown up on the communicator, I wouldn't be more surprised.)

"Sorry to bother you," he says, "but somebody broke into my apartment."

Hey, I *was* looking for an excuse to get out of here…

CHAPTER SIX

Pro wrestling and travel have always gone hand in hand. Even when the business was largely made up of regional territories, a territory would usually run shows six or seven nights a week, so wrestlers spent a considerable amount of time in the car. If they were working a larger territory or, later on, a national promotion, they would be lucky to get home one or two days a month. They lived out of a suitcase, tried not to spend all their money on food, hotels, and booze (to say nothing of recreational pharmaceuticals), watched their kids grow up without them, and their spouses become more and more a stranger. Hence, the concept of home became rather foreign to a lot of wrestlers.

I remember seeing an interview with a retired wrestler. He said friends who didn't know the wrestling business would ask him how hard it was to adjust to living his whole life on the road. He'd tell them, "Hell, I was doing that since I turned twenty. When I retired, I had to adjust to being at home."

Given my status as a confirmed home body, you can see where this aspect of pro wrestling is hard for me to connect with.

I assume that's just one of the many differences between me and Bobby Cronus. He's spent practically his entire adult life on the road. As such, he probably has little consideration for whatever place he calls home for the moment. Doesn't mean he wants it broken into, though. Cronus lets me know the burglar is no longer there and that he's going to call the police. I assure him I'll stop by.

Getting out of the Piper's house proves rather difficult, as Frankie corners me and asks to make out (we almost got there, but her father made a timely appearance) and Lars tries to finalize his drug deal with Fabio. Still, we make it out of there with Dr. Piper's dry assurance that he'll think about our proposal. Weird that I'd consider that a victory, but that's show business for you.

There's no sign of a squad car when we pull into the parking lot of the Techwood Complex. We dash up to Cronus's apartment. Again, there's bass thumping coming from one of the apartments. (It's early enough in the evening that I should have expected that.) Cronus whips open the door a split-second after I knock. He wears his usual non-gimmick black t-shirt and sweats. He ushers us inside.

"Thanks for coming," he says, looking askance at Lars in his Nehru jacket, "Wasn't sure who to call. Gordon is the next best thing to useless. And you have friends in the St. Paul Police Department."

I scratch my head. "Uh, *friends* might be an overstatement…"

"I just called the police," Cronus says, "They should be here any minute."

"What happened?" I ask.

Cronus shrugs. "I've been at the arena since this morning. When I got back here, the door was a little ajar. Looks like they forced their way in."

"You mind if I look around?" I say.

"Feel fucking free," he says, "It's not like you're going to mess up the place."

He's right there. The place has been pre-messed. The cushions have been thrown from the threadbare couch. All the cupboard drawers are open, and foodstuffs tossed around the kitchen. In the bedroom, the bedclothes have been tossed from the mattress. All the dresser drawers have been pulled out and emptied on the floor. The medicine chest in the bathroom has been ransacked. No doubt. The place is a friggin' mess.

"What did they take?" I ask, when I get back to the living room.

"That's the fuck of it," Cronus says, "They didn't take anything."

"No memorabilia?" I ask, "I heard you were a pretty big collector."

"All my valuable stuff is back in Louisville. I only brought what I needed up here. I don't have anything here worth taking."

I look around the room. "They didn't take anything. Meaning they were looking for something and didn't find it." I turn to Cronus. "Who knows where you're staying? Anyone outside the promotion?"

That gets a scoff. "I kept in touch with my mom until she passed away and all my ex-wives until they became my ex-wives. Those are the only people outside the business I *ever* kept in touch with."

Before we can get any further, the police arrive. There's a quick knock and an announcement of their presence. At first, it appears to be only a couple of uniformed cops. As soon as they walk in, though, they reveal someone behind them.

"Counselor," Pike says, "why did I know you'd be here?"

He's one up on me because I had no idea *he* would be here. But I should have. Cronus is a suspect. A call comes in that his place has been broken into. Naturally, Pike is going to check things out. He strolls around, trying to be unassuming. Cronus drops on to the sofa and puts his head in his hands. Lars stands in the corner, humming. The two uniformed cops question Cronus about the break in. One of them goes over to the door and examines it.

"Kicked in," the cop says, looking over the doorframe, "Although most of the damage is at the top. Whoever it was must have just leaned into the thing. Hard." He looks back at Cronus. "Any idea who it could be?"

Cronus shakes his head. "None."

They take him through the usual questions about whether anything is missing. Pike gets my attention and walks toward the tiny kitchen. I follow him, moving carefully amongst the debris. Pike glares at me over his wire-rim frames.

"Any idea what this is all about?" he asks.

"None," I say, "Came completely out of the blue."

"You think Cronus staged it?" Pike asks.

"For what possible reason?"

"Throws the suspicion off him, doesn't it?"

"And how's that working out for him?"

Pike's face tightens. "Why would someone break in here?"

"I don't know," I say, "But they were looking for something. They trashed the place but didn't take anything. Don't ask me what they were after."

Pike keeps his thoughts to himself. Maybe he sees my point about Cronus. Maybe he's trying to figure out another way to pin it in on him. That's a thing about Pike: once he gets the bit between his teeth, he refuses to let go. I imagine that makes him a hell of an asset when he's going after the correct target. When he's not, it just makes him a pain in the ass.

Speaking of pains in the ass, Lars has apparently been exploring the bedroom. (The fact he hasn't stepped into the kitchen to make himself a sandwich can be considered progress.) He tries to get my attention. Pike doesn't notice anything. I lightly flip my hand toward Lars, as if to say *What the hell are you on about?* Lars responds by opening his Nehru jacket, revealing a bong as big as a toddler's leg. He then reaches up one sleeve and comes out with a syringe and a length of rubber tubing. (If he's taking up magic, he's picked a shitty way to do it.) He manages to hide the items again before the cops notice him.

"You really think this guy is on the up and up?" Pike asks.

My look snaps back to Pike. "I don't think he killed Lance Mack, no."

Lars gets into a position where Cronus can see him, but the cops can't. He shows Cronus the drug paraphernalia. Cronus's eyes get wide. One of the cops looks toward Lars, who closes the jacket before the cop can see the goods.

"Everything okay?" the cop asks.

"Fine," Cronus says, "Just worried about my apartment."

"We're going to take a look around," the other cop says, "You okay with that?"

The apartment isn't that big, so it's not going take forever. One cop handles the living room while the other disappears into the bedroom. Footsteps are audible in the hallway outside. Apparently, the neighbors are gathering. Pike is lost in thought. I hold my hands out toward Lars, silently asking him what the hell is going on. Lars gestures toward the bedroom, indicating he found the stuff in there.

"Something's going on here," Pike says.

"No shit," I mutter. Then add, "I agree."

Cronus frantically gestures toward Lars, trying to tell him what to do with the paraphernalia. Lars looks confused. Cronus repeats the gesture. I can't make head nor tail of it, either. Based on the available evidence, I think Cronus is telling Lars to get that shit out of his apartment. But that's not clear to Lars. He takes out the bong and the tubing and offers them to Cronus, who swings an open-hand slap that only narrowly misses Lars. Cronus nods toward the front door. Lars wanders toward it and opens it slightly, as if someone is knocking. The cops don't seem concerned. Lars looks back at Cronus, confused. Cronus makes a *big* signal to get the stuff the hell out the door. Lars smacks his forehead.

"Oh, I get it," he says, "Get rid of the drug shit."

Cronus looks as if every fiber of his being is invested in Lars's gruesome and untimely death. I drop my hands on to the kitchen counter and try not to swallow my own tongue. Pike steps out of the kitchen.

"What the hell is going on?" he asks.

Lars, who has never cozied up to the police in general or Pike in particular, adopts an air of haughty indifference. "And what business is it of yours?"

"I'm a police officer," Pike says.

"You'll have to do better than that, my friend," Lars says, adding a sniff.

I've made it clear that I'm not the bosom friend of Sergeant Frank Pike. But I know him well enough to know that's not the kind of thing you say to him, as a joke, on a *good* day. (Assuming he has good days. I've seen little evidence of that.) Pike walks over to Lars.

"I get the feeling you're up to something," Pike says, his voice murderously quiet.

Lars tries to laugh it off. "It's just your paranoia. Common to police officers, I'm told. Maybe you need some professional help with that." Lars lays what I'm sure he thinks is a helpful hand on Pike's shoulder.

Pike looks to his shoulder. "Do you know you have your hand on me?"

Lars withdraws the hand so quickly you'd think a marionette was doing the work for him. Unfortunately, this movement causes the bong to fall out of Lars's jacket. He swings a hand down stop it, which dislodges the tubing and the syringe. Pike surveys the scene.

"What are those?" he asks.

"Nothing," Lars says, "Certainly nothing that need concern the authorities."

Pike reaches down to grab the items. Lars tries to get there first. Their heads collide. Lars gets the worst of it. He steps backward, holding his head, and trips over a displaced ottoman. He tumbles backward to the floor, legs and arms flying in every direction. Pike simply checks his head and, not seeing any blood on his fingers, points toward the paraphernalia.

"You want to explain this?" Pike asks.

Lars stares at him, vacantly. "Explain?"

"Yes," Pike says, "Why are you carrying drug paraphernalia? And where did you get it?"

The other cop has come out of the bedroom and now both uniformed cops have an interest in the proceedings. After a few seconds, Lars comes to a decision. He gets to his feet, summoning up what little dignity he can muster.

"I choose to keep that information to myself," he says.

Pike turns to the uniformed cops. "You two want to handle this idiot?"

The uniformed cops don't appear enthusiastic, but Lars is summarily cuffed and hauled out. The cops tell Cronus they'll get back to him if they find anything (though it's doubtful they will). Once Lars has been ushered out, Pike turns to me and Cronus.

"Last chance," Pike says, "You want to tell me what was really going on here?"

Cronus's jaw tightens. "You know as much as I know."

Pike looks toward me. I just give him a headshake in return. He takes in a breath through his nose. "Then you can play it like that," he says, "But I'm going to find out."

Pike turns on his heel and strides out of the apartment. Cronus tries to close the door behind him, but the damn thing won't work.

"That asshole is going to help get me out of this?" Cronus says, "I don't think so."

"You're right," I say, "I think *I'm* the asshole who's going to get you out of this."

That doesn't bring Cronus a lot of comfort. I can't say I blame him. It isn't doing much for me, either.

***

"You think there will be a hotel party?" Mike asks, fussing with his black suitcoat, "The hotel parties Nick

Diamond had back in the day were legendary. Remember when he gave out his hotel room number right before the big card in Baltimore? I heard that party was insane."

It's hard not to share Mike's enthusiasm, even if the prospect of meeting Nick Diamond is a little terrifying. We're in a corner booth at The Block restaurant. It's in a converted brick building and leans toward being a sports bar. Big screen TVs adorn the corners. A large patio sits beyond the windows. That will be great in the summer, but it's not ready for occupancy on a chilly, misty April night. There's a square bar area in the center of the main room, drawing halfway decent business. I tug at my blue dress shirt, knowing I won't match the sartorial splendor of Nick Diamond.

"Remember the whole goal is to chat with him," I say, "If there's any partying to be done, we can do it later."

Mike gives me the stink face. "Aren't you a fucking good time?" He checks his reflection in the picture window, fussing with the collar of his black dress shirt. "Speaking of good times, I take it Lars is out on bail?"

"He was released this morning," I say, "He's got a court date. It's a petty misdemeanor."

"First offense?"

"Shockingly, yes. And he wasn't even caught with his own paraphernalia. I convinced Lars to keep covering. Cronus doesn't need this added to his other troubles."

Mike fusses with his cuffs. "Someone must have planted that stuff in Cronus's apartment. Trying to frame him."

"Funny way to go about it," I say, "Planting the drug paraphernalia makes no sense. Unless someone is trying to imply that Cronus has a drug problem and might go off half-cocked and kill Lance Mack. It's a reach, but after planting the murder weapon, they might not have anything else to work with."

"Cronus doesn't have a reputation for drug use."

"I wonder if Lance Mack did?" I say.

"Not according to Ashley," Mike says, "There are some rumors about some guys but not Mack. UWE is a publicly traded company. They look down on anyone with a drug problem. It's why Ashley is so concerned about staying straight edge."

Our server approaches the table and offers to take our drink order. (Oh, thank you, kindly inn-keep.) "Do you need some menus?" she asks.

"We'll see," I say, "We've got someone joining us. I'm not sure if he's going to want to eat or just stick with the drinks."

Mike snorts. "I seriously doubt he'll want food to get in the way of the drinking."

The server hugs the serving tray to her chest and gives us a quizzical glance. I give her a little chuckle.

"The guy joining us is Nick Diamond," I say.

"Nick is coming in tonight?" the server says, her eyes lighting up, "I was hoping he would. He's been in practically every night the last few weeks. He buys drinks for everyone. He's the greatest guy."

"That's what I've heard," I say.

"That's so awesome," the server says, "I'll get those drinks for you and see about the menus when Nick gets here."

The server leaves us to our trepidation. Sure, you've heard Canelo Alvarez packs a hell of a punch, but are you ready to go three rounds with him? And try to question him about a murder while you're doing it? I can't shake the feeling I'm out of my league.

Mike picks up on my vibe. "We're going to be fine. I saw him drinking in here the night I met Ashley and he, uh, he got a little nuts. But it's not like we're Ned Flanders and Mike Huckabee over here."

A perceptible buzz runs through the restaurant. News of Nick Diamond's imminent arrival is starting to spread. I grab a napkin and tear little bits off it.

"Did you see Ashley last night?" I ask.

"Yep. I pretty much saw all of her."

"Somehow, I knew that line was coming."

"Speaking of which…"

I hold up a hand, stopping him. "Just let it go, Dirk Diggler. I'm going to be sitting across the table from her father in a few minutes. I don't need the mental image of you and Ashley rutting while I'm doing that."

"How do you think I feel?" Mike says.

I *did* bring the subject up, so I can't get too far up on my high horse. I keep shredding the bar napkin. "Things are going well?" I ask.

"Most definitely. She's as sexy as hell and she's really sweet, too. And she's been through some stuff."

"I imagine. Given her upbringing and what happened with her brother."

"She's made some bad decisions," he says, "Had some really bad guys in her life."

"I see. And you think of yourself as a step *up*?"

"Hey dick—or perhaps Richard—you want to be nice?"

"Mea culpa." I set the shredded napkin aside. "Has your boss gotten suspicious yet?"

"Suspicious, yeah. We were supposed to go out last night and I cancelled. Said I was sick. I never cancel on her, so she got suspicious. Next time I see her, she's going to have to get the sex of a lifetime."

"Who are you going to hire to do that?"

"Shut up." Mike runs a hand through his hair. "Brigid wouldn't be bad if it wasn't for her ego. She's full of herself. To the point where she's…delusional. She's smart, but in her mind, she's a cunning genius. She's good-looking, but she thinks she's the hottest woman on planet Earth. And so on. In a weird way, it's the reason I haven't gotten into bigger trouble. Brigid is suspicious but at the same time, she can't fathom the idea I'd find any other woman attractive."

"Her ego has brought balance to The Force."

"And you saw what happened to the last person who tried to bring balance to The Force. That's what I'm going to be dealing with if Brigid finds out I've been sneaking around on her." He lets out a breath. "But it's totally different with Ashley. She takes me at my word. It makes me feel strange, though. Sort of down, kind of."

"I think that's called *guilt*."

Mike scratches his goatee. "Wow. That's what that is. It's unpleasant. I'm going to have to avoid it in the future."

I'm sure he will. I could lecture Mike about the tangled web we weave, but Nick Diamond makes his appearance in the bar. Business, to borrow the phrase, is about to pick up.

"Hey, that bar open or is it just for decoration!"

Diamond struts into the room, wearing a black coat (that's *got* to be cashmere) and a gray custom-tailored suit. He may have aged, but the strut from the old days remains unchanged. You half expect him to have models on each arm (just like the old days). The customers and staff greet him with a loud cheer. He strolls to the bar and loudly addresses the bartender, a tall guy with a brush of black hair.

"You got the makings of a Kamikaze?" Diamond asks.

"We do," the bartender says.

Diamond rubs his hands. "Big man, set me up with a tray of those."

The bartender starts throwing the Kamikazes together. "You buying for the room?"

"Eventually," Diamond says, "but these are for me."

The bartender nearly drops the shaker. Then he goes back to his work. Nick Diamond is still living his gimmick: the rich playboy enjoying the high life. It's a sight to behold, like watching Ernest Hemingway down Mojitos. Diamond slams the Kamikazes as fast as the bartender can pour them. Between drinks, he spots our table. He picks up the tray and makes his way over.

"Joe Davis?" he asks.

"That's me," I say, making room for Diamond, "This is my friend Mike."

"Pleased to meet you both," he says, putting the tray down and sliding easily into his seat. He shivers, ostentatiously. "Chilly out there. I don't get to Minnesota much anymore. I forget how cold it gets." He picks up two of the shot glasses, "Join me, all right?"

I manufacture a smile. "Sounds like fun."

We take the shots from Diamond. He holds his up in a toast. Up close, his hands are gigantic, practically engulfing the glass. The server arrives with beers for me and Mike. There's a definite buzz in the restaurant. Even the people who don't recognize Nick Diamond figure this guy has to be _somebody_. Mike folds his hands on the table, trying to contain his excitement. Diamond looks up at the waitress and slides a Kamikaze toward her.

"Join us, my dear," Diamond says, "The more the merrier."

The server is clearly torn. She's not in the habit of accepting drinks from customers and certainly not customers who scream _Aging Lothario_. On the other hand…Kamikaze.

"I may have to wait until later," she says.

Diamond downs the shot himself. "I'll be looking forward to that." He scoops up another shot. Mike and I are quick to join him. "Here's to living the good life," Diamond says, "All the time."

We clink glasses and knock back the shots. It goes down smooth. The taste is fruity with a trace of bite in the aftertaste. Like drinking Kool-Aid. (This is why I prefer my vodka on the rocks or in a martini. If I'm drinking hooch, I want to know what I'm getting myself into.)

Mike smacks his lips and turns to the founder of the feast. "Thank you, Mr. Diamond."

"None of that *Mr. Diamond* stuff," Diamond says, "Call me Nick." He knocks back another shot then puts two more in front of us. "Bobby tells me you're writing an article."

"I am," I say, waiting for the effects of the shot to hit me. (Nothing yet. I'm not sure if that's a good thing or a bad thing.) "It would be great if you were part of it."

"Sounds good," he says, downing another shot, "What do you want to know?"

I take out my cell phone and show it to Diamond, getting his permission to record the conversation. He gives me the go-ahead. At first, I stick with some general background information, allowing him to relax as the alcohol hits. I get his general resume. Born in Minnesota, to a wealthy family. Educated in private schools. Played football at the University of Minnesota. Got involved in pro wrestling in Minnesota, mainly working opening matches. Then a wrestler passing through the Minnesota territory recommended him to a promoter in Georgia. He went down there, dyed his hair blonde, and became the Diamond Stud. The rest, as they say, is history. Throughout the interview, Diamond's voice is calm and casual, a sharp contrast to the larger-than-life personality he uses in the ring.

"I know I'm long in the tooth to still be doing this," he says, and I'm not sure if he means professional wrestling or binge drinking, "Sure, the IRS keeps me on the move. But even without that stuff, it would be hard to give up. The crowd reaction. Being around the boys. All of it. What can I say? I love being the Diamond Stud." He looks at ceiling. "I used to have this place out in the middle of nowhere, in North Carolina. Big damn house. Everyone in town knew who we were. But they were respectful. I'd go to places like Chicago and Philly and never get a minute's peace. I could go to the grocery store down the road from my house and nobody would say boo to me."

"Now you're helping out Bobby Cronus," I say, trying to get things back on track.

"Bobby's an old friend," Diamond says, "We go all the way back to the PWA. He was a bright kid. Still is." He downs another Kamikaze. "There was no one I wanted to train Ashley other than him."

Mike looks toward the ceiling. "Ashley's really got great…potential."

"She does," Diamond says, "She's going to be huge. She's going to change women's wrestling. She's got that kind of potential. She's a natural."

"Like father, like daughter?" I say.

"Maybe," he says, "But she's going to be her own kind of star. She deserves that." Diamond brings another Kamikaze to his lips. He pauses, staring at the table. "It's what *we* deserve. Our family." He knocks back the Kamikaze and slides more shots our direction. His voice takes on the familiar booming quality used when Diamond cuts a promo. "Grab another round. Let's go. To the good life and all that shit."

It doesn't sound like a request. We down another round of shots. We're only two drinks in, but I'm starting to feel it. Dammit. *This* is why I avoid fruity drinks. Diamond has no such scruples. He lets out a little shout and downs another shot.

"Love it!" he shouts, "Love it!" His voice gets calm again. "I'm very proud of Ashley. But she has to be careful."

"With the backstage stuff?" I ask.

"Exactly," Diamond says, "The politics. The social stuff. The backstabbing. That shit. It can mess with your head. I've seen a lot of guys start running with the wrong crowd, get used up by them. Guys who could have made real money in this business and their careers just went down the shitter. I don't want that happening to Ashley. Look, I don't want to talk out of school, but Ashley's made some bad decisions in her life. I'm not putting it all on her or her mom. They did they best they could. I...I wasn't there for her. Or the other kids."

He sweeps back his thinning dyed blonde hair. "But I can be here now. If I can keep her out of trouble, that's what I'm going to do."

"Was Lance Mack trouble?" I ask.

Some coldness creeps into Diamond's tone. "Why do you say that?"

I grab my beer glass (and hope like hell Diamond doesn't offer me another shot). "I talked to Bobby Cronus last week. Watched a little of the training session. You seemed to get nervous when Ashley was talking to Lance Mack. Then I saw the two of you arguing. I figured it was about him."

Diamond picks up another shot but doesn't drink it. "The guy made me nervous. I've seen his type before. In it for himself. Doesn't care about the business. Just likes what the business can get him. I wanted to keep Ashley away from that. She gets pissed sometimes. She can be headstrong. But I know this business. And I know trouble when I see it."

"You were there, right?" I say, "The night Lance was killed? You were in the arena?"

Diamond signals for another round. (And dear God, by *another round,* I think he means another *tray* of kamikazes.) "I was there. It was a party. A lot of people were there."

"But you were there at the end of the night," I say, "I think Gordon Russell told me that. You and Ashley and Jack Blades and, obviously, Lance Mack."

"And Bobby Cronus," Diamond says.

"And him," I say, "Did you see anything with Mack? Anything unusual?"

"Why you need to know that? Is that going in the article?"

Everyone wants to know that. "I can't really leave it out," I say, "Lance Mack's death. It's kind of a big story."

"I get that," Diamond says, "I can't tell you much. I talked with Ashley a little. I went into the office and talked with Bobby Cronus. Then I left and came here for a while."

"About what time did you leave?"

"I don't know. Maybe ten after twelve. Somewhere in there."

"What did you and Bobby talk about?" I ask.

"Just shot the shit about the old days."

"Did you leave with Ashley?"

"No. She went off somewhere. I lost track of her."

Diamond stares at me, steadily. His attitude has gotten suspicious. Fortunately, the server arrives, setting another tray of kamikazes in front of us. Diamond's head swings her direction.

"You given any more thought to that drink?" he asks.

The server gives him an indulgent look. "I'm still going to have to wait on it."

"Your choice," Diamond says, "Don't leave without spending some time with us, okay?"

"Sounds like fun," she says, her gaze lingering on Diamond before she walks away.

Diamond puts shots in front of us and offers another toast. Mike and I join him. At this point, I'd rather shotgun a bag of candy corn than have another kamikaze pass my lips. Sadly, I don't think fate is going to indulge me on that one. Nick Diamond downs another shot then does a little war whoop. I try to prop an elbow on the table, but I miss and nearly fall into Mike's lap. Diamond puts more shots in front of us. "Drink up, boys. Party's slowing down."

This is the equivalent of a kid getting caught smoking and having to smoke an entire pack of cigarettes as punishment. Except Mike and I didn't do anything wrong. (Specifically. Karmically, we've got this coming.) I notice the server standing at the bar, waiting for an order. A thought occurs to me. I stand up (or a reasonable facsimile).

"I'm going to the restroom," I say, "I'll be right back."

"Take your time," Diamond says, "I'll have another round by the time you get back."

Mike gives me a forlorn look, as if he can't figure out why I'd abandon him. I stumble to the bar. The room is lurching one way, I'm lurching the other. (Maybe together we're sober.) The server looks up as I approach.

"Having fun?" she asks.

"That's…one word for it," I say, "I'm wondering about something. Maybe you can help me out. I'm doing an article on Nick Diamond and the company he's working for right now. Just trying to check a few things, make sure I get them straight." I lower my voice. "Nick has some trouble remembering details."

"I'm not surprised," the server says, "He can really put them away."

In the same way Donald Trump can tell a fib or two. "Mr. Diamond says he stopped in here last Sunday night. Were you working then?"

"I was. I saw him."

"What time did he get here?"

The server looks up. "I'm going to say about one. In fact, I'm positive of that. He got here just in time for last call. Of course, for him, last call was two trays of kamikazes."

I'm slightly sick at the thought, but I manage to tamp that down. One o'clock arrival. According to Diamond, he came straight here after leaving the arena. More than forty-five minutes to go a couple of blocks? That doesn't add up. I check with the server again and she's firm on the one o'clock arrival time.

"Thanks for that," I say, "I'm sure I'll be seeing you soon."

I return to the table as Mike and Diamond are doing another round of shots. Mike is turning slightly green. Diamond puts a shot in front of me as soon as I sit. Then he downs another one and follows that up by standing and doing a little spin and strut. It gets some cheers from nearby patrons. Diamond laughs.

"A thing I was wondering about—" I say.

Diamond, though, is done with our interview. "Enough of this article shit. Let's have some fun. To the good life and all that."

"I'm not sure that—" is all I get out.

Diamond downs three shots in succession then shouts toward the bar. "You just keep 'em coming, okay?" That gets a positive response from the staff. "Why don't we really get this party started, huh?" Diamond stands on one of the tables and drops his pants. He's wearing a pair of purple bikini briefs (thank ye gods). He holds up a Kamikaze. "How about a round for the house?" That gets a huge cheer from the patrons, who are now totally into his act. "Let's all get comfortable," Diamond says, "Ladies, feel free to join in."

Diamond downs the shot, takes off his suitcoat and goes to work on the tie. Mike and I sag at the table. Suddenly, I'm not worried about keeping Bobby Cronus out of jail.

I'm more concerned about keeping *me* out of jail.

CHAPTER SEVEN

There is a word you never use around professional wrestlers unless you wish to be insulting or have an unusual desire to get your ass kicked. And that is the F word. No, not that *F word. I mean* fake.

By strict definition, professional wrestling is fake, in that what's being presented to you is not exactly what it seems. The preferred term is work, *because the wrestlers are* working *on the audience's emotions, manipulating them into reacting a certain way. (By contrast, a* shoot *means that on some level, shit just got real.)* Fake *is an insult because it implies that nobody really gets hurt. That's not the case.*

Wrestlers get hurt all the time. Punches or kicks land with more force than intended. Guys get dropped on their heads. Cartilage or ligaments get torn or strained. The simple act of hurling one's body through space for a number of years eventually takes a toll. Wrestlers have a history of abusing painkillers or alcohol; things they needed just to get through a day relatively pain-free. It's a lifestyle that's taken a large number of wrestlers away from us far too soon.

That, sadly, is a shoot.

As far as I know, Nick Diamond's drug of choice is—and always has been—alcohol. That might explain why he's lived longer than some of his contemporaries, having avoided the ravages of prolonged cocaine, painkiller, or steroid abuse. Still, if last night's performance is any indication, I can't believe he made it a week drinking like that, let alone thirty or forty years.

Carol leads the way to our seats at the Sportatorium. "Must be nice to know that Nick Diamond's reputation isn't bullshit," she says.

I'm just glad my headache is finally gone. "Please remember to say that at my funeral."

Carol gives me a look of disapproval. It's not as if she's above imbibing herself (she got into some serious trouble on that score last fall) but she never misses an opportunity to lecture me or Mike.

"When do you think you'll feel better?" Carol asks.

Mike looks toward the lights as he thinks. "Let's see. It's just about seven o'clock now, so I'd say…in about three days. I'm just glad I stopped throwing up."

"When was that?" I ask.

"About an hour ago."

I must return to my policy of never meeting my heroes. Once upon a time, Mike and I thought the closest thing to heaven would be going on a bender with Nick Diamond: the women, the wild parties, the glamour. It would be like hanging with a less mob-connected Rat Pack. We never pictured getting thrown out of a Lyft after either Mike puked on the floor or Nick Diamond and the server were trying to have sex in the backseat. (It might have been both. I'm a little hazy on the details.) This morning, ibuprofen and greasy hash browns were all that stood between me and total system failure.

Carol looks at Mike like she's a disappointed parent. "Did you make it into the office?"

"I did not," Mike says, "Brigid was not pleased. And she's getting even more suspicious. I may have to make it up to her."

"Tonight?" I ask.

Mike blow out a sigh. "Yeah. I have to get out of seeing Ashley tonight."

"Tell her you have diarrhea," I say.

"I'm not going to do that!"

Carol shoots him a look. "Or you could tell her you're shtupping your boss in order to get preferable treatment."

Mike considers this. "Diarrhea, you say."

Carol must once again give up hope that Mike or I will, even at an advanced age, reach anything close to maturity. "Did you at least get anything interesting out of all this?" she asks.

"There's a little gap in Nick Diamond's alibi," I say, "According to him, he left here at about twelve-ten. According to the server, he didn't get to The Block until one a.m. Doesn't take fifty minutes to go a couple blocks."

"You sure he left when he said he did?" Carol asks.

"Bobby Cronus saw him go," I say, "I suppose it's possible Diamond left and came back. He's got the keys to the place." I run a hand over my face. "According to Gordon Russell, Diamond was tending bar that night. And Lance Mack had roofies in his system. Diamond would have been in the perfect position to spike Mack's drink."

"You think it was him?" Carol asks.

"I don't know," I say, "If Mack set his drink down at some point, anyone could have gotten to it."

We plop down in the front row. It's the weekly show, so no announce table and seating is available everywhere in the arena. The crowd files in steadily. All sense of momentum toward *WrestleShock* has disappeared and been replaced by a sense of dislocation. Hopefully, things will be cleared up tonight. I look over the program.

"Ashley's in a tag team match," I say.

"Her and some chick against Vanessa and some other chick," Mike says, scratching his goatee. "It's, uh, it's going to be interesting."

"How so?" I ask.

"Can't tell you," Mike says, "Kayfabe."

Cripe. Now *Mike* is kayfabing me? I'm the intrepid reporter and lead investigator and I'm the only one being kept out of the loop. Ashley's match comes up right before intermission. As advertised, she is part of a tag team match involving her and a cute young wrestler (I say this not to be sexist but because she plays up the *cutie pie* aspects of her gimmick) named Sienna. Vanessa, the Women's champion, is on the opposing team. Her partner is a muscular woman named Alexandra Micelli. Ashley and Vanessa are the stars of the show. The referee is forced to separate them before the match.

It's entertaining and fast-paced. Vanessa, in the fine tradition of chickenshit heels everywhere, continually avoids being in the ring with Ashley, tagging out whenever necessary. The crowd chants *Gutless!* Vanessa shouts at them to shut up and covers her ears when they won't comply.

Ashley misses a flying splash in the corner and winds up flat on her back. Vanessa tags in and lays the boots to her. Ashley, though, uses her long legs to land a kick to Vanessa's head, stalling her attack. When they get to their feet, Ashley stalks toward Vanessa, backing her into a corner. Just as Ashley launches her attack, Vanessa pulls the referee between them, causing Ashley to wipe out the ref.

"Uh-oh," Mike says, "Here it comes."

"What?" I ask.

He hangs his head. "Just watch."

Vanessa hits Ashley with a cheap shot. Sienna jumps into the ring but is attacked by Alexandra Micelli. The two of them go to the floor. Vanessa drives Ashley back into the ropes then pulls the middle rope over both the top rope and Ashley's arms. Ashley is effectively tied up in the ropes, helpless. Vanessa slaps Ashley for good measure.

"This looks bad," Carol says.

Vanessa slides under the bottom rope and reaches under the ring. She comes up with a large pair of scissors and brandishes them to the crowd. She gets back into the ring and stands in front of Ashley, who offers only a few feeble kicks in return. Vanessa grabs Ashley's head and cuts off a lock of her hair. Vanessa shows it to the crowd, then tosses it aside and goes after Ashley again. She slices away another lock. Ashley fights furiously but can't get loose.

Sienna gets away of Alexandra Micelli. She makes her way around ringside and frees Ashley from the ropes. The second that happens, Vanessa drops the scissors and runs for the hills. By the time Ashley tears across the ring, Vanessa and Alexandra Micelli have disappeared into the heels' dressing room. Ashley picks up the scattered locks of her hair and looks toward the heels' dressing room, giving it a murderous glare.

"Wow," Carol says.

"Ashley wasn't thrilled with the idea," Mike says, "Looks like she came out okay."

He's right on that. Vanessa was kind enough to cut the two hanks from the longer part of Ashley's hair. There's a slight dent in her flowing locks, but it's not like she's sporting a Larry Fine. She gives Sienna a brief hug, thanking her for her help, then stalks off to the faces' dressing room. Carol turns toward Mike.

"I take it Ashley's going to get revenge for that?" Carol asks.

"Oh yeah," Mike says, "I'd tell you more, but…"

"I know," Carol says, "Kayfabe."

Intermission comes. Lars doesn't seem to be doing his usual working the crowd, so we head into the lobby. Mike goes to the concession stand for a beer (a little hair of the dog, I guess). Carol and I are alone in one corner of the lobby.

"Are you doing anything on Sunday night?" she asks.

"Oh, the usual," I say, "Meet with the press, black tie fundraiser, fashionable martinis on the yacht with a scantily-clad Gal Gadot."

"When you will actually be…?" Carol asks.

"Watching a *Doctor Who* marathon after the Twins game. Why? You got a better offer?"

Carol musters her strength. "Would you like to have dinner with me and Rick?"

My eyebrows go up. "You've cleared that with the man of the house?"

"*I'm* the man of the house. So, yes. Rick would like to see you."

"I may not be able to rustle up a date by Sunday night. Okay if I'm the third wheel?"

"It doesn't bother me if it doesn't bother Rick."

"Good. I'm looking forward to it."

Carol doesn't say anything to that. Mike returns with a couple beers for us and a candy bar for Carol. The thought of alcohol turns my already queasy stomach. But I know this will help. I take the cheap beer and sip at it as best I can. Mike sees something in the corner.

"You think Mr. Russell knows what's going on with the main event tonight?" he asks.

Gordon Russell stands by the black curtain separating the lobby from the hallway to the heel's dressing room. Even though he's not announcing tonight, he's wearing his usual suit and tie. He gazes at his phone then drops it into his pocket.

"I can ask him," I say.

"Fine," Mike says, "Just don't tell him I knew about Ashley getting her hair cut."

"Of course," I say, "I'll just tell him you two are sleeping together and see if he'll tell her father about it."

I'm sure Mike wants to yell at me, but he can't do that without letting the entire lobby know he's sleeping with Ashley Diamond. (Something would do gladly if not for the complication with his boss.) I make my way over to Gordon Russell. He looks up, startled.

"Hi Joe," he says, "How is the article coming along?"

"Progressing," I say, figuring that sounds vague enough, "I was wondering if I could get some help with it."

"Help in what way?"

"I'd like to talk to Jack Blades," I say, "Do you think you could set something up?"

"I'm sure I could," Russell says, "Were you thinking about a phone call or…"

"I'd rather talk in person that can be arranged."

"I'll see what I can do."

Russell's phone buzzes. He digs it out of his pocket. A smile plays at one corner of his mouth. Then Bobby Cronus pokes his head out of the curtain.

"We're going to be ready to go in five minutes," Cronus says.

Russell nearly drops the phone. He shoves it back into his pocket. "Sounds good, sounds good. I'll get the audience back into the arena. Thanks for letting me know."

"Everything okay?" Cronus asks.

"Completely, completely," Russell says, "Why wouldn't it be?"

Cronus doesn't have time to answer that. He slips behind the curtain without another word. Russell powerwalks across the lobby. The lights flicker and the audience is told the second half of the show is about to begin. We return to our seats.

The second half of the show starts. The two matches leading to the main event are rather forgettable. A tag team match of little consequence and a couple future contenders whose futures are a *long* way down the road. Mike looks over the program.

"Jack Blades isn't on the card," he says, "Isn't that kind of strange?"

"It is," I say, "I know he's still in town. Russell's going to set up a meeting for us."

"Did he tell you what's going to happen in the main event?" he asks.

"Didn't get a chance to ask," I say.

Mike sets the program aside. "I guess we'll find out."

A trifling incident, perhaps, but enough to make long-time fans like Mike and me suspicious. A booker as detailed as Bobby Cronus doesn't bring in a legend like Jack Blades and leave him off the card. Something is going to happen. Blades is almost certainly going to play a role in the main event. It's just a matter of how.

Lars hops in the ring and gets ready to introduce said main event. Before he can start, though, Bobby Cronus strolls down the aisle from the heels' dressing room and stands near one of the ring posts. A chorus of boos follows him. The Midwest Championship Belt sits prominently on his shoulder. Lars gives him a confused look as Jackson Darkfire's music starts playing. Darkfire slinks into the ring and takes a seat in one corner. Nick Diamond's music hits and the crowd goes crazy. Diamond walks down the aisle, showing no ill effects from last night's binge drinking. He steps into the ring without looking at Bobby Cronus. Lars waits for the hoopla to die down. While he's doing that, Bobby Cronus makes his way into the ring and snatches the mic away from Lars.

"Why don't you sit this one out, Purple Suit?" Cronus says, drawing further ire from the fans, "Let someone who knows what they're doing handle this."

Lars glares at Cronus then slowly turns away and steps out of the ring. He plunks down in his usual ringside chair. Cronus turns toward the audience.

"Ladies and gentlemen, this is your main event of the evening!" Cronus says, "It is…" He stops, but the crowd continues with a chant of *One fall.* "Y'know, it would be worth booking a two-out-of-three falls match just to get you idiots to stop doing that." The crowd cheers their own ability to get under Cronus's skin. "It is for the *vacant* Midwest Heavyweight Championship." Cronus stretches out his left arm and his voice loses any sense of enthusiasm. "In the corner to my left, two hundred thirty pounds, parts unknown, Jackson Darkfire." The last part comes out almost as a mumble. The crowd rewards Darkfire with a healthy round of applause. Cronus puffs himself up and grandly throws his right arm out. "And in the corner to my right, the former PWA, UWE and GAWF World Champion, PWA World Tag Team Champion, United States Heavyweight Champion, Missouri Heavyweight Champion, Carolinas Heavyweight Champion, Florida Heavyweight Champion and Georgia Heavyweight Champion. One of the greatest wrestlers in professional wrestling history and a close personal friend of mine. He weighs in at two-hundred-and-forty pounds and hails from Beverly Hills, California—" The change of hometown from Diamond's actual hometown to his gimmick hometown does not go unnoticed by the fans. "The Diamond Stud, Nick Diamond!"

The crowd still gives Diamond a huge round of applause. The man is, after all, a legend. Cronus gives Diamond a handshake and then adds a hug. That done, Cronus leaves the ring without acknowledging Jackson Darkfire. The bell rings and the match gets underway.

It's a scientific match through the early portions, both men exchanging holds and escapes. It looks like a turbo-charged amateur match. A couple of times, they wind up in the ropes, forcing the break of a hold. Each time, Diamond breaks cleanly, refusing to hit Darkfire with a cheap shot. The crowd applauds the sportsmanship. However, Diamond finally backs Darkfire into the ropes and, after being told to break, unleashes a terrific chop to Darkfire's chest. He follows with a knee that drives Darkfire through the ropes. The crowd is stunned but doesn't turn on Diamond. After all, this is a guy who once billed himself as the Dirtiest Dog in the Yard. You have to expect that sort of thing.

Diamond takes over, getting a couple of near-falls on Darkfire. The younger man tries to make a comeback. He throws a couple of right hands that back Diamond up. Darkfire then throws himself into the ropes, but Cronus grabs Darkfire's foot and trips him. Diamond goes back on the attack before Darkfire can go after Cronus. The crowd boos, sensing the fix is in. (A good sign, given the entire sport is fixed, that they've achieved Willing Suspension of Disbelief.)

The match continues like this; Darkfire making the occasional comeback and Diamond cutting him off, usually with unsolicited help from Bobby Cronus. Diamond finally slaps on the Diamond Clasp. Cronus struts around ringside, ready to hand the championship belt over to Nick Diamond. The crowd is conflicted, both cheering and booing.

Suddenly, Jack Blades runs out of the heels' dressing room. Nick Diamond spots him and drops the Diamond Clasp. Blades gets up on the ring apron. Diamond confronts him. The referee tries to keep the two apart. Meanwhile, Cronus throws the title belt to Darkfire, gets up on the opposite apron and calls to the referee. The ref runs to Cronus and gets into an argument with him. (Remember the rules about wrestling referees.) Darkfire hefts the belt preparing to hit Diamond with it.

Lars jumps out of his seat and slides into the ring. Mike and Carol and I are on our feet. What the hell is Lars doing? Jack Blades hops off the ring apron. Darkfire swings the title belt at Diamond. Lars jumps in front of Diamond and takes the hit for him. Lars is laid out, flat on his back on the mat.

"They've killed Lars!" Carol shouts.

"Those bastards!" Mike says.

While Diamond is distracted by Lars's fall, Darkfire hits him with a clean shot from the title belt. Diamond winds up flat on his back, out cold. Darkfire tossed the belt away and goes for the cover. Blades hauls Lars's carcass out of the ring. Cronus hops down from the apron, freeing the referee to make the count (and to never suspect something untoward might have taken place in the meantime).

The crowd boos all through the referee's count. The hope that Diamond will miraculously kick out is dashed. The ref completes the three count. Darkfire rolls off Diamond and gets to his feet, thrusting his arms into the air. Cronus steps into the ring, holding the Midwest Title belt. He raises Darkfire's hand and puts the belt around the winner's waist. Darkfire turns to Cronus and embraces him. Blades rolls into the ring and throws an arm around Darkfire. The crowd boos the entire time. Cronus produces a microphone.

"Like I said, it's time for a little quality control with the Midwest Title," he says, ignoring the popcorn and beer cans being thrown into the ring, "What you're looking at here is the future. That—" He extends a hand toward Nick Diamond. "Is the past." He turns to Jack Blades. "Jack, do me a favor. Get that piece of crap out of my ring."

Blades picks Diamond up by his hair and tosses him through the ropes to the ring floor. He lands next to Lars. (Nice grouping.) Cronus turns to the crowd.

"Thank you all for coming," he says, "Have a great night."

Cronus, Darkfire, and Blades dash out of the ring. It takes a handful of Ace Security guys to get them through the crowd. Some wrestlers emerge from the faces' dressing room and attend to Nick Diamond and Lars. Diamond gets to his feet and stumbles to the back. Lars is carried out by a couple of the wrestlers.

Carol puts a hand to her mouth. "Do you think he's okay?"

"I'm sure he's fine," I say, "It's just commitment to a bit."

"Gentleman and lady," Mike says, "we have officially been swerved."

"Quite nicely at that," I say.

Carol holds her hands out. "Swerved?"

"We expected one outcome," I say, "We got another."

"Common piece of booking," Mike says, "Works best if it makes sense."

Carol shoots an inquisitive look toward the ring. "Did it make sense, though? Bobby Cronus turns on an old friend for no apparent reason?"

"We'll probably get the answer when they tape TV on Tuesday," Mike says.

"I don't want to wait that long," Carol says.

I point at her. "Now you know the essence of good booking."

Carol stamps her foot. She's getting into this wrestling thing. Whether she likes it or not.

★★★

"And Beans gets the damn mule as far as the door to the gym," I say, setting my glass of wine down on the table, "He's *this* close to getting it into prom. But Mr. Somrock is working the door. He says, 'You can't bring that ass in here.' Beans goes, "Hey, don't talk to my mule that way.' Mr. Somrock says, 'I was talking to the mule.'"

Rick and I explode in laughter. It's weird. We were both there for the whole *Beans Madden tries to bring a mule to the prom* incident and Carol is hearing it for the first time and yet we seem to be more amused by it than she does. Rick and I are holding our sides and Carol is just a step above polite laughter. Guess you had to be there.

We're at a corner booth in the restaurant area of The Tav. It's the classier end of the place. Nice tables and booths. Tablecloths and cloth napkins. Clean silverware. Mood lighting. Servers with white dress shirts and black slacks. Nary a big screen TV nor a pool table in sight. Perfect for a date or a semi-formal get together. (I feel guilty for constantly holding my fantasy football league draft here. It's like taking the guys from *Animal House* to Spago.) The restaurant is not busy, lending a sense of intimacy.

Carol toys with her glass of cabernet. "Whatever happened to Beans Madden?"

Rick looks toward the ceiling. "I honestly don't know."

"I think he sells medical supplies," I say.

"That make sense," Rick says.

Carol cradles her wine glass. "And what about the mule?"

"I'm not sure," I say, "Never found out about that."

Rick smiles, displaying a mouth full of straight white teeth and a couple dimples. "Knowing Beans, we should be thankful he didn't get it pregnant." That gets another round of laughs out of Rick and me (and polite laughter from Carol). Rick holds up his wine glass, offering a toast. "To the mule."

Carol and I raise our glasses and join Rick in the toast. This is nice. I wasn't sure what to expect. Rick and I haven't hung out in forever. I'm surprised at how easy it is. It's like no time has passed. Certainly, his looks haven't changed much. His brown hair is worn a tad shorter. The face is more gaunt, as if it's lost some baby fat. He's filled out a little in the torso, but still looks lean and still moves with an athlete's grace. The ratty flannel shirt and tattered jeans have been replaced by a black suit and a black shirt, open at the neck. He has a goatee, but it is immaculately trimmed. He looks like a man doing well.

Rick drains the rest of his wine. "Small world, isn't it? I meet this incredibly attractive woman at a fundraiser, and she winds up being friends with a buddy of mine from high school."

Carol blushes. She's resplendent in her wine-colored blouse and black skirt. Her hair flows past her shoulders and she wears a hint of makeup. The server comes by, and we order another round. Rick sets his arms on the table.

"So, you got that column," he says to me, "What else you got going?"

"Oh, the usual. Jaywalking. Throwing rocks at police cars. The occasional acid flashback."

"You thought of doing anything else?" Rick asks.

"Never once."

He holds up his hands. "I don't mean you should start writing textbooks or anything. It's just that people have heard of you. You've got a good start on a brand."

"I've heard that from other people," I say, "Ex-girlfriends, mostly."

"It might allow you do other things that are fun," Rick says, "You ever thought about doing a podcast?"

I open my mouth for the usual smartass response but hold off. The podcast idea intrigues me. I have absolutely no idea how one creates or distributes a podcast. I don't know if my bosses at *The Daily Bugle* would want a cut. (I'm going to assume so. Beneath that alternative-hippy bullshit beats the hearts of some ruthless capitalists.) I don't even know what the subject of my podcast could be. But I don't want to dismiss the idea.

"I'm thinking about it now," I say.

"I might have some contacts for you," Rick says, "And if you want to do some other writing, I might be able to help you there, too."

"What kind of writing?" I ask.

Rick sips his wine. "I've read your column. I know you're interested in politics. And my boss is looking for speechwriters."

Oy. This could be an uncomfortable conversation. "Your boss is Bill Longson, right?"

"He is," Rick says, hesitant, probably picking up on the tone in my voice.

"Unless I'm *really* mistaken, he's a Republican." I say.

"He's a populist," Rick says, "More of a libertarian."

"But he identifies as Republican," I say.

"Yes," Rick says, "he's a part of the Republican Party."

I knew that, of course. Bill Longson is a U.S. Senator, currently campaigning for a second term. He's not exactly the shy, retiring type. He started life as an entrepreneur, parlaying the family construction company into a string of real estate developments. He put his name on most of these developments. He then invented (or more accurately, put his name on the invention of) a space age mattress that brought him national attention. He used the celebrity (and the money) from that to gain entry into politics, despite having as much experience as your drunk, racist uncle. And his politics views aren't much different than your drunk, racist uncle. It's the sort of thing that plays well in the rural sections of Minnesota, as well as the lily-white suburbs. This re-election campaign might be the prelude to a presidential run. God help us.

Obviously, I'm not entirely thrilled with what Rick is floating. Or that he's even involved with a guy like Longson. I keep that last part to myself. Carol has decided to stay out of it. I take a quick sip of my wine.

"I'm not sure I'm your man," I say.

"You don't have to have the same views as the Senator," Rick says, "I get that. I don't either."

"I'm glad to hear that," I say.

"You just do your job, keep your head down, and collect your pay. There's nothing to it."

"There would be for me," I say, "I can't disassociate myself from the stuff I write. I appreciate the offer, but…"

"It's okay," Rick says, "Not everyone's gig. No worries."

Carol shifts in her seat, uncomfortable. I'm sure she's similarly dismayed about Rick's employer. Rick not being in sympathy with Longson probably makes it more palatable for her. (And maybe Rick has other charms that make it more palatable as well. But I'm not going to get into that.)

"If I can ask," I say, "What do *you* do for Longson?"

"A little of this and that," Rick says, "Truth be told, I'm a glorified—but very highly paid—errand boy. Keeps the job from getting boring, I'll give it that much."

Thankfully, our food and a new round of drinks arrives. When the server has stepped away, Rick raises his glass of wine in another toast.

"Here's to old friends," he says. Then he turns to Carol. "And new."

Carol and I join him in the toast. I spread the cloth napkin on my lap and start in on my Dijon Chicken Sandwich. Carol daintily picks at her sea bass. (When not on a date, she eats like a damn lumberjack.) Rick carefully slices his pesto chicken. He asks me a few polite questions about the case but doesn't have anything new to offer. That done, a thought occurs to him, and he starts to laugh.

"Did Joe ever tell you about the homecoming football game, senior year? What happened with our quarterback?"

"No, he didn't," Carol says, "He doesn't talk much about high school."

Rick's wineglass stops short of his lips. "Really?"

"Just never seems to come up," I say.

Carol tilts her head. "You never make much of an effort to bring it up."

I let that go without comment. So does Rick, which is a relief. I don't want him to take my hesitation to talk about high school as a personal attack, no more than I would want other friends from high school to take it that way. What better solution than to turn it around?

"I'm sure Rick's told you about *his* high school days," I say.

"Not really," Carol says, "Other than the two of you knowing each other."

My glass of wine stops short of my lips. "But you know his big claim to fame, right?"

I'm sure Carol imagines it's some story about stuffing a guy in a locker or TPing the assistant principal's house. Rick has a stricken look, telling her it's something else.

"I don't think I've heard this story," Carol says, now possibly wondering if she's been knocking boots with the Son of Sam.

I plow forth. "You're sitting next to the guy who scored the game-winning goal when Porter's Bay won the state hockey championship."

Carol is not a huge sports fan. Yes, she participates in my fantasy football league every year and spends Sundays in the fall watching football with me and Lars and Mike. But she doesn't follow the wide world of sports. Still, even *she* knows the importance of the Minnesota state hockey tournament. She turns to Rick as if she just met the dude.

"I didn't know this," she says.

Rick flicks his hand. "It was no big deal."

I laugh at that. "It sure as hell was at the time."

"At the time," Rick says, quietly.

Carol clears her throat. "It was, what, seventeen years ago. I'm sure it's still a big deal up in Porter's Bay—"

"It is," I say, "But not just there. Take a look on YouTube under *Greatest hockey goals ever* and it will be one of the first that comes up."

"*Ever?*" Carol asks.

Rick says nothing. He seems embarrassed and I'm not sure if it's because he hasn't told Carol this or if there's another reason. And yet, one of these days there's probably going to be a statue in front of Memorial Arena in Porter's Bay depicting Rick Michaels flying through the air, his body parallel to the ice as he somehow makes contact with the puck and slaps it into the net for the state championship goal. But that isn't a comfortable topic at this table.

I say, "Anyway, it's out there if you want to look it up."

Carol doesn't say anything. We eat the rest of the meal in uncomfortable silence. When we're done, Carol sets her napkin on the table and slides out of her chair.

"I have to run to the restroom," she says, "I'll be right back."

Rick and I stand as Carol gets up. (I follow his lead.) She crosses the restaurant and disappears down the hall to the restrooms. Rick stares at the picture window. I drum my fingers on my wineglass.

"Sorry about that," I say, "I just assumed she knew about the goal."

"It's no big deal," he says, "Everyone asks me about it sooner or later. The Senator has even talked to me about it. He's a big sports fan."

"I assume when he makes a campaign stop in Porter's Bay, you'll put in an appearance?"

Rick's eyes cut toward me. Then he shrugs. "Maybe. They don't let me in on that stuff."

I regret opening my mouth. For some reason, Rick's claim to fame is a sore spot for him. I'm not sure why (he and I didn't have many conversations after it happened) but I respect his feelings. And I shouldn't take shots at his boss, as much fun as it may be.

"You and Carol make a nice couple," I say.

That brightens his face. "Thanks, man. It's cool that you guys are friends." He sips his wine. "How long have you two known each other?"

"A little more than six years."

"How did you meet?"

"She was dating my best friend," I say.

"Was it serious?"

"He thought it was." I pick up one of the dinner mints (they're wafer thin). "Carol and I stayed friends after she and Mike broke up."

"Is she still friends with this Mike guy?"

"More or less," I say, "Mostly less."

Rick sits back in the seat, frowning. I get the feeling I've stepped in it. Again. See how brilliantly I've managed this little reunion? Rick rolls his wineglass between his palms.

"Did this Mike guy talk about…stuff with Carol?" he asks.

"I know he was really into her and—"

"No, like…intimate stuff," Rick says, "Locker room talk. That kind of thing."

I get it. It's that insecure *What do you know about my girlfriend?* thing that guys occasionally go through. I want to placate Rick and make up for taking shots at his boss and exposing some history he'd rather not have known. I ignore the *Danger, Will Robinson* signals going off in my head.

"Mike didn't talk much about that," I say, "I imagine if there was something to tell, he would have told me. He just mentioned the thing about having people watch and that's that."

Rick cocks his head. "Having people watch? What do you mean?"

"I don't mean people actually watched them," I say, "She just liked to imagine they were. Like if the curtains were open, she'd ask, 'Do you think anyone can see us? Do you think they're watching?' That sort of thing. It's something you do in the heat of the moment. Like the thing with the mirror."

"Mirror?"

"She liked to watch her and Mike…y'know, in the mirror. Just…when there was one available."

Jesus Christ on a cracker, what did I just say? It's like my mouth was moving and my brain didn't want to interrupt. I have absolutely no idea what possessed me to tell that stuff to Rick. (I still have no idea what possessed Mike to tell that stuff to *me*.) Carol comes back to the table, thus sparing me further embarrassment. (I wish I could same the same for Carol.)

"Having fun?" she asks, sliding back into her seat and lacing fingers with Rick.

"Sure," I say.

"Absolutely," Rick says, almost right on top of me.

Neither of us make eye contact with her. Rick, in fact, is looking toward the picture windows, as if uncomfortable that just anybody can walk by the restaurant and get a look inside. Carol's eyes narrow. Yep, we handled that brilliantly. Right out of the Don Knotts Seminar on How to Win Friends and Not Arouse Suspicion.

"Glad to hear it," Carol says.

Things get quiet. It's an interesting bouillabaisse of emotions: suspicion, confusion, regret, annoyance, what have you. We make a few stabs at conversation, but they die quickly. The check comes, and Rick offers to pay. (I do the Minnesota thing of pretending to protest before accepting the gift of free grub.) We grab our coats and make our way to the door, pausing when we get to the parking lot.

"Good seeing you again, Joe," Rick says, thrusting a hand toward me.

"You, too, Rick," I say, briefly shaking his hand, "We should do this again sometime."

Carol and Rick say nothing at first then (disingenuously) agree to the idea. They scurry to the car. Carol looks back, her blue eyes giving me a Sodium Pentothal Glare. There's a question in them. *What did you do?* I turn away.

Solve Lance Mack's murder? Sure. But who is going to solve mine?

***

The Tav is walking distance from my building, but the willingness to walk it depends on the time of year and the weather. This is one of those nights when the weather feels decent at first. You think, *Oh, I'll be fine walking.* It's a decision you reconsider right about the time it's too late to do anything about it. I huddle into my coat and powerwalk, trying not to shiver.

I go through the front door of my building and up the main stairs, flexing my fingers and reminding myself I'll be hanging out on the deck in another month. I open the door, flip on the lights, and start to unbutton my coat.

And get clobbered from behind.

CHAPTER EIGHT

Believability has become a sore point in wrestling. Some will argue—with a certain justification—that pro wrestling has never *been believable. Show me another sport in which someone is allowed to wear a mask to disguise their real identity. How often does someone get thrown into a metal post and* not *wind up unconscious for the better part of an evening? And doesn't every other sport stop the proceedings when a referee is knocked out? This line of thinking has led to the current trend of ironic deconstruction in wrestling. Why not be absurd and create comic parodies of wrestlers? Why not have someone wrestle a blow up doll or the invisible man? Nobody thinks this stuff is real anyway.*

The lack of believability, however, need not be taken to absurd lengths. Sometimes, there's just a simple gap in logic. Take that old standby, the Beatdown, *for example. The Beatdown occurs when one wrestler—usually a heel—attacks another out of the blue. This frequently occurs in the ring because that's where the fans can see it easily. It happens so often in wrestling that fans have gotten immune to it. But that's due to how it's handled.*

Modern day, you frequently see a heel carry the Beatdown to extremes; everything up to (and possibly including) ass rape is inflicted on the babyface. No referee attempts to break it up. The announcer doesn't call for help from the back. There's no security to separate the wrestlers. Hell, they don't even ring the bell to alert someone that something untoward is happening. In an age in which TV monitors are ubiquitous in a backstage area, wouldn't you think someone would notice assault and battery going on in front of ten thousand people?

That's where the old and new schools diverge. Old school recognizes that a certain amount of willing suspension of disbelief is required. But you can't waste that. A prolonged Beatdown does just that. And if you don't have that willing suspension of disbelief, what exactly are we doing here?

Sadly, I can tell you from experience that the *Why isn't somebody helping that poor guy?* sensation applies to real life as well. I'm experiencing it right now.

I catch a break in that whoever clobbers me doesn't get me in the back of the head. If that were the case, I'd be out cold or at least knocked silly. In fact, it's more of a shove. I hit the floor, knees-first. Pain knifes through my legs. I grope for something to help me get up, only to be kicked in the ribs. It isn't the hardest blow I've ever been hit with. Whoever is coming at me is taking it easy. If for not the breaking in and the attacking, I'd be grateful.

A voice is close to my ear. "Stay out of it."

It's muffled and gravelly. I look up and see the intruder is wearing a ski mask and shades. From this perspective, they could be anywhere between six and nine feet tall. I curl into a fetal position, hoping to avoid further damage to my body.

"Stay out of what?" I say.

The intruder delivers another boot to my ribs. This one doesn't have any more force than the last one. I must be tougher than I think. The intruder hovers over me. They have something in their hand. It's a golf club.

Oh shit.

"Stay out of it," the intruder says, wielding the club, "You understand me?"

My front door opens. The intruder swings the club at the door. Whoever is coming in scurries back. The intruder has momentarily forgotten about me. I grab a framed photo off the hall table and frisbee the damn thing at them. It catches them right between the eyes. I'm sure the ski mask absorbs some of the blow. They shout an oath and drop the golf club.

A voice comes from behind the door. "You okay, brother?"

I'm not sure if Lars is talking to me or the intruder. I get to my feet. The intruder looks between me and Lars, realizing they're outnumbered (for what that's worth). They turn and run down the hallway to the backdoor. They yank it open and disappear into the night.

I slump on the arm of the futon. The cats come out of the bedroom and make their way over to me. Lars pokes his head in the door.

"Brother, if you were going to have company, why didn't you tell me?"

***

"But what did the guy *look* like?" Carol asks.

I pull my Saturn Ion into a parking space at the curb. "I didn't get a look at him. Or her."

Carol muses on the other end of the line. "You think it might have been a *her?*"

I pick up the phone from the cupholder and take it off *speaker.* "They might have been disguising their voice. It had a weird, kind of gravelly sound to it."

"Like maybe a woman in disguise?"

"I have to leave open every possibility," I say, getting out of the car and walking toward the paybox, "It was dark, and they were wearing dark clothes. Not to mention they spent most of our interaction trying to beat the piss out of me."

Carol pauses. (I suspect she's eating licorice, a habit when under stress.) "I don't suppose you're going to call the police."

"I already did," I say, "They sent over a beat cop, and I made a full report. Pike called me this morning to follow up. I couldn't tell him much, so he didn't promise me much. I left out the part about the golf club because Pike would just think it was Cronus.”

“And you don’t think it was?”

“Doesn’t make any sense,” I say, “I’m trying to *help* Cronus. Why would he attack me? The golf club is supposed to create doubt. Or maybe remind me what happened to Lance Mack. I don’t know.” I finish paying for the parking space, “I have to go. I’m having lunch with Jack Blades.”

There’s a pause on the other end of the line. “You’re having lunch with that lunatic? What variety of human flesh is on the menu?”

“I’m sure he’s a decent guy,” I say.

“For a serial killer, yes.”

“I’ll be fine, mother.”

Carol doesn’t rise to that bait. She waits a moment then asks, “Did something happen with you and Rick last night?”

Glurk. I have to play dumb. There are only so many assaults I can handle in any calendar year. “Nope,” I say, “Just two old friends catching up.”

“Because Rick was acting weird when we got home. He kept checking the windows, making sure the blinds were closed tight. You didn’t talk too much about your case, did you?”

“No,” I say, silently relieved Carol is on the wrong track, “I don’t think something like that would bother Rick.”

Carol doesn't sound convinced. "It was really weird. And it all started after I left you two alone."

I laugh that off (glad that Carol can't see the flop sweats I'm breaking into). "You're just being paranoid. It was a great time. Let it go at that."

"Fine," Carol says, drawing the word out, "But if you think of something, let me know."

"Absolutely. Wouldn't dream of doing anything else."

"Great. Have a nice lunch. Enjoy eating Raoul."

I drop the phone into my pocket, trying not to collapse from relief. I'm not sure what will happen when I talk to Jack Blades, but it can't be any worse than Carol knowing the truth about my chat with Rick. I cross the street and walk toward Jack Blades' building.

I'm not sure this even counts as a compliment in today's world, but Jack Blades is what my friend Robbie would describe as a *grown ass man*. He played college and professional football and worked as a bouncer before discovering professional wrestling. He doesn't generally grant interviews, and I'm not sure if he's going to stay in gimmick during ours. But he's agreed to meet me, so that's a step in the right direction.

Toward that end, Blades has agreed to meet me at his air B-n-B: an apartment in downtown St. Paul. It's in a high rise building on the eastern edge, not far from Highway 94. I'm not an architectural expert, but the place seems to have been built sometime in the Seventies. The building, like a lot of downtown St. Paul, looks sleepy and depressing, especially in the rain. I step into the foyer and buzz Blades' apartment. He lets me in without acknowledging me on the intercom. The apartment is on the fourth floor. The building is neat and clean, if not inspiring. I easily find Blades' apartment. He answers after one brief knock.

"Pleasure to meet you," he says, giving me a firm handshake, "Jack Blades."

I'm well aware of who he is, but he gives me his full name by way of introduction, sort of like an old school calling card. It's the kind of thing my father would appreciate, so I can't help but be charmed by it.

"Joe Davis," I tell him.

"Come on in, Joe," Blades says, stepping away from the door, "Lunch is almost ready. You hungry?"

I'm a Minnesotan, born and bred, so a certain economy of expression is expected, particularly regarding food. I go with the old reliable, "I could eat."

"Good to hear," he says, "I'll take your coat. Just leave your shoes by the door."

Blades deposits my peacoat in a small coat closet. He walks down a short curving hallway that extends from the front door. He moves slowly, using the same bow-legged walk he uses on his way to the ring. He wears a plain white apron over faded jeans and a flannel shirt. A certain pleasing aroma hits me.

"Chili?" I ask.

"That's right," he says, "Cornbread's in the oven. Should only be another minute. I got milk in the fridge. You're going to want that."

Blades' ring persona creates an expectation that his apartment will look like a cross between a bunkhouse and a condemned building. Instead, the hallway opens on to a place that's clearly been renovated since the 1970's. A huge breakfast island separates the kitchen from the living room. Picture windows along two walls afford a view of the nearby buildings and the highway beyond. A small patio wraps around the windows. It's too cold and wet to hang out there now, but the place must be fantastic in the summertime. The housekeeping is immaculate. The hardwood floors have been swept. There's no trace of discarded clothing or beer cans. The kitchen sink is clear of any dirty dishes, and the counters are spotless. Save for the giant stainless-steel stockpot sitting on the stove and the bowls, spoons and napkins resting on the island, you'd think the place was completely unoccupied. Blades uses a large wooden spoon to deftly remove the lid of the stockpot.

"That's looking good," he says, "I'll just keep the lid off."

"Let it thicken," I say.

Blades looks back, amused. "You make chili?"

"It's one of my favorite things to make."

He gives that a grandfatherly chuckle. "Chili in Minnesota. That must be interesting."

I let it pass without comment. Yes, I could argue we make damn good chili in Minnesota because we're damn cold most of the time. But Blades is a Texan. They take pride in their chili. I won't tell him how to make chili, and he won't tell me how to make chicken wild rice soup. To each their own.

Blades slips on a couple of oven mitts and fetches the cornbread. I take a seat at the breakfast bar. I move carefully, the neatness around me planting the irrational thought that I might break something. (I wonder if I people feel like this at *my* apartment? Then again, I don't care.)

"This is a really nice place," I say.

"I try to find decent places if I'm going to be around a few weeks," Blades says, "I've stayed in enough cheap hotels. I've earned a little comfort."

I run my fingertips along the countertop. "You keep the place clean, too."

"Something my dad taught me," he says, "Leave a place cleaner than you found it. Some of the hotels I stayed in, that wasn't too hard to do."

Against all odds, Jack Blades is a man after my own heart. He pours two glasses of milk, then dishes up two bowls of chili and cuts off two hunks of cornbread. When he's done, he takes off the apron, folds it neatly and sets it in a drawer. He sits on the other side of the island, wincing from old injuries as he lowers himself on to the stool.

"It's real cornbread," he says, "Got the recipe from a guy in east Tennessee. It's not the box mix you get at the store. That stuff is corn *cake*."

"I look forward to it," I say, picking up a spoon, "No beans in the chili?"

"I'll pretend you didn't say that," Blades says, "Keep the milk handy."

"I make a pretty spicy chili myself."

"Keep the milk handy."

I indulge Blades and take a bite. It's good chili. Flavorful. And just a little…holy fuck! Fire ants are setting off bottle rockets in and around my tongue. I try to look unhurried as I grab the milk and take a healthy drink.

"Good stuff," I say, unable to keep the rasp out of my voice.

"This is how my momma used to make it." He takes a little sip of the milk, but otherwise shows no effects from the chili. "You're writing an article on the wrestling company, eh?"

"I am," I say, keeping the spoon alongside my bowl, "It's Gordon Russell's idea. But I'm a huge fan. Have been since I was seven."

"How old are you now?"

"Thirty-five."

Blades does the math in his head. "When you were seven, I was…"

"The PWA Champion," I say, "I remember reading about it in the wrestling magazines. Then you came up here and defended it at Minnesota All-Star Wrestling."

"Did you come to the match?"

"I couldn't. We lived four hours from the Twin Cities and my dad owned—owns—a hardware store. He had to work."

"Working man," Blades says, "Sounds like my dad."

While I record the conversation on my phone, we talk about Blades' early career: breaking in with a small promotion in Texas, rising up through various territories until he was a main eventer, a run with the PWA World Title, multiple retirements and comebacks, his current status as an aging legend. Blades is polite and self-deprecating. You'd think he spent a few years in the business and hadn't accomplished much rather than being a legend who has worked all over the globe.

"Sounds like a lot of time on the road," I say.

"It was," Blades says, pouring me another glass of milk, "That's why I liked Japan. You could make a damn good living doing a couple tours every year. Twelve weeks of work and that was all the money you needed."

"But you didn't work exclusively in Japan."

"It wasn't just about money. Too much time away from the ring and I'd start to go crazy. My wife would finally say, 'Virgil, would you find someplace to go for a few weeks?'"

"She called you Virgil."

"Only the boys and the fans call me Jack. My wife married Virgil Robley, so that's what she calls me."

"What does she think of Jack Blades?" I ask.

"She thought that's how I made a living. She understood the difference. She told me when she would give me a ride to the airport, I'd say goodbye to her and my daughter and when I'd walk toward the gate, she could tell by the way I was walking—just from looking at my back—that Virgil was going away and Jack Blades was taking his place."

"Was that a good thing or a bad thing?"

"Depends on who you ask, I guess." He looks down. "That's a thing a lot of guys can't let go of. They know the gimmick, but they don't know themselves. I love Nick. He's one of my best friends in this business. But he can't let go of being the Diamond Stud. He doesn't know who Nick Wisniski is. And he doesn't want to know."

An unpleasant thought, but one I observed on my own. We go back to the chili. Just when I think I'm getting used to the spice, another five-alarm fire rages in my mouth. Blades is clearly amused but says nothing. I pick through the ingredients. There's steak, ground pork, onions, peppers, and probably some unnamed spices (Napalm prominently among them, if I had my guess). I set the spoon aside.

"Why did you come to Minnesota this time around?" I ask.

"Bobby Cronus," Blades says, "He's a good guy. He can call me up anytime, and I'll do him a favor if you can."

"Are you, uh…" I look for the words. "I don't want to offend…"

"Just ask it, son."

"Are you thinking about retiring?" I ask, "Permanently? Because you can't do this forever, right?"

"I've tried to move on. I tried being a movie stuntman, putting money into restaurants. Even tried being a bounty hunter for a minute-and-a-half. Some of it was interesting, but none of it was wrestling." Blades sips his milk. "I tried getting into promoting. Did a couple of cards in Dallas. It didn't work out."

"What happened?" I ask.

"I trusted Lance Mack."

Isn't that an interesting wrinkle? I try to keep things casual. I'm tempted to take another bite of chili but there's no way *that* will keep things casual.

"What happened with Lance Mack?" I ask.

Blades pushes his chili aside. "I put him on the first card I promoted in Dallas. Lance broke in down there, so he's got a decent following. I put him up against Chris Reed. You heard of him?"

"English wrestler," I say, "A legend down in Dallas."

"That's right," Blades says, a little impressed, "I figured the best thing was to match Lance up with a veteran who could show him the ropes. Except the bastard no-showed."

"Why?"

"Lance said he was injured. If I had to guess, he got a better offer. He left town and sent me some pictures of his ankle. It looked fucked up all right. Then I heard he was working in Virginia the next night. I don't know whose ankle was in the pictures, but if Mack was back wrestling the next day, it wasn't his."

I cringe. "You took a bath on the show?"

"Not that first one, no," he says, "I found someone to fill in for Mack. But when fans think you've pulled a bait-and-switch, they aren't going to come back. We took a bath on the *second* show. After that, I got out of promoting. I'd just be throwing good money after bad."

"Did you talk to Mack about this?" I ask.

"Didn't seem to be a point," Blades says, sliding his chili back in front of him, "He'd just stick to his story. And what good would it do? It wouldn't bring back my promotion."

I stir my chili, still trying to keep things casual. "You were in the arena the night Lance was killed. Am I right?"

Blades gives me a steady look. "I was."

"What do you remember about it?"

"We had a party. There were a few of us left at the end. I made some chit-chat, walked around a little. Then I left and came back here. That was that."

I take a bite of the cornbread (which is delicious, by the way). "Ashley Diamond said you were talking to her. That you left the arena and came back."

Blades looks out the window. "Talked to her about her dad. She thinks he's getting too controlling." He picks at the chili. "It's a hell of thing, having potential like Ashley's. She spends a lot of time trying not to screw up. And she's getting into a business where it's pretty damn easy to do just that. Ashley pretty much grew up without her dad around. Happens to a lot of second-generation kids in this business. They hate it because it's what took their dad away. But they get into it because it's a way to get closer to their dad. You get that?"

"Yeah, I do."

"You going to take over your dad's hardware store?"

"No, my younger brother is," I say, "He's probably the best one for the job. Don't tell him I said that."

"But your dad is happy about that?" Blades asks.

"I think so."

His face grows serious. "That's what Shane, Ashley's brother, wanted. The kid had some talent. The UWE was willing to sign him, but he couldn't pass a drug test. And then…I'm sure you read about what happened."

I did. Shane Diamond's overdose made its way through the headlines. Given the number of arrests and other scrapes that preceded it, it wasn't surprising. But I wish it had been. Blades drops his spoon into the bowl and leaves it there.

"I don't think Ashley had any intention of getting into this business until her brother died," he says, "But she did it smart. She got herself clean, and she's kept herself clean. That's a lot of pressure on someone. And if she's feeling pressure now, think what it's going to be like when she gets to the big time." He flips a hand. "Anyway, I think she just needed someone to talk to."

"She chose you," I say, "I didn't realize you two knew each other so well."

"We do, and we don't. I've known her since she was a little girl. Watched her grow up. I guess if she can't talk to her dad, one of her dad's friends is the next best thing."

"And that's all you talked about? Her dad?"

"That was it."

"You didn't talk to Mack that night at all?" I ask.

"No, sir," Blades says, "Nothing to say to him. I saw him talking to Ashley, but I don't know what it was about."

Huh. I don't remember Ashley saying anything about talking to Lance Mack that night. Under normal circumstances, I wouldn't think anything of it. But these are hardly normal circumstances. I'll have to take that up with Ashley Diamond another time.

"What time did you leave?" I ask.

"About midnight," Blades says.

"And when did you come back?"

"Maybe five minutes later. Ashley said she wanted to talk to me, and I had forgot about it. I came back."

"You didn't see anyone on your way out?" I ask.

"I don't think so." Blades' eyes narrow slightly. "Why do you want to know all that?"

I want to know so I can determine if anyone can confirm his alibi. But judging by the look I'm getting, it might be time to back off.

"No big deal," I say, "Just trying to get the full picture of the situation. Might help with the article. Probably won't."

Blades accepts that explanation. I steer clear of further questioning. Instead, we spend the time chit-chatting about *WrestleShock* and Blades' possible involvement in it. (He refuses to give me spoilers.) I'd love to ask him about some of the nuts and bolts of working, but he's old school. Not inclined to give away the magician's secrets. While we chat, Blades puts the chili pot in the refrigerator, rinses out the bowls and places them in the dishwasher. I thank Blades for his time, and he walks me to the door.

"I could send some of the chili with you," he says.

"No, that's okay," I say, "I wouldn't want to deprive you."

Blades gives that a little chuckle. He knows better. He moves with an arthritic limp and admits the rain aggravates it. He hands me my coat. I thank him for his time and pause with my hand on the doorknob.

"Just do me a favor," I say, "If things get physical, keep an eye out for my friend Lars. He breaks easily."

"I'll do my best," Blades says, "But it ain't ballet."

A corner of his mouth flicks up. I feel like I've passed whatever test he was giving me. I'm not sure if said test was a rib or if Blades genuinely wants to trust me. Either way, I passed. That's the important part.

That and finding some Rolaids as fast as humanly possible.

***

"Unbelievable," Carol says, "You've talked to everyone involved in this company and you *still* don't have any idea what's going to happen tonight?"

I look away, disguising my amusement. Carol has fallen victim to the *But I want to know what happens next* syndrome that makes pro wrestling (and the spoilers contained therein) so popular on the internet. We've got front row seats for this week's TV taping. The arena is again set up for TV, with only three sides used for seating, Gordon Russell doing his duty at the announcer's table, and the production truck in the parking lot. We're halfway through the taping and we still haven't gotten the full fallout from last Friday's events. Ashley Diamond has cut a promo vowing revenge on Vanessa for the hair-cutting, but nothing has been heard from the participants in the main event.

"They're tight-lipped," I say, "On that subject and most everything else."

Carol winces. "No progress on the…" She pauses because she hates using this word. "Investigation?"

"Not really," I say, "Everyone was in the arena that night, but nobody saw anything. At least nothing worth talking about. Everybody has an alibi. Nearly everybody was seen leaving the arena. Since they all have keys, it's possible the murderer left and came back. And none of them liked Lance

Mack. That's what I've got." I run a hand through my hair. "It would be easier getting answers out of mob guys."

Mike, who spent the last segment glued to Ashley Diamond's vow of revenge, finally pops out of his sex-induced fugue state. "Professional wrestlers *are* like mob guys. They don't trust anyone outside the business."

He's got a point. This little code of Omertà certainly works in the favor of the guilty party. It's not doing much for Bobby Cronus, though. Carol turns to me.

"What are you going to do next?" she asks.

"Not sure," I say, "The only lead I've got is Ashley talking to Lance Mack the night of the murder. I don't remember her mentioning that before. Might be worth another chat with her."

Mike, as can be expected, pricks (which is the absolute appropriate word) up his ears at the sound of that. "Hey, don't go bothering Ashley. She doesn't like that sort of thing."

I mime picking up a phone. "Hi, Brigid? You don't know me, but I'm a friend of—"

"All right, fuck you," Mike says.

Fortunately for Mike, the conversation stops there. A celebration is being set up. A huge sheet cake sits on a small table in the middle of the ring. Lars waits for the cue and when he gets it, he seems less than enthusiastic.

"Ladies and gentlemen, please welcome Midwest Championship Wrestling general manager, Bobby Cronus," he says.

Cronus emerges from the heels' dressing room, wearing a red suit with a navy blue shirt and a yellow tie. As if the outfit couldn't get more garish, he's also sporting a pointy party hat. Jack Blades walks behind him, threatening the fans. He also wears a party hat, which contrasts his usual wild-eyed look. (Hard to believe this is the guy I had lunch with.) They climb into the ring and Cronus snatches the mic away from Lars.

"Go stand in the corner, nerdlinger," Cronus says.

Of course, the fans react badly to this. Not throwing-crap-in-the-ring badly but a definite round of boos. Cronus drinks them in.

"That's right, humanoids," Cronus says, "Get it out of your system."

That only increases the booing. Blades counters it with a blast from his noisemaker. It's ineffective, but you can't fault the effort. Cronus waits for the din to die down slightly.

"Ladies and gentlemen, let me be the first to introduce your new Midwest Heavyweight Champion," Cronus says, "Now hailing from Louisville, Kentucky." A huge number of catcalls for that. "He is the brightest star in the future of our sport. Here is Jackson…Darkfire!"

Darkfire, sporting aviator shades, a black suit, a silk scarf and slicked back hair, emerges from heels' dressing room. He strokes the title belt, lest anyone forget who the champion is. He ignores the crowd as he walks to the ring, though this is probably for the best. He's not getting a lot of love. When Darkfire gets into the ring, he and Cronus share a hug, which draws a further round of boos. Cronus punctuates this with a kiss on Darkfire's cheek (an old trick designed to draw the homophobic ire of the crowd, though it probably works better in the South than in Minnesota). Cronus looks at the audience, as if to say *Hey, what's wrong with that?* Give the man credit. He's playing his greatest hits.

"Like I said on Friday night," Cronus says, "We need to think about the future of Midwest Championship Wrestling. Now that Lance Mack is gone. Ah gee. What a shame." The crowd boos lustily. "When you think about the future, the last person you think of is Nick Diamond. Nick, if you thought I was going to raise a finger to help you win this title, I'll tell you this: if brains were gasoline, you wouldn't have enough to power a flea's motorcycle around a raindrop." This inspires some chants of *Fuck you, Cronus!* (Those will have to edited for TV.) Cronus turns to Jackson Darkfire. "Mr. Darkfire, I always thought you had something special in you. You just had to stop caring what these idiots out here think of you. You needed a little guidance. I'm here to give you that." He throws an arm around Jack Blades, who is frozen in position. "Welcome to the family," Cronus says.

He hands the mic to Jackson Darkfire, who slowly removes the aviator shades and gives the paying customers some thinly disguised contempt. "Thank you, Mr. Cronus. It is my pleasure to be here." He sweeps an arm toward the crowd. "And of course, it's *your* pleasure to have me here." The crowd greets this with a *You suck!* chant. "You're right, Mr. Cronus. I knew I had potential. But something always seemed to be holding me back. I couldn't figure out what it was. I couldn't quite get over the top. Couldn't quite beat a guy like Lance Mack. May he rest in peace. Or whatever." More boos. Darkfire ignores them. "Turns out, I just had to listen to Mr. Cronus. *The* greatest manager in wrestling history. Now, finally, I can live up to my full potential." The crowd takes up a chant of *You sold out!* "You're right. I *am* selling out. Every arena, every night, for the rest of my career."

Darkfire hands the mic back to Cronus and slides his shades back on. The crowd, having run out of chants, just boos the living hell out of them. Cronus pretends to conduct them like an orchestra. He brings the microphone to his lips.

"Okay, enough of these morons," Cronus says, "This is a party. We've got this beautiful cake. Let's help ourselves. Sorry for the rest of you. There won't be enough to go around."

Cronus blows into the noisemaker. Darkfire plays to the crowd. Blades yells at some heckling fans. Cronus picks up the cake cutter. The crowd starts buzzing. Nick Diamond dashes down the aisle and into the ring. He sneaks up behind Cronus, grabs his hair and slams Cronus's face into the cake. The crowd explodes. Blades runs at Diamond. But Diamond grabs a handful of the cake and slams it into Blades' eyes, blinding him. Cronus flails about, his face covered in icing. Blades punches at the air. Darkfire turns back and sees Nick Diamond closing in on him. Darkfire scurries out of the ring and runs for the hills. Diamond lets him go. He walks around ringside, slapping hands with the fans, then returns to the dressing room. Cronus flops about for several more seconds, then Blades helps him out of the ring. They stagger toward the back.

"The old sheet cake attack," Mike says, "Classic."

Carol shoots him a look. "He's done this before?"

"At least four times that I know of," Mike says, "And we were here to see this one. It's like watching Zeppelin do *Stairway to Heaven.*"

Lars climbs out of the ring and comes over to us. The crew is busy cleaning the ring. We're at a commercial break (or at least where the commercial break will go). Lars puts his hands on the fan barrier.

"Greetings and salutations and stuff and things," he says, "Having a good night so far?"

"Better than Bobby Cronus," I say.

Lars grimaces slightly. "I need something to cheer me up. The situation with Peter and Les Bos is not going well."

Mike and Carol sit, leaving me to handle this. "What's happening now?"

"Chuck had the idea to hire some muscle," Lars says, "We figured if Peter wasn't willing to listen to reason or legal arguments, maybe he could be coerced through…other means."

Given that Chuck was involved, we should just be glad it doesn't involve a famine or a plague of locusts. Then again, I may have spoken too soon.

"Did you try to follow through on that idea?" I ask.

"Try? Yes," Lars says, "Succeed? No."

Thank heaven for small favors. "Who did you ask?"

"Guipetto Intantolla."

No wonder it didn't succeed. For those not in the know, Guipetto Intantolla is a local thug noted for two things: a taste in French cuisine and the nickname The Guppie. It's suggested you don't mention the latter to his face if you wish to come out of the conversation with the same number of orifices you had when you entered it. As thug work goes, he would be a good guy to call. There's just one problem.

"Wasn't he one of the investors in your original club?" I ask.

"That was the problem," Lars says, "He wouldn't help us out. Threatened to throw me out if I didn't leave on my own."

"Tough break," I say.

"You're telling me?" Lars says, "We were in *my* apartment at the time!"

We are each in various stages of cringe. No one comments, beyond Carol offering a feeble, "Sorry to hear that."

"I just don't get it," Lars says, dropping his hands into his pockets, "The Guppie and I have known each other for a long time. I've always considered him a friend. He certainly wouldn't object on moral grounds. I don't understand why he won't help."

"Maybe because he lost money on the club," I say.

"What's a few dollars among friends?" Lars says, "Chuck thinks we need to skip the middleman and talk directly to Peter."

"Haven't you tried that already?" I ask.

"There's talking and there's…talking."

He tries to emphasize his point by cracking his knuckles. He fails and lets out a sissy cry when he bends one of his fingers too far back. I try not to roll my eyes.

"If you had a lawyer, I'm sure he'd advise against that," I say, "If you had a lawyer."

"I hate to break this to you, brother," Lars says, "but Perry Mason ain't walking through that door. I'm going to have to handle this myself. Can you help me out?"

"With what?"

"Be there to back me up," Lars says, clapping me on the shoulder, "That's all I need."

"That's it?" I say, "Just stand there and be a witness?"

"Maybe get me out of trouble, if need be," he says, "But I don't think that will happen."

On the contrary, I'm absolutely certain it will happen. I've known Lars too long. (His penchant for stupid plans is something that can be divined after knowing Lars for only ten minutes, so seniority doesn't have a lot to do with it.) He moves on down the line, looking for further victims, uh, fans. Carol turns to me.

"How do you think that's going to go?" she asks.

"Like backing up Custer at Little Big Horn," I say, "Hopefully, with fewer casualties."

"Hopefully," Mike says.

"But nothing is guaranteed," Carol adds.

Lars climbs into the now-cleared ring to prepare for our return from "commercial break." I glance toward the back and see Bruno Harvey, the owner of rival Minneapolis

Wrestling Federation skulking about. He better hope Bobby Cronus doesn't see him. In the ring, the fans join in Lars's jovial mood.

"Wasn't that great?" he asks. The crowd roars its approval. "You never know what you're going to get on *Midwest Championship Wrestling*."

Lars consults his notecards to announce the next match. Before he can do that, though, Bobby Cronus storms out of the heels' dressing room followed closely by Jack Blades. He's wiped his face, but some of the cake icing still clings to it. He stalks into the ring and rips the microphone out of Lars's hand.

"Go lay by your dish," Cronus tells him, "I got something to say."

The crowd boos this slightly. But they're still so filled with mirth at Cronus's appearance, they largely let it go. Lars dutifully steps over to the corner, though he still seems amused. Cronus ignores him and turns to the crowd.

"Nick Diamond! You think that was funny?" Cronus shouts, "You come out here looking like Methuselah in his retirement years and think you're going to humiliate me? Nick Diamond, you are going to pay! I am going to get my hands on you personally. You get yourself a partner, you reject from the Over-the-Hill Gang! And on April 30, at *WrestleShock*, me and

Jack Blades will end your miserable career! You hear me? You're going to pay! You're going to…"

At this point, Cronus has worked himself into a state where he's damn near tears and can't even form words. It resembles a fiftysomething toddler throwing a tantrum. One of Cronus's old standbys. He lowers the mic and turns to Blades, who puts a hand on his manager's back. Cronus hugs Blades, literally crying on his shoulder. Blades looks like he's barely tolerating this but doesn't stop Cronus. The audience jeers them. Lars stands in the corner, doubled over laughing. Cronus breaks from Blades and looks over at Lars.

"What the hell are you laughing at?" Cronus says, "You think this is funny?"

Lars thinks about it. Then he takes the mic and says, "Yeah, I really do."

The crowd roars. Cronus gets up in Lars's grill. Lars lowers his head and takes the abuse. Cronus punctuates the yelling by slapping Lars in the face. Lars snaps him a look. Cronus, though, is oblivious. He continues the berating, his nose only about an inch away from Lars's. Finally, Lars has had all he can stands, and he can't stands no more. He puts two hands on Cronus's chest and shoves the portly manager to the mat. The crowd explodes. Mike, Carol, and I are on your feet.

Carol is the first to find her voice. "Lars, what the hell are you doing?"

The cheering is cut short when Jack Blades hits Lars with a forearm shiver. Lars goes down as if shot. Blades and Cronus put the boots to him. The crowd rains boos and beer cups down on them.

"Cronus, you suck!" Mike screams. It's a sentiment shared by most of the crowd.

Suddenly, Nick Diamond runs down the aisle, swinging a baseball bat. Blades and Cronus flee the scene. Diamond stands in the ring, yelling for them to come back and face him. Nothing doing. Cronus and Blades disappear into the dressing room. Diamond turns back to check on Lars.

Carol leans over the railing. "You think he's okay?"

"He's fine," Mike says, "If there was anything seriously wrong, Diamond would be giving a signal."

"What kind of signal?" Carol asks.

Mike crosses his arms, forming an X. "The international signal for a legit injury. Diamond's not doing that, so this is all kayfabe."

Carol doesn't look convinced. After a few seconds, Diamond picks Lars up in a fireman's carry and takes him from the ring. The crowd applauds them both as they make their way back to the dressing room. Judging by the general lack of activity from Gordon Russell at the announce table, we're at another "commercial break."

Gordon Russell powerwalks past me, heading toward the back. I follow him. Maybe this will be something interesting. Bruno Harvey is there, standing in the entryway to the arena. Russell takes him by the arm and escorts him deeper into the lobby. I get to the lobby in time to hear the end of things.

Harvey is doing the talking. "…the money for Mr. Olani."

"I don't care," Russell says, "Believe me, it can't be worse than what will happen if Bobby sees you here."

Harvey allows himself to be shoved out the front door. Although, Russell stands half a head taller, so I don't know how much permission he needed from Harvey for said ejection. That done, Russell spins around and walks back toward the arena. I start back as well, hoping Russell didn't notice me. When I get back to my seat, he blows right past me and returns to the announce table. I guess my secret is safe. Mike, Carol, and I sit down.

"Anything interesting there?" Mike asks.

"No," I say, "Just throwing Bruno Harvey out. Like you do."

Mike turns his attention back to the ring. He strokes his goatee as he does some high-level thinking (an activity he normally performs strictly on the crapper).

"Nick Diamond is supposed to get a partner for *WrestleShock*," Mike says, "Blades and Cronus against Nick Diamond and…oh shit."

I sit back in my chair. "Lars?"

"That looks like where they're going," Mike says.

"Crap," I say, "You think he'll let us know for sure?"

"Probably not," Mike says.

"Kayfabe," Carol says.

Yep. She's learning.

***

An hour later, we find ourselves in a select group still in the arena. The place is quiet and echoey. There are some vestiges of the crowd's energy detectable in the air. Gordon Russell is breaking down the announcer's table. Bobby Cronus has come in from the TV truck. His jacket is gone and his tie hangs loosely around his neck. He drops heavily on a chair in the front row and wipes some icing from behind his ear.

"It's a good angle," he says, "But I'm getting too old for this shit."

Gordon Russell walks over from the announce table, putting his phone in his pocket as he goes. "It came off great. But…are you sure about involving Lars in this?"

"It will be fine," Cronus says.

"You realize Lars has pretty much no athletic ability to speak of?" I say.

"Not going to matter," Cronus says, "I've done this plenty of times. You get three guys who can work. We carry the guy who can't. I've done this with high school principals, football coaches, police chiefs, fire chiefs and Baptist ministers. Sure, some of the matches were the drizzling shits, but we made it work. As long as the guy is over, we're fine."

Russell looks toward the ring. "There isn't another main event we can do?"

Cronus shakes his head. "Jack and Nick would be great, but the fans have seen it a hundred times already. Darkfire and Nick is a no-go. Nick isn't going to be around after *WrestleShock,* so he can't go over. The original plan was for Lance to go over Nick and then turn babyface. We can't do that with Darkfire. We just turned him heel. And we still need a happy ending. You saw the crowds. That ring announcer of yours is the most over guy we've got."

Russell doesn't seem convinced, but he's long since learned the futility of arguing with Cronus. His phone buzzes. He looks toward Cronus, who doesn't seem to notice. Russell powerwalks back to the announce table. Cronus looks toward us.

"You're going to keep all this quiet, right?" he says, "No telling your friends. No writing about it in your column. Right?"

Mike, Carol, and I all agree to stay quiet. Cronus heads for the heels' dressing room. Russell is still on the phone; his back is to us. I wonder who exactly he's talking to. (Okay, it's none of my business. When has that ever stopped me?) I slink closer.

"That sounds good," Russell says, his voice low, "Tomorrow night would work great. Seven o'clock. Here at the arena. And please don't let Bobby know about it. He'll have to deal with it sooner or later." There's a pause while he listens to the other party. "I think we can make the money work. Bobby won't be a problem."

There are a few more pleasantries, then Russell hangs up the phone. He puts it into his pocket, then turns and sees me. His face whitens.

"Some…something I can help you with?" he asks.

I scratch the back of my head. "I saw Bruno Harvey here earlier. Looks like you had to give him the bum's rush."

"Bruno's fine," Russell says, "I just know Bobby doesn't appreciate him being around here. Thought it best to avoid a scene."

"Why was Bruno here?"

"He likes talking to the wrestlers. He keeps trying to bring guys over to his promotion."

I've heard that said. I guess that works as an explanation. "Do you know if Lars is okay?"

"He's just fine," Russell says.

"How do you know?"

"Because he's right over there."

I spin around and, sure enough, Lars is strolling out of the faces' dressing room. He moves with a certain sashay and shows no ill effects from his attack.

"How did it look?" he asks.

Mike slips on his leather jacket. "Like you got your ass kicked."

Lars taps the ring apron. "Exactly how we wanted it to look."

"You sure you're up for this kind of thing?" I ask.

"I'm in it now," Lars says, hunching his shoulders, "I'm enjoying it. Brings out a new side of me. Something I didn't even know was there. I can handle this thing with Peter now." He turns to me. "Does Saturday night work for you?"

I run it through my head, hoping against hope I've got something going on. Sadly, I do not. (Stupid dating slump.) "That's fine," I say, with the same enthusiasm I show regarding a trip to the dentist.

"Excellent," Lars says, turning to Mike. "How about you, brother? You want to join us? The more, the merrier."

"No can do," Mike says, "I've got a date that night."

"With who?" Lars asks.

Mike opens his mouth to answer then shuts it. "That's a good question. I should probably get that straightened out."

This probably won't end well. (I'm talking about Lars's situation, but it could just as easily apply to Mike's.) We decide to take off. I lead the way back to the lobby. We've just gotten there when I see movement in the office. Maybe Bobby Cronus is back from the heels' dressing room. I walk over to the office.

Nick Diamond is going through the filing cabinet on the far side of the room. He doesn't realize I'm there. I'm so surprised to see him, I don't say anything. Diamond slams one of the drawers shut. He pulls out the middle drawer. *Then* he notices me. There's a second where he looks at me as if Bigfoot just strolled in. He flips the middle drawer shut.

"Hey," he says, because what else would he say?

"Hi," I say, because what else would I say?

A moment goes by, then Diamond asks, "You looking for Bobby? I think he's in the locker room."

"No, no," I say, "I was just…on my out."

Another moment. My friends line up behind me, but I don't think Diamond can see them. He taps the desk with his knuckles.

"I'm looking for a schedule," he says, "I thought Bobby mentioned something about some spot shows this week. I want to make sure I don't miss anything, you know?"

"Um, yeah. Totally."

We stand there. I think Diamond is hoping we'll walk away and let him continue ransacking the office. I'm not leaving until he vacates the place. Our weenie Mexican standoff continues until Diamond gives up the ghost and steps out of the office.

"Maybe I'll just ask Bobby about it," he says.

Diamond crosses the lobby and disappears through the curtain leading to the heels' dressing room. Carol seems suspicious. Mike seems nervous (as you will be in the presence of your clandestine girlfriend's father). Lars seems hungry (a perpetual thing with him).

"We should get something to eat," Lars says, "Getting my ass kicked gives me an appetite."

I know how he feels. Or if I don't know it now, I'll probably find out in the near future.

CHAPTER NINE

A thing music and professional wrestling have in common is that the idea of home *becomes a nebulous thing. The typical view of home, of course, invokes Norman Rockwell-like images of hearth and family and all that crap. But for the people in the businesses I mentioned, home is a stopover on the way to other gigs. A permanent address so you can at least stay on the grid. But maybe, just maybe, the actual concept of home is found in an entirely different place.*

Travel has always been a part of the pro wrestling business. Back in the days of the territories, travel could easy or hard, depending on the territory. Some territories were referred to as "short-drive territories." This meant the territory ran most of its shows within a small geographical area. It allowed the wrestlers to spend most of the day at home and be back in their own beds that night. Larger territories didn't offer that luxury. Some required drives of several hours just to get to one town, which almost certainly meant you were going to spend the night there. Larger territories paid better, though. It was just a matter of surviving the territory and not starting to hate the wrestling business while you collected your money.

Once the territories went away and the big companies were running shows all over the country, there was no longer any such thing as a "short drive territory." The wrestlers generally flew from town to town and got home even less than they did before. (One weekend a month, if you were lucky. It was like the reverse National Guard.) Hotels, rental cars, and airplanes became home turf for the wrestlers.

There's a moment in the movie Almost Famous *when William, the kid reporter, says, as he's sitting on the tour bus, "I've got to go home." Penny Lane, the groupie, says, "You are home." It's a romantic moment. Problem is, it usually only happens in the movies.*

For me, the concept of home *does* apply to the place I live. My little apartment might not be much, but it's cozy and it's where I like to hang out.

While I've gotten a lot of grief from my brothers over the years regarding my multiple domestic skills, I'm grateful to have them. There's something calming about doing work around the house. And I don't find anything as relaxing as cooking.

"What's that going to be?" Mike asks, sitting at the breakfast bar, sipping his grape soda.

I finish slicing up the carrots, then I add them and some sliced potatoes to the beef and onions simmering in water. "Beef stew. One of my mom's recipes."

"You going to eat all that yourself?"

"Of course not. It's going to make a huge pot. And I've got biscuits in the oven."

"Homemade biscuits?"

"Is there any other kind?"

Mike looks away. This is one of those uncomfortable moments where he can't quite admit what he's thinking: if I was a woman, he'd marry me. I cover the awkwardness by grabbing a bottle of Grand Maibock out of the fridge and joining him at the breakfast bar.

"You figured out who you're seeing on Saturday night?" I ask.

"It's Ashley," he says, "I'm going to have to break things off for good with Brigid."

The man has finally seen the light. "Going to make the temp job rather difficult, won't it?" I ask.

Mike gives me a smug grin. "Not if *she* is the one to break up with *me*."

Oh, this ought to be good. "You have a plan for this?"

"Already in motion. I just have to reach into the Bad Boyfriend Bag of Tricks. Being rude. Not bathing. Tanking it in the sack. It's not hard to be a bad boyfriend."

"Not for you, anyway."

Mike ignores me. "I'm not a big fan of putting the break-up ball in Brigid's court. But I don't have much of a choice. I just have to hope for the best."

"Assuming *best* is the word you want to use there."

"But I'm not worried. I've got plenty of material."

Of that, I have no doubt. I set the beer aside and check on the stew. Mike strolls to the fridge and gets a beer of his own (leaving his empty soda can on the breakfast bar, even though the damn recycling bin is *right here*). He cracks the beer, throws the cap in the recycling (thank heaven for small favors), and leans against the kitchen counter.

"What do you suppose Nick Diamond was really doing in the office last night?" he asks.

I put the lid back on the pot. "That's an excellent question. You think we can take him at his word? That he was just looking for a schedule?"

Mike winces. "He seemed pretty startled to see us."

We take our beers into the living room. I look longingly at the cement lip extending past the arch windows at the front of the apartment. I call it *the front stoop* and when the weather is decent, I throw a couple lawn chairs out there and use it as a makeshift patio. But the temps are in the low forties and there's a light rain falling. The front stoop will have to wait for another day. Mike parks it on the futon while I drop into the comfy chair.

"What do you think is going on?" Mike says, "You've talked to everyone by now."

"No idea yet," I say, "Cronus didn't kill Mack. I'm positive of that. I think someone is trying to frame Cronus, probably the same person who killed Mack." I prop my chin on the beer bottle. "Jack Blades had an old grudge against Mack for no-showing him and torpedoing his promotion. Nick Diamond is protective of Ashley and had a bad feeling about Mack. Ashley talked to Mack the night of the murder. Gordon Russell was in the building that night, but he left early. Besides, Mack was his biggest star. He had no motive to kill him."

Mike rubs his jaw. "What else have you got?"

I sit back in the chair. "I'm pretty sure the murderer left and came back. Ashley is the only exception to that. She only left the building once, though nobody saw her go. Beyond that, I've got Nick Diamond going through the office. I've got somebody planting drug paraphernalia in Bobby Cronus's apartment. I've got somebody jumping me here. And I've got Gordon Russell going to a meeting he doesn't want Cronus to know about."

Mike perks up a little. "What meeting?"

"I overheard Russell talking about it on the phone. Didn't hear the other end. And I didn't ask him about it. Apparently, the meeting is at seven o'clock tonight. At the arena."

"Might want to take a look at it."

My beer bottle stops short of my mouth. "What? You mean spy on him?"

"No. I mean bring him some coke, some broads and some firearms and get real nuts. Yes, I mean spy on him, you moron."

"We don't know if the person he's meeting is involved in all this," I say.

"And we won't know until we see him."

I wince. "I don't know. Spying on someone? That feels a little sleazy."

"Sleazier than eavesdropping? You really want to die on that hill?"

Shit. He's got a point. Not that it makes me feel any better. But I have no counterargument and nothing else going on with this investigation. (I picture Carol doing the annoying air quotes thing around *investigation*.)

"Might as well," I say, "Let's just avoid getting caught, okay?"

"Hey, what's there to worry about?"

Cute. He asks that like he's never met me.

***

While Mike and I have hung out in many places, I can't think of many less interesting than the parking lot of the Gas 'n' Go across the street from the Sportatorium. But it affords a damn good view of the building. It's closing in on seven o'clock. We've got another hour of daylight, but the cloudy weather makes it seem just about dark. That works to our advantage. From across the street, you'd have to be Superman to get a clear look into my Saturn Ion. So far, there's been no sign of activity. I take out my phone.

"Six-fifty-five," I say, "Apparently, Russell doesn't believe in being early."

"Just give him a minute," Mike says, casually sipping the crappy to-go coffee he bought from the Gas 'n' Go. (Hey, supporting a local business makes loitering more acceptable. At least, that's what I keep telling myself.) If this meeting is so important," Mike says, "You think he's going to miss it?"

Jeez, I must be jittery if *Mike* is talking me off the ledge. At six-fifty-eight, Russell's car pulls into the lot. He walks to the front, looking around, furtively. About a minute later, a black Audi with Tennessee license plates pulls up to the curb. Clearly a rental. A rotund guy with a florid face and shaggy blonde hair gets out. He ambles over to Russell. The two of them shake hands and walk into the arena.

"You recognize that guy?" Mike asks.

"No," I say, drawing the word out, "but he looks kind of familiar."

"Yeah, to me, too. But I can't place him."

"Well, that was extremely enlightening," I say, "What the fuck do we do now?"

Mike rubs his jaw. "Probably more than one way into that arena."

"I think there are two side doors. Why?"

"Plenty of nooks and crannies," Mike says, "Pretty good acoustics, as I recall."

Oh shit. I'm surprised it took me this long to figure it out. Mike wants us to break into the arena and eavesdrop on Russell and his guest. That's completely ridiculous. Risking life, limb and incarceration to eavesdrop on a meeting that might have nothing to do with Lance Mack's murder. But we're back to question one: what other plan do we have?

"You think we can pull that off?" I ask.

"Follow my lead," Mike says, "Everything will be fine."

I neglect to tell Mike that *fine* has never resulted from me following his lead. He hops out of the car and starts toward the parking lot. I hasten to follow him. The rain has let up. Mike crosses the parking lot, steps around a few puddles in the dirt and swings around to one side of the arena. We move through the shadows. He stops at a metal door near the back.

"This is one of them, right?" Mike asks.

"Looks sturdy. You think you can get in?"

Mike scoffs, vaguely offended. "Just keep a look out, okay?"

A thing I should probably mention: when we were in college, Mike had a sideline career as a cat burglar. He wasn't exactly a one-man crime spree. He'd grab small-ticket items, and only do it when he was short of cash and couldn't hit up his parents for money. As far as I know, that whole thing ended when he graduated. Then again, I've had need for his skills in the last couple years and he hasn't exactly looked…rusty. Probably best not to think about it. I keep a look out while he goes about his fiendish work. A few seconds later, the door pops open.

"After you," Mike says, waving a hand inside.

I slip through the door, which Mike closes *very* carefully behind me. We're in a hallway that leads past the heels' dressing room and into the lobby. We're mostly in darkness, but there's some light spill from the arena, enough to see our way around. I inch toward the heels' dressing room. Voices come from the arena. I can't make out what they're saying. A few bits come through here. "Cronus…" "Won't be a problem…" As we reach the entrance next to the heels' dressing room, we can hear everything clearly.

"…a thing with Bruno Harvey?" the guest asks.

"It's not going to be a problem," Russell says, "He even cancelled the show he was running against *WrestleShock.*"

What's not going to be a problem? Maybe we can find out. If we situate ourselves right, we should be able to hear the conversation without being seen.

If Mike doesn't a trip over a shovel, that is.

The shovel in question is a wide, yellow snow shovel. How Mike didn't see it is beyond me. The clattering of its fall sounds like a grenade going off.

"Is somebody back there?" Russell calls out.

Neither of us say anything. Mike is still on his feet, which is more than you can say for the shovel. We hug the wall nearest the dressing room. Russell's footsteps are audible, coming toward us. Mike and I cross the opening to the arena. No one sees us. We hustle down the hallway, toward the lobby. The curtain to the lobby looms in front of us. Before we get there, a shadow can be seen at the bottom of the curtain. Someone is waiting for us, maybe even about to come through the curtain. Meantime, Gordon Russell is closing in on the entrance to the heels' dressing room.

We're fucked.

Then something pulls me backwards. I find myself in a little nook near the support pillars. There's enough room to hide and still keep an eye on the hallway leading to the heels' dressing room. Mike and I huddle there, trying to control our breathing. Russell goes into the heels' dressing room. His guest comes into view but doesn't look our direction.

Russell steps out of the dressing room. His voice comes down the hallway. "You see anything?"

"Nothing," the guest says, "You have an alarm system on this place, don't you?"

"We do," Russell says, "But we practically never remember to arm it." There's a moment of quiet, then Russell says, "There's a shovel over here. Maybe it just fell down on its own."

"Maybe," the guest says.

Another pause. The guest doesn't move. A few seconds later, Russell comes into view. Mike and I get further behind the pillar.

"Should we get back to it?" Russell asks.

"Works for me," the guest says.

They start down the hallway toward the heels' dressing room. I move to my left and keep an eye on Russell and his guest without leaving the safety of the shadows. They are about to go back into the arena when the front door is heard, distantly. They both freeze.

"Who the hell is that?" the guest asks.

Russell tugs at his mustache. "It might be Bobby. I have no idea what he'd be doing here. He said he was going to take the night off."

"Looks like he didn't," the guest says.

The door to the lobby opens and closes. Footsteps head toward the arena, mostly muted by the rubber flooring. Russell peeks into the arena. He starts powerwalking down the hall, corralling his guest by the arm.

"It *is* Bobby," Russell whispers, "Our ring announcer is with him. They must be training."

"You need to train your ring announcer?" the guest asks.

"It's a long story," Russell says, "We need to hide. I know where to do it." They make a beeline toward where Mike and I are hiding.

Oh shit.

Mike and I slide all the way to the other side of the pillar, but it's a temporary hiding place at best. Soon, Russell and his guest will be hunkering down with us and possibly asking some awkward questions. And all I will have only awkward answers.

Something whistles past my ear and pings off one of the support beams under the bleachers. Russell and his guest turn that direction. Mike and I run for the lobby. We get through the curtain, unnoticed.

"What the hell did you throw?" I ask.

"Car keys," Mike says.

"You really threw your car keys?"

"Of course not. I threw yours." I stop. Mike pushes me toward the door and says, "I'm kidding. It was a fucking washer I found on the floor."

Just before we get to the door, I spot something in the office. Lying against Cronus's desk is a golf club. That's not unusual, obviously, given that it's his gimmick. In this case, though, the golf club is bent and scratched. As if it was used in an attack. I look toward the arena.

"Holy shit," I say.

Mike sees what I'm looking at. But he keeps pushing me toward the door. "I get it. But you can deal with it later. Let's go."

We make sure the door closes gently. We do the same with the front door. We haul ass across the street, returning to the safety of Mike's crappy car. He pulls out of the parking lot. I sit back in my seat.

"That told us…very little," I say.

"I'm pretty sure I recognized the guy," Mike says, "I just don't know from where."

"Whoever it is, Russell wants to keep him away from Bobby Cronus."

"Looking at the golf club in Cronus's office," Mike says, "I don't blame him."

I get that. As far as I know, I've already had an up-close-and-personal with the club in question. I'm positive it wasn't Cronus. But who was it? And what was it doing in Cronus's office?

Really, I should just be glad it's not wrapped around my head.

CHAPTER TEN

Because the wrestling business gets more mainstream attention now, some think it must be more popular than it was back in the day. After all, they see images of UWE selling out a stadium and think this must the golden age of wrestling. That's a fallacy.

See, UWE might sell out one stadium a year. Maybe two. They run a couple house shows every week but rarely sell them out. Therefore, you're looking at UWE drawing maybe thirty thousand people a week for about fifty weeks a year. That's a total of one and a half million fans per year. Throw in those couple of stadium shows and maybe it's closer to one point six million. Pretty impressive, right? But that's one promotion with almost no competition.

Now, in the territory days, a typical territory ran up to nine shows per week (seven nights a week with one or two matinees on the weekends). Most of those shows would draw at least a couple thousand fans, with at least one major city drawing up to ten thousand. Therefore, right around twenty-five thousand fans per week. But that's one territory. Back in the day, there could be fifteen to twenty territories in the U.S. alone. If you multiply twenty-five thousand fans per week by twenty territories, you get five hundred thousand fans per week *and twenty-five million fans* per year. *By every metric, wrestling was a* far *more lucrative business in the old days than it is now.*

But hey, Americans aren't going to think if the media can do it for them, right?

I watch the crowd filter into the Sportatorium and think Midwest Championship Wrestling must be doing pretty well for itself. It's the weekly Friday night show, the last one before *WrestleShock.* If we have any questions about Cronus's good taste and judgement, we're clearly in the minority. The show is a sellout. I'm glad our ringside seats are reserved. Bobby Cronus is, of course, nowhere to be found (probably in the back, handing out match finishes). Gordon Russell stands on the far side of the lobby, greeting fans. There's no sign of his guest from the other night. Lars strolls into the lobby, wearing his customary purple suit, and greeting some fans as he goes. He runs a hand through his quasi-pompadour.

"Greetings and salutations," he says, his voice tight and his pace quick, "Big night, huh?"

"Big night," Mike says, "You're not going to tell us what's going to happen?"

"Not at all," Lars says, "Sorry, brother. My hands are tied. Lot of pressure on me. Not just from the fans. We've got special guests tonight."

"What kind of special guests?" I ask.

"Frankie and Fabio," Lars says, "I thought they'd enjoy it."

My entire body goes into a clench. Just in case we haven't done enough to completely blow this movie thing, Lars decides to cinch the deal. I grab his arm.

"You really think that's a good idea?" I ask.

"They'll love it," Lars says, waving away my concerns, "Trust me." He throws a shadow punch at nothing in particular (not even his shadow). "I'm trying to prepare. Mr. Cronus says my punches are a little…tentative."

That makes sense. Lars is not a man of violence, despite his attempts to toughen up. I imagine that's been the focus of his training with Bobby Cronus. We wish Lars good luck. He accepts it then walks back to the faces' dressing room. Carol, Mike, and I make our way to our seats. The arena is configured for the weekly show (seating on all four sides) and is filled to the rafters. I drape my coat over the back of my chair. Mike buries himself in the program. Carol looks over at me.

"Rick is coming to *WrestleShock*," she says.

"Sounds like fun," I say.

Carol waits for me to expound, but she gets nothing. I look toward the ring, keeping my eyes clear of her. Finally, Carol speaks slowly and with more than a hint of acid in her tone.

"Sure," she says.

I look around the building, tugging at my t-shirt, looking for something to distract me. Sadly, I spot something after only a few seconds. Frankie and Fabio are in the bleachers, near the entryway from the lobby. Lars's friend Chuck is sitting with them. While Frankie and Fabio chatter away, Chuck sits there, looking like the result of a Cro-Magnon Man mating with a VW Bug. This does not make me feel better about our chances of getting this movie off the ground.

Lars emerges from the faces' dressing room and the place explodes. He slaps hands with the fans as he makes his way to the ring. He's showered with chants of *Purple Suit! Purple Suit!* He flips on the mic and brings it to his mouth.

"Ladies and gentlemen, *welcome* to Midwest Championship Wrestling! Our first—"

That's as far as he gets before Bobby Cronus's voice booms over the P.A. "Hold it, hold it, hold it!" Cronus appears in the aisle near the heels' dressing room. He wears his usual Crayola box of colors outfit: green jacket, white shirt, yellow pants, blue tie. Hired security guys flank him as he approaches the ring. The fans yell and spit. Lars lowers his mic. Cronus gets into the ring. "Why don't you take the night off, beanpole?"

Lars spreads his arms wide and looks to the fans as if to say *Do you believe this shit?* He turns toward Cronus and asks. "Who's going to do the ring announcing?"

"*I* will be doing the ring announcing tonight. You get the hell out of here. Now!" He turns to the security guards. "Get this piece of crap out of my ring."

The security guards move toward Lars. He stands his ground, unwilling to go down without a fight. One of the security guards, a burly guy with a mustache, seems to talk reasonably to Lars. Cronus shouts at them, pushing them to do their job. The security guard seems annoyed but continues. Lars allows himself to be escorted out of the ring. The crowd cheers Lars until he disappears into the dressing room.

"Humanoids of all ages!" Cronus says, "Welcome to Midwest Championship Wrestling!" It's met with a solid wall of booing. Cronus's face crinkles up. "Ah, shut the hell up." Which, of course, inspires the crowd to do just the opposite.

That establishes Cronus's style of announcing. The heels are given lavish introductions while the babyfaces settle for a few mumbled words, interspersed with insults. The crowd's ire is rising (which is exactly what Cronus is after). The first half of the show is pretty meat-and-potatoes. The highlight is Vanessa defending the women's title against Sienna. The match itself is nothing much. But after Vanessa wins, she ties Sienna in the ropes. She gets out a pair of scissors and starts cutting Sienna's hair. This ends when Ashley charges out and chases Vanessa from the ring. Vanessa brandishes some of Sienna's locks as she backs toward the heels' dressing room. Ashley points at Vanessa, as if to say *Your day is coming.* Vanessa merely smirks. Cronus waits until Ashley and Sienna have cleared out before stepping into the ring.

"Okay, it's intermission," Cronus says, "Go spend some of your welfare money at the concession stand and be back here in fifteen minutes or we'll start the show without you."

The crowd boos but does as Cronus says and files toward the lobby. I glance toward the bleachers. No sign of Chuck or the Bobbsey Twins. Maybe they didn't make it through the first half. Maybe they're out pillaging the countryside. I join Mike and Carol and head for the lobby.

The temperature has gone up (still rainy and drizzly but at least an indication that spring is coming) and the arena is a little humid, particularly when bodies are in close proximity. We join some of the other fans in stepping outside for intermission. We've just found a place on the sidewalk when I hear a voice squealing nearby.

"Joe Davis!"

Oh boy. This is either a female fan or that paternity suit I've been dreading. I turn and see Frankie coming straight at me. Fabio is behind her and Chuck slouches in the rear. These are the times when I wish I could tap a comm badge and say, "One to beam up." Frankie greets me with a hug that nearly knocks me over.

"Joe Davis," she says, "Great to see you!"

"Hi Frankie," I say, gently prying her off me, "Good to see you again. These are my friends Mike and Carol."

Frankie doesn't so much as look their direction. "Okay, great," she says. Then she grabs my forearms. "Isn't this so cool? Can you believe Lars in there? He's great, isn't he?"

"He's something all right," I say.

Frankie leans in. "He's coming back later on. He didn't want me to tell you that, so don't say anything."

"Got it," I say. We'll keep this between us and whoever else she mentioned it to.

"We're going out with him after the matches," Frankie says, "Someplace called The Block. You want to come along?"

I hope Mike and Carol will find a way to get me out of this. But they don't say anything. Treacherous bastards.

"Let me see what my friends want to do," I say.

Frankie's smile fades slightly. "Okay, I guess. Just let me know." She lowers her voice. "We were just doing some coke with Lars. You want to piece of that?"

What are the odds she's talking about Coca-Cola? Or even metallurgical coke? Very small. And certainly nothing I want a piece of.

"Can't right now," I say, "Have to stay sharp in case I see something I can write about."

"Suit yourself," Frankie says. Then she leans close to me, whispering in my ear. "By the way, the offer from the other night still stands. Think about it."

She punctuates that with a slap on my ass then walks away with Fabio and Chuck (worst band name ever). Once they're gone, Carol and Mike are willing to acknowledge my presence.

"Those are your investors?" Carol asks, "They look like they couldn't produce a kidney stone. I thought she was going to strip down right here."

Mike ponders this. "Spectacular hooters, though."

Carol's head spins toward Mike. "*That* was your takeaway from this whole…of course that was your takeaway. You're a mechanical penis. What else should I expect?"

Mike doesn't react to the *mechanical penis* crack, likely because he takes it as a compliment. The crowd moves back into the arena, so we join them. I can't help wondering if I should intervene with Lars and the Bobbsey Twins. I let it go. Lars is a (theoretically) grown man and can take care of himself. Besides, why would I risk the comedic potential of a coked-up Lars possibly inserting himself into a wrestling match? Once we get back into the lobby, Mike decides to grab a beer. Carol and I wait for him in the corner. Out of the blue, Carol pins me in the corner and speaks through gritted teeth.

"I want you to tell me what happened with you and Rick," she says, "He's been completely paranoid lately. He's even started wearing a t-shirt when we're…intimate. This only started after you had your little chat with him at dinner. What the hell did you two talk about?"

Carol is not going to buy any bullshit from me (which is a shame because I'm selling it at a reasonable rate). I have two choices: talk to her or set fire to the building and run for the exit. (Decisions, decisions.)

"It really wasn't anything important," I say, "We were just talking about old times."

"Uh-huh. So, it was just about sex?"

"Right, just…" Fuck. I walked right into that one. "Yep, it was about sex."

Carol takes in a breath through her nose. "And what, specifically, about sex? I'm assuming it involved me and if you try to deny it, I will terminate the existence of your testicles. Do you understand?"

"Yes, you've made that rather clear." I lower my voice. "It was about having sex. And…people watching."

It takes a second for that to sink in. When it does, Carol's eyes bug out. "You think I like having people watch?"

"That's just what I heard."

"Where did you hear…fucking Mike. Right? That's what I get for, well, fucking Mike."

This is bad on a number of levels. Rick is likely in trouble for having privileged information. I'm definitely in trouble for sharing said privileged information. And Mike—who's always in trouble with Carol—is in deep sewage for being Patient Zero in the current TMI epidemic. Carol clenches both fists.

"May I ask how in the hell *that* came up in conversation?" she asks.

"I honestly don't remember. We were making small talk and I just blurted it out."

"You blurted it out? What happened? Did you have a series of small strokes?"

I position my hands in front of me, as if that will stop the assault to come. "I'm sorry. It was one of those things that once it's out there, you can't reel it back in."

After a few seconds, Carol says, "Isn't that just swell?"

"Is there anything I can do to make it up to you?" I ask.

"Of course. Just get in the time machine, go back to dinner at The Tav and smack yourself in the head before you open your pie hole. That would clear everything right up."

Okay, I'm clearly on Carol's shit list, though I do applaud her use of the term *pie hole*. I fumble for something to say. All I come up with is, "I'm sorry."

"You've heard the expression about *sorry* and *not feeding the bulldog*, right?" Carol says, "Now, everything makes sense. Thanks to you idiots, my boyfriend thinks I'm a sicko."

"You're not a sicko," I say, "You're maybe sick-ish...."

The look I get from Carol tells me I'm not a comfort. (That's never been my specialty.) Mike returns from the beer garden. Carol snaps him a look. He freezes in place.

"Problem?" he asks.

Carol lets a breath out through her nose. "I like having people watch?"

Mike's jaw drops. "I thought that was just between you and me?"

"Apparently, it was between you, me, and Joe."

He shoots me a look. "You told her that?"

Carol stamps a foot. "No, he told my boyfriend that. *Then* he told me. But I'm interested in who started the whole daisy chain."

"I see," Mike says, "So, you're taking full responsibility?"

She kicks the wall, managing to do it without breaking her foot. Mike backs off, holding his beer in front of his groin. I'm backed against the wall, wishing I could just vibrate my molecules and go right through it, ala The Flash. A few people turn to look, but we're not creating a scene. Carol sticks a finger in Mike's face and then in mine.

"I'd like to thank you two idiots," she says, "Almost every relationship I have gets fucked up by at least one of you. Just know this: I am going to get you. I don't know how, but I'm going to get you."

With that, Carol storms out of the lobby and then out the front door. I guess we're on our own for the second half of the show. Mike steps over to me, looking where Carol has gone.

"I guess she's pretty upset," he says.

"Can't say I blame her."

"She'll get over it," Mike says, "Let's watch the second half."

We make our way back to our seats in time for the end of intermission. As per usual, the first few matches are forgettable. Prior to the main event, the most memorable moment is the Super Destroyer (Bill Walker) attempting a dive outside the ring, tripping over the middle rope and damn near going straight down on his head. (The ring apron breaks his fall. And possibly portions of his anatomy.) You can practically hear Bobby Cronus shouting "Goddammit!" from somewhere in the back. Indeed, Cronus looks a little peeved when he returns to the ring to announce the main event. (Then again, he always looks a little peeved, so who's to say?)

Cronus starts to raise the microphone to his mouth then pauses. His eyes are focused on something in the back. Gordon Russell's guest from the other night is standing in the entryway to the arena. The guy uses his middle finger to push up his oversized glasses. Cronus's face turns red, but he regains his composure (or a reasonable facsimile).

"This is your main event," he says, still glaring toward the back.

The main event is a rematch between Jackson Darkfire and Nick Diamond for the Midwest Title. Traditionally, the champion is introduced last, but in this case, the challenger is an absolute legend. Screw tradition. Cronus launches into his Darkfire spiel before his man even makes an appearance.

"Introducing first," Cronus says, "He is *now* the Real Main Event, the Showstopper, the Straw That Stirs the Drink…your reigning, defending Midwest Heavyweight Champion…Jackson Darkfire!"

Darkfire struts to the ring. A black and silver robe has replaced the leather jacket. His hair is slicked back and there's no trace of goth makeup. Cronus holds the ropes for him as he gets into the ring. Darkfire throws open the robe, revealing the Midwest Title Belt around his waist. The crowd greets him with catcalls. (Although, there are a few scattered cheers from those who didn't dig the whole goth gimmick thing. Or just like to root for the bad guy.) Cronus helps him out of the robe and gives him a hug and a kiss on the cheek (again trying to rouse the homophobic element in the crowd). Once that falderol is completed, Cronus brings the mic up to his mouth and mumbles, "And his opponent's Nick Diamond."

Despite the lack of a proper introduction, the crowd explodes at the mention of Diamond's name. He wears an ornate green robe, which he puts on full display with a little turn on the ring apron. Once in the ring, he walks toward Cronus, who hides behind Darkfire. Diamond directs several less-than-friendly remarks toward Cronus. I don't catch all of them, but the ones I do seem preoccupied with removing Cronus's various body parts and stuffing them up certain orifices. Cronus stands on the apron to address Diamond.

"You stay the hell away from me, Nick Diamond!" Cronus says, "Unless you want to end up like Lance Mack!"

The crowd reaction is akin to someone telling a joke and getting a *Whoa, they went* there*!* reaction. It's part shock and part anger. Then it turns to mostly anger, with fans tossing beer cups in the general direction of Bobby Cronus. I drop my head into my hands, trying to avoid getting hit with a stray beer cup. Cronus turns his back to Nick Diamond and brings the microphone to his mouth.

"You want to keep throwing stuff at the ring, that's fine," Cronus says, "I'll just disqualify Nick Diamond and we can all go home. That sound good?"

Despite wrestling fans' general inclination to be contrarians, the announcement *does* stop the flow of beer cups. The wrestlers and the referee kick aside the cups while Cronus provides a little help with his golf club. The bell rings and the crowd has something to take their minds off their ugly mood.

The first part of the match gets over Jackson Darkfire's new persona as a chickenshit heel. He ducks behind the ref, frequently rolls out of the ring and takes cheap shots whenever the opportunity presents itself. Diamond gets frustrated. He argues with the ref once or twice, hoping to neutralize Darkfire's tactics. At one point, Darkfire backs Diamond into the ropes and as the referee tries to get them to break, Darkfire hits Diamond with a poke to the eyes. It was one of Diamond's classic moves when he was the top heel in the business. The crowd responds with appropriate hostility.

Diamond throws himself into the ropes and gets tripped by Bobby Cronus. Darkfire seizes the moment and proceeds to beat what I'm certain Bobby Cronus would call *the teetotal shit* out of Diamond, climaxing with him tossing Diamond out of the ring. While the referee reads Darkfire the riot act, Cronus jabs Diamond in the stomach with the golf club, then throws him into the ring post. Diamond comes up bleeding from the forehead. (You knew that was coming.)

Diamond gets back into the ring and keeps getting beaten. The referee checks the cut and asks Diamond if he wants to stop the match. Darkfire prepares to hit Diamond with his finisher, but Diamond counters with a low blow. Darkfire crumbles into the corner. Cronus hops up on the ring apron and shouts at the referee. Diamond makes a rush at Cronus, who scurries away. Darkfire stumbles toward Diamond, who greets him with a kick to the knee.

"Here we go," I say.

Diamond lays waste to Darkfire's knee. It's all the old tricks: kicking the back of the knee, sitting down hard on it, slamming the knee into the ring post. Darkfire howls in pain throughout. Cronus paces back and forth. It's only a matter of time before the Diamond Clasp is applied and the match is over.

I look toward the heels' dressing room. "Something's going to happen. Bobby Cronus isn't going to let Nick Diamond win. Not this easily."

The crowd is going crazy. Darkfire is flat on his back. Diamond grabs Darkfire's legs and grapevines them around his own. He looks out to the crowd.

"Time to take it home!" Diamond shouts.

The crowd erupts. It's an old line of Diamond's, one he used when he was about to put someone away. A second later, he flips Darkfire over on his stomach, stepping over him as he does, and squats down, fully applying the Diamond Clasp. Darkfire screams in pain. Cronus tries to get the referee's attention. The ref, however, ignores him and checks with Darkfire, waiting for him to tap out.

"Here it comes," I say.

Cronus turns toward the heels' dressing room. Darkfire raises his hand, ready to tap out. Jack Blades runs toward the ring. Nick Diamond doesn't see him coming. Blades slides under the bottom rope, charges toward Diamond, and levels him with a clothesline from behind. Diamond sprawls out on the mat. The referee calls for the bell. Darkfire loses by disqualification, but he keeps his title. (In wrestling, titles don't change hands on a disqualification.)

The crowd boos and beer cups fly toward the ring again. Mike and I cover up, since some of the projectiles are lobbed by those with bad seats and bad arms. Cronus rolls into the ring and joins Blades in laying the boots to Nick Diamond.

The crowd roars. Ashley Diamond runs to the ring. Before she gets there, though, Darkfire rolls out and grabs her. He can't do much more than hold her in check, but it's enough. Blades picks up Nick Diamond and pins his arms behind his back. Cronus slaps Nick in the face. The crowd is reaching a fever pitch. Suddenly, someone comes tearing down the aisle from the lobby. He leaps the fan barrier and slides into the ring.

It's Lars.

Cronus turns just as Lars hits the ring. He draws back the golf club and swings at Lars's head. Lars easily ducks it then hits Cronus with a right hook. Cronus flies through the air, awkwardly, and hits the mat, flat on his back. The crowd roars.

Nick Diamond throws a back kick that hits Blades right in the groin. Blades falls to the mat. Darkfire lets go of Ashley and turns toward the ring. Ashley takes advantage of the situation and swings a mighty kick into Darkfire's nuts. (It's so nice to see a daughter taking after her father.) Cronus crawls out of ring, holding his jaw. He hooks up with Blades and Darkfire, both reeling from their own attacks. I can just make out what Cronus is saying.

"The dumb son of a bitch potatoed me," Cronus says, "I think he broke my fucking jaw."

Blades and Darkfire help Cronus up the aisle to the heels' dressing room. Nick and Ashley Diamond and Lars stand in the ring, triumphant. Nick grabs a mic from ringside.

"Hey Cronus," he says, "You want me to get a partner for *WrestleShock*? I got one. Here he is!"

Nick and Ashley grab Lars's arms and thrust them into the air. The crowd goes wild. Cronus shouts at the ring, but he's drowned out by the crowd. He looks toward the lobby and a different kind of irritated look comes over his face. He stalks back to the dressing room. I look toward the lobby and see Russell's guest is still in presence. Mike follows my look.

"Looks like the guy is back," Mike says, "What do you suppose that's all about?"

Gordon Russell ushers the guest toward the front door. Russell looks as if he'd love to crawl under a table and then into the earth itself.

"I don't know," I say, "But I get the feeling business is about to pick up."

***

A half hour later, Mike and I are standing in the lobby. One again, the place seems eerily quiet after the noise of the wrestling card. Gordon Russell tugs his mustache. The guest has disappeared. Lars pokes his head into the lobby. He looks around to make sure the fans have cleared out then glides up to us. His eyes are bright and his movements quick. Clearly, the cocaine is doing its job.

"Everyone enjoy the show?" he asks.

Mike pats him on the shoulder. "I did. I'd say more, but I'm seething with jealousy."

Lars gives us the closest thing he's got to a self-deprecating grin. "It was a truly funky moment, no doubt." He looks around. "Where's Carol?"

"Don't ask," I say.

Lars lets it go at that. "Let's celebrate. Fabio, Frankie and Chuck are at The Block."

As festive gatherings go, that one sounds somewhere on the level of root canal. I don't wish to offend our potential investors, but there's unfinished business here. And I don't want Frankie to try and finish business with me. I give Lars a (faux) mournful look.

"Sorry, I can't," I say.

Fortunately, the conversation stops there. Unfortunately, it's because Bobby Cronus has stormed into the lobby. His face is red, and his eyes are bulging. His jacket and tie are absent. He charges up to Russell and slams his golf club to the floor.

"What the fuck was Bruce Johnson doing here!" Cronus says.

Russell's eyes flick toward the front door, as if he's contemplating making a break for it. "We're working on a deal."

"A deal?" Cronus says, "What kind of fucking deal?"

"A development deal," Russell says, "The UWE wants to use us as a developmental territory for their new talent."

"And you agreed?" Cronus asks.

Russell fumbles with his glasses. "It's in discussion. But there's interest. On both sides."

"And my interest doesn't matter?"

"I was going to tell you," Russell says, "But I thought if I told you right away, you'd want to kill the deal."

"You're fucking-A right I'd want to kill it!" Cronus says, "I've worked for those fuckers. You can't trust them."

"I...I don't know if I'd..." Russell says, speaking mostly into his shirt.

"Bruce Johnson, that smug motherfucker. If I never saw his fat, lying face again, it was going to be..." Cronus stops. "How long has this been going on?"

Russell tugs at his mustache. "A...a couple of months now."

Cronus's eyes bug out. "A couple of *months*? And you're just fucking tell me now? You aren't *even* fucking telling me. I had to find out for myself. Did you think Bruce Johnson was going to roll in here and I wasn't going to notice?" He straightens his glasses. "The deal is already set, isn't it? Because otherwise, you wouldn't take a chance on me seeing him."

"Yeah, it's done," Russell says, "They start sending us talent right after *WrestleShock*."

Cronus's cheeks puff out as he breathes. "Motherfucker," he says. He starts back toward the arena. He stops when he sees Lars. "And you, you cocksucker. You nearly broke my fucking jaw. I taught you how to do that shit safe. Fucking use what I fucking taught you!"

Lars wipes his nose. "Will do, Mr. Cronus."

Cronus disappears into the arena. From somewhere in the darkness comes the sound of something being kicked, followed by Cronus crying out in pain and swearing. Russell slumps against the wall, looking like a guy who's just been released from the electric chair. I walk over to him.

"That went okay," I say, "Assuming Bobby didn't break his foot." I slip my hands into my coat pockets. "Why didn't you tell him sooner?"

"You know that old saying about how it's easier to ask forgiveness than permission?" Russell says, "That's what I was thinking. I've wanted to get into the wrestling business full-time since I was a kid. Now, here I am, fifty-two years old and I finally have the chance. I figured Bobby would either accept it or he wouldn't. Personally, I'm hoping he will. But I had to make the deal."

I'd love to share Russell's optimism about Cronus accepting the deal, but Bobby Cronus isn't known for his flexibility. He *is* known for holding a grudge and wanting to piss on the graves of his enemies. A thought occurs to me.

"Mack knew about the developmental deal, didn't he?" I say, "He was threatening to leave if you didn't fire Cronus. That would have messed up the deal, right?"

Russell shoots me a look. "How did you know that?"

I could confess to eavesdropping, but that might not be my smartest plan. "I hear things," I say, hoping that's vague enough.

"Yes, Lance knew about the deal. If he had gone elsewhere, he would have taken a lot of the talent with him. That would have killed the deal. It's why I wanted to work things out between he and Bobby. Bobby's not only a great booker, he's a great trainer. I wanted us to put our best foot forward."

I look toward the arena. It's not hard to picture Cronus stalking around, looking for something to throw and/or destroy. Russell gives it a concerned look of his own. (Which makes sense. Most of the stuff in there belongs to him.) The front door opens. Bruce Johnson, the representative of UWE, strolls in and approaches Russell, ignoring the rest of us.

"How'd he take it?" Johnson asks.

"About how you'd expect," Russell says.

"He'll get over it," Johnson says, "Let's go get a drink, you and I."

They walk out the door without a look back. With Russell gone and Cronus in no mood to talk, there's not a lot left for the rest of us to do. We leave as well. Lars puts his hands into the pockets of his purple suit.

"Hell of a night, eh?" he says, "I think I'm in a pretty interesting angle."

Mike rubs his jowls. "Might get a hell of a lot more interesting."

***

I'm not certain how much positivity this conveys, but we've come to describe certain close friends as our *Ride or die*. I'm not sure Lars has ever fallen into that category for me, and yet, here I am, riding in his piece of crap car with an opportunity to die.

"We're going to The Saloon?" I ask.

"We are indeed," Lars says, "You ever been there?"

"Once. It wasn't pleasant."

"We're not going there to have pleasant time," he says, "There's work to be done."

Great googly-moogly. I'm only coming along on this mission to keep Lars out of trouble (which might be its own variety of fool's errand). Midwest Championship Wrestling just had one main eventer die. They don't need another to follow.

"You're sure this is the only way to handle it?" I ask, "It's a little…"

"Proactive?"

"Criminal."

Lars flips a hand at that. "I'm just going to point out the potential grievous bodily harm that might result from Peter pursuing this revival of Les Bos. Does that sound criminal to you?"

"That sounds like the very definition of criminal."

When Lars told me about this idiot plan, I tried to talk him down from the ledge. But he had already talked to Chuck and once that happens, there's no force in heaven and earth that will move him off that ledge.

"This is really the last resort?" I ask.

"I'm afraid so, brother. We tried hiring a private investigator. Figured we'd dig up some dirt on Peter. Maybe use it against him. But we had no luck."

"What happened?" I ask.

Lars drums his fingers on the steering wheel. "I *will* give the P.I. credit. He was both efficient and thorough. He got back to us with a very detailed report."

"And…?"

"And his report dug up a lot of very compromising and embarrassing information. Unfortunately, it was all about Chuck."

I swing my head toward Lars. "Chuck?"

"The P.I. got confused. He's very detailed and very thorough but also has very serious short-term memory issues."

"Where did you find this guy?"

"Chuck's friend George Gadaski recommended the guy. Apparently, Gadaski once hired the guy to tail his wife. He thought she was cheating on him. The P.I. got the information, and it was very incriminating. But it turned out the guy tailed Gadaski's mistress and caught Gadaski in the act."

"Then why the hell did Gadaski recommend him?"

"I'm starting to think Gadaski doesn't like Chuck. A little matter of Chuck screwing over Gadaski on a car repair. But then, the motivations of people are a mystery at best."

Lars pulls into the parking lot of The Saloon. The place is in Frogtown, a not particularly reputable neighborhood that stretches out behind the State Capitol. The Saloon is a two-story operation. There's a downstairs bar that best resembles the set of *Mean Streets*. The upstairs bar is a little more welcoming, with its bandstand and dancefloor. I haven't been here in a while, but I can't imagine the place has changed much.

We try the downstairs bar first, but Lars doesn't see Peter. We decide to look around upstairs. I follow Lars up the steep flight of stairs. The lighting gets dusky. There's usually a blues band playing up there. Instead, I hear a scramble of up-tempo beats. Is that techno? At The Saloon? That's like spraying potpourri in a biker bar. What's going on here? Everything is clear when we get to the top of the stairs, and I see a dick on stage.

And by *dick*, I don't mean the metaphorical kind of dick one generally meets at the DMV or the Republican National Convention. I mean the penial portion of the male anatomy. The gentleman in possession of the aforementioned penial unit is dancing onstage, wearing leather chaps, a leather vest and nothing else. Lars and I take in the scene. The dance floor and the surrounding tables are filled with gentlemen who appear to be…with each other. Some have interesting piercings and wear leather, chains and similar accoutrement. Whirling multi-color lights fly about the room. There are more mirrors here than I remember. A mural featuring Bette Midler, a classic Madonna, and Cher stretches along one wall. The DJ on the far side of the stage may or may not have been a member of Frankie Goes to Hollywood.

"Lars," I say, "when did The Saloon become a gay bar?"

"I'm not certain," Lars says, "but we can't let that throw us. We're here on a mission."

"Fine, but you try to hold my hand, I'll slug you."

I should be very clear on this: I have no issues with the LGBTQIA+ community. They can consider me a strong ally. That part of my personality, it should be noted, comes from living in a very open-minded metropolitan area for the last decade or so. There is, however, this other part of my personality: the part that spent his first few decades in a small town in northern Minnesota. *That* part of my personality has a tendency to feel uncomfortable in situations in which your average white heterosexual is not in the majority. I know that feeling is wrong and I'm working on it. But for the moment,

I'm going to face facts: I find any penis that's not mine to be rather gross. (And I'm not entirely sold on my own.)

Lars, though, is comfortable in any setting. He sashays about the room, lightly bopping his head to the music. "No luck here," he says, "Let's try the bar area at the back."

The back area is separated from the main room by an archway. The bar area is small, with a bar on one wall and a few tables on the other. Neon and glass dominate the decor. (*That*, at least, is a holdover from the old days.) Lars comes to a halt.

"There he is," Lars says, "Down at the end of the bar."

The dude in question is short and barrel-chested. He has a hawk nose, piercing eyes (made more piercing by the eyeliner) and a rim of white stubble on his shaved head. He wears tan slacks and a striped button-down shirt and nurses a martini bigger than my car. He appears to be alone.

Lars hunches his shoulders, tensing for a fight. "It's go time. You ready to do this?"

"Ready as I'm going to be," I say.

Naturally, Lars doesn't pick up on my lack of enthusiasm, which is fine. He's got enough for the both of us. He marches down the bar. I lag behind him. Peter spots Lars when he's a few feet away and visibly stiffens. Lars leans on the bar.

"Peter," Lars says, staring down his nose, "it's good to see you again."

"What are you doing here, Lars?" is how Peter greets him, his voice surprisingly guttural.

"What's with the hostility, my friend?" Lars says, "Here we are, stopping into this fine establishment for a drink. We see an old friend. We approach him. And *this* is how we're greeted? Not a good look on you, my friend."

"Blow it out your ass, Lars," Peter says, "You're here about Les Bos. You know it and I know it. Quit fucking around and say what you have to say."

Peter must not know Lars all that well. Fucking around and not really saying anything is Lars's specialty. My idiot friend's mind struggles to his planned script.

"If that's how you want it," Lars says, squaring his shoulders, "I want you to end this plan to open your own Les Bos."

"Nothing doing," Peter says, "You and your friend Chuck are a couple of bumbling fucking idiots. No one ever should have trusted their money with you."

The insults bounce right off Lars. "There is the principle of—"

"Don't talk to me about principles," Peter says, "There's no principle involved. You and Chuck fucked up your business and now it's open season on that idea. Let someone who knows what they're doing make money. Go fuck yourself."

Peter returns to his martini. Lars lays a hand on Peter's shoulder and tries to spin him around. However, he only causes Peter to spill his martini. Peter shoves Lars away and bounces to his feet.

"What the fuck are you doing?" Peter says

"I don't want this to get ugly," Lars says.

"Fuck you!" Peter says, nudging Lars with his chest, "You're paying for that drink!"

Lars takes a step back. "I don't think you understand what's going on here."

"No, I understand perfectly," Peter says, poking Lars in the chest with one of his stubby fingers, "I understand you're going to be wearing your ass for a hat."

"Hold on a second," Lars says, "I don't think this is necessary. I—"

"Kiss my ass!"

Lars keeps backing up. I join him. And Peter keeps coming. Whatever passes for Lars's tough guy routine is completely gone. The bartender tries to get their attention.

"Hey fellas," he says, "We can't have that in here!"

That isn't getting through to Peter. He makes a grab at Lars and narrowly misses. Lars jumps through the archway leading to the main room. Peter follows. I let him pass. (Hey, he's not after *me*.) By this time, the other fellas in the place are noticing the ruckus.

A guy in a sparkly vest asks: "What's going on, Peter?"

"This asshole is trying to muscle me," Peter growls.

Whispered conversations run through the surrounding tables. The music stops. The dancer stops. The stillness is making me nervous. Someone in the background speaks up.

"Kick his ass, Peter!"

Great. I don't know anything about Peter, but fighting is not Lars's specialty. Neither is running, come to think of it. Lars backs toward the stairs with Peter in hot pursuit. I'm a few steps behind them. The guests crane their necks to get a peek at the impending carnage. Lars trips over a chair and tumbles to the floor. He flips over and gets on all fours, trying to regain his feet. Peter takes the opportunity to boot Lars hard in the ass. Lars is thrown forward and disappears down the stairs.

Holy shit, he killed him.

Peter stares blankly at the stairs; stunned, no doubt, by the power of his own literal ass-kicking. There's a moment where he debates going after Lars. Then he walks back toward the bar, drawing applause from the other patrons.

I charge down the stairs. I don't see Lars right away, leading me to irrationally wonder if he was vaporized in the fall. When I get to the bottom of stairs, I find him crouched in the corner under an empty high-top. I crouch down next to him.

"Are you okay?"

He's glassy-eyed. "Oh, hello, Joe. What are you doing at the prom?"

I offer him my hand. "Can you get up?"

"I think so." Lars rolls out from under the table and allows me to help him to his feet. He feels around and checks the movement in his limbs. "Nothing broken. Everything moving as it should. I think I'm good to go."

I look up the stairs. "I'm amazed you didn't get hurt."

"It's like being in a car crash. You keep your body limp and go where gravity takes it. Minimizes the damage."

"Have you been in a lot of car crashes?"

"Enough to know," Lars says.

I'll defer to Lars on that one. I realize we're being watched by most of the patrons. (Guy comes tumbling down the stairs, it's going to draw attention.) We decide to get out of there and make our way out into the night. The chill hits us and a breeze comes off the rain-slicked streets. Lars shivers. He's skinny as a rail and not cut out for any temperature below *balmy*. Once he starts the car, he turns up the heat. We've just pulled away from the curb when my cell phone rings. It's Sergeant Pike. I answer, tentatively.

"Trump Accounting Services. You book 'em, we cook 'em. This is Junior speaking. How may I help you?"

As usual, Pike pushes past my attempt at humor. "Thought you might want to know, counselor: Lance Mack's apartment was just broken into."

Poor Lars. Gets his ass kicked and it isn't even the most noteworthy event of the evening.

CHAPTER ELEVEN

As I've pointed out, the key to any Swerve is logic. It must make sense. Maybe you can't see a Swerve coming, but when it's executed right and explained correctly, you wind up going, "How did I not see that coming?" The ideal Swerve will pick up on events that took place and clues that were dropped.

Let's take a heel turn for example. Babyface A is gunning for a title he lost. During a match against the Heel Champion, the champ pulls some shenanigans. Babyface A's friend, Babyface B, runs out to stop the cheating. But in the process, Babyface B gets Babyface A disqualified. Babyface A is disappointed but understands that Babyface B was just looking out for him. Then Babyface B gets a title shot. During the match, Babyface A comes down to ringside. Just when it looks like he's going to save Babyface B from the same shenanigans, Babyface A instead turns against Babyface B, costing him the title. Babyface A thus becomes Heel A.

But if the swerve is to play out in a sensible way, it has to be a slow burn. Heel A can't immediately become a drooling monster. He has to justify his actions and become a bit bitchy when no one seems to _understand him. He takes an attitude of_ Hey, why are you booing me and cheering this guy? Isn't he the one that cost me the title in the first place? _Heel A goes farther and farther in his attempts to get revenge on Babyface B. Remember, all of history's greatest villains, from Genghis Khan to Darth Vader to Dr. Roberts, my college history professor, thought they were in the right and completely justified in whatever heinous actions they might take. Being a heel is a slippery slope, but the fall has to be gradual._

I'm not sure if someone is trying to swerve us with the break-in at Lance Mack's but it certainly seems like the work of the villain behind all this. I wonder if they feel justified in doing it.

Lance Mack's former (temporary) abode is also in the Techwood Complex, just a few buildings over from where Bobby Cronus is housed. (Probably good that he and Mack were kept somewhat apart.) Pike is waiting outside when we get there. He looks like he was roused out of a light sleep, but then he always looks like that. He leads the way to Mack's apartment on the main floor. The door is open, and cops are milling about inside. One of them is a heavyset guy I recognize from previous experience. He fills the doorway as we arrive.

"These guys with you, Sergeant?" Officer Bukowski says.

"They are, Chuck," Pike says, "Let them in but keep an eye on them."

"Got it, Sergeant," Bukowski says. I half-expect him to throw Pike a salute.

Pike makes his way into the apartment. The place looks like a mirror of Cronus's: a living room with threadbare carpeting, a tiny kitchen, a hallway leading to a bedroom and bathroom. And like Cronus's place when it was broken into, it's been tossed thoroughly: couch cushions, foodstuffs, posters, all scattered about. Pike searches casually. He might be browsing magazines in a store for all anyone would know (and I firmly believe Pike still reads print magazines). I doubt anything escapes his notice. Lars leans toward me.

"Who do you think did this?" he asks.

"Could be anyone." I clear my throat, trying to get Bukowski's attention. "I was just wondering: who called in the break-in?"

Bukowski jerks a thumb toward the wall. "Next door neighbor. She got home from work and saw the door hanging open. Saw the place had been broken into and called us."

I thank Bukowski, though I doubt he cares. He's preoccupied with scratching the stubble on his jowls. My eyes scan the room. I take a few steps away from Lars. The police take little notice of me. (I assume the cops are like The Borg. As long as I'm not perceived as a threat, they ignore me.)

I look through the wreckage on the floor. There's a pile of papers and fast-food containers. (I'm betting the place wasn't neat even before it was tossed.) A scrap of paper gets my attention. It looks like it was torn from a flip notebook. Something is written on it. I bend over and hold my lower back, as if stretching it. The cops pay me no never mind. The scrap of paper has the words _Windham County_ written on it. Windham County. That sounds familiar. Pike comes out of the hallway.

"You want to take a look in back?" he asks.

"If you're cool with it," I say.

"I'm going with you," Pike says, "and don't touch anything."

I follow Pike to the bedroom. It's in a similar state of disarray. The bedclothes have been tossed on the floor. The drawers have been pulled out of the nightstand. The contents of the closet are scattered about the room. Give whoever broke in here credit. They did a thorough job.

"Has anything has been taken?" I ask.

"Not exactly," Pike says, running a hand along his jaw, "The TV is still here. So is the stereo system. Mack had a laptop and a cell phone, but those are in an evidence locker. Part of the investigation."

"This wasn't your garden variety break-in."

"No, it was not," Pike says, "Whoever did this was looking for something specific."

"You think they found it?"

"Your guess is as good as mine. They certainly weren't subtle about it."

I stroll around the room, trying to see what I can spot. Not easy, since I can't touch anything, and Pike has an eye on me. There's nothing of note, anyway. Just an assortment of crap. Mostly clothes and stuff. Something hanging in the closet catches my attention. It's Lance Mack's vest, the same one he wore the last night I saw him wrestling. It's covered in buttons and other things, just like I remember. But something is missing.

"There's a new sheriff in town," I say.

Pike steps over to me. "Find something?"

"This is Lance Mack's vest," I say, "He wore it to the ring. What's it doing here?"

"Hanging, from the look of it."

So glad I bring out the comedian in this miserable S.O.B. "It wasn't with his ring gear?"

"His ring gear wasn't at the arena. Just his street clothes."

That makes sense. The wrestling card in Mankato was in the afternoon. The party was at night. Mack would have come back here and dropped off his wrestling gear. I study the vest.

"Something's missing," I say.

"What's that?" Pike asks.

"It had a big badge," I say, "Mack would point to it and say, 'There's a new sheriff in town.' But it's not here."

"Maybe he lost it. Is it relevant to anything?"

"Probably not." I run a hand through my hair. "Maybe I'm just desperate to find something interesting."

"Other than a dead man's apartment being ransacked?"

"Yeah, other than that."

Pike leads the way out of the room. We rejoin Lars at the front door. Lars pointedly looks away from the police. I turn toward Pike.

"You'll keep me updated if you find anything?" I ask.

"No," he says.

"Ah. Then I'll just have to keep bashing away at this thing on my own? Maybe irritating the hell out of you?"

"Same old, same old," Pike says.

He steps past us and down the hall. Lars and I follow. Lars looks back as we stroll away from the apartment.

"Who could have done that?" he asks, "And why?"

"I'm not sure," I say, "Could be that whoever killed Lance is trying to cover something up. Could be another reason entirely. I'll know for sure when I know who the murderer is."

Lars receives that in silence. I don't think he has a lot of confidence in that proclamation. I don't take it personally. I don't have a lot of confidence it, either.

***

"Given the sheer number of broads who've broken up with me over the years," Mike says, pacing my living room, "you'd think it would be easy to get one to break up with me."

"Particularly when you call them *broads*," I say, staring at my computer screen.

Carol, sitting the breakfast bar, raises her hand. "You want me to give her pointers?"

Mike gives us both the stink face. His hair is disheveled, and his dress shirt hangs halfway out of his pants. Carol's mouth is tight. On the bright side, she's speaking to us again. Unfortunately, she's also glowering at me, still angry about my conversation with Rick. Meantime, Mike is stewing over his various relationships. This isn't how I saw happy hour going. Then again, I'm not the greatest of hosts. I'm at the desk, a beer in front of me, researching *Windham County*. Mike's pacing takes him back my direction.

"I've got to do something," he says, "Brigid kind of dropped a bomb on me today."

I spin around in my chair. "She's pregnant?"

Mike stops pacing. "No!"

Carol leans forward. "Is it a venereal disease?"

"No!"

"You're getting married?" I say.

"God, no," Mike says, "She wants to come to _WrestleShock_."

The _Oooh_ that runs through the room is unstated but palpable. Carol and I lean back, as if we want nothing to do with this. Mike sinks on to the arm of my futon. I scratch my cheek.

"I assume Ashley is still going to be at _WrestleShock_?" I ask.

"Of course she is, you fucking moron!" Mike says, "Ashley and I are supposed to go out after the matches. What am I going to do?"

Carol studies her reflection in the hall mirror. "I suppose being honest with them is off the table?"

"It's not even in the room," Mike says, "Not even in the same state." Mike wrings his hands. "I have to bide my time. Until Ashley gets called up to UWE and I can be her—"

"Hanger on?" I say.

"Private leech?" Carol asks.

"Personal manager," Mike says, drawing the words out, "Until then, I need the temp job."

My beer glass stops below my mouth. "You're going to be Ashley's personal manager?"

"She's going to need someone to look after her," Mike says, "And that someone is me."

"You're sure you're ready for that kind of commitment?" I say, turning back to the screen, "Or *any* kind of commitment?"

"Of course he is," Carol says, "If there's one thing Mike should be, it's committed."

Mike gives Carol a dirty look but says nothing. He decides to do some thinking, stalking down the hall to the bathroom. (Swell.) As soon as the bathroom door closes, Carol makes her way over to the corner.

"What are you doing?" she asks.

"Looking up Windham County," I say, "I found a mention of it on a scrap of paper in Lance Mack's place. I remember Nick Diamond used to live in Windham County. I'm just not sure why Lance Mack would have that information."

"And what have you found out?"

"That there's a hell of a lot of nothing in Windham County. As backwoods as you get."

Carol peers over my shoulder. "Population one-hundred-and-fifty. Right in the middle of North Carolina. That's got a *Deliverance* feel to it."

Mike returns from the restroom. Judging by the look on his face, he thinks we're still talking about *his* problems. He walks over to the futon and again sits on the arm.

"Anyhoo, you got any ideas about the stuff with Ashley and Brigid?" he asks.

"I do not," I say.

Mike slaps his thigh. I continue my research. Carol returns to the breakfast bar. After a few seconds, Mike peers over my shoulder.

"What are you looking into?" he asks.

"Your girlfriend," I say.

There's a slight pause. "That, uh, that covers a little bit of—"

"Ashley. And her dad. I noticed Ashley talking to Mack once, then Jack Blades mentioned she was talking to him the night of the murder. Has she ever told you what they might have been talking about?"

"Nope," Mike says, "I try not to bring it up. Kills the mood if you talk about dead guys."

I go back to my research, though I'm not getting far. Mike grabs another beer out of the fridge and returns to his seat on the arm of the futon. Carol spins on the stool to follow Mike.

"Did Ashley ever talk her growing up?" she asks, "Friends she might have had? Stuff she did. Anything like that?"

Mike looks up as he thinks. "Not a lot. She played volleyball in high school and college. Looked like she was a hell of a player."

I spin around in the chair. "Ashley mentioned a friend of hers once. When I talked to her at the Tav. You remember her name?"

"Tricia," Mike says, "Tricia Dumas. Ashley showed me her high school yearbook. Tricia's picture was in there. Cute girl."

"Did Ashley say anything about her?" I ask.

"Nope," Mike says, "She closed up the yearbook and put it away. End of conversation."

I punch Tricia Dumas's name into a search engine. I check the results then sit back in my desk chair. Mike perks up.

"You find something?" he asks.

"I did," I say, "I think I'm going to have to talk to Ashley about it."

Mike grabs my shoulder. "Why? What did you find?"

"Tricia Dumas is dead."

CHAPTER TWELVE

I've talked about how wrestlers lived an almost impossible lifestyle, particularly after wrestling became a national business. Beyond the toll it took on their families, there's the toll it took on them.

Once they were working for a national promotion, wrestlers' lives became an endless cycle of catching planes, picking up rental cars, getting to the hotel. Maybe a nap before the matches. Then you go back to the hotel to get some sleep and start over the next day. If you had time off, it was rare.

Sadly, this lifestyle contributed to drug and alcohol problems. Trouble staying awake? Grab some amphetamines. Trouble going to sleep? Pills and alcohol solve that. No time to workout? Steroids will maximize what you can do. In constant pain from throwing yourself on the mat? Pain pills cure that. It's a wonder any of them survived. Quite a few of them did not.

As far as I know, Ashley Diamond hasn't spent a lot of time on the road yet. But she's done her share of hard living and knows it isn't all that romantic.

As is the case with every other member of the Midwest Championship Wrestling roster, Ashley Diamond's apartment is in the Techwood Complex, not far from the arena. We park near the building and make our way to her apartment. Mike knocks on Ashley's door. She answers quickly, excited to see Mike. She's less excited to see me.

"Hi, Joe," she says, balancing awkwardly on one foot, "What are you doing here?"

I didn't really expect a hero's welcome. "I was hoping we could talk."

Ashley remains in the doorway, keeping the door mostly closed. "About what?"

"Tricia Dumas," I say.

The second the name comes out of my mouth, Ashley looks stricken. Her eyes widen, and her mouth drops open. "What about her?"

"I think you know," I say, "It's about what happened in Windham County."

There's a long moment where nobody says anything. Ashley opens the door wider and steps aside. "You should probably come in," she says.

I ignore the Death Glare 2000 that Mike is giving me and make my way into the apartment. Unlike Cronus or Mack, Ashley has taken the time to decorate her place. Plants line the windows. Framed posters of Taylor Swift and Harry Styles adorn the walls. She's even got a few magazines on the coffee table. (And who the hell reads those anymore?) I assume she and Mike spend most of their time here, since one look at the *No Farting* poster in Mike's apartment might cause her to rethink the relationship. Ashley and I sit on either end of the sofa while Mike hovers nearby. Ashley picks up a bottle of water from the coffee table.

"What do you want to know about Trish?" she asks.

"I found something going through Lance Mack's stuff," I say, "A reference to Windham County. I did the research from there. I know Tricia Dumas is dead. I know you were talking with Lance Mack. That you were upset. And I'm guessing Lance had information you didn't want getting out."

The air seems to go out of Ashley. A vacant look comes into her eyes. Mike sits next to her, perched on the arm of the sofa. When Ashley finally speaks, her voice is quiet.

"Even after Lance is gone," she says, "he's still harassing me."

"What was going on?" I ask.

Ashley leans back on the couch. Mike puts a hand on her shoulder. She slips her hand over his without looking at him.

"Tricia was my best friend," she says, her voice small, "Back in high school. We'd hang out all the time. We were on the volleyball team together. We'd spend nights at each other's house. Double date. That sort of thing." She takes a breath. "And we'd get wasted together. One night, we went out for a drive. Wasted. We used one of my dad's cars. A Ferrari." Her eyes well up. "It went so fucking fast. We just wanted to have a good time."

"Who was driving?" I ask.

"I was," Ashley says, "Tricia was a little scared, but we had the top down, and it was a beautiful night and I felt like going fast." A breath. "I wasn't in control."

"And there was a crash," I say.

Ashley stares at the wall. "Tricia wasn't wearing her seatbelt. I was. Don't ask me why I thought to do it, but I did. It's why I lived."

"And she didn't," I say.

There's no response to that. Tears spill on to Ashley's shirt. Mike puts an arm around her. I fight off the feeling I'm a shit-heel for dredging all this up. Ashley wipes the tears away.

"I don't remember a lot of it," she says, "It was a blur and then I woke in the hospital. My dad was there. He said he'd take care of everything." A wheezy breath in. "And he did."

My mind works quickly. Nick Diamond said he'd take care of things. His daughter was in an accident that left a friend dead. Ashley, as far as I know, never spent a minute in jail, though she confessed right here to driving recklessly and under the influence. How did Nick Diamond manage to take care of things? Rural county. Money. One good possibility.

"The sheriff," I say.

"Dad knew him," Ashley says, "They made it look like Trish's fault." She cradles her head. "I felt so bad for Trish's parents. For everything. But…I let it happen."

I lean back on the sofa, fidgeting. This whole thing gives me a sick feeling. Tricia Dumas's parents must have suffered her death, but they suffered it thinking their daughter was responsible and Ashley Diamond was lucky to be alive.

"How did Lance Mack find out about it?" I ask.

"He didn't tell me," Ashley says, "But he was going to use it to ruin my career. Unless…he got something from me."

"What was that?" I say.

Her face reddens. "He wanted…me."

Son of a bitch. Mike and I weren't fans of Lance Mack to begin with. This bit of info certainly isn't going to change that, particularly on Mike's end. I lean toward Ashley.

"And, uh…did you?" I ask.

"No," Ashley says, shaking her head, "I couldn't."

"Take me through it."

Ashley slides out from under Mike's arm. "Lance told me what he knew. And what he wanted. That was before the party. He gave me time to think about it. When I got to the party, he pulled me aside and told me that he wanted me that night. I had to make up my mind. Either we got together that night or he'd release the information the next day."

Mike clenches his fist. "What a guy."

"I didn't have a choice," Ashley says, "If that stuff got out, it was going to end my career. The UWE would never hire me. I would let my dad down." Her throat catches. "I would let Shane down."

I try to keep my equilibrium. "How was it supposed to work?"

"We were going to meet in the heels' dressing room," Ashley says, "His idea. I don't know why. He said we wouldn't be disturbed. We went about our business at the party. When the time came, I met him in the heels' dressing room."

"What happened?" I ask, wishing I didn't have to.

"We…fooled around a little," Ashley says, "He was acting weird. Kind of spacey."

Pike said there were roofies in Mack's system. That might explain his being spacey. I move delicately toward the next question.

"And did, um…"

"I couldn't do it," Ashley says, "Not even to spare my dad or Shane. I broke it off and got out of there. I walked out of the building and went home."

"And that was it?" I ask.

"That was it," Ashley says.

"Did anyone see you leave?"

"Not that I know of," Ashley says.

"And no one else knew about this?"

"No," Ashley says, "I talked to Jack Blades a little. I thought about telling him, but I just couldn't. Maybe he knew something was wrong, but I don't know." She wipes her eyes. "I went out looking for my dad. I don't know. I just needed to talk to him. I couldn't find him."

"What time did you leave the arena?" I ask.

"I honestly don't know," Ashley says, "I was just so freaked out."

"But it was later than 12:15, wasn't it?"

"Yeah, it was."

Things lapse into silence. I don't have a lot left to ask her, other than *You sure you don't want to confess? It would really make my job easier.* (And I already know how she'd answer that question.) I get up from the couch.

"Thank you for talking with me," I say.

Ashley's eyes are still glistening. "Are you going to write about this?"

Good question. My first thought is that I'll only write about it if Ashley is the murderer. Shockingly, I don't think that's going to be of any comfort to her. I hesitate.

"I don't think so," I say, "It was just some information I came across and I had to follow up on it. I don't see any reason to write about it."

Ashley looks shocked. Her opinion of the press (or the ancillary press like me) must not be high. She grabs my hand and says, "Thank you."

We stand there, awkwardly. I look at Mike, who indicates he's going to stick around. I pat Ashley's hand and gently disengage from her. I walk to the door. Ashley's voice stops me.

"You're not going to tell my dad, are you?" she asks.

If Nick Diamond knew that Lance Mack was blackmailing his daughter, he's got a surefire motive. But how do I ask him that? If he *didn't* know about the blackmail, there's no way to ask him without giving it away. I turn back toward Ashley.

"I doubt it," I say.

She exhales, relieved. I leave. I'd love to tell Ashley that I won't, under any circumstances, tell her father about what Mack did. Unless, of course, he's the one who killed Lance Mack.

Nick Diamond isn't above the law. No matter what he thinks.

***

Once upon a time, watching wrestling was a ritual in my house. When I first moved to the Cities and didn't know anybody and was dirt poor, that ritual was about the only thing that got me through the week. The UWE was good in those days and their show aired every Saturday night. I'd set aside a little money (spare change mostly) and save up for dinner. Come Saturday night, I'd run over to Fong's (best Chinese restaurant in the city), pick up some Orange Peel Beef and eggrolls and haul them back to my tiny studio apartment to watch wrestling. I don't look back on that period of life with a lot of fondness, given the lack of friends or money, but I *do* fondly remember those Saturday nights.

So, it feels strange to not be excited about watching wrestling on TV. Even when my friends are gathering at my place.

It's Wednesday night. Mike, Carol, and Lars are over. We've got a feast from Fong's and are preparing to watch *Midwest Championship Wrestling.* The actual show was taped last night and will be airing tonight. This is what is termed the *go-home* show, the last TV right before a big event. Even though Mike, Lars, and I were at the taping last night, we're curious to see what it looks like on TV.

Carol is at the breakfast bar, helping me open various to-go containers. Mike sits at the bar, nursing a beer and letting us do the work.

"Gotta admit," Mike says, "It's kind of hard to see Nick Diamond as a babyface now."

"On the bright side," I say, "it's really easy to think of Lance Mack as a douchebag."

Carol frowns but doesn't say anything. Just when she was starting to become a wrestling fan, she hears about Lance Mack blackmailing Ashley, years after her father covered up a fatal car accident that was Ashley's responsibility. It's put a damper on her enthusiasm.

"You haven't talked to Nick Diamond about this?" she asks.

"Not yet," I say, "I tried to talk to him after the matches last night, but he had taken off."

Carol takes a pair of tongs and begins setting the eggrolls on a platter. Mike reaches for one, but Carol bops his hand with the tongs. He holds his hand.

"You think Nick Diamond might be the murderer?" he asks.

"No idea," I say, opening a container of jasmine rice and dumping it into a large serving bowl, "He certainly has the motive. Assuming he knew Mack was blackmailing Ashley."

Mike steps away from the breakfast bar and plops down on the couch. Lars bursts in the front door, wearing a black bowling shirt and gray slacks; a far cry from the purple suit we'll be seeing on TV shortly. The cats, lounging on the shelf over the radiator, give him a brief look before going back to their all-important snoozing. Lars swings over to the breakfast bar and tosses a piece of paper down.

"I don't see how I can stop him," he says, as if this is what we've been talking about the whole time.

"Stop who doing what?" I ask.

"Peter," he says, tapping the paper, "and the club."

Carol and I look over the paper. It's a flyer for the grand opening of Les Bos. I'll be honest: with the blue and white color scheme and the color photography, it's a classy piece of work. But that won't bring Lars any comfort. I hand the thing back to him.

"Sorry about that, man," I say.

Lars aggressively shoves the flyer into his back pocket. "It's an outrage. I don't know how Peter thinks he's going to get away with this."

"Free and clear from the look of it," Carol says.

Lars ignores her. "I'm not giving up yet. Yes, it looks dark right now. But it's always darkest before the dawn."

"Anything dawning on you?" I ask.

"Not at the moment, no," Lars says, "But it will. Believe me."

I let him have that delusion. Carol stays silent. Mike gets off the futon and joins us at the breakfast bar.

"If you need me for any kind of demolition work, let me know," Mike says, "Meantime, the show is about to start."

I put some cream cheese wontons on the appetizer platter. Carol puts the kung pao chicken into another large bowl. Mike and Lars do nothing (which, to be fair, is their specialty). I slide four white square plates, some cutlery, and a handful of napkins into position. (Only Carol is adept with chopsticks.)

"Soup's on," I say.

We all dish up hastily. By the time the opening credits are over and Gordon Russell has done his introduction, Mike and Lars are parked on the futon, Carol is in the comfy chair, and I've placed the straight back chair next to the futon. On the screen, Bobby Cronus is cutting a promo about Nick Diamond and his new tag team partner, Purple Suit.

"Skinny dork!" Lars says from the futon, taking offense at one of Cronus's insults. Then he looks down and says, "Oh yes. Skinny."

The rest of us would agree more with the *dork* part of that assessment, but we don't bring it up. Cronus goes on, saying he's going to fire Purple Suit. Purple Suit himself comes to the ring to confront Cronus. Before he can do that, Jack Blades shows up. Then Nick Diamond runs out. It's a Mexican standoff of sorts. Diamond gets on the mic.

"Hey, Bobby, Bobby, Bobby, calm down," Diamond says, "Why don't we add a little juice for Friday at *WrestleShock?* We put in a stipulation. If you and Jackie boy over there win, then Purple Suit here is fired and I will leave Midwest Championship Wrestling." The crowd howls its opposition. Diamond holds up a hand, asking for quiet. "But if *we* win, Purple Suit keeps his job and you, Bobby Cronus, step down as general manager."

The crowd cheers. Cronus looks around, goaded by the cheers and the smug look on Nick Diamond's face. He stabs a finger at Purple Suit.

"You think I'm afraid of that little nitwit?" he says, "Fine, Nick, have it your way. You want that stipulation? You got it!" Again, the crowd roars. Cronus holds up his hand for quiet and surprisingly gets it. "But I think your boy needs a little warm up. I'm going to do him a favor and give him a chance. Tonight, he's going to wrestle Jack Blades in the main event!"

The crowd isn't into this idea. But Purple Suit grabs the mic from Nick Diamond.

"That's fine," Purple Suit says, "I'm not afraid of Jack Blades and I'm not afraid of you. Bring it on!"

I'm impressed. Purple Suit threw some gravel into his voice. Cronus sticks out his jaw, looking not unlike a toddler about to throw a tantrum, and slaps Purple Suit across the face.

The cheers die down. Purple Suit bends over, holding his mouth.

"Nice selling," Mike says.

"It comes naturally to me," Lars says, taking a triumphant bite of his cream cheese wonton. Then he adds, with his mouth full, "Especially when you get potatoed."

"Potatoed?" Carol asks, "What's that?"

I jump in. "A potato is a punch or a kick that lands with full force. Sometimes accidentally. Sometimes not."

Carol swings her head Lars's direction. "He hit you for real?"

"It was payback for me potatoing him last Friday," Lars says, "It was a…what did he call it?"

"A receipt?" Mike says.

"That's it!" Lars says, spitting out a few wonton crumbs, "Hurt like hell. But it was great."

On screen, Purple Suit throws a slap of his own, one that takes Cronus completely off his feet. The crowd again goes wild.

"Nice hit," I say.

"I can thank Mr. Cronus for that," Lars says, "He inspired me to put some real *oomph* into my return slap. And boy, can Bobby Cronus take a bump. He even started bleeding from the nose and broke his glasses." He stops to think. "That might not have been planned."

"You may have another receipt coming," Mike says.

There's a commercial break. I try to get Mike and Lars to use their coasters. (My success is…indifferent.) Then the show returns, and the action starts up again. Ashley has a match against some no-name woman (a jobber, or as the modern lingo prefers it, enhancement talent). She puts the no-name woman away in short order and stays in the ring for a promo.

"Vanessa," Ashley says, "Looks like you had your fun, cutting my hair. Cutting Sienna's hair. Well, you're going to pay for that, honey. Why don't we up the stakes for Friday? Not only will our match be for the Midwest Women's Championship. Why don't we make it a hair-vs-hair match?"

Judging by the crowd reaction, they're into it. By way of answer, Vanessa appears in the ring and hits Ashley from behind with a forearm. Ashley drops to the mat. Vanessa pulls a pair of scissors from her coat and prepares to cut more of Ashley's hair. However, Ashley spins around and clotheslines Vanessa. The scissors go flying. Ashley picks them up and brandishes them for the audience. Vanessa scurries under the bottom rope and grabs the mic.

"That's fine, Ashley Diamond!" Vanessa says, "If you want hair-vs-hair, let's do it!" The crowd roars. Vanessa pushes right past it. "And after Friday night at _WrestleShock_, your pretty little head is going to be completely bald!"

Vanessa throws down the mic and stalks off. Ashley pumps her fists and drinks in the crowd's adulation. That takes us to commercial. Carol slides forward in the comfy chair and looks over at Mike.

"Ashley isn't really going to get her head shaved, is she?" Carol asks.

Mike stirs, uncomfortably. "I don't know. Ashley told me about the hair-vs-hair match, but she won't tell me what the finish will be." He looks over at Lars. "You don't know what the finish will be, do you?"

"They haven't told me the finish of *my* match," Lars says, "Sorry."

That sends Mike into a pout. "This could be a problem. Ashley is great and all, but I can't be getting it on with Mr. Clean."

The show returns. There are promos (all hyping *WrestleShock*) and a meat-and-potatoes tag team match. There's a shot of Frankie and Fabio in the crowd. Lars pats the arm of the futon.

"Frankie and Fabio are looking forward to Friday night," he says, "So are their parents."

I stop chewing my eggroll. "Their parents? Why are their parents looking forward to Friday night?"

"They're coming to *WrestleShock*," Lars says, as if it should be obvious. (And it is. I just didn't want it to be true.)

"Fabio and Frankie have been thrilled by the action, and they think their parents would dig it as well."

I don't know what's worse: the sheer nightmare fuel provided by our potential investors taking in a professional wrestling show or the way Lars is so serenely unconcerned about it. Either way, I'm certain it will kill our nascent film deal.

"You're going to talk them out of this, right?" I say.

"Why would I?" Lars says, "It's going to be a hell of a show. Frankie and Fabio know their parents well. I assume. What's to worry about?"

Plenty. Knowing their parents would require the kind of awareness—self or otherwise—that has not been evident in Fabio's and Frankie's behavior to date. (Similarly, awareness is not Lars's strong suit.)

"If the parents show up at *WrestleShock*, they're not going to let us have any money to make the movie," I say, "In fact, they might demand to take what little we already have."

Lars dismisses my concerns. "You worry too much, Joe. You just have to trust that everything will work out as it should."

"I don't like doing that," I say, "I'm a control freak. That's why I'm a writer."

I can't carry this conversation any further. It's impossible to talk Lars out of something once he's convinced he's right. On top of that, the main event is about to start. We go back to the wrestling while I try to tamp down my feeling of doom.

Jack Blades comes to the ring first, wearing the usual vest and cowboy hat. He threatens a few ringside fans then climbs in the ring. He stalks past Bobby Cronus, who is doing the ring announcing, and climbs the turnbuckles in one corner of the ring. Cronus gives him the usual florid introduction. Something about Blades' attire hits me, just as it did last night. But I can't put my finger on it.

Love Gun by Rick James kicks in and out comes our babyface. Purple Suit is dressed in black tights, a purple t-shirt, kneepads, elbow pads and tennis shoes. He doesn't exactly look athletic, but he looks *exactly* like a ring announcer competing in a wrestling match. The crowd goes wild. He gets to ringside, puts on a white headband and a mouthguard, and rolls under the bottom rope. He gets up on one of the turnbuckles and strikes a pose. It best resembles The Thinker sitting on the crapper, but the crowd eats it up. He drops back to the ring and turns to face Jack Blades. Bobby Cronus finds all this very amusing.

"Who in the hell do you think you are?" he asks, nearly doubled over with laughter.

Purple Suit takes the mic from him. "Who do I think I am? I think I'm the next guy to bust you right between the eyes."

He rears back and slugs Cronus in the face. Cronus takes a huge bump. The fans go wild. Jack Blades tries to get at Purple Suit. The referee keeps him back. Cronus rolls out of the ring, holding his mouth. Gordon Russell is on commentary, trying to sum up the situation.

"The fans are happy Purple Suit got a shot in on Bobby Cronus," he says, "But once the bell rings, I'm afraid this is going to be a bludgeoning. Nothing more than a bludgeoning."

Blades tries to push past the referee. Purple Suit stands in the corner, trying to look determined (though he looks more terrified than anything). Then *Pomp and Circumstance* kicks in. The crowd explodes. Nick Diamond marches to the ring and grabs the mic from Cronus.

"If you don't mind, Bobby," Diamond says, "I'm going to hang around and keep an eye on my tag team partner."

Blades shouts at Diamond, who shouts right back. The referee struggles to keep them separated. Purple Suit and Cronus jaw as well. The referee finally gets control of the situation, ordering Cronus and Diamond out of the ring and Purple Suit and Blades to their separate corners. That done, he orders the bell to be rung and the match to start.

Blades comes right at Purple Suit, who ducks out of the way and dances around the ring. Blades turns to go after him. Before he can get anywhere, Diamond reaches into the ring and trips Blades. Then Diamond backs away as if to say

Hey, I didn't do anything. Purple Suit hits Blades from behind with a flying knee, knocking him out of the ring. The referee admonishes Purple Suit. While he's doing that, Diamond throws Blades into a ring post. Blades is busted open and dazed. It's an even match.

Not that it does Purple Suit a lot of good. He throws some punches and kicks, but they don't do any damage. Blades hits Purple Suit with a clothesline. Purple Suit rolls around on the mat. The referee asks him if he wants to quit. Blades throws himself into the ring ropes. Diamond clubs Blades in the back. Blades goes down. Purple Suit tries for a pin. Blades kicks out at two. Purple Suit throws himself into the ropes. Cronus trips him. Diamond chases Cronus around ringside. The fans cheer him on. Blades reaches out of the ring, trying to get to Diamond. Purple Suit grabs Blades and tries to roll him up. Blades kicks out before the ref can even start the count. Purple Suit tries a clothesline but misses. Blades hits Purple Suit with a clothesline of his own, then goes for the cover and gets the three count.

"Ah, that's a bummer," Carol says, watching the TV, "I'm sorry, Lars."

"That's okay," Lars says, with a flip of his hand, "I put up a good fight."

Bobby Cronus slides into the ring. Nick Diamond is still in pursuit. Cronus runs past Blades. As Diamond tries to pass, Blades hits him with a cheap shot. Now, both Purple Suit and Nick Diamond are laid out.

"This doesn't look good," Carol says.

Blades and Cronus go to work on the babyfaces. Cronus uses the golf club on Purple Suit. Blades grabs his branding iron and starts in on Diamond. Of course, Diamond comes up bleeding. Surprisingly, so does Lars. Mike shoots a look at him.

"You learned how to blade?" Mike asks.

Lars waves a hand toward the TV. "As you see."

I look to Lars. "You guys did it hard way, didn't you?"

That takes some of the superiority out of Lars. "Yeah, Mr. Cronus handled it."

Carol tilts her head to one side. "Hard way?"

"It means Lars didn't have to cut himself," Mike says, "Bobby Cronus was nice enough to bust him open."

"You're kidding," Carol says, recoiling slightly.

"The proof is onscreen," I say.

On said screen, Blades has torn off Diamond's polo shirt and is beating him over the back with his branding iron. Cronus chokes Purple Suit with his golf club. Cups and cans, some of them half-full, are tossed in the ring. Those are the images we're left with when the show goes off the air.

"Looks like the start of a riot," Carol says, setting aside her food.

"It damn near was," I say, "We were lucky Cronus and Blades cleared out when they did. They might have had to call a SWAT team."

"But that's how you do it," Mike says, slugging his beer, "You build up heat for the heels before the big show. Then anyone who might still be on the fence will line up to get tickets."

We finish our dinners in silence. Carol and I collect the plates and put them in the dishwasher. (Here we are again: parents to these idiot man-children.) Carol rinses off the dishes and carefully hands them to me while I do the loading (glassware on top, plates on the bottom; I have a system). She studies me for a moment.

"You're worried about this thing, huh?" she asks.

"I am," I say, "I'm getting information, but nothing that's right on…the…"

I stop what I'm doing. An answer to a thing that's been bothering me has started to dawn. Carol seems worried I'm going to drop a plate.

"Joe?" she asks, "Joe, are you okay?"

"Fantastic," I say. I snap out of it and put the dish in the dishwasher. I hustle out of the kitchen and into the living room. "We DVR'ed the show, didn't we?"

"It looks like it, yes," Lars says.

"Bring up the main event," I say.

He looks confused but does the honors anyway. We get to the part where Jack Blades is coming to the ring. He gets up into a cameraman's face. The shot gives me a good view of the vest he's wearing.

"Pause it!" I say.

Lars does as he's told. I walk over to the screen and study the image. I stab the screen with my forefinger, aiming at a spot on Blades' vest.

"That badge," I say, "That belonged to Lance Mack."

Mike and Lars close in on the screen. Carol comes from the kitchen and does the same. I'm pointing at a big, garish badge, the one Mack would point to and say, *There's a new sheriff in town.*

"You sure it's the same one?" Mike asks.

"Positive," I say, "It was missing from Mack's vest and now it's on Jack Blades' vest. Hell of a coincidence, don't you think?"

The meaning of it sinks into everybody. Blades broke into Lance Mack's apartment. He also had a longstanding grudge against Mack. What else has he been doing? I turn off the TV.

"I need to chat with Jack Blades," I say, looking toward Lars, "You think you can set something up?"

Lars scratches his face. "Maybe. I'll have to talk to Mr. Cronus. Now that I'm an active wrestler, there's kayfabe to consider."

Oh, dear Lord. Lars is no more an active wrestler than my brother Owen and I were when we'd play-wrestle in the living room. (In fact, Bobby Cronus would probably think Owen and I were better. We figured out how to do combat without hurting each other.) But appealing to reason isn't going to get me anywhere with Lars.

"When are you going to see Cronus next?" I ask.

"Tonight," Lars says, "A training session at the Sportatorium. Just the two of us."

I gesture toward the remains of the meal. "You have a training session with Bobby Cronus, and you just ate a huge meal?"

Lars seems nonplussed. "I need to keep up my strength. I don't know if you're aware of this but wrestling takes a lot out of you." He punctuates this with a belch.

I clench my fists. I'm reaching the end of my tether with Lars lecturing me about something I've loved all my life. But I need his help, so I'll omit my concerns about his training to Bobby Cronus.

"What time do you have this training session?" I ask.

"In about a half-hour," Lars says.

"I'm coming with you," I say.

Mike raises his hand. "So am I."

"No can do, brother," Lars says, "And brother. You guys can't see me working out. There's—"

I hold up a hand, stopping him. "Lars, I swear if you *kayfabe* me one more time, I'm pounding you through the floor and into to your own apartment."

He holds up his hands. "Okay, brother. No need for the hostility. I'm a pacifist, remember?"

Right. Perfect for the wrestling business. "I'm just going to talk with Bobby Cronus," I say, "Then we'll leave the two of you to your training. Does that sound good?"

Lars puts a finger to his chin as he thinks. "That sounds proper. As long as we make it clear to Mr. Cronus that this was your idea. After all, I'm going to be in the ring with him. I don't want him to get angry with me and take liberties."

Yeah, I wouldn't want that to happen. I might enjoy the hell out of it.

***

By the time we reach the Sportatorium, the rain has stopped falling. Wet streets reflect the streetlights. Lars, Mike and I wait in the car. Yes, Lars has a key, but it feels better to let Bobby Cronus lead the way in. The wait is not long, though. Cronus's car pulls up in front of the Sportatorium. Lars, Mike, and I dash across the street. As could be expected, Cronus looks askance at the presence of me and Mike.

"I thought you knew to come alone," Cronus says, looking at Lars and not me.

Lars, always overestimating his persuasive powers, holds a hand up. "It's all good, Mr. Cronus."

Cronus cuts him off. "Oh, it is? Tell me how."

That brings Lars up short. "You see, my friends here needed, um, needed to talk with you—Joe, in particular—and I didn't really see that I was in a position to…y'know, to stop them, really, so…"

Cronus rolls his eyes, exasperated. This has gone south quickly. I feel more out of place than at any time since my sophomore year of high school. Mike hangs back, hands in the pockets of his leather jacket. The chill in the air is growing considerably.

So, the alarm in the arena going off seems like a good thing.

As soon as it sounds, everyone recoils. Even outside the arena, the thing is audible and loud. It's got to be earsplitting inside. Cronus runs toward the building.

"Someone's using one of the side doors," he says.

"Where are they?" I ask.

"There's two," Cronus says, going in the front door, "One by each dressing room."

We run through the lobby and into the arena. Cronus sprints toward the heels' dressing room. I push Lars to follow him. Mike and I run toward the faces' dressing room. I stop for a second, wondering what to do. The intruder is either in the dressing room or leaving by the side door. Mike pushes past me and into the dressing room. He pops back out a second later.

"Empty," he says.

We run down the hall to the side door. I push through the heavy door and find myself in the parking lot. There are only a few cars in the lot. Beyond the lot is a copse of trees screening the arena from the neighborhood around it. Someone is running for the trees. He wears a dark jacket, pants, and cap. I run after him. It's hard to get a good look at the guy. If not for the streetlights bleeding into the parking lot, I probably wouldn't see him at all. I'm gaining fast. Question, of course, is what am I going to do? It's like a dog chasing a car. Not catching the car is a problem. Catching it is a bigger one.

The guy disappears into the trees. The ground is wet. I'm a fast runner, but I get leery on unsure footing. The guy runs across a lawn, heading for a nearby church. I plunge into the trees. Wet branches slap at my arms and head. It's like running through a car wash. I come out with a minimum of damage. The guy doesn't have a big lead on me. The lawn dips slightly then curls up toward the church. The guy is trying to climb but isn't making a hell of a lot of progress. I hit the hill. The guy is big. A little taller than me and much thicker. He's nearly to the top of the hill. I dive at the guy's legs, scoring a direct hit. He crumples nicely, going face first into the wet grass. For a guy who never played tackle football, I do all right.

Once I've got the guy down, though, he doesn't have the decency to surrender. He flips on his back and swings an open hand slap, cuffing me on the side of the head. My ear is ringing. I roll away, holding my head. The guy gets to his feet. Then somebody else tackles him.

I recognize the skinny arms and the quasi-pompadour. Lars throws punches but doesn't appear to be doing any damage. I join in the attack. There's a lot of flailing and shouting. No one lands anything. It's the Ali-Frazier of Kindergarten Slap Fights. Suddenly, the guy jackknifes and lets out a shout.

"Motherfucker!" he says, "You got me in the fucking nuts!"

Lars gets to his feet. He shakes a finger at the guy. "Let that be a lesson to you."

I get a clear view of the guy's face. My breath nearly seizes up.

"Nick Diamond," I say, "Fancy meeting you here."

CHAPTER THIRTEEN

The goal of any heel worth his or her salt is to get what is called heat. *Heat is that anger and disdain the audience pours out on a bad guy. Ideally, the better the heel, the more heat they can get. While it may not sound appealing to have large groups of people spitting on you and openly hoping for your death and/or (but preferably* and*) dismemberment, it's the best thing that can happen to any heel. The more heat, the further up the card you go. The further up the card you go, the more money you make. Garnering heat is a good thing.*

At the same time, there are varieties of heat. Real heat means the audience is invested in the heel, even if that investment best resembles an urge to maim. Go-home heat means they don't even want to see this SOB on their TV screen or in their arena. Certain clueless bookers will confuse the latter with the former. Boos don't necessarily mean the audience is invested. It could just as easily mean, "Screw it. I don't want to see this mother-humper. I'm going to the can." A clueless booker will only see the difference when there aren't as many people watching their product anymore.

Nick Diamond has experienced plenty of heat in his career, most of it *real heat*. Right now, though, he's got *go-home heat* with me.

Once Diamond's been outed, so to speak, the fight goes out of him. He lets us lead him back to the arena, not saying a word as we go. When we get there, Bobby Cronus has turned off the alarm and the arena is quiet. Cronus's jaw drops when he sees Nick Diamond.

"What the fuck is this?" Cronus asks.

"This is who set off the alarm," I tell him.

Cronus looks at Diamond. "You're fucking with me. What the fuck is going on, Nick?"

"I'm sorry, Bobby," Diamond says, his voice barely above a whisper, "I forgot about the damn alarm. It started beeping and I couldn't shut it down."

"Only me and Gordon have the code," Cronus says, "And he always forgets to turn the damn thing on. It's usually my job." He looks toward Diamond. "What were you going to do?"

Diamond doesn't answer. Cronus seems to think I'm supposed to have the answers. I fold my arms.

"Bobby, you should probably call the police," I say.

Diamond snaps a look at me. Mike and Lars are stunned. Cronus bobs his head, unsure. This is not a popular idea.

"I don't want to get anyone in trouble," Cronus says.

"Mr. Diamond was trying to break into the building," I say, "He's trying to *create* trouble. That's worth calling the cops about."

Diamond's eyes are hollow. "I'm not trying to create the trouble."

"Then what *were* you trying to do?" I ask.

That's met with silence. Cronus won't make eye contact with me. I'm on my own. I take my cell phone out of my pocket and start dialing. Diamond reaches toward me.

"Whoa, whoa, whoa," Diamond says, "What are you doing?"

"I'm dialing the police," I say.

Diamond throws his hand over the face of my phone. (Glad he did it quickly. It's not easy to run a bluff when there are only three digits to dial.)

"I didn't do anything wrong," Diamond says, "What are you going to tell the cops? That I broke into a place I work?"

"That you set off the security alarm and started running," I say, "I'm sure they'll be interested in that. Unless you can give me a decent explanation."

Diamond hangs his head. "I was breaking in to…plant some stuff."

"What stuff?" I ask.

"Evidence," Diamond says, "Evidence against Bobby."

Cronus throws his arms out. "Evidence against me? Why the fuck would you do that?"

"To protect Ashley," Diamond says, quietly, "I want this whole investigation shut down and I thought the best way to do it was to…prove that Bobby's guilty."

"What the blue fuck?" Cronus says.

If I didn't know better—and I don't—I'd think Cronus was going to take a swing at Diamond. Instead, he stalks away. Diamond's hair falls forward, revealing his bald spot. If Ashley is involved, this conversation is going to get uncomfortable. We shouldn't have it in front of the others. I step toward the office.

"Why don't we go in there?" I say.

Diamond and I step into the office, and I close the door behind us. Diamond sinks into the chair behind the desk. I lean against the wall. We're quiet. I break the silence.

"*Is* Ashley guilty?" I ask.

Diamond snaps me a look then looks down again. "I don't know. Lance Mack was bad news. Kept asking her why she got sober. Like it was a dumb idea. She told him she didn't want to get drunk and she wasn't interested in him. End of story." He draws a breath in through his nose. "At least, it should have been."

"What do you mean?"

"I think he…might have known something," Diamond says.

"About Windham County?"

Diamond's eyes widen. "What do _you_ know about that?"

"I know a friend of Ashley's was killed in a car accident. I know Ashley was behind the wheel and she was drunk. I know you and the sheriff covered it up."

"Son of a bitch," Diamond says, as much to himself as anybody, "How did you find all this out?"

"I found something in Lance Mack's apartment. It mentioned Windham County. Then I did a little digging. Then I asked Ashley. She told me everything."

Diamond lightly slaps his hand against his thigh. "Mack _did_ know about it?"

I'm thrown by the question. "He did. He was blackmailing Ashley with it."

"Motherfucker!" Diamond says, clenching both fists, "I knew that slimy piece of shit was up to something. How the hell did he know? How did he find out?"

"I don't know," I say, "But that's what he was using against Ashley." I focus on Diamond. "You really had no idea?"

"I knew something was up. But every time I asked Ashley about it, she told me not to worry. I didn't ask Mack. The prick would only lie to me."

Huh. If Diamond is a suspect, it largely depends on his knowing that Mack was blackmailing Ashley. He certainly suspected it. Of course, he could be lying to me. The only way to test it is to tell him what I know and check his reaction.

"Ashley had a meeting set up with Mack," I say, "The night he was killed. He, uh, he wanted something from her."

Thankfully, Diamond doesn't make me expound on that. The office is silent. Diamond is barely audible. "Motherfucker."

"It didn't happen," I say, "Ashley says she left and went home. That was that."

Diamond's body sags. "Thank God."

"You were afraid Ashley killed Lance Mack. So you were trying to frame Bobby Cronus and shut down the investigation."

"That's right."

"What made you think Ashley might have done it?" I ask.

"Something was bothering her," Diamond says, "She wouldn't tell me what it was. Then Mack turns up dead." He throws up his hands. "It's probably fucking stupid, but your mind goes to the worst-case scenario."

"You didn't see Ashley before you left?" I ask, "The night of the murder?"

"No," he says, "I tried talking to her, but I didn't get anywhere. I should have tried harder." He lets a long sigh. "Story of my life. Everyplace but in the fucking ring." He pinches the bridge of his nose. "I'm not proud of trying to frame Bobby. He's a good guy. Bad temper, but fuck, I've seen way worse. I was desperate. I figured if the police were ninety-nine percent sure Bobby did it, maybe I could push them that last little bit. Save Ashley."

It dawns on me. "You broke into Cronus's apartment? You planted the drug paraphernalia?"

"Yeah, that was me," Diamond says, "I thought it best to keep Bobby out of the way. Get him arrested for possession of paraphernalia. Then I'd be free to…set stuff other up."

"And you broke into my apartment and attacked me. Tried to get me drop the investigation."

Diamond's eyes get wide. "No! No, I didn't do that. I don't even know where the fuck you live."

Snake eyes on that. Assuming I can believe him. And I'm taking a leap there. I'm not sure I can even buy the story about framing Cronus to protect Ashley. Maybe he killed Mack to protect Ashley and is framing Cronus to protect himself. I look toward the lobby.

"You broke in here to plant evidence?" I ask.

"I had a couple threatening notes that Lance Mack received. Well, he didn't really receive them. I made them up. I was going to put them in Bobby's desk and then give the police a tip." He tosses a hand in the air. "Didn't really work, did it?"

No, it didn't. He got caught by a couple of nerds. Speaking of which, Bobby Cronus's voice floats in from somewhere in the lobby. Apparently, he and Lars are having a conversation, and it isn't going well.

"Let me see if I get this straight," Cronus says, "I put you in the main event of my biggest wrestling show and you turn around and get your ass kicked in a gay bar?"

Lars's voice falters. "There were circumstances, you see..."

"Back in the day, you'd get fired for a thing like that," Cronus says, "Hell, you'd probably get fired for being *in* a gay bar."

"I'm sure nobody from the bar will be at the show. Are, uh, are you going to fire me?"

Cronus turns away. "One disaster at a time."

Diamond and I step out of the office. Cronus turns away from Lars. His face is red, and his glasses are askew. He looks from Diamond to me.

"Where are we at?" Cronus asks.

"Pretty much where we left off," I say, "Mr. Diamond broke in here to plant evidence to frame you for Lance Mack's murder. And it wasn't the first time he's tried framing you."

Cronus holds his hands out. "Why?"

"I'm sorry," Diamond says, "I was trying to protect Ashley."

"From what?" Cronus says.

I jump in. "Did you know Ashley and Mack were still in the building the night of the murder? They were here when you left."

Cronus's jaw drops slightly. "I had no idea. I didn't do a walk through because Gordon had already done one. What were they doing here?"

I scratch the back of my head. "Probably nothing. At least, that's Ashley's story." I cut my eyes toward Diamond. "Apparently, her father wasn't quite so sure. Hence, the planting evidence."

Diamond stares at the floor. "It wasn't anything personal."

"I've got to tell you: I'm taking it kind of personal," Cronus says.

I turn toward Cronus. "You going to call the police?"

That brings Cronus up short. "You think we should have Nick arrested?"

"Breaking and entering," I say, "Tampering with an investigation."

Cronus adjusts his glasses. "He's also in the main event of *WrestleShock*. That's a couple days away. I can't re-do the main event now."

My jaw drops. "So, he gets a pass?"

"I'm going to have to fine him." He looks toward Diamond. "Pay envelope's going to be a little light on Friday."

"I get it," Diamond says.

Cronus walks out of the lobby and into the arena. Diamond follows him. I'm wondering when was the exact moment was that I entered the Bizarro Universe. Mike, Lars, and I are alone in the lobby. Mike throws his hands out.

"What the hell is going on?" he asks.

I shrug. "Apparently, when you're headlining a wrestling event, you have the equivalent of diplomatic immunity."

With nothing left to accomplish here, we decide to call it a night. Lars shuffles behind me and Mike as we leave the building. The rain has started up again. Lars kicks a rock down the sidewalk.

"I've got to be honest," he says, "I thought pro wrestling would be a lot more fun."

And *I've* got to be honest: he's not the only one.

***

Part of the problem with talking to professional wrestlers is just finding them. They won't acknowledge you if you track them down in a restaurant or a store. You have to get an invite to meet at their houses. And you dare not enter the dressing room if you value your life. So, it takes a little legwork.

In this case, I stake out Jack Blades' apartment in downtown St. Paul. Blades leaves around noon and drives up to the Grand Avenue area, not far from my place. (Dammit. I could have practically stayed home and done this stakeout.) His destination is a little bakery called Le Boulevard. We both park on Grand. I sit in the Saturn and watch him cross the street and disappear inside the bakery. Then I hop out of the car and race after him.

The interior of Le Boulevard is rather cozy, particularly on a cold, rainy day. There's a black and white design on the tile floor. Knick-knacks and books line metal bookcases. Small, round, black tables dot the floor. Behind the huge bakery case, workers in white uniforms prepare the goods. The scents of sugar, flour and bread fill the air. Under all that is the unmistakable aroma of fresh coffee. I can't believe I haven't been here before. The place is half-full, mostly with those from the Church of Latter Day Yuppies. (Maybe that's why I haven't been here before.)

Jack Blades is at the counter, chatting up a middle-aged woman with a pinched face and glasses. He props an arm on the bakery case and is chuckling at some joke between the two of them. I approach.

"Good morning, Mr. Blades," I say, "I was hoping we could have a word."

He looks over his shoulder and frowns. "What about?"

"The badge on your vest," I say, "The one that belonged to Lance Mack."

Blades takes a breath in through his nose. He turns to the woman at the counter. "I'm going to take my coffee and éclair to a table, Rose. It's been nice talking to you."

I order a to-go cup of French Roast. We make our way to a table near the picture window. Rivulets of rain bleed down the glass. Blades carefully sets his mug of coffee and the plate with the éclair on the table, situating them just so.

"You know about the badge," Blades says, "This going in the article?"

Jeez, am I ever going to ask a question without getting *that* question in return? But I'm developing a stock answer. "That depends on what I find out," I say, "You were the one who broke into Lance Mack's place."

He takes a bite of his éclair and nods. "The badge belonged to me in the first place. Mack stole it. But it wasn't just about the badge. There was something else he stole."

"What was it?"

"A belt buckle. Belonged to a friend of mine."

"A belt buckle?"

Blades sips of his coffee. "You ever heard of Eddie Hammond?"

I jog the internet-inspired memory banks. "Promoter out of Houston, right? Former wrestler, too."

"Good," Blades says, "He was the guy who broke me into the business. Trained me. Pushed me into the main event. Talked other promoters into using me. Put me up for the PWA Title. Even taught me a little about booking and promoting. He was a hell of a guy. Like another father to me."

"I get that."

"Eddie was in rodeo before he got into wrestling. Won a couple of things. One of them was a big belt buckle. He loved that thing. Had it on the wall of his office at home. When he passed away, the family gave it to me. Meant a hell of a lot." Blades takes another bite of his éclair, dabbing his lips with a napkin. "I put Mack up at my place once, before the card he no-showed. He stayed in the guest room where I kept the belt buckle. When he left, the fucking belt buckle was gone. I called and asked him about it. He denied it. I was convinced it was him."

"Did you find the belt buckle? When you broke in?"

"I did. It's back in my apartment. It was worth it."

"Even though it would look suspicious?" I say, "You breaking into the Lance's apartment shortly after he's murdered. It would look like a cover up."

"I get that now," Blades says, "I just wanted that damn belt buckle back."

"Did you find anything else of interest?" I ask.

"I did," Blades says.

He reaches into the pocket of his tan duster and extracts a folded piece of paper. He tosses it on the table in front of me. I pick it up and unfold it. It's a flyer for the Minneapolis Wrestling Federation's *Mill City Mat Wars* on April 30. The show that now won't happen.

"This is the show Bruno Harvey was going to run opposite *WrestleShock*," I say.

"That's what it looks like. I heard Mack was using that to blackmail Gordon Russell."

"I heard that, too," I say. Then I hold up the flyer. "Okay if I keep this?"

"All yours," Blades says.

I tuck the paper into the pocket of my peacoat. I take a moment before moving on to our next bit of unpleasantness.

"Did you go through Lance Mack's stuff the night of the murder?" I ask.

"Wasn't me," Blades says.

I should have expected that would be his answer. It still gives him some motivation for disliking Mack. Though I'm not sure it gives him reason to kill him. Not that I'm short of questions on that front. I watch the rain through the picture window.

"You talked to Ashley," I say, "Did she tell you anything about her and Mack?"

Blades snaps me a look. "What about her and Mack?"

"He was blackmailing her. Over an accident that killed a friend of hers."

I said I'd keep it out of my column. I didn't say I'd keep it to myself. Blades stares at me, maybe wondering what sorcery I used to get this info.

"You know about that?" he asks.

"Yes, I do," I say, "Apparently, so do you. You just gave that away."

Blades finishes his éclair and dabs at his mouth with a napkin. He gathers the crumbs together on his plate and places the napkin over them. He largely speaks to the tabletop.

"I knew about it years ago," I say, "Not long after it happened."

"Nick Diamond told you?"

"No. Ashley." He lets out a breath. "She's always talked to me. Things she couldn't talk to her dad about. She told me about the accident and how Nick covered it up."

"Mack found about it. And was blackmailing her."

"Yeah, he was," Blades says, glancing up briefly, "She said he wanted something from her. Wasn't too difficult to figure out what that was. I told her not to do it. To give it some time. Think of a way out of it. She didn't seem sold on that."

"Did you deal with Mack?"

"Ashley wouldn't let me," Blades says, "Took some doing. It was my fault in the first place."

I pause in taking the lid off my coffee. "How is it your fault?"

Blades looks past me, out the picture window. "Mack knew about Windham County because he heard it from me."

"You told him?"

"I didn't do it on purpose," he says, "It happened when Mack was staying with me. Nick called. Ashley wanted to get into the business. Nick wanted her to do it, but he was worried about what happened in Windham County. Mack must have heard my end of the conversation. I saw him running up the stairs after I hung up with Nick. I asked Mack about it, but he said he didn't hear anything. Mack was a weasly little bastard. I should have known he was lying."

I consider the situation. Blades is a confidant of Ashley's. He has a vested interest in her well-being. If said well-being is tied to her career, he's going to look out for her. What steps might he take, particularly if he has a grudge against Mack in the first place? But how far does that concern go?

"My friend Mike is seeing Ashley," I say.

Blades snaps a look at me. There's a little blood in it. Then he relents. "Good for him. Hope he's decent to her."

I keep my pessimism to myself. "I'm sure he will be. Ashley is nice. She's attractive. All the qualities Mike—or any other straight male with a pulse—might appreciate."

"I guess," Blades says.

"You'd have to be a pretty hard guy to ignore that sort of thing," I say, "Especially when she confides in you. Knows you'll understand and sympathize. No one could ignore that."

Blades glares at me. "You got something to say, why don't you say it?"

I didn't really earn points for subtlety there, did I? Glad we're surrounded by witnesses. "Your interest in Ashley," I say, "It's more than just friend-of-the-family stuff, right?"

"I'm married. And I'm old enough to be her dad. Hell, I'm *older* than her dad."

"Doesn't mean you're dead, though, does it?" I lean forward. "She leans on you when she's upset. You'd have to be less than human to ignore a thing like that. I don't think I could if I was in your position."

Honestly, I could probably resist it now because she's dating Mike. If I was in in my fifties, it might be a different story. Odds are, the sex drive would still be in place, but I'd be too old and decrepit to have any game. (Assuming, of course, I can lay any claim to currently having game). Blades' eyes drop to the tabletop.

"I'd do anything for Ashley," he says, quietly, "I really would. I know it's stupid and it's nothing more than an old man flattering himself. But that's how I feel." He taps his coffee cup against the table. "Knowing that make you feel any better?"

No. It makes me feel worse. "I just wanted to know." Before he can ask, I tell him, "And no, it's not going in the article. It's not anybody's business but yours."

"Thank you," Blades says, "But I know what this also means."

"You've got a motive for killing Lance Mack," I say.

"What are you going to do with *that* information?"

"Keep it to myself. For now."

Blades says nothing. He finishes the last of his coffee, gathers his plates, then gets up to leave. I put the lid back on my coffee, and decide to walk him out with him, though he seems indifferent to the offer. We draw a few looks as we walk to the door. I wonder if it's because the patrons recognize either of us as a sort of celebrity or if they think we're going to brawl on the sidewalk. Once we get outside, Blades' shoves his hands into the pockets of his tan duster.

"You going to tell Ashley any of this?" he asks.

"It doesn't seem necessary," I say, "Unless I find out something she needs to know."

"Like what? That I killed Lance?"

"Something like that."

Blades looks out at Grand Avenue, in its raw, drizzly glory. With his craggy face and duster, Jack Blades could not look more out of place than he does in this corner of what passes for a city. He should be someplace in the past. Back when he could have gunned down Lance Mack down and nothing of it. Instead, he's here in this miserable time and place, getting interrogated by a weenie like me. The drizzle drips off his beard.

"Nice seeing you again," he says, without looking at me.

I reach out to shake his hand, but Blades is already crossing the street. I should be getting home. I should be writing another column. I should be finding out who killed Lance Mack.

Or maybe I should just be minding my own business. I don't think anybody would object to that. Including me.

CHAPTER FOURTEEN

I know this viewpoint has already been expressed by Randall in Clerks, *but it applies to me as well: I hate people, but I love gatherings.*

Maybe gatherings *isn't entirely accurate. I like* happenings. *I like to know there's a street fair or a music festival or a carnival or a sporting event going on somewhere in the world. I just want to enjoy them from the fringes. Or maybe only in theory.*

But I do like the energy that surges through a crowd, the welding of psyches, the communal experience. Maybe people don't literally link arms and sing Kumbaya, *but they do it in spirit. It's one of the most powerful things in which we can engage. How can you not be drawn to that?*

*Until said public gathering turns into a riot. Then f**k it, you're on your own (which is kind of the point of a riot).*

The excitement in the Midwest Championship Wrestling Sportatorium is palpable. The crowd, from the ticket line to the lobby to the arena, is alive with anticipation. The stands are teeming with humanity. The concession stand is loaded with new merchandise. The absence of Lance Mack has not hurt *WrestleShock*. Midwest Championship Wrestling is in clover. We just have to hope they still have their booker by the end of the evening.

"This is going to be awesome," Mike says, sporting an Ashley Diamond t-shirt.

Carol is wearing a Purple Suit shirt (a purple shirt that resembles the front of Lars's usual suit) under her dark coat. "You're joining us at ringside?"

"Absolutely," he says, "I talked to Brigid earlier. I'm in the clear. Told her I had to be with a friend tonight. Someone going through a hard time."

I step past two dudes in Nick Diamond t-shirts. "Which friend and what hard time?"

"I picked you," Mike says, "Sorry to hear your grandma died."

"My Grandma Davis is eighty-six years old and alive and well," I say, bristling.

"Does Brigid know that? No," Mike says, "Grandma Davis can take one for the team."

I open my mouth to argue but don't. Grandma Davis is a good sport. She might have qualms about Mike's attempts to deceive, but she'd enjoy being included in the adventure.

"Fine, I'll cover for you," I say, "But you get one use of Grandma Davis, and this is it."

"Great," Mike says, "I'll remember that. As long as it helps with Brigid."

We move into the front row. Special banners reading *WrestleShock* are decked out around the arena. We drop into our seats and Carol plunks her purse down on the fourth chair.

"Is Rick joining us?" I ask.

"Eventually," Carol says, tugging at her ponytail, "He's got something going at work. He should be here before intermission."

"You better hope you can hold that seat until he gets here," Mike says.

Carol scoffs. "I'd love to see someone try to take it from me. They don't need that kind of pain, blues, and agony."

Mike and I stifle laughs. Whether she likes it or not, Carol is into this whole professional wrestling thing. I lean toward her.

"Things okay with you and Rick?" I ask.

"They're fine," Carol says, smirking, "Better than fine, really."

What the hell is that about? I'd ask Carol for more information, but I'd rather not talk about one of Carol's boyfriends with Mike around. We're likely to watch enough bloodshed tonight without me adding to it.

I scan the arena. Gordon Russell, sporting a tux for the occasion, goes over his notes at ringside. Thanks to Lars's participation in the event, Russell has to pull double duty as the play-by-play man and the ring announcer. No sign of Bobby Cronus. But the guy trying to put him behind bars is visible.

"Pike's here," I say.

Sergeant Pike stands in the entrance to the lobby. His hands are in his pockets, and he's leaning against the wall. I have no doubt he's taking in everything he sees, even in the chaos of the arena.

"I wonder if he'll even wait until the show is over," I say.

Mike bobs his head. "I wouldn't bet on it. I wouldn't bet against it, either."

As if that wasn't encouraging enough, a further scan of the audience reveals Frankie and Fabio sitting in the bleachers. Their parents are next to them, looking as if they're judging the local dog shit competition. Frankie sees me, then licks her lips and pulls aside a little of the low-cut t-shirt she's wearing to reveal the lacy black bra underneath. Her father throws a look at her. I turn back to the action.

"Your investors are here?" Carol asks.

"That appears to be the case," I say.

Mike is also checking out the arena. "Look at this crowd, man. I wonder if Bruno Harvey would have drawn this kind of crowd if he'd have gotten Lance Mack?"

Excellent question. Lance Mack negotiated that one like a genius, playing two promotors off each other to get what he wanted. Actually, he didn't get what he wanted. He died first. But he was on the right track. Although…

I'm interrupted when something gets Mike's attention. It stiffens him like he's frozen in carbonite. "Brigid is here," he says, in a voice not unlike the walking dead (which viewed from a certain angle…)

It's not hard to spot Brigid. She's dressed professionally (black jacket and skirt, white blouse) and looks out of place. (Sort of like a malevolent version of Carol.) Her brown hair flows past her shoulders and she lurches forward slightly, accenting her already hawk-like appearance. Her large, piercing eyes search the room. Her movements are jerky and bird-like. You can practically see her vibrating. Mike tries to hide behind me.

"I think she's spotted you," I say.

"Motherfucker," Mike says.

Brigid pushes her way through the crowd. Mike is likely debating greeting Brigid and running for the hills. He comes down on the side of greeting Brigid. He throws his leather jacket on and zips it up, completely covering his Ashley Diamond t-shirt. He meets Brigid in the aisle. I look to Carol.

"Guess you don't have to save that seat for Rick," I say.

Carol shakes her head. "Oh, what a tangled web…"

Brigid takes Mike's arm, smiling, and they start back toward us. Mike looks not unlike a man on his way to a colonoscopy. This ought to be interesting.

"Good news," he says, his voice tight, "Brigid is going to join us until Carol's boyfriend gets here."

"That *is* good news," I say, sounding slightly forced. (I was never a great actor.)

Brigid looks toward me. "You're Joe, right? Mike's friend? I thought your grandmother died. What are you doing here?"

I silently check with Mike to make sure he hasn't already provided an excuse. The bulging of his eyes tells me he hasn't. Great. I'm on my own here. I take on what I hope is an appropriately somber look.

"She was a huge wrestling fan," I say, "She would have wanted me to be here."

Brigid accepts my excuse. She doesn't express her condolences, which I find a little irritating, even though my grandma isn't really dead. One could express a little genuine concern over the completely bogus death of a beloved relative. Carol takes charge of the situation.

"How about you, Brigid?" she asks, "Are you a big wrestling fan?"

Brigid clutches her purse. "Actually, I've never been to one of these things."

"You'll have a great time," Carol says, "I wasn't sure what to make of it at first. But Joe and Mike have been pretty good about filling me in."

Clearly, Brigid has no interest in Carol's support. Her face puckers as if someone just farted in her general direction. She leans toward Mike and mumbles something about *That bitch you used to date.* Carol doesn't catch it. I'm glad for that. It wouldn't exactly create a festive atmosphere in our row.

Fortunately, the big card starts, giving us something to concentrate on. Lars makes his way into the ring, wearing his usual purple suit. Apparently, he's going to start as the ring announcer before becoming an active wrestler. The crowd greets him with a chant of *Purple Suit! Purple Suit!* Lars pumps his fist then lifts the mic to his mouth.

"Ladies and gentlemen, *welcome* to *WrestleShock!*"

And we're off and running. The atmosphere in the building is electric. Even if the first few matches are forgettable, the crowd is buzzing. Lars gives way to Gordon Russell as ring announcer. Mike sits next to Brigid, looking like a man waiting for the electric chair to kick in. It's not going to get any better when the third match arrives. Russell climbs into the ring, his voice booming.

"This next match is a hair-versus-hair match for the Midwest Women's Championship!"

The crowd gives it an enthusiastic response. Mike looks like he's about to swallow his tongue. Vanessa comes down the aisle first, wearing a leather jacket over her black and white wrestling trunks. The Midwest Women's Championship belt is slung over one shoulder. Once in the ring, she mounts a turnbuckle and holds the belt aloft.

Russell continues. "And the challenger…"

Barracuda kicks in and Ashley Diamond struts out of the faces' dressing room. The crowd explodes. When she reaches the ring, she and Vanessa are immediately in each other's faces. The referee sends the combatants to their separate corners. Ashley grabs the corner ropes and rocks back and forth, readying for battle. She takes a quick look toward Mike. For a second, the warrior's mask drops from Ashley's face, and she tilts her head to one side, confused. Mike shrinks in his seat. Ashley's staring is interrupted by Vanessa hitting her with a knee to the face.

Vanessa dominates the first part of the match, working over Ashley's knee. Ashley sells like a champ. The crowd chants her name. Every now and again, she gets a punch in, looking like she's ready to make a comeback. But every time, Vanessa gets in a cheap shot and takes control of the match again. When she's near the ropes, Ashley looks our direction and scowls. I'm torn between enjoying the match and fearing for Mike's safety.

While Ashley is against the ropes, Vanessa hits her with a clothesline, causing the two of them to tumble over the top rope. Vanessa lands cleanly on the floor. Ashley stays in the ring and finds herself tied up in the ropes. Vanessa reaches under the ring and comes out with a small gym bag. She extracts a large pair of scissors from the bag. Then she gets back in the ring and stalks toward Ashley. Apparently, the hair cutting will start early.

"Oh God, no!" Mike shouts. Everyone, Brigid most particularly, looks Mike's direction. "That poor young lady!" he says, "Oh, the humanity!"

Brigid eyeballs him. Mike focuses on the ring. I privately wonder about the best receptacle to handle Mike's remains. Vanessa is ready to work on Ashley's hair. The referee, however, snatches the scissors out of Vanessa's hand, much to the delight of the crowd. Vanessa confronts the ref, but he refuses to give the scissors back. Vanessa turns toward Ashley and is greeted with a kick to the stomach. Vanessa doubles up. The referee frees Ashley from the ropes. The tide turns.

Ashley's attack includes slaps, hip tosses, and good old-fashioned punches and kicks. Vanessa tries a few counterpunches but misses each by a mile. She staggers around the ring. Ashley hits Vanessa with a clothesline, knocking her to the mat. Ashley grabs Vanessa's legs and applies the Diamond Clasp. Vanessa grabs the ropes, forcing Ashley to break the hold.

"Gutless!" Mike shouts. Then he notices Brigid and slumps down in his seat.

Vanessa sweeps Ashley's knee, taking her down to the mat. The champ then goes for a pin, putting her feet on the ropes for extra leverage. The crowd howls, trying to get the ref's attention. He looks up at the two count and sees Vanessa's feet on the ropes. He makes her break up the pin attempt. Vanessa argues with the referee. Ashley grabs Vanessa and rolls her up for a pin attempt of her own. Vanessa kicks out at two. The crowd groans.

"So close," Carol says, dropping back into her seat.

Vanessa takes a swing at Ashley, who ducks. Ashley grabs Vanessa's leg, hoists her up, and gives her a knee-breaker. Vanessa crumples to the mat. Ashley slaps on the Diamond Clasp. Vanessa writhes in agony. The crowd screams for her to tap out. Vanessa's hand comes up and hesitates. Ashley sags, her own bad knee bothering her. Then she finds a second gear and straightens up again. Vanessa's hand slaps the mat, surrendering.

The crowd explodes. Ashley lets go of the hold and drops to the mat, exhausted. The ref takes the hair clippers from Gordon Russell. Vanessa tries to get out of the ring, but Ashley grabs her by the trunks and pulls her back in. Vanessa tries a swing at Ashley. Ashley ducks it, grabs Vanessa around the head, and drives her into the mat, face first. Vanessa is knocked silly.

"Get her, Ashley!" Mike says, drawing a look from Brigid.

Ashley fires up the clippers and starts in on Vanessa's hair. Vanessa's dark locks fall to the mat in clumps. Every now and again, Ashley throws one to the crowd. Mike snags one. It takes all of one look from Brigid for him to throw it back. Ashley glares at Mike and Brigid. She nearly takes Vanessa's ear off at one point. Brigid, for reasons passing understanding, puts an arm around Mike and gives him a possessive squeeze. Ashley finishes shaving Vanessa's head, leaving her humiliated and bald on the mat. Ashley bolts from the ring and runs over to us.

"Who the fuck is this?" Ashley says, waving a hand toward Brigid.

Brigid lets go of Mike and asks, "Who the fuck is *this*?"

"I'm Mike's fucking girlfriend!" Ashley says.

"Bullshit," Brigid says, "*I'm* Mike's fucking girlfriend!"

They look to Mike to settle the issue. Mike works his jaw, but no words come out. He's sweating and nervously chuckling. We're the center of attention.

"Tell her we're dating, Mike," Brigid says.

"Get your hands off him, you bitch!" Ashley says.

Brigid squares off with Ashley. "Fuck you, whore!"

Ashley clocks Brigid with an open-hand slap. Brigid buries her hands in Ashley's hair and attempts to slam her head into the metal fan barrier. Ashley resists, so Brigid tries to choke her instead. Ashley attacks Brigid with hands like claws.

Mike tries to get between them. "Ladies! Ladies, please! I'm not worth this!"

"He's really not," Carol says, keeping her distance.

The crowd is quiet, wondering what the hell is going on. Ace Security rushes to ringside. Somehow, Mike's appeal for sanity breaks through the ladies' wall of crazy. They both look to Mike. Then they attack him.

Carol and I stand frozen. The ladies rain blows upon Mike while taking the occasional moment to swipe at each other. There is a lot of screaming and crying and I think most of it is coming from Mike. Security is having trouble controlling the situation. Vanessa, covered with bits of hair that were once on her head, leaves the ring to help separate the combatants. Ashley is picked up off her feet and moved toward the aisle to the faces' dressing room. She kicks her legs and hurls a stream of threats at Mike and Brigid. Security gets a hold of Brigid and escorts her toward the lobby. She spews an equal amount of invective at Mike and all of Mike's works. For his part, Mike is left disheveled. I help him to his feet.

"You okay?" I ask.

Mike is glassy-eyed. "I'm fine. Just a little dazed. And kind of turned on."

Carol's head drops. Hoping for remorse from Mike is, at best, a fool's errand. I look toward the lobby, where Brigid is being hauled out.

"You going after her?" I ask.

Mike swallows hard. "Y'know, I might just give that one a miss. Let Brigid calm down."

I don't think that's going to happen, but I'll let the cowardly bastard talk himself into it. Gordon Russell steps into the ring, clearly wondering what in the blue hell just happened, and announces that intermission is at hand. We stroll back to the lobby. Pike is there, cop face firmly in place. I step away from my friends and make my way over to him. He watches me arrive.

"Was the assault and battery on your friend part of the show?" Pike asks.

"It was part of *a* show," I say, "Speaking of which, are you enjoying yourself?"

"I'm strictly here on business," he says.

That doesn't sound comforting. "You going to arrest someone?"

"I can't comment on an ongoing investigation," Pike says.

"Horseshit," I tell him, "If you didn't comment on ongoing investigations, we wouldn't talk at all."

Pike closes his eyes. "Hang on. I'm just going to fantasize about that for a second."

Asshole. "You're going to arrest Bobby Cronus?"

He gives me the cop stare. "You got a better suspect for me?"

"I've got suspects. Just none that I can point to for sure."

"I can give you one piece of information, for what it's worth," Pike says, "Ashley Diamond is no longer a suspect."

Holy shit. Talk about burying the lede. "Why is that?"

"Two things. First, we got ahold of the surveillance footage from the gas station across the street. The front door of this building can be seen in the background. It confirms that Ashley Diamond left the building at 12:23 a.m. "

"And the second thing?" I ask.

"Lance Mack's cell phone. There's a call to Ashley Diamond at 12:25 a.m. Two minutes after she left the building."

"Meaning Lance Mack was still alive when she left."

"That would be the case. Yes."

That's good for Ashley. And maybe Mike, though I wouldn't bet the farm on the future of that relationship.

"This security tape," I say, "did it tell you anything else?"

"That everybody left the building when they said they did. Including Bobby Cronus."

That confirms my theory that the murderer left and came back. Unless Lance Mack chose a particularly involved form of suicide. I glance back toward the ring, a thought occurring to me.

"You find out anything about the ten-thousand deposited in Mack's account?" I ask.

"We looked into the holding company," Pike says, "Everything was legit. Money was sent through guy named Olani. And it was on behalf of Gerald Whippleman."

"Who the fuck is Gerald Whippleman?"

Pike's mouth tightens, as if embarrassed to have this information. "In wrestling circles, I believe he's known as Bruno Harvey."

I shouldn't have assumed any self-respecting parents would choose *Bruno Harvey* as a birthname. Still, Bruno Harvey was the one who sent Lance Mack ten grand the day before Mack died. That's interesting.

"Did you talk to Bruno Harvey?" I ask.

"We did," Pike says, "He has an alibi and says the transfer was wrestling related. He has nothing to do with anyone at Midwest Championship Wrestling. We had no reason to pursue him. That was that."

Still, that's a lot of money, at least at this level of the wrestling business. But I doubt Pike is interested in standing here, trading theories. I step away from him.

"Thanks for the info," I say, "Enjoy the rest of the show."

"Oh, it's going to be a damn blast," Pike says.

I walk back to my friends. Rick has joined us. Carol tries greets him with a hug, but he casually sidesteps her, looking around nervously. Mike ignores him and strolls to the beer garden. I throw out a hand.

"Good to see you, man," I say.

Rick shakes my hand but doesn't make eye contact. "Good to see you, too," he says, tightly. He drops the handshake and turns to Carol. "Let's go in."

Carol sees the look on my face. "Go ahead, Rick. I'll be there in a second."

Rick scurries into the arena. Carol and I find a relatively quiet corner. I look toward where Rick left.

"Okay, what the hell was that?" I ask.

"Nothing, really," Carol says, her tone light, "I just told him about your thing with the whipped cream."

My guts turn to water. "My thing with the whipped cream?"

"Oh yes. I know all about it. Sicko. And now, so does Rick. I thought it only fair that he should know."

"How did *you* find out?"

"From Mike," she says, "He mentioned it in passing while we were dating."

"For what possible fucking reason?"

"I don't know. Mike trashed you quite a bit in those days. I think he was trying to make himself look better."

My face is warm; the international signal my blood pressure is rising. There are certain things you tell a dude on the understanding that this information will not be shared with anyone, even significant others. I was naïve to think Mike would keep such a thing from Carol. Particularly when his own interests could be furthered.

"Yeah?" I say, "Let me tell you a few things about Mike."

"I already know." She sighs. "Believe me. I know."

Dammit. How do you get revenge on a guy when there's no way to shame him or embarrass him? Even now, I can picture Mike shaking off the front row catfight and moving on with his life.

"That's why Rick seems freaked out?" I ask.

"That's my guess" Carol says, "I would like it noted that I didn't make you drag that explanation out of me."

Carol walks back into the arena. I slump against the wall. Great. A guy I liked in high school, who apparently used to admire me, now thinks I'm a filthy pervert. That's the kind of thing that sticks with you.

I look toward the hallway to the faces' dressing room. The entrance is closed off by a curtain. The Guppie is standing there, talking to someone. I angle my head and see Lars wearing a bathrobe (to cover his wrestling trunks, I'm guessing). Lars and The Guppie are talking? What is that all about? Then again, it's probably better I don't know.

Someone pops into my line of sight. It's Frankie. I try to step back but realize I'm up against the wall. Frankie presses her chest into me.

"Joe Davis," she says, "It's good to see you here."

"Um, you too, Frankie," I say, "You enjoying the show?"

Frankie glides a hand down one of my hips. Given the close quarters—and the black tights she's wearing—she's going to feel an immediate response. "I'm digging it," she says, "Just wondering what I'm going to do afterwards."

I try not to sweat. "Are, uh, your parents enjoying the show?"

"I guess," Frankie says, frowning, "Why do you want to know that?"

"Because your dad is standing right over there. And he's watching us."

Frankie tosses a quick look over her shoulder. Her expression is halfway between sad and exasperated. It's the same look my high school girlfriend, Lisa, would get when we were making out on the couch, and her parents would pull into the driveway. Frankie takes a step back.

"He is *such* a cockblock," she says. Then she leans close to me. "Just think about it. We could really have some fun. Okay?"

"Uh…sure."

Frankie gives me an air kiss, then walks away, pointedly not looking at her father. Dr. Piper balls his hands into fists. For a few seconds, I think he's going to come over and take a swing at me. But he just walks away. Dodged that bullet. For now.

Mike strolls up, carrying two beers. He hands one to me. "Where's Carol?" he asks.

"She and her boyfriend went back at the seats," I say, "Which reminds me…" I splash the beer on Mike's crotch and hand him the empty cup. "I'll see you inside." I walk away, leaving Mike to appear as if he's pissed his pants.

The second half of the show doesn't do much for me. There's a tag team match that bores me. Then Darkfire successfully defends the Midwest Title in a match nobody really thought the other guy had a chance to win. The atmosphere on the front row doesn't add to anything. Rick won't look at me. Carol is failing to get any physical attention from Rick. Mike is stewing in failure and beer. His leather jacket covers his lap and, needless to say, he's not speaking to me. I'm on my own here.

I let my mind drift on to the case. What is the killer's profile? They drugged Lance Mack with roofies. They left the arena and returned. If they had gone in the front, the security camera at the gas station would have caught them. They had to use a side door. They had to know Mack was in the heels' dressing room. They needed the golf club to kill him. I'm momentarily pulled out of my reverie by the crowd reacting to something. I'm annoyed. The noise is…the noise…son of a bitch. But why?

"That guy wasn't even in Darkfire's league," Carol says, "He was running out of gas."

My body jerks. *All* of it comes together in a flash. Leaving and coming back. *Gas*. The money. It all makes sense, doesn't it? It's got to be right. I turn to the others.

"I've got to run an errand," I say, "I'll be right back and…ah hell, none of you are speaking to me, so fuck it."

I run back into the lobby and stand at push past the curtain separating the lobby from the hallway to the heels' dressing room. I look to the pillars near the lobby. I step behind one and look down the hall. Perfect view. Just like I thought.

Then I get grabbed from behind.

CHAPTER FIFTEEN

One thing that's been lost in modern wrestling is the art of the Sneak Attack.

Back in the day, most sneak attacks had to take place in the arena or the TV studio. Just telling fans that some dastardly heel had jumped a poor defenseless babyface in a parking lot somewhere didn't have much impact. Hostilities were put on hold until the antagonists were in full view of an audience. In the modern era, though, we find cameras in the back more often. Strangely, this had made things less *rather than* more *believable.*

The problem is the very presence of the camera. The babyface is giving a backstage promo and he or she gets jumped by the dastardly heel. We're given stunning footage of the ensuing asskicking. But there's the small matter of the camera crew. Why are they just standing there? Nobody is calling security or the police or at least an ambulance. Nobody even bothers to say, 'Hey, don't do that." They just watch a felonious assault and do nothing. Yes, there's such a thing as journalistic integrity and not becoming part of the story but come on.

And that's before you ask yourself, "Why the hell is there a camera backstage? Can't they just do the interview out in the arena?"

Right now, I'm less concerned about the presence of a camera and more concerned about the presence of my attacker.

Before I realize what's happening, I'm spun around and slammed up against the wall. I'm staring at a big guy in black tights and a black wrestling mask. It takes a second, but I recognize him. It's the Super Destroyer AKA Bill Walker.

"What the fuck are you doing back here?" Walker asks, "It's wrestlers only."

"I get that," I say, "But I'm looking into something. Something you might know about."

Confusion clouds Walker's eyes. "What do you mean?"

"I mean you're the guy who broke into my apartment and attacked me. Right?"

For a second, the confusion is replaced by panic and that gives the game away. Walker might not be the sharpest tack in the drawer (and other cliches my father is fond of), but he seems to sense that, too.

"Fine, fucker," he says, "if this is how you want to do this."

Walker swings a looping right hand at my ribs. I try to cover up like Muhammad Ali doing a Rope-a-Dope. The punch lands. And doesn't hurt at all. He follows with a looping left to the other set of ribs. Same result. I peek out from the Ali position.

"Are those working punches you're hitting me with?" I ask.

Walker stops and says, "I, uh, I don't really know how to fight."

"I get it," I say, "I never really learned how to fight, either." Then I kick him in the balls.

To be clear: I'm not a big *kick somebody in the balls* guy. Much as I disrespect authority, there are certain rules I feel should be followed. A gentlemen's code, if you will. And somewhere in that code, it states, "Thou shall not, with malice aforethought, during any variety of physical confrontation, endeavor to strike a hail-fellow with a boot to the noogs." So obviously, I have my scruples about doing such a thing. But time is short. I need to wrap up this conflict and get on to exposing the murderer.

Walker goes straight down on his knees, curling around his groin. His mask isn't laced up, so he's able to pull it off in quick motion. He must need air. It doesn't make me feel any better, but hey, the guy was trying to pretend beat me up. I squat down over him.

"You didn't kill Lance Mack," I say, "But you're working for the guy who did."

He speaks through gritted teeth. "Yeah, I am. I was told to keep an eye on you." Walker sits up, slowly recovering from the nut shot. After a couple deep breaths, he asks, "What are you going to do?"

Good question. "The murderer is who I think it is, right?"

I give Walker the name. He confirms it. Then he confirms why the murderer did it. After another few seconds, I have a vague idea of a plan. I stand and say, "Come with me."

Walker follows me, reluctantly (although that may be the groin pain), back to the lobby. Pike stands in the entryway to the arena, more interested in this wrestling stuff than he'll admit. He turns as Walker and I approach.

"Counselor," he says, though he's eyeballing Walker, "Who's your friend?"

"He's a professional wrestler and a friend of the late Lance Mack. He's also working with Mack's murderer."

Pike's body tenses. "Oh? And who is…"

That, sadly, is as much as Pike gets out before Walker takes off running. It isn't the smoothest run, what with him cupping his injured fellas, but it's getting the job done.

All I can do is mutter, "Son of a bitch." Walker is out the front door before Pike and I can do anything. Pike starts toward the door then glances back at me.

"You know who killed Mack?" he asks.

"I do."

"You have proof?"

"Yeah," I say, "Most of it just ran out the door."

Pike draws his gun and disappears into the entryway, moving faster than I would have expected. I bounce on the balls of my feet. I could go after Walker as well. But Pike doesn't need my help. And I have to confront the murderer. I march into the arena.

Bobby Cronus and Jack Blades have already gotten into the ring. Blades yells at the crowd and brandishes his branding iron. Cronus, dressed in a red-and-black full body suit (sadly, form fitting), smugly brandishes a golf club. Gordon Russell does the ring announcing. Nick Diamond and Lars have just started their entrance. Diamond wears a stunning blue sequined robe. Lars wears a purple robe over his tights and purple t-shirt. The audience gives them a rousing welcome, punctuated by chants of _Purple Suit! Purple Suit!_ My bullshit plan is still forming in my head. I run toward the ring.

"This is the main event of the evening!" Russell says, drawing cheers from the crowd, "It is one fall with a one-hour time limit."

I jump past the fan barrier at ringside. Security doesn't immediately react. I climb up to the apron then hop between the ropes. Any self-congratulation over entering a wrestling ring without falling on my ass is washed away by the knowledge that every eye in the place—including the six men in the ring—is on me. Russell looks stunned then throws out a hand.

"We have a celebrity on hand tonight," Russell says, "You know him from his *Cup o' Joe* column in *The Daily Bugle*. He is Joe Davis!"

That merits a polite round of applause. (*Polite* in the sense that no one throws a beer can at me. But give them time.) I give the crowd a quick wave, then hold my hand out toward Gordon Russell, silently asking for the mic. That does nothing to abate Russell's confusion, but he hands it to me. I address the crowd.

"Uh, thank you," I say, "As you all know, Lance Mack was originally supposed to be in the main event tonight. And we all know why he's not here. Now, we've got a great main event. No question about it." That gets a little round of applause, but it's mostly anticipatory. "Before that main event can happen, though, we've got to get clear on a few things."

Cronus steps over to me. "What the fuck are you doing?"

"Saving your ass," I say, my hand over the mic.

He backs off. "Make it fucking good."

I turn back to the crowd. "I know we all felt a certain way about Lance Mack. Some of us bought into his persona and hated him. Some admired his abilities in the ring. But when he was killed, we all felt a great talent had been lost. Maybe that's true. But we certainly didn't lose a great *person*." The crowd grumbles, clearly thinking I'm part of the evil heel plot to discredit Lance Mack. "You see there are some unsavory things I've found out about Lance Mack. He was a thief and a liar. And a blackmailer. And one of those things got him killed."

The crowd is quiet. I've never had this level of undivided attention. I'm gaining confidence. I push forward.

"See, Lance Mack was on his way to the big time. The UWE was interested in him. And they had their eyes on Midwest Championship Wrestling. There is a deal in place to make MCW a developmental territory for UWE."

That gets a shocked round of applause. Russell's face is red with embarrassment. Cronus stares a hole through me. I bring the mic back to my mouth.

"But Lance Mack was the key to the deal," I say, "If he left MCW and went to another independent promotion, he would take most of the MCW talent roster with him. The only thing they'd have is a general manager who isn't on speaking terms with UWE. It would have killed the deal." I turn toward Cronus. "Lance Mack *was* threatening to leave. Unless Gordon Russell fired Bobby Cronus. Gordon Russell was trying to work that out when Mack was killed." A confused mumble moves through the crowd. "Lance's death was a break for Bobby Cronus since he kept his job. But it was a break for

Gordon Russell as well. Because Lance Mack *was* leaving Midwest Championship Wrestling, Bobby Cronus or no."

There's a stirring in the crowd. Gordon Russell tugs at his mustache. Mike, sitting in the front row, mouths *What the fuck?* I keep rolling.

"Lance struck a deal with the Minneapolis Wrestling Federation," I say, "The MWF sent him ten-thousand dollars to be at the show they were supposed to run tonight. He was trying to get Bobby Cronus fired and he still planned to leave and take most of the wrestlers with him. Gordon Russell found out. And it made him mad. Mad enough to kill Lance Mack." I turn to Russell. "And that's what you did. You killed Lance Mack."

CHAPTER SIXTEEN

One of the key components to a pro wrestling match is the Comeback. This occurs after the heel beats the living hell out of the babyface, likely using many varieties of chicanery. The crowd pulls for the babyface, hoping he'll get the upper hand. There might be a few spots where the babyface looks as if he's going to take over on the heel. But the heel will find a way to get the advantage back. This merry dance continues throughout the match: the babyface with a moment of hope, the heel crushing it. The crowd pines for the babyface to give the heel his well-deserved comeuppance.

Then it finally happens. Maybe the babyface starts shrugging off blows from the heel, maybe they duck a big move, maybe they cheat a little in return. Whatever it is, the babyface starts laying waste to the heel, delighting the fans and bringing the match to its conclusion. The only question is whether the heel will find a way out of this mess and still come out on top or if the babyface can keep the momentum and win the match.

The key component to the Comeback is timing. You need to work the audience to a fever pitch, the absolute peak of their frenzy before the babyface comes back. Wait too long and the audience loses interest. Go too soon and they aren't invested enough. That's why old school wrestlers prefer to call matches in the ring rather than work them out beforehand. You have to feel the audience. It can't be planned in advance. As some old schoolers put it: "What if the audience wasn't in on the meeting?"

Judging by the audience's stunned silence, my timing, at least, is perfect.

After my pronouncement, no one moves or says anything. Gordon Russell's hand falls to his side. He sways slightly and I wonder if he's going to faint.

"I didn't do anything," he says.

"I'm afraid you did," I say, "You found out about Lance Mack's deal to go to the Minnesota Wrestling Federation and no-show *WrestleShock*. The night of the murder, you left the building and came back. You had drugged Mack while you were running the bar earlier. You saw him go into the heels' dressing room, then you went to the faces' dressing room and got Bobby Cronus's golf club. You had your murder weapon. By the time you got to the heels' dressing room, Mack was nearly out from the drug. Then you killed him with the golf club, wiped the club clean and left it beside the body."

The crowd looks from one to the other. Russell totters backward a little. The ropes keep him on his feet. Cronus's head swivels from him to me. Nick Diamond and Jack Blades are standing next to each other, not moving. Even Lars is stunned. I focus on Gordon Russell.

"You had Mack dead," I say, "You had a perfect suspect in Bobby Cronus. And you still had your deal with the UWE. Everything you wanted. You were willing to kill for it."

Russell must realize the jig is up. He's been exposed in front of a large crowd of people and the accusation has been taped for broadcast later. I'm not sure if Pike has caught Bill Walker, but I can handle Gordon Russell. I hold out a hand toward Russell.

He responds by punching me in the face.

Okay, as a guy who has inflicted exactly zero beatings on any other member of the human race, I had no business taking Gordon Russell lightly. I'll own up to that. But no one could have known Russell hits like a damn mule kicking. He catches me just above my left eye. My head snaps to one side and I'm vaguely aware of stumbling backwards. The ring ropes hold me up. My vision takes a second to come back into focus. When it does, I realize Gordon Russell has vacated the scene. He's running up the aisle toward the lobby. Nobody—fans or security—makes a move toward him. The reason becomes clear when Bobby Cronus walks over to me.

"Is this whole thing a work or a shoot?" he asks.

"Just start the fucking match," I say, tumbling out of the ring.

And when I say *tumbling*, I'm not exaggerating. I fall through the top and middle ropes, bounce off the ring apron, and land on my ass at ringside. I hop up and stagger toward the aisle. Russell's punch has rung my bell. No one in the crowd touches me.

Still, I close on Russell. (I'm twenty years younger and a hell of a lot faster. Also, Russell has the most unathletic run this side of Lars.) He's on the other side of the lobby when I get there. The front door opens and Pike steps back in, Bill Walker in tow. Russell changes direction and runs toward the hallway to the heels' dressing room. I follow him.

Russell runs for the side door next to the heels' dressing room. He looks back, wild-eyed, and sees me gaining. He's not going to beat me out the door. He stops and rears back, ready to hit me again. I duck the punch and bury my shoulder into his mid-section. We go flying and hit the concrete, hard. Russell lets out a gasp. I'm thrown clear on impact. Russell rolls to one side. I put a hand on his shoulder, trying to roll him back toward me.

And Russell buries a punch into my mid-section.

My insides seize up and my vision gets blurry. Russell struggles to his feet. He swings a kick at my ribs. I throw my hands out to block it. I hold on to the foot and yank his leg, throwing Russell off-balance. He puts a hand against the wall, steadying himself. I've got a clear shot at his balls. I've got to take it.

I throw a straight right at his crotch. Before it lands, Russell's hand swings down and bats the punch away. Dammit. (Then again, I *was* violating the gentleman's code.) He tries to stomp my balls in return, but I'm able to slide back. I keep sliding and Russell keeps advancing.

Russell steps into the heels' dressing room. I freeze in place, wondering what the hell is going on. Russell can't escape through the heels' dressing room. He must be out of his mind.

The door to the heels' dressing room opens. Gordon Russell steps out, holding a golf club. I guess Bobby Cronus keeps a spare around. Russell hoists the golf club over his head and brings it straight down at me. I roll to one side, the club narrowly missing me, then scramble to my feet. Russell swings sideways, like he's going after a fastball. I duck and the golf club clangs off the door. I stumble up the hallway, holding out a hand.

"You don't want to do this," I say.

Russell responds by taking another swing at me. I jump back and avoid it. Okay, I guess he *does* want to do this. I have to buy some time.

"It's true, isn't it?" I say, "Mack was going to double-cross you."

Russell's voice is a rasp. "Yes, he was. How did you know?"

"Bruno Harvey paid him ten grand the day before Mack was killed. Mack had a flyer for the MWF show. Based on Jack Blades' experience working with Mack, I could put it together. Bill Walker pretty much confirmed it for me."

"That bastard," Russell says, his lip curling.

"You had Walker under your thumb, right? I saw him talking to Bruno Harvey and I overheard the word *gas*. I didn't get it right away. But *gas* is steroids. There were rumors of drugs going around. You knew Walker was on steroids. If you passed that along to your new friends at UWE, Walker was never going to work there. That was the carrot you were dangling."

"Mack was garbage," Russell says, "I was doing everything I could to make him a star with the UWE. And that was how he was going to pay me back?"

"When did you find out?" I ask.

"The night of the party," Russell says, "I overheard Walker talking to Mack. They talked about the money from Bruno Harvey. I knew I had to do something."

"Killing him was taking a risk, though," I say, "You might lose the deal with the UWE."

"Yes, it was a risk," Russell says, "But without Lance, Minneapolis didn't have anything I didn't have. I could keep all the talent Lance was going to take over there. I could keep the UWE deal together." Russell brandishes the club, "Lance kept roofies on him. That was the kind of guy he was. I went through his stuff and found them. Then I slipped them into his drink."

"You left and came back," I say, "While you were gone, Cronus set the alarm system. You and he were the only ones who could disarm it."

"That's right. I watched everyone leave. I went in the side door and grabbed Bobby's golf club out of the faces' dressing room. When I went to the heels' dressing room, I saw Ashley and Lance going in. They nearly saw me, but I hid behind the pillar."

"And you watched Ashley leave," I say, "Then you had your chance with Lance Mack."

Russell lowers the golf club slightly. "I don't remember much after I went in there. I don't know if I've blocked it out or if I just went crazy. But then it was over."

"You were going to let Bobby Cronus take the blame," I say, "You never really objected to this whole *Cronus is glad Mack's dead* angle, did you?"

"Of course not," Russell says, "It would just make Bobby look more guilty. And the fastest way to make up Bobby Cronus's mind about something is to disagree with him." Russell holds his hands out, almost pleading. "I couldn't let the deal with UWE go south. I worked for my whole life for it."

"But now it's over."

"Yes," Russell says, hefting the golf club again, "I don't have anything to lose."

He swings the club again. Great work, Joe. You've moved him from panicked to completely unhinged. I stumble back and fall on my ass. Russell stands over me, legs on either side of me, pinning me in. He lines up for a swing. This is the end, my only friend. The end.

"Stop!" a voice shouts.

At the end of the hall stands my savior: Sergeant Frank Pike of the St. Paul PD. His gun is drawn and he's perfectly still. His eyes bore a hole into Gordon Russell. Great. Now, I'm going to owe him one.

"Put the golf club down and get on your knees," Pike says, slowly, "Hands behind your head. You got me?"

I scoot away, giving myself some breathing room. Russell drops the golf club. It clatters to the floor. He raises his hands slightly. Then he runs into the arena.

They can never come along quietly, can they?

Pike lowers the gun. I hop to my feet. Russell is running down the aisle toward the ring. Pike is suddenly next to me.

"Goddammit," he says, "I can't risk a shot." He starts back toward the lobby. "I'll see if I can cut him off. You stay here."

Like that's going to happen.

I run down the aisle in pursuit of Gordon Russell. The crowd is on its feet and screaming. Then they see me and Russell and a different buzz sweeps the place. Apparently, they think this is part of the show. Diamond and Blades are in the ring. Cronus, who has sweated through his red and black suit, sees us from the ring apron and does a doubletake. Lars, on the opposite ring apron, walks along the ropes to get a better look. In the ring, Nick Diamond lays in a corner while Jack Blades stomps him. Blades sees the chase and pauses in mid-stomp. Diamond stops selling and watches the action.

Russell runs around the ring, past Carol and Mike. Mike reaches out and grabs Russell's coat. It doesn't stop Russell, but it slows him down. And leaves him without a coat. Carol jumps over the railing, ready to join the chase. Security closes in on all sides. They're coming for Carol, but Russell doesn't know that. He thinks he's surrounded. He decides to take refuge in the only place he can think of.

The ring.

Russell rolls under the bottom rope and pops to his feet. The action in the ring, already paused, comes to a complete halt. The crowd quiets. Russell looks around, as if another escape route is available to him. I slide under the bottom rope. Bobby Cronus steps into the ring. Russell turns to me.

"No," he says, his voice quiet and disconnected.

He swings a roundhouse right at me. I do a Jon "Bones" Jones lean back and the punch misses me. It throws him off-balance. He stumbles toward me. I do the only thing that comes to mind: I throw a forearm shiver.

To be honest, if I had hit Nick Diamond or Jack Blades or maybe even Bobby Cronus with such a shot, they might have laughed it off (maybe not Cronus). But the blow knocks Russell backward and he crashes into Bobby Cronus. Cronus then collides with Jack Blades. Blades falls back against the ropes, selling in that cartoony way of his. Diamond turns to Lars.

"Go home," Diamond says, just loud enough for those of us in the ring to hear him.

Blades falls forward and his head appears to crash into Cronus's. Cronus's body bucks from the collision. Diamond tags in Lars, then reaches over the ropes and picks him up for a scoop slam. He tosses Lars through the air, causing him to land on top of Bobby Cronus. Diamond grabs Jack Blades and slaps on the Diamond Clasp. Russell starts to get up. I leap over Lars and Cronus and crash land on Russell. His body sags, the fight going out of him. I have him pinned. The ref drops to the mat. The crowd counts along.

"One...two...three!"

The place goes bananas. Lars rolls off Cronus. Diamond releases Blades. I stay on top of Russell, keeping him in place. Mike and Carol jump up and down, celebrating. Pike has strolled to ringside. He waits to take possession of Russell, letting the folks in the ring have their moment. Diamond grabs Lars's hand and raises it, along with his own. The crowd gives them a huge round of applause. Ashley Diamond runs into the ring and embraces her father. Lars grabs my arm and holds it up. I get goosebumps as the crowd cheers.

Okay, *now* I understand how wrestlers get addicted to this.

EPILOGUE

A thing that occasionally hits me as a wrestling fan is how things never really end. Just like a soap opera. Or life.

See, an angle might come to an end, but the participants will always find themselves in another angle. The babyface will have a new villain to confront. He or she may have won a title, but there will be another nefarious heel trying to take it from them. The heel might be bested but will soon find another babyface to terrorize. The end of one big card just means it's time to start planning for the next one. The wheel never stops.

And that's fine. That's how the business makes money. And why fans spend it.

Nobody in the lobby of the Midwest Championship Wrestling arena seems to think their money has been poorly spent. There's a clamor of excitement, even though the TV taping is over. Mike, Carol, and I stand in a corner of the lobby and watch the crowd drain out. A few fans hail me as they walk past. I give them a faux-modest wave, causing Carol to roll her eyes. Mike wears a hangdog expression and slouches against the wall.

"Nick Diamond is going to Texas next week," he says, "Working for an indie in Dallas."

"He's still got the IRS to pay off," I say, "You hear anything about Jack Blades?"

"There's an indie in North Carolina that's advertising him for their next show," Mike says, "I guess we've seen the last of him, too."

Carol twists her mouth to one side as she thinks. "Once Nick Diamond and Jack Blades leave, the houses are bound to go down."

"I'm sure they'll figure something out," Mike says.

I lean toward Carol. "You're really getting into this, huh?"

"It grows on you," Carol says, "Just like the two of you. Or a fungus. But I don't know if it's going to last."

"We'll always have Paris," I say.

The last person in the lobby is a thin dude with a bad haircut and creepily intense eyes. He's Chet Alfred, the new play-by-play man for the *Midwest Championship Wrestling* TV show. He meets Bobby Cronus coming in from the production truck.

"How did it go?" Alfred asks, eager to please.

Cronus drops a weary hand on his shoulder. "You did fine. Come in the office. We'll talk about a few things."

They close the office door behind them. Carol, Mike, and I wait for Lars. Carol nods toward the office.

"Where did they get the new announcer?" she asks.

"From the Minneapolis Wrestling Federation," Mike says, "He was doing play-by-play for them. Cronus threw some money at him. And he mentioned the deal with UWE."

"They're going forward with that?" Carol asks.

"That's what it looks like," I say, "Even without Gordon Russell."

The founder of that particular feast is currently in jail, awaiting trial. Russell didn't have the money for bail and the judge didn't seem inclined to set an amount at the initial hearing. We'll see what happens next with Midwest Championship Wrestling. Russell probably won't be able to maintain his ownership. Bobby Cronus will have to sort it out. Lars glides into the lobby, resplendent as always in his purple suit. We give him a round of applause. He stops and bows.

"Thank you, my friends," he says, "I hope you enjoyed the show."

"We did," Mike says, "How about you? Tough going back to being a ring announcer after being a main event star?"

"No sir," Lars says, "I'm just fine doing what I'm doing. A man has got to know his limitations."

Those are words I never thought would come out of Lars's mouth. *Not* knowing his limitations has been his M.O. for as long as I've known him. I'm hesitant to bring up an unpleasant subject, but curiosity has gotten the better of me.

"You heard any more about Les Bos?" I ask.

Lars adopts a superior air. "I don't think we'll have to worry about that anymore. Les Bos will not be opening."

"Not opening?" I ask, "What happened?"

"Peter's licenses have been pulled," Lars says, "Apparently, someone at city hall isn't a fan of his enterprise."

I'm stunned. After the night at The Saloon, I didn't think there was any chance Lars could stop Les Bos from going forward. He's sporting an insufferable grin, telling me he's responsible for this development.

"How did you pull that off?" I ask.

"I guess someone has connections at city hall," Lars says, "Turns out they know a city councilman with some fairly shady business dealings. Not the sort of thing they would want the general public to know about. A little influence was wielded, and Peter is out of luck."

"So, blackmail?" Carol asks.

"Blackmail is an ugly word," Lars says.

"Extortion?" I say.

Lars points at me. "That has a much nicer ring to it. But yes, that's how we got it done."

"Who's *we*?" I ask.

"Mostly The Guppie," Lars says, "I acted in an advisory capacity."

"The Guppie?" I say, "That's why he was at *WrestleShock*? I thought he hated you."

"Everything is negotiable," Lars says. He spins toward Carol. "By the way, Carol, The Guppie wanted you to know how much he enjoyed your date, once upon a time."

Oy. About a year and a half ago, Lars persuaded Carol to go on a date with The Guppie, mainly to prevent The Guppie from rearranging Lars's internal organs. I never heard how the date went, largely because Carol refuses to discuss it. I *have* noticed The Guppie adopting a dopey expression whenever he sees Carol. Lars waggles his eyebrows. Carol gives him a deadpan look in return.

"I'm not going out with The Guppie again," Carol says.

Lars's head snaps back. "I see. That's, that's going to create a new problem."

He's smart enough not to venture any farther along that line. It's not going to get him anything, save for a punch in the stomach (the stomach if he's lucky) from Carol. We're interrupted by the office door opening and Bobby Cronus emerging with his new play-by-play announcer. He sends the guy on his way then waits for him to leave before joining us.

He's back to wearing his black t-shirt and black sweats. I turn to him as he approaches.

"Good show tonight," I say.

"Just setting up angles," Cronus says, "We got a bunch of UWE trainees coming in next week. We'll see what becomes of that. Or if I'm around long enough to see what happens."

That sends a little charge through the group. "You're leaving?" I ask.

"Not right away," Cronus says, "We've got to get the ownership situation straightened out. We have a possible buyer. Rich kid whose daddy will buy the company for him because the kid's always wanted to be in the wrestling business. Thinks he can book because he played with his wrestling dolls as a kid."

Mike frowns. "Are you going to another promotion?"

"No, I think it's time I got out of the business altogether," Cronus says, "I looked at Gordon and how it drove him insane. There were times when I was in the same boat. I'm going home to Louisville." He folds his arms. "I've got all those collectibles in storage. Maybe I can open a business, sell some of that. Or do a podcast."

"Or both," Mike says.

"Or both," Cronus says, "But it's time to do something else."

I'm not sure what to say. Part of me would be sad to see Bobby Cronus get out of the business. But the part of me that still admires him knows this is for the best.

"Good luck with that," I say.

Cronus looks down. A moment passes, then he sticks out his hand, not making eye contact. "I, uh, want to thank you for helping me out. It, uh, it was…thank you."

I give him a quick handshake. Cronus drops the hand and walks to the office. He closes the office door behind him. I can't help wondering what life will be like for him. Being an average citizen will be thornier than he supposes. I look to my friends.

"Shall we take a stroll?" I ask.

We step out the front door. The air is warm and dry. A good night for a walk. We're all wearing our lightest coats. Soon, it'll be shorts and t-shirts. I take in a deep breath. Carol looks over at Mike.

"Couldn't help noticing Ashley wouldn't look at you during the taping," she says.

Mike shoves his hands in the pockets of his jeans. "It's over. Soon as she saw me and Brigid at *WrestleShock,* she knew she couldn't trust me."

"Can you honestly say she was wrong?" Carol says.

"She could have trusted me." Mike says, "Eventually."

"I guess things are over with Brigid as well?" I say.

Mike bobs his head. "Depends on what you mean by *over*. We're done fucking. She made that pretty clear. But I still have a job."

My eyebrows go up. "Brigid didn't fire you?"

"Nope, she kept me on board," Mike says, "To be the company whipping boy. I've been kicked out of my office."

Lars falls in step behind Mike. "You're back to a cubicle?"

"No, I'm at a desk in the corner," Mike says, "Actually, it's more of a table. A really small table. With a rickety chair. In the flow of traffic."

"No more preferential treatment?" I ask.

"No, I'm *really* not getting that," Mike says, "I'm expected to handle a work quota that's twice as high as anyone else's. My lunch hour has been cut down to fifteen minutes. And I'm expected to run Brigid's personal errands."

Carol's head swings Mike's direction. "Can Brigid really get away with all that?"

"She can as long as I'm working there," Mike says, "There's no way I can go to management and tell them I'm being treated unfairly without telling them *why* I'm being treated unfairly. If they know I was sleeping with Brigid, we'll *both* get fired. Then I'm still out of a job. And Brigid will be, too. And I'm pretty sure an unemployed Brigid is a Brigid with time to hunt me down and do bodily harm to me. Best to take it until I can find a new job."

Nobody comments on that. Yes, we feel bad for Mike. But it's a bed he made for himself. What's more, with his track record of sleeping with co-workers and their family members, a new job might not be the solution. Oh well. I'll let *him* stress about that. I look over at Carol.

"I didn't see Rick here tonight," I say, "Didn't he enjoy *WrestleShock?*"

A shadow falls over Carol's face. "No, he liked it just fine. But Rick and I broke up."

"Really?" I ask, "What happened?"

"TMI," she says.

"Oh, sorry," I say, "I didn't realize it was that personal."

"No, TMI between me and Rick," Carol says, "We found out too much about each other. Once he knew the thing…that you told him."

"That you fantasize about doing it in front of other people?" Lars asks.

Carol's jaw tightens. "Yes, Lars, *that*. Between that and the thing I told him about Joe, Rick thought he should share something with me."

"Sounds fair," I say, with a due sense of trepidation, "What did he tell you?"

"I'm not getting into it," Carol says, waving her hand as if erasing a blackboard, "Let's just say it involved Wonder Woman and bondage and stripping. It was very…involved."

Mike, Lars, and I are silent, not sure what to say. Mainly because we're trying to picture it ourselves. I'm the first one to get it together.

"You broke up with him because of that?" I ask.

"Not really," Carol says, "But after that, it became pretty clear we couldn't keep dating. When you can't make eye contact with somebody, it's hard to keep a connection going."

We all agree with that. Sex, of course, doesn't necessarily require eye contact, but it's difficult to get it on when you can't talk with someone and don't particularly want to undress in front of them. Makes for an awkward scene, you understand.

"That's a shame," I say.

"Shame or no, I'm done dating any of your friends."

"Really? That's too bad. I liked you and Rick as a couple."

"Maybe the two of you can hang out sometime," Carol says, "Swap ideas about Wonder Woman and whipped cream."

"Sounds good" I say, "Maybe you watch us while we do."

That gets snickers out of Mike and Lars. I'm sure they're amused by Mom and Dad arguing about embarrassing stuff. The fact they have resumes neither Carol nor I could touch in that department doesn't occur to them. (Self-awareness never being a strong suit for either.) Lars loosens his tie.

"I guess I'll be out of a job shortly," he says, "If Mr. Cronus and Mr. Russell are gone, I can't see myself continuing. Besides, I need to focus on the movie."

Ah. That brings up a question I've been avoiding for a few days. "Have you heard from Fabio and Frankie?" I ask.

"I have indeed," Lars says, "They had a long conversation with their parents after *WrestleShock*. The parents are on board for funding the movie."

That brings everyone to a halt. If Lars said the Vulcans had arrived and made first contact in his apartment, this news could not be more unexpected.

"You're kidding me," I say.

"I am not," Lars says, "The parents loved the wrestling show. The pageantry, the intensity, the excitement, the unexpected twists and turns. They wanted to know if our movie would be like that. Fabio and Frankie assured them it would be. The parents are on board."

Everything is quiet. Then Carol says, "That's unbelievable."

"Oh, you can believe it, sister," Lars says, "They *did* have one caveat, Joe. They would like you to stay away from Frankie. Dr. Piper was particularly insistent about that."

That much, I can agree with. Wholeheartedly. "I think we can make that work."

"Good thinking, brother," Lars says. He drops a bony arm around my shoulder. "We're going to have to discuss the script. I've got some big ideas. Now, this vampires-from-the-inside-out thing is cute. But if we're going to involve vampires, we need blood. Buckets of blood. Something to put that river in *The Shining* to shame. And we need sex. Lots and lots of sex. Fortunately, I know several actresses who are perfectly willing to do nude scenes. Well, when I say *actresses*, it might be a little closer to *prostitutes*, but I'm sure we can fit them in the budget. And we're going to need a big, scary house. Preferably one that's condemned because, oh, we're going to beat the living hell out of it. Which reminds me, *Living Hell*. What do you think about that for a title?"

I think I want to go home, crawl under my bed, and not come out until *next* spring. For not the first time in the last few weeks, I wonder what the hell I've gotten myself into. And how, exactly, I'm going to get myself out of it.

And that's a shoot.

FINAL BELL

Randall J. Funk is the writer of the Joe Davis Mystery series. He is also an actor, director and playwright. His plays include *The Hound of the Baskervilles*, *The Mudslinger Party*, and *Bring Me the Head of Dominic Papatola*. He lives in St. Louis Park, MN, with his son Ben.